Carole Matthews

Million Love Songs

Leabharlanna Poiblí Chathair Baile Átha Cliath
Dublin City Public Libraries

SPHERE

First published in Great Britain in 2018 by Sphere
This paperback published in 2018 by Sphere

Copyright © Carole Matthews 2018

1 3 5 7 9 10 8 6 4 2

A CIP catalogue record for this book
is available from the British Library.

ISBN 978-0-7515-7196-7

Typeset in Sabon LT Std by Palimpsest Book Production Ltd,
Falkirk, Stirlingshire
Printed and bound in Great Britain by Clays Ltd, St Ives plc

Papers used by Sphere are from well-managed forests
and other responsible sources.

MIX
Paper from
responsible sources
FSC® C104740

Sphere
An imprint of
Little, Brown Book Group
Carmelite House
50 Victoria Embankment
London EC4Y 0DZ

An Hachette UK Company
www.hachette.co.uk

www.littlebrown.co.uk

Carole Matthews is the *Sunday Times* bestselling author of thirty novels, including the top ten bestsellers *The Cake Shop in the Garden, A Cottage by the Sea, Paper Hearts and Summer Kisses, The Chocolate Lovers' Christmas* and *Calling Mrs Christmas*. In 2015, Carole was awarded the RNA Outstanding Achievement Award. Her novels dazzle and delight readers all over the world and she is published in more than thirty countries.

For all the latest news from Carole, visit www.carolematthews. com and sign up to her newsletter. You can also follow Carole on Twitter (@carolematthews) and Instagram (matthews.carole) or join the thousands of readers who have become Carole's friend on Facebook (carolematthewsbooks).

Chapter One

Hello, I'm Ruby Brown. It's a pleasure to make your acquaintance. What do you need to know? Let's see. I'm thirty-two and I live at Princess Sparkle Palace, Great Holm, Costa del Keynes. It's one of the nicer areas of the city and I live in an enormous four-bed detached home which overlooks a lake.

Well, I actually have a self-contained apartment over someone's garage. Someone who is a lot richer than I am. OK, even that's over-egging it. I essentially live in a rented granny annexe that you can't swing a cat in. It's not sparkly. It's not a palace. It's a granny annexe. But it's *my* granny annexe, mine alone. And the lake is real. I try to convince myself that what my home lacks in size it makes up for by having a great view. Every morning I wake to the sound of quacking ducks. That has to count for something, no?

My birthday is 6 June. So I'm a Gemini. That makes me sociable, communicative and ready for fun. Frankly, a fat lot of good that's done me. It doesn't say 'gullible' anywhere on the list of Gemini Traits, but I am. Really, I am.

I'm actually trying really hard to be my most sociable, communicative and ready-for-fun self at the moment, as I'm recently divorced from my husband and am starting out on a New and Exciting Life as a footloose and fancy-free single woman once more. At least, that's the plan. Though I have to confess that I'm currently feeling a little daunted by the whole thing. Simon and I had been together for five years and you kind of get out of the habit of being by yourself, don't you? I feel as if I've lost one of my limbs. One that I'll be able to manage without in time, obvs, but it's still bloody tough getting used to it.

When Simon and I parted – more acrimoniously than was probably needed – I walked away from my job, my home, my friends, my everything. Madness, I know. But I was heartbroken – still am – and felt cut loose. I needed a fresh start where no one knew me, where my pain didn't say hello before I did.

If you met me, you'd think that I was the most staid and responsible person on the planet. I'm not known for my irrational behaviour or my impulsiveness. I'm good old reliable Ruby. Look how far that got me! So I decided that I was going to become a new and different version of me. One that was open to adventure, spontaneity and fun. So I set about shaking it all up a bit.

My old job in finance at the council was the first major thing to go. I was comfortable in that job. It paid well and I'd accrued a ridiculous amount of holiday entitlement and an enviable, gold-plated pension pot. Though, in truth, I hated every minute I spent there. I hated the work, I hated my colleagues, I hated the beige carpet, I hated the group huddle we had every morning for fifteen minutes to discuss how we could 'as a team' improve our working practices. The whole thing made me want to claw my own eyeballs out. No one – except me – thought that stopping the stupid group huddles would be the best way forward. I did it because it was a 'good' job with virtually zero chance of being made redundant. And because I was a little bit frightened of change. That's no reason to stay anywhere, is it?

As part of the New Year, New Me vibe I felt the world of local government finance would be better without my contribution. My boss would probably tell you that he felt much the same. There are better ways, I think, to spend your nine-to-five. I wanted to get out into the world, meet new people. New people who didn't think that a suit from Asda was the height of fashion. I'm still young – relatively speaking – but I feel ancient and dull. I want to get out there and mix it up a bit before I am *actually* too decrepit to enjoy it. In the words of Freddie Mercury, I want to break free!

So I've entered the heady world of hospitality instead. I know you're thinking Event Organiser or Wedding Planner, something exciting like that. What I've actually done is become a waitress at a posh gastropub on the outskirts of Milton Keynes. Which seems to mean nothing more than having a lot of pancetta and butternut squash on the menu and writing said menu on a chalkboard. The pay is terrible, the holidays even worse. Yet, strangely enough, I love it. I enjoy meeting new people every day. The customers are fun, mostly, and the team I work with is great. I know what you're thinking. So ask me again if I still like it in a year's time. However, this really is only a stopgap job until my confidence in myself is restored and I decide what I'm doing with my new and exciting life.

What else can I tell you? I love music, films and anything containing copious calories. I love Kylie Minogue, though I am probably twice her height and size. Unfortunately, the only thing I share with Kylie is that I have the same penchant as her for picking The Wrong Guy.

In my younger days, I did my share of dating truly dreadful men. Though, much like Kylie, I never actually managed to spot how dreadful they were until after the event. I even went as far as marrying one of them – the aforementioned Simon. More fool me. Though he wasn't horrible when I married him.

He was lovely. We laughed a lot. He bought me roses. Only from the local One Stop Shop, but that's more than a lot of men do. We were good together. I thought he was the love of my life. It was such a shock when it all went horribly wrong.

But all of life is a lesson. So now I'm done with relationships. I've given up on men, the lot of them. I'm concentrating on being Single and Fabulous. Though, at times, it feels like a steep learning curve. I'm opening myself to new opportunities. I'm going to be like that bloke who said yes to everything for a year. I'm going to see where life takes me.

I need to get a bit of a wiggle on with it, too. I feel as if time is running out for me to fulfil my dreams. And I have dreams, you know. I'd like my own home one day, a car that starts without me having to swear at it, more money coming into my bank account than goes out of it, a job that suits my skill set – whatever that might prove to be. They're not big dreams in the scheme of things, I admit. They're probably quite small. But they're my dreams.

Though, one day, I do hope to own a unicorn.

Chapter Two

Actually, back in reality, I'm thirty-eight and feeling so disillusioned that I'm not even sure that I believe in unicorns any more.

Chapter Three

So. What are the first things you do when you find yourself unceremoniously divorced? I tell you what you do. Change your job. We've already covered that. Then you drastically change your hairstyle, lose some weight and take up some reckless and possibly life-threatening pursuit.

Ergo, my long brown hair is now a sharp-cut blonde bob. I might as well see if it's true that blondes have more fun. If I'm honest, I think they just take more selfies. They also spend a lot more time dyeing their hair. On the weight front, I've dropped a stone simply due to the inability to eat while crying. I'm thinking of marketing it as the Next Big Thing diet plan. *Weight Loss the Weeping Way!* Believe me, the pounds drop off. Life-threatening pursuit? I've signed up for scuba-diving lessons. I know.

I'm not sure that the opportunity for scuba-diving is that widespread in Milton Keynes, but I tried Zumba and found my musical coordination abilities are seriously lacking. When everyone else was whooping and grapevining to the right, I was shimmying to the left all by myself. Plus they were all wearing tight, multi-coloured Lycra clothing that jingled when they moved. That's never going to be a good look. To add insult to injury, the instructor was nineteen, size six and shouted a lot. When is that ever going to do anything for your self-esteem? Plus, doing Zumba isn't exactly a life challenge, is it? Whereas scuba-diving might well be – given, especially, that I'm frightened of water. Particularly going under it.

At this point, I'm thinking that rally driving might have been a better idea. Thought I do already have many points on my licence as another part of my End of Relationship Rehabilitation was to buy a sports car. Don't get carried away and imagine a Porsche. This is an ancient and well-loved Mazda something or another that has more rust in evidence than polished chrome and smells vaguely of mould. The boot has a bag of those silica crystals in it to extract moisture – put there by the previous owner, I hasten to add. The moisture issue hasn't just been since I took possession. It's the sort of car that middle-aged, recently divorced women with no money drive. But it's *my* Mazda, rather like *my* granny annexe. Even though there are dents on every body panel, it shows that it's seen life and I love it just the same.

I should fill you in a bit more on my marriage, then you'll understand where I'm at and why. I'd been with Simon for five years. A year of dating, a year of living together in a rented house in downtown Leighton Buzzard before we wed. So we hardly rushed into it. I met him in real life, at a work conference – unusual in these days of Tinder and e-dating, I think you'll agree. He was in local government too. Traffic Management. It's more interesting than it sounds. Well, not that much.

We met at a Social Responsibility weekend at a posh hotel. After all the boring presentations about initiatives to assess and take responsibility for the company's effects on environmental and social well-being, he bought me a drink in the bar afterwards. Three drinks, actually. Then we got a bit socially irresponsible together back in my room which was quite nice. My heart went pitter-patter and everything. All the things it's supposed to do when it clocks true love. After that, we started seeing each other regularly and I fell in love. I thought he did too.

When we got married, it wasn't a big do. We had a quickie register office ceremony with a few friends and family. Our wedding breakfast was a finger buffet at my parents' house afterwards. Maybe that should have told me something. Simon wanted no fuss, the smallest wedding possible. Turns out he may have even preferred it if *I* hadn't been there.

I was seeing stability, lasting love, buying a home, a mortgage, joint bank account, pensions, kids. Turns out, Simon was seeing the woman from the local One Stop Shop where he went to buy my roses. The one who wore false eyelashes with little pink crystals on them. I also found out during one of our more heated break-up arguments that she had similar pink crystals on her vajayjay too. Classy. I might have gone to certain somewhat unsavoury lengths to attract a gentleman in the past but, believe me, I've never resorted to crystals on my lady parts. Serves me right for asking what she had that I didn't. TMI. Still, five years down the swanny for that, so what do I know.

I found out about Simon's infidelity on Christmas Day. He sent one of those heartfelt texts, full of declarations of love and signed with a dozen kisses and sexy emoticons. It just wasn't for me. I was the one who got the Lakeland spiralizer and a seventy-nine pence card from Card Factory.

The first Christmas we were together, he bought me a box of After Eight mints with a diamond pendant hidden in one of the packets. Cool, eh? Romantic even. It wasn't exactly the Koh-i-Noor, but it was so unexpected and thoughtful of him that I was bowled over. I find that a solo, surprise jewellery purchase is always a good thing in a man. This year, spiralizer. I think that says all it needs to about how far our relationship had declined in a short space of time. Not that I haven't used my Lakeland spiralizer quite a lot. It's great. The number of things you can do with a spiralized courgette is simply amazing. You just don't want one as a major gift from your loved one, right?

Simon left on Boxing Day. Packed a box – I'm sure it's not called Boxing Day because of that – and went to live with The One of the Crystalled Vajayjay. I couldn't bear to stay in that house on my own – the one which we'd shared together. Where we'd loved, laughed and made our plans. Neither, quite frankly, could I afford the rent on my salary.

So I handed the keys back to the landlord and moved away to Milton Keynes without a backward glance. Not a million miles – barely ten miles down the road. And I know what you're thinking – *Milton Keynes*! Why not the golden sands of Cornwall or the fabulous hills of Lake District or the heather-strewn borders of Scotland? Somewhere you'd go on holiday and yearn with all of your heart to go back. Why Milton Keynes? No one aspires to live in Milton Keynes. But, you know what, it's flipping great here and sometimes too much change is unsettling. Everything else was up in the air. I needed somewhere different but familiar, if you know what I mean. Plus I needed a new job and quick. Milton Keynes has everything you'd ever want. Good shopping, good theatre, a surfeit of lakes and more trees than you can shake a stick at. The concrete cows. Don't mention the cows – everyone does. IKEA is a three-minute drive from my house. What's not to love? How far do *you* have to go for your BILLY bookcases? Think about it.

My granny annexe is great too. Honestly. I can have it all decorated from one end to the other with a super-size can of magnolia and a free weekend. At least in theory. I have, of course, yet to put this to the test. It's not exactly Princess Sparkle Palace yet – but, believe me, when it's all nice and freshly decorated it will be both sparkly and palatial.

Cleaning? An hour tops. My kind of housework. I still need some bookshelves putting up and my wall art from Next is still stacked behind the sofa awaiting attention, but I'm pretty much settled in now. Sadly, the thing I miss most about Simon is his ability with power tools. I can tell you now that's not a euphemism for *anything*. It might have taken months of cajoling, but when he set his mind to it he was a demon with a Bosch hammer drill. And that's, essentially, the hardest thing about being single. You have no one else to do . . . well . . . *anything*. You fly solo with finances, decisions, outings, holidays. All of it. The grind of being the only one is relentless. I have to think about everything. Sometimes I think my brain will go into overload with all it's got to hold in there. Yet it's infinitely better than being with someone who thinks having a sparkly noo-noo is more important than a sense of humour or integrity. I must remember that.

Anyway, I'd better get a move on or I won't have my shiny new job to go to. I grab my bag and jump into the car which only requires three f-words before firing into life. Maybe it needs a new battery or alternator or something else under the bonnet which may not be quite right. Another thing that guys are very useful for. I'm perfectly capable of doing it, but when you're a couple you kind of automatically fall into Blue Jobs and Pink Jobs, right? I'm already sorted with putting out the bins myself and if I had any grass, I'd be perfectly fine about cutting it. I'm just going to have to get used to googling car maintenance stuff.

I'm on the late shift at work today which means I go in for four o'clock and am lucky if I'm home at midnight. The plus side is that I get most of the day to myself to chill out, read, watch telly and put off the hour's housework for as long as I can. You win some, you lose some.

The pub is called the Butcher's Arms and is one of a chain

of five similar pubs in the area owned by a small, family-run company. It's set in the lovely village of Great Blossomville, about a ten-minute drive out of Milton Keynes' city limits and into the leafy Buckinghamshire countryside. It has a thatched roof, overlooks the village green and usually has about three hundred top-of-the-range cars parked outside it – making our relationship with the long-suffering residents of Great Blossomville somewhat tetchy. Inside, it's all stripped wooden floors, chalk blackboards and artfully arranged things made out of hopsack.

The drive is lovely and I take the time to turn up my music, letting Kylie soothe me, and enjoy the countryside around me – while fully maintaining my concentration on the road at all times, obvs. It's spring and the hedges are coming shyly into bud. The sun's out in force today and the worst of the winter feels long behind us. Everyone feels better in spring, don't they? It's all that new life, new hope shtick. I'm happy to buy into it, though. It makes your heart soar just a little bit, doesn't it? I won't be downtrodden and disillusioned. I'm going to be bright and filled with optimism. You heard it here first!

This year, for me, is onwards and upwards.

Chapter Four

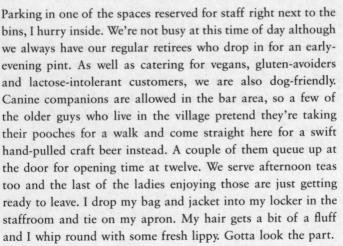

Parking in one of the spaces reserved for staff right next to the bins, I hurry inside. We're not busy at this time of day although we always have our regular retirees who drop in for an early-evening pint. As well as catering for vegans, gluten-avoiders and lactose-intolerant customers, we are also dog-friendly. Canine companions are allowed in the bar area, so a few of the older guys who live in the village pretend they're taking their pooches for a walk and come straight here for a swift hand-pulled craft beer instead. A couple of them queue up at the door for opening time at twelve. We serve afternoon teas too and the last of the ladies enjoying those are just getting ready to leave. I drop my bag and jacket into my locker in the staffroom and tie on my apron. My hair gets a bit of a fluff and I whip round with some fresh lippy. Gotta look the part.

When I head out into the restaurant, Charlie Clarke is at the desk, taking a phone booking.

'Hi,' I say, when she hangs up. 'Cut it a bit fine today. Sorry.'

She shrugs. 'Lunch was a bit manic, but we haven't exactly been rushed off our feet since.'

Charlie has been a great friend since I started here. You know some people you just bond with instantly and become firm friends for life? Well, Charlie is one of those. She's the same age as me – thirty-eight pretending to be thirty-two or less – and we have the same silly sense of humour.

Despite my bravado, I can confess to you that I felt so low when Simon left that I didn't know what to do with myself. In fact, I barely recognised the person I became. Despite the fancy haircut, the new job, the new apartment, I'd completely lost my confidence. I think I have a lot to offer in a relationship, yet my husband's head was turned by a sparkly noo-noo. That's got to hurt. Charlie has been such a tonic though. We've shared so many laughs together that she's helped me through some dark hours. Mostly because she's as jaded with life as I am. We are both bruised and a little bit broken.

Charlie's small and curvy. She'd be the first to tell you that. Our mutual muffin tops are a constant topic of conversation. She has a cheeky face and there's always a beaming smile on it, even if she's feeling rubbish inside. Her hair is her pride and joy and I can't tell you how much or how long she spends on it. It's long, dark and lustrous. She straightens it within an inch of its life and has one of those flash hairdryers which cost a few hundred quid. For a *hairdryer*. Makes my twenty-quid Babyliss look a bit pants. For work she has to tie it back in a ponytail which she resents with every fibre of her being. She's not married. Never has been. Charlie is resolutely single, but that's not to say she isn't hopelessly in love. Hopeless being the operative word.

My dear Charlie only has eyes for Gary Barlow, he of Take That mega-fame. She's been a serious fangirl since they first came on the music scene. No other nineties band will fit the bill. You can keep your Wet Wet Wet and your Westlife, thank you very much. Whenever you get in Charlie's car or go to her flat, the hit tunes of Gary and the lads are blasting out. She follows Gary to gigs all over the country but, in certain circles, isn't considered a truly hardcore fan as she's never travelled abroad to see him. Mainly due to lack of funds rather than lack of inclination. I think, if she could, she'd go to the ends of the earth for Mr Barlow. She has a cardboard cut-out of him in her living room. The first time I went back to her place, late at night, he scared the bejaysus out of me. I thought she was being burgled. She's the only person I know who looks forward to the beginning of every month simply because she gets to turn over a new Gary on her calendar. She can't wait for August because he's doing a yoga pose wearing very small black shorts.

'I've got to shoot off sharply when I'm done.' Charlie gets a tray and starts tidying the nearby tables while I scan the bookings for this evening. Tonight's steak night, which is always popular. Two steaks and a bottle of decent red for forty quid. 'I'm seeing the Take That tribute band tonight. Take Off.'

See? Total fangirl.

We both launch into the first few lines of 'Could it be Magic'. In my short time here, I've been tutored well. 'I'd forgotten it was tonight.'

'Shame you couldn't come. It's a good crack.'

'I would have loved to. I couldn't get anyone to swap shift.'

'You need to be on your toes later.' She pauses, cloth in hand. 'Our dear lord and master is in da houzz. Apparently.'

'Mason Soames?'

'The one and only.'

Wow. This is my Big Boss. The one I've yet to meet, despite having been here for two months already. 'What's he like?'

'A twat,' she says. 'But a handsome twat. He looks a bit like that movie star bloke – Tom HigglePiggleBum.'

'I know he's supposed to be my boss, but I haven't met him yet.'

'That's because he's never around.'

'Why is that?'

Charlie shrugs. 'I guess being the owner's son bestows on him a certain amount of largesse. If he was in any other business he'd probably be given the boot.' My friend rolls her eyes. 'He's supposed to be our Events Director yet he seems to spend most of his time in Klosters or Monaco or somewhere. Nice work if you can get it.' More eye-rolling.

'What does he actually do?'

'Do? Good question. Mostly he turns up in his Aston Martin and gets on everyone's tits. That's what he does. Whenever we have an event, Jay and I organise it. Shagger generally sweeps in when it's all sorted and takes the glory.'

I laugh. 'I still can't believe you all call him that.'

'Not to his face, obvs.' Charlie laughs too. 'That's probably a sackable offence. Still, you'll know why when you do meet him. He's a smooth sod. He's probably tried it on with every single female that comes through those doors. I don't think he can help himself.'

I shake my head, dismayed. 'Now I *really* can't wait to make his acquaintance.'

'Don't take your eyes off his hands or they'll be down your pants before you know it.'

'Thanks for the warning.' A lecherous boss. Lovely. Just when it was all going so well.

Chapter Five

I make sure that everything's spick and span in the restaurant. I smile brightly at the customers as I greet them at the desk and bustle about all evening being generally efficient and bright. Before I get a chance to turn around, it's eleven o'clock and the last of the stragglers are leaving as I'm wiping down the tables. It's at that point when Mason Soames finally rocks up.

He needs no introduction. Instantly, I can tell it's him. A throaty engine and a shower of gravel in the car park announces his arrival. I glance out of the window and there's some slick silver beast in one of the reserved parking spots. A moment later the door swings open and a vision in a light grey suit strides in. Charlie's right – he does, indeed, favour Tom Hiddleston. He's tall, over six feet, lean and more handsome than is good for a man. As Charlie pointed out, he is, no doubt, a smoothie but she hadn't managed to convey quite how good-looking he is. His fair hair, with just a hint of curl, is swept back but he runs his fingers through it as he comes through the door nevertheless. His features are fine, almost delicate, his skin lightly tanned. Mason Soames carries himself with the air of a man who never has to try too hard. He's certainly quite classy – even given some of the posh stuff we get in the restaurant. I bet he'd look fabulous in a tuxedo.

I'm standing with a pile of menus in my hand and become aware that I'm staring. Our eyes meet and he smiles widely at me. I try to recover my composure as I give him a professional smile back.

'Hi. I'm Mason.' His gaze is steady, searching when he extends a hand to shake mine. 'You must be . . . er . . .'

'Ruby,' I supply. 'Ruby Brown. Your new waitress. Well, new-ish.' I might not have met the boss yet, but I already feel like part of the furniture.

'Ah. Right. Yes. Of course.'

'I've been here for two months now.'

'Right. And I haven't.' He's still beaming at me and his smile is quite disarming. 'I've been skiing for the season.'

'Why wouldn't you?' I say.

'But now I'm back.' He claps his hands together. 'Is Jay around?'

'No. Night off. I'm in charge.'

'Fine. You're the very person I need then. Why don't we shut up shop together and you can tell me what's been going on here while I've been away?'

I don't point out to Mason that it's nearly my home time and maybe he should have come in a bit earlier for this chat. Still, there are just two tables left to leave and one party is getting their coats on already, so I won't be long. The couple in the corner are so wrapped up in each other that they might get down and dirty on the table and I don't want to be wiping up after that. I think I'll take their bill over to them.

'Give me another ten minutes to finish up here and then I'm all yours.'

Mason raises an eyebrow.

That came out wrong.

Flustered, I tap in the bill for the happy couple and hurry it over, interrupting their footsie. They take the hint, pay up and leave. I lock the door behind them, clear their table and turn off the lights in the restaurant. When I go through to the bar, Mason has dimmed the lights in there and is standing behind the counter. He's taken off his suit jacket and has rolled up the sleeves of his crisp white shirt, showing off tanned arms with a down of blond hair.

'What's your poison?' he says, leaning on the bar and fixing me with eyes that are the colour of summer sky – now that I come to look. They glint at me even in the low light. Always beware of a man with twinkly eyes. Charlie has told me as much.

'Diet Coke, please. I'm driving.'

'Ha. Me too. I'm making myself an espresso,' he says. 'I've a party to go to later and need something to put some life into my bones.'

'Later?' I laugh. 'I like your style. It's a long time since I went to a party that started after half past seven.'

'Join me? The more the merrier. It's just a small gathering.'

'I'd better not.' What on earth would I have in common with Mason Soames and his posh friends?

'A coffee, then? I'm a wizard with this machine.' He certainly moves around it like he knows what he's doing.

'Just the cola, thanks. If I have coffee, I'll be buzzing until dawn.'

'That's exactly why I want it.'

I laugh at that. 'Good luck to you.' I have enough trouble sleeping as it is as my mind goes into overdrive the minute my head hits the pillow and, anyway, it feels ridiculous to have decaf espresso. Isn't the very point of an espresso to make you wired?

He pours out half of a diet Coke and pushes it across the bar to me. I get a straw and try, unsuccessfully, to look cool

18

while I sip it. Mason rattles about with the cups and coffee machine, pulling levers, pushing buttons, until it spits out a double espresso. I hate the blasted thing and try to avoid it as much as possible.

'Sit?' He nods to one of the tables. 'You're not in a rush to get away?'

'No.' I wonder if he's checking out whether I've got a husband or a family waiting for me and then I think I'm maybe a bit too jaundiced by Charlie's opinion of him. I'd say that Mason Soames is no more than thirty-two or thirty-three at most, so I'm a good few years his senior. He looks like the type of man who likes his women younger and preferably of supermodel status. And why not? In his enviable situation, I'd probably be exactly the same.

We sit at the nearest table and Mason stretches out his long legs. Even with him wearing a suit, I can tell that his thighs are made for skiing. The thought of which makes me gulp down my drink. He takes a mouthful of his coffee and stretches back, comfortably. Whereas I'm not entirely sure what to do myself at all. I fuss with taking off my apron, then I'm not sure how to arrange myself in the chair. It's clear that I'm being subjected to his scrutiny and, while I'd like to tell you that I couldn't care less, I find myself hoping that I meet with Mason's approval.

'So,' he says. 'How are you finding it working here?'

I shrug. 'I like it. It's very different to what I was doing before.'

'Which was?'

Even if he read my CV, he's clearly forgotten. It was Jay, our manager, who took me on. 'I was in finance. At the local council.'

Mason nods sagely. 'Is that as interminably dull as it sounds?'

'Yes,' I admit.

He gives a guffaw and, call me stupid, but it makes me glow to think that I've made him laugh.

'I only watched you in action for a few minutes,' he says, 'but I liked what I saw. You're a natural.'

'Thanks.' My cheeks burn and I'm glad that the lights in the bar are turned down low.

'Why the sudden change of course?'

'Oh, you know.' I'm a bit reluctant to reveal my mid-life meltdown, my divorce, my lack of direction. 'New year, new me. All that. Thought it was time for a change.'

'Well, I'm glad that you ended up here in the Butcher's Arms.' He makes it sound terribly salacious. Is he flirting with me?

'I can't think of a better place,' I bat back.

Mason checks his watch and swigs back his coffee. 'I'd better be making tracks or I'll be in trouble.'

A very large part of me thinks that someone like Mason Soames is probably in trouble quite a lot. And likes it that way.

'Sure you won't change your mind?'

'No, thanks.'

'I'm going to be around much more from now,' he says as he stands. 'I want to develop the business here. We could do so much more. We'll have time to get to know each other better.'

There it is again.

'I've got to grab my bag and my jacket from the staffroom.'

'I'll wait,' he says. 'We can lock up together. I'll get the lights.'

So I go through to the back of the pub and gather my belongings, such as they are. Back in the bar, Mason has turned off the lights and is standing waiting for me in the darkness. I tell you for real, his bloody eyes are *still* twinkling.

'Ready?'

I nod. Which is stupid because he probably can't see me clearly at all.

As I pass, he rests his hand gently on the back of my waist and steers me towards the door which he holds open. Outside, the night air is cold, the moon full and bright. Mason walks me to my car and I try not to fumble with my keys as I open the door.

'Enjoy your party,' I say.

'I'd rather be going home to bed,' he replies and, again, it's ridiculously loaded. He winks at me. 'Sleep tight. Don't let the bed bugs bite.'

In a moment, he's back in his own car and roaring out of the car park. I sigh. I know which of the residents will come in and complain about that tomorrow.

I sit in my own less sleek and less shiny Mazda, gripping the wheel, waiting for the rapid beating of my heart to slow down. *He was cute*, I think. Young and cocky, but also cute. I feel myself smirk into the darkness.

This is bad, Ruby Brown. Very bad.

Chapter Six

I'm not on the same shift as Charlie the next day. Which is a good thing, I think. I'd have to confess to her that my thoughts about Shagger Soames aren't exactly in keeping with her own. He seemed nice. Too smooth, I'll give you that. Though he was much more charming and entertaining than I'd imagined him to be. Flirty even. But then Charlie said he flirts with anyone with a pulse. It wouldn't do to tell my friend that I was actually quite taken with him.

In keeping with my recently divorced status, I told you that I'd rashly booked a course of scuba-diving lessons – which, of course, I am now slightly regretting. Actually, *very much* regretting. Still, in for a penny, in for a pound. I've paid up now and won't get a refund if I bottle it, so I might as well give it a go. I could have gone for a Discover Scuba-Diving taster evening – that would have been the sensible thing to do. Right? Try it out, see if I like it. But no, fool that I am, I signed up for a full-on PADI Open Water Diver Course. Why did I do that? Because I was feeling reckless and independent and wanted to show the world that just because my man had left nice loyal me for a total slapper, I wasn't through with life. Great plan!

Though I'm currently wondering why I didn't prove that I am a rock chick by joining the local knit-and-natter club or booking Indian cookery lessons.

My first session with the Wolverton Sub-Aqua School is tonight after I've finished work and anxiety is gnawing at my stomach already. Lunch and afternoon service goes without a hitch. No breakages, no complaints, no hissy fits from the chef. Fabulous. I'm out of the Butcher's Arms on time and head straight to the leisure centre, bag ready and waiting on the passenger seat. Organised or what?

At the swimming pool, I get changed in the cramped and slightly chilly cubicle, realising that it's several years since a swimsuit has graced my body. This is an ancient thing found in the very dark recesses of my wardrobe and it's a miracle that it even still fits me. Reluctantly, I emerge in public, thinking that burkinis are, in fact, the most excellent thing ever invented. I catch sight of myself in the mirror and whilst my swimsuit might fit, just about, the Lycra is stretched to the limit and is struggling to contain the more comely of my curves. This is borderline obscene. I try to cover as much as I possibly can with my cheery towel and, worrying about whether I'm going to take some other scuba-diver's eye out with my puppies, I head off to meet my fate.

The pool area is brightly lit to an intimidating level. I feel as if a spotlight is following my every move and my stomach is a churning mass of regret and terror. I rue ever signing up for this and I'm terrified of going underwater. Surely they won't make you do that on your first lesson? Perhaps we'll just have a little paddle about in the shallow end while discussing the finer points of scuba-diving. That would suit me. While my mind is urging me to get dressed again and make a run for it, I take a shower and tiptoe my way through the hideous water bath – which, far from making me feel cleansed, always remind me that there are *veruccas* lurking *everywhere* – and on to the

23

side of the pool. I'd forgotten what chlorine smells like too. It hits me like a wall and starts me off sneezing.

At the far end of the pool, there's a group of men huddled together and no one else in sight, so I'm guessing that these are my fellow novice divers. No other women. Just blokes. That either makes me a rufty-tufty go-getter or an idiot. The only comforting thing is that the majority of the blokes look worse in their swimmers than I do. Secretly, I was hoping they might be all off-duty lifeguards or firemen, all pumped and ripped – but no. These are the male diving equivalent of the Lycra-clad, middle-aged ladies at Zumba.

All except one and he steps forward. 'Hi. Welcome.' This man is tall, handsome, broad in the shoulder and lean in the waist. There is a six-pack very much in evidence and he wears his swimmers rather more pleasingly than the rest. He holds out a hand and I shake it. 'I'm Joe Edwards. I'll be running the session this evening.'

'Hi. Ruby Brown.' I remember to give his hand back.

'Good timing. We're just about to get started.'

Which I read as *Cutting it fine there, love.* I pull my towel a little bit tighter around me.

Without further preamble, Joe takes us through the equipment we're going to use, his voice echoing the way voices do in swimming pools. There seems to be an awful lot of stuff we need and I learn that those massive flipper things that you put on your feet are actually called fins by those in the know. Who knew? He gives us a run-through of some safety basics and then, before I'm quite ready for it, he says, 'We've got some really experienced guys here to help you, so let's get into the water and we can show you some more.'

Water? So soon? I thought it might be lesson two or maybe even three before the dreaded water would be introduced into the mix.

While everyone else picks up their equipment and partners up, Joe sees me dithering and comes over. 'OK?'

'Just nervous.' I try to stop my teeth chattering.

'Your first go at diving?'

I nod.

'It's easy. You've just got to be methodical, safety-conscious and stay chilled. I'll buddy up with you for this lesson. You'll be fine.'

Hmm. I think I'll be the judge of that. Though the idea of buddying up with Joe does have a certain appeal. He gets my equipment while I stand there like a wet fish. Joe patiently explains what it's all for, one more time, while he loads me up but I'm not sure that I take any of it in as terror has turned most of the information he's imparting to gibberish. First the fins go on and then a weight belt which weighs a ton and makes me wonder how I'll manage to move at all. Then I'm kitted out with air tanks which weigh even more and I'm feeling like a beached whale rather than the vision I previously held of sporty sleekness cutting a dash through the water. I tell you, I'm going to drown, not scuba-dive.

'This is the glamourous bit.' Joe raises an eyebrow. 'Now you need to spit into your face mask and smear it around.'

'Seriously?' I'm sure I gag a bit. When I was a child, my mum used to spit on a tissue and rub it round my face to clean it – didn't all mothers? Totally gross. I don't think I've ever recovered from the trauma. Thank goodness some bright soul invented Wet Wipes.

'You'll thank me for it later when your mask doesn't steam up.'

'There's no other way?'

He shakes his head. Someone ought to patent a waterproof mask gel or something for moments such as this. I compromise and lick my finger then rub it, reluctantly, round the inside of my mask. Joe laughs.

'Wait until we do a cold open water dive and you need to wee inside your wetsuit to keep warm.'

That day is *never* going to happen, I can tell you now. If I'd known that scuba-diving involved being bathed in your own urine, I'd never have signed up. More than ever, I am finding the thought of extreme crocheting or a bit of macramé more and more appealing. However, I'm here now, so what else can I do other than subject myself to it?

Finally, I splat my way towards the pool in eight tonnes of gear, fins flailing. Joe climbs in first. He doesn't look anywhere near as ungainly as I do. He waits for me at the bottom of the steps as with much huffing and puffing I go down backwards into the water, not entirely unaware that my own derrière is descending perilously close towards his face. Joy.

Chapter Seven

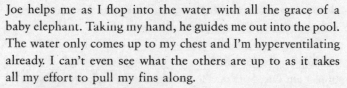

Joe helps me as I flop into the water with all the grace of a baby elephant. Taking my hand, he guides me out into the pool. The water only comes up to my chest and I'm hyperventilating already. I can't even see what the others are up to as it takes all my effort to pull my fins along.

'The first thing we'll do is put our masks on and sit on the bottom of the pool.'

That doesn't sound too onerous. I can do sitting down. In fact, I'm something of an expert in it.

'I'll give you this sign to check that you're doing all right.' He makes OK with his fingers. 'If you're feeling good, you do the same. If you're unhappy, thumbs down and we'll come straight up again.'

'OK. OK. OK.' Breathe. Breathe. Breathe. 'I can do this.'

'Masks on. Breathing tube in your mouth. Just take normal, relaxed breaths. Easy does it.'

I follow Joe's lead, trying not to think how my face must look squashed into my mask, my mouth beautifully distorted by the tube. A moment ago, Joe looked very handsome; now he looks like something out of a horror film. An underwater horror film, obvs. So there's no way I want to see how I look in a mirror. He gives me the OK sign as I try not to spit out the tube. It feels as if I've got a pair of socks wedged between my tongue and my tonsils.

He takes my hand and signs that we're going to sink beneath the surface of the water and we do so in harmony. I can hear my breathing in my ears and I know that it's too rapid, but I'm surprised how much I can see beneath the water. This is not particularly a good thing. The swimming pool is clearly the place where all Elastoplast go to die. There's surely more silty stuff on the bottom than can be classed as hygienic and I wonder how many little kids have weed in here. But I try not to think about that and concentrate instead on relaxing and enjoying the moment. Actually, the last bit is a step too far. I concentrate on surviving and trying not to scream.

Joe and I sit cross-legged on the bottom of the pool, still holding hands. He gives me the OK sign and I echo it back to him. I am OK. Sort of. However, he didn't tell me the sign for 'I'm barely coping'. We sit and sit a bit more and, eventually, my breathing returns to a more even keel. I know it's one small step for man and all that, but it does feel like a giant step for me. It's the first thing I've done in a long time that's all *my* idea. I'm not doing it because some bloke enjoys it and if I want to see him at all, I need to tag along.

Despite all the weights I'm laden down with, my bum keeps bobbing up from the bottom of the pool and making a bid for the surface. Believe me, it's surprisingly hard to sink when you need to.

Joe signals that I should try to slow my breathing and I do. He gives my hand a squeeze and I take it to mean that I'm doing all right and I get a little thrill from that. Get me, Ruby Brown, fearless scuba-diver! Joe gives me the thumbs up and my bum touches the floor of the pool once more. He puts his fins on top of mine and we sit perfectly still for a few more moments. As I finally start to relax, he gives me the sign that we're going to the surface and I feel surprisingly disappointed that it's all over.

We come up together and Joe helps me to take my mask off. 'You did well, Ruby.'

'That was completely brilliant.' Well, I wasn't quite so keen on it when I was down there, but once it's stopped, I want to do it all over again. Immediately! I have a rush of something – blood, adrenalin, testosterone – that makes me feel more buzzy than I have in a long time.

Joe laughs. 'Good. Think you'll come back next week?'

'Definitely.'

'Excellent. I've never lost a student yet.' He shrugs out of his gear and then helps me with mine. For a moment, Joe looks hesitant and then he says, 'We normally go to the pub afterwards. Just a few of the lads. If you fancy joining us.'

'Sounds like a plan.'

'Great,' he says. 'I'll wait for you in reception.'

So I hurry off back to the changing rooms, run round the shower, letting the warm water dispel my goosebumps. I use a lot of shower gel in the hope that I don't still smell of chlorine. I give myself a quick rub round with a towel and blast the hairdryer over my sodden locks so that I don't drip in the pub. Not sure I can count it as a hairdo, but I can't really keep Joe waiting for too long while I style it properly.

Still carrying a faint whiff of Eau de Bleach, I hurry into reception.

Chapter Eight

Despite my attempt at speed changing, Joe is, indeed, already standing there. He's reading notices on the board in the manner of someone who's pretending to be busy and isn't really. He spins round when I say, 'Here I am.'

For a brief moment, the sight of him takes my breath away. He's dressed in a black hoodie over a white tee and jeans and, for some reason, he looks a lot more handsome than he did in the pool. Could be that his face isn't squashed out of shape by a mask. Just guessing. Or perhaps I was too traumatised by my impending ordeal to take a proper look. Well, now I'm getting an eyeful and very pleasant it is too. He has dark hair, almost black, curly and long into the nape of his neck and there's a shadow of dark hair along his strong jawline as is the fashion. I think he's probably a couple years older than me. I'd make a stab at forty-two or three. He's got a strong, vibrant face, though his eyes seem tired if you look closely.

'The others have gone on ahead,' he says. 'It's just us two.'

'I had to do my hair,' I offer apologetically. It must be so much easier to be a scuba-diver if you're a baldy.

'No worries. The pub's only round the corner.' Joe holds the door open for me and we head out into the cool evening, falling into step side by side. There's hardly anyone around as we walk up the side street towards the main road in Wolverton. A few lads hanging around by the school look as guilty as hell as we pass and there's the heady whiff of cannabis coming from their general vicinity. I'm wondering whether I should have left my car parked by the leisure centre or whether I should have driven to the pub. I hope Joe walks me back.

As if I haven't got enough to worry about, I'm fretting about catching pneumonia or pleurisy by going out with damp hair – the things that your mother tells you leave scars for life – when Joe says, 'You did well tonight. You were nice and calm. Not everyone does so well on their first session.'

I get a rush of pride. 'Thanks.' We make our way along the street of slightly downtrodden terraced houses before turning onto the main road. It's dusk now and the street lights are flickering into life.

'Have you always wanted to have a go at diving?'

'No,' I admit. 'It was recently added to my To Do List. I'm currently embracing the whole post-divorce, independence, new-me thing.'

'Ah,' he says. 'I can empathise. I've also found myself recently single and staring at divorce papers.'

'Me too.' Even as I say it, a secret evil part of me is glad to hear that he's not happily married. He kind of looks as if he would be. That doesn't necessarily mean that he's on the market, of course. 'Sucks, doesn't it?'

'Yeah,' he agrees. 'It's certainly a steep learning curve.' Joe shakes his head, sadly. 'You sort of assume that when you sign up for life it won't all fall apart in fifteen years.'

'Fifteen years. Wow. Is that how long you were together?' Seems like a Herculean effort when compared to my paltry attempt at forever.

31

'Even longer, I suppose. As usual, we were together a few years before we took the plunge.'

'I only lasted five in total with Simon. I'm trying to see being single again as a new challenge rather than an abject failure.'

'I think if I was on my own, I'd probably do the same. Unfortunately, I have two children who are very bewildered and hurt by it all.'

God, what an idiot I am. It never occurred to me that he'd have kids to think of. 'I'm sorry to hear that. It must be a nightmare when there are children to take into account. Kids are remarkably resilient though.'

'That's what everyone keeps telling me. I'm not so sure.' He sighs and jams his hands into the pockets of his hoodie. 'I can understand Gina walking away from me if she'd had enough, but how do you turn your back on your kids?'

'How old are they?'

'Old enough for them to be taking it badly. Tom's fifteen and Daisy's twelve. Tough ages at any time, without all this as well. They should be into kids' stuff and not having to deal with our problems.' He shakes his head, baffled. 'Tom's doing all right. On the surface. But Daisy's not happy. I know it. She needs her mum around. It breaks my heart.'

'It will all work out.'

He laughs, but it's not without humour. 'If I had a pound for everyone who said that to me, I'd be buying myself a yacht in the Bahamas.'

'Good diving out there, I hear,' I tease.

'At this rate, I'll never find out,' Joe says as we arrive at the pub. He stops under the light of a street lamp and turns to me. 'That was a pretty heavy conversation for openers.' He grins at me and I notice that he has a beautiful smile. It softens his face and takes years off him. 'Sorry about that.'

I grin back. 'How very un-British of us. We should have been talking about the weather.'

'Sorry,' he says again. 'There's no one I can really talk to about it. My mates just think my ex is an out-and-out bitch yet I'm trying my best to keep a slightly more balanced view of the situation for the kids' sake.'

'That sounds like a healthier option.'

'Yeah,' he agrees. 'It's a noble sentiment, but some days it's easier than others.' He opens the door to the pub and we step inside. 'I'll buy you a drink by way of apology for bending your ear with my break-up woes.'

'I'll just have a diet Coke please. Driving.' I'm going to end up looking like a glass of this stuff if I drink much more of it, when I'd really rather look like a glass of champagne.

He steers me to the group from the dive club and introduces me. 'This is Ruby, lads. She completed her first session tonight with flying colours.' Then he leaves me to chat to them while he pushes through the crush of people to the bar and gets our drinks.

My eyes follow him. Hmm. It would be very easy to fall for someone like Joe Edwards. Someone exactly like Joe Edwards but who wasn't recently divorced and had two kids.

Remember that, Ruby Brown.

Chapter Nine

If you were looking for a quiet pub in which to have a romantic get-together, this isn't the place. It's rough, it's noisy and the heavy metal music's turned up loud – no Kylie or Take That here. Oh no. The base level is Led Zeppelin and it seems to get heavier from there up. It's also accompanied by a constant clank from the bank of fruit machines on the far wall. However, the crowd from the sub-aqua club are friendly and I note with relief that a few more women have joined the group.

Joe comes back, hands me my drink and, thankfully, stays by my side to chat. A number of people come over to say hello and it's clear that he's a popular member of the group. He has an easy way with him, a ready smile. Some people are natural team leaders and, from what little I've seen, my guess is that Joe is one of them. I listen to chatter about air tanks, dry suits and rebreathers and understand none of it. No idea. Every sport, it seems, has its jargon and diving is clearly no exception.

'Did you finalise the dive day, Joe?' someone asks.

He nods. 'Yeah. We're off to Quarry Hill Cove again. You need to get your name on the list. It always fills up quickly.' Joe turns to me. 'You should come with us.'

'Me? After one session in the pool? I'm not sure I could cope with that.'

'You won't be ready to dive in open water, but come along for the ride. It will give you more of an idea of what it's all about and you can get to know some of the other people in the club.'

'I don't want to be a spare part.'

'We're always happy to have an extra pair of hands to help with the equipment. There's a nice pub there and we get something to eat afterwards. It's not a bad day out, if the weather's good.'

'There seems to be a lot of socialising involved with this diving lark.'

Joe laughs. 'We do our best. Come,' he urges. 'I have a spare seat in my car. I'll give you a lift, if you like. You don't even have to drive.'

'It's sounding very tempting,' I admit. 'I'll have to check my shifts though. When is it?'

He reels off a date that's tantalisingly close. 'Call me tomorrow, if you can make it.'

'I'll do that.' He reels off his number and I punch it into my phone. Then he downs his drink. 'I've got to shoot. I'm picking the kids up. One's at football practice, the other's at her friend's house and they've probably both got homework that they haven't done yet. Do you want me to walk you back to your car, Ruby?'

'Yes,' I say, thinking of the gang of young lads that could still be hanging around there. 'I should be going too.' Though I have nothing but an empty flat waiting for me. I need to get a goldfish or something. A cat seems like too much responsibility and too much like giving up on the world.

So I say goodbye to my newfound diving mates and follow Joe out into the night air. There's a briskness to his pace and

I realise that he must be running against the clock. I hurry to keep up with him.

'Do you have a lot of help with the kids?' I sound slightly breathless in my bid to match his brisk pace.

'Hardly any.' He sighs. 'My family are scattered all over the place, so I can't call on them. Mum and Dad moved down to Taunton to be near my sister, so they're too far away. My brother's working in Canada on contract for the next couple of years. Not that he'd be much use. He's got four of his own to keep him occupied.' He raises an eyebrow. 'Some of the mums of Daisy's friends have been great. They'll step in for taxi duties if I'm stuck and the kids both go to after-school clubs which helps. I don't like to push it though. I work shifts – not that unsociable – but there are times when I can't be around for them.'

I guess I'm lucky that most of my family are all local. I couldn't have managed without them when I split with Simon. Sometimes, though, they can feel a bit *too* close. Do you know what I mean? I can't move without my mother wanting to know what I'm up to. Still, as I'm mainly at work or watching telly, she doesn't have too much to worry about.

'What do you do?' It hadn't occurred to me that Joe might have a day job as well as being a scuba-diving instructor. 'I thought this was your work.'

'Diving? No. I wish it was. Diving is my sanity. It's the only thing that I do for myself. I'm trying to hang on to that. I only volunteer as an instructor. If I know I've got people waiting at the pool for me, I've an excuse not to miss it. I'm the manager of a community for supported living. That's what pays the bills.'

'Sounds interesting.'

'It's a great place but it's fairly full-on. We house mainly adults with learning disabilities. At the moment, we have a lot of Down's Syndrome residents and they're fantastic, but they'd have me there 24/7 if they could. You should see the timetable I have to do each week for me and the kids. I've got full custody of the children, but Gina's supposed to have them every other weekend and one night in the week.'

'You're having to keep a lot of plates spinning.'

'Yeah. My ex seems to be spending a lot of time on romantic little weekend breaks when it's her turn to have them. Though she tries to tell me it's to do with work. I wish my job took to me to Rome, Paris and Vienna.' He smiles grimly. 'That must sound very bitter and twisted.'

I can't really deny it as there was a definite edge that crept into his voice, but it seems as if he might have good cause. However, there are always two sides to every story.

'She changed her job a year ago and ended up going off with the guy who's her boss. He's rich, slick and has no family commitments. I think Gina sometimes forgets that she still has children.'

'It all sounds very raw.'

'I'd like to be able to tell you that it wasn't acrimonious, but I'd be lying to you. It's tough maintaining a civil relationship when you get the impression it's all one-sided. I feel as if I'm running round like a headless chicken while she's swanning about as if she hasn't a care in the world.'

'I'm sure you'll get it sorted out given time.'

'Yeah.' He doesn't sound convinced. 'All I can do is try to protect Tom and Daisy from the fallout.'

'And what about you?'

'Right now, I'll settle for those plates staying in the air and not coming crashing down on my head. I'm always terrified I'll forget something.'

'I'm sure you're doing the best you can. No one can ask more of you.'

He clears his throat before he says, 'I don't have much time for anything else in my life.'

You're telling me. There's a bit of an edge to his voice and if he thinks that he's warning me off any kind of notion I might have about becoming romantically attached to him, then there's really no need. If there's one thing I've learned this evening – apart from buoyancy, bottom time (not what you might think) and equalisation of the ears – it's that this man's life is complicated. I've no idea how he manages to cope with all that he does. And I admire him for it. I just don't want to be part of it. There's no way that I want to be getting involved in another relationship. Not me, no sir! This is my time for fun. Sheer, unadulterated, especially uncomplicated fun. I'm just waiting for it to begin! I don't want to be dealing with someone else's heartbroken kids and bitch ex-wives. Noooo way.

While I'm still trying to work out whether I need to spell that out to him, we reach our cars which are thankfully still intact outside the leisure centre. He walks me to the door of mine.

'I'll see you next week for your lesson, then?' He grins as he says it.

'Yeah,' I agree. 'You will. I enjoyed it. In a vaguely terrified way. You're a very patient instructor.'

'And you'll let me know about Quarry Hill Cove?'

'Yes,' I say. 'I'll ring or text tomorrow. I won't be taking up the space of a diver?'

'No. It will be great to have you along.'

Then I climb into my car and he goes to his.

There's no way that I'm going on the dive outing. Why would I? I'll just let it slide for a few days and there won't be room for me, anyway.

Joe's nice, I think, as I watch him walk away in the direction of his car. Very nice. But he's made it very clear – even if I was interested – that he's got no room for romance. Well, me neither. I don't need a man in my life. All I'm looking for now is fun, fun, fun.

Chapter Ten

'How was the scuba-diving?' Charlie asks.

'Wet,' I tell her. 'Mainly wet.'

We're in the Butcher's Arms, waiting to start our shifts. It's a warm day, so we're out by the bins behind the kitchen. Charlie and I are perched precariously on a rickety bench that has a couple of screws missing from the arms and even more broken slats. I'm not entirely sure what's holding it together. It's been dragged out of the garden before some poor unsuspecting customer plonks themselves on it and ends up in a heap on the floor and then sues our arses off for a broken back or neck or something. Now it's headed for the local tidy tip as soon as someone can remember to take it up there.

Chef has made us both bacon butties – on sourdough, of course. I don't think he even knows what a white sliced loaf is. We're having a sneaky coffee too – latte for Charlie, cappuccino for me – so all is well in the world. The sun is warm on my face and it's nice to think that summer will soon be here.

When Charlie finishes her butty, she goes through the complicated rigmarole of smoking an e-cigarette. No one looks cool vaping, but I don't tell her that. She rummages in her little pouch full of preferred flavours of liquid and what-not, then fusses and fiddles. It's like watching a heroin addict getting ready to shoot up. She drags on her e-cig and puffs out a huge cloud of water vapour. I wave it away. Smells nice though. Vimto, if I'm not mistaken.

'No hotties in ridiculously small Speedos in the manner of Tom Daley?' Charlie regards me through the fragrant mist.

'No.' I get an unbidden flashback of Joe's rather fine six-pack.

'Were there any hotties at all or were they all middle-aged men suffering a midlife crisis?'

'Mostly the latter.'

'Mostly?' she queries. You can't get much past Charlie.

'Well, my instructor was actually quite fit,' I admit. 'I went to the local pub with him afterwards.'

'Oh, really?'

'With a group of other divers from the club. Not like a date or anything. He didn't single me out. Don't get over-excited, we're not planning to get engaged.'

'Shame. I could do with a party to go to.'

Me too. I need to do something to kick-start my party-party lifestyle. 'Downside: he's recently separated and has a couple of kids. That's *definitely* not on my shopping list.'

'It seems pertinent to remind you that there are very few guys out there of our age who don't have history of some sort.'

'Yes, but he's right in the thick of it. They still sound as if they're at war. Besides, he has full custody of his kids and I'm not really child-friendly. I think the mothering gene has passed me by.' I can't say that I've ever had a maternal pang. Perhaps that's because the men in my life to date have all taken more looking after than a kid.

'You and me both. Though I might have made an exception for Gary Barlow. I'd have been quite happy to push out a football team if he'd asked nicely.'

We both have a good giggle at that. 'You know he's a very happily married man.'

'Of course I do and that's part of the attraction. You know that he's good husband material.'

I suppose she has a point.

Then Charlie adds, somewhat darkly, 'Besides, things change.'

They certainly do. She's right about that if nothing else. One minute you can be happy and settled, the next minute you're not. Someone waves their crystal-encrusted chuff at them and they're off. Though I think the chances of Charlie ending up with her unattainable pop star are about the same as me finding a nice, uncomplicated, child-free man to love.

'It's a shame, as this instructor is quite cute,' I say rather wistfully. 'If he was by himself, I might be quite interested.'

'Don't go overboard with praise,' Charlie quips.

'You know what I mean. I think he could become a friend if nothing else. He's nice to be with. And, while he's not romance-appropriate, he seems like a good instructor. So I'm going to give scuba-diving another go.'

'Foolish woman.'

I grimace and try not to think how panic-stricken I was on my first lesson. Confidence will come in time, I'm sure. I just need to try to stick with it. I'm not a good sticker. I have a history of flitting about from thing to thing. Maybe I've just never found my niche before.

'There's a day out to a dive place coming up which I've been invited to. I've checked my shifts and that's my weekend off. I don't know if it's my thing though.'

'I guess you never know until you try it.'

'The same could be said of many things,' I point out.

'Go. There might be some other hot stuff single dive bloke *without* kids that you haven't met yet. If you've nothing else on that day, what have you got to lose?'

'True.' Plus it means I can put off painting the granny annexe for yet another week.

'So the scuba-diving lesson wasn't a complete waste of time?'

'Far from it. I'm prepared to admit that I didn't exactly enjoy the whole diving thing while it was actually happening, but I felt exhilarated afterwards.'

'You could be talking about the last time I had no-strings-attached sex.'

We find a filthy guffaw for that.

'Speaking of no-strings sex,' Charlie continues. 'How did you get on with Shagger?'

Ah, moment of truth. 'I quite liked him,' I confess, wincing as I wait for the backlash.

Charlie looks at me aghast. 'Awh, come on! He's a complete sleazeball. What's wrong with you, woman?'

'Sorry.' I cringe a bit more. 'He's a smoothie, no doubt. But he can rock a sharp suit and he has a certain charm too.' Charlie rolls her eyes at my obvious lack of taste. 'I know, I know. Maybe I'm on heat or something. Is it a full moon? I've had my head turned by two men in the last couple of days. That usually doesn't happen in a couple of *years*.'

'I don't want you going anywhere near Shagger. Seriously. He's had every gullible woman that's come through this place.'

'Including you?' I tease.

'I said *gullible*,' she stresses. 'I'm totally immune to Shagger's charms. I only have eyes for Gary. You know that. It's you I'm worried about.'

'I've met men like him before, Charlie.' I feel slightly piqued that she thinks I'd be so easily fooled by a bit of flattery. 'Many, many times. I'm a woman of the world. I know how to handle him.'

'Yeah, so did the last assistant manager. Yet she was on that bar with her knickers round her ankles before you could say "inappropriate".'

'Oh my God. How do you know?'

'CCTV is a very cruel and revealing thing.'

'Nooooo!'

'Oh, yes. Everyone in the staffroom saw it. Her resignation was on Jay's desk the following morning.'

'Poor woman.'

'Silly, silly girl, I'd say.'

'Harsh, though.'

'That's what our Shagger is like.'

'Well, you don't have to fret. I'll steer well clear.'

'Chef said he's coming in again later. I don't know what we've done to deserve two visits in quick succession. We normally only see him once every blue moon.' She gives me a probing look. 'There must be some new attraction.'

Then, mercifully, her phone pings which distracts her. 'Hey, babe,' she says and, while she's busy chatting, I turn my attention to my own phone. I take the opportunity to tap out a text to Joe and, despite my qualms, tell him that I can make the dive outing to Quarry Hill Cove. Anxiety prickles in my stomach as I type. I don't want him to think that I'm interested in him more than the diving. Not that I'm really interested in the diving, but I can hardly say that I'm coming to check out the talent – if there is any. Before I can think better of it and change my mind, I press send.

When Charlie hangs up, she says, 'That was one of my GB Army mates. We've scored a bunch of tickets for one of the live shows of *Let it Shine* on Saturday.' One of those Saturday night talent shows – this one featuring, of course, Take That. 'It's up in London. Do you fancy coming along?'

'Deffo. It's my weekend off. I've just agreed to go to the dive day out on Sunday, but I'm free on Saturday.'

'Perfect. It'll mean a seriously early start.'

'I can do that. I'll set double alarms.'

'We should be outside the studio for about six o'clock to make sure we get near the front.'

I look at her, horrified. 'Six in the *morning*? You're kidding me? I've seen this on telly. The show's not until the evening.'

'I know, but there's no point going if you're at the back. Gary can't see me then.' She has a point, I suppose. 'How will he know I'm there?'

'You could text him?'

She shakes her head at me. 'You are an innocent in the world of fandom.'

'Does he have to know that you're there?' I ask somewhat weakly. I know the answer already. Charlie looks at me as if I am more stupid than Mr Stupid. 'Will there even be trains at that time of day?'

'I'll drive in. We can park up at Euston and get a Tube or taxi across to the studio.'

That sounds a bit more civilised. I glance at my watch. 'We'd better get back inside, Charls, or Chef and Jay will have our guts for garters.' Charlie packs away her e-ciggie and I knock back the dregs of my coffee, now cold. We jump down from the bench, glad that it hasn't collapsed under our collective weight. She links her arm through mine as we walk towards the restaurant, saying goodbye to the sunshine for the rest of the day. 'We can play Take That's Greatest Hits all afternoon to get us in the mood.'

'Fab.'

Together we break into the chorus of 'Pray' and throw in some of the dance moves.

'See. I'm teaching you well. You wait and see, I'll induct you into the GB Army yet.' Charlie gives me a smug smile. 'I *am* his future wife, you know. If not in this life, then in the next. I'm prepared to wait.'

I laugh at that. 'That's so creepy and not a little scary, The Future Mrs Barlow.'

'Yeah,' she says. 'Even for me.'

Chapter Eleven

As predicted, Shagger Soames does turn up. Right in the middle of evening service. We are totally rammed with not a table to be had and lots of disgruntled customers who've been waiting in the bar for over forty-five minutes. Our diners are intent on hogging their tables tonight and there's nothing I can do to rush them.

I'm feeling red in the face and just a little bit fractious when I see Mason swing in to the restaurant out of the corner of my eye. I'm delivering drinks to a table who've already had the wrong order and I have to give them my full attention, but I still manage to catch that he's wearing a black shirt and jeans which look mighty fine on him. I really don't like what that does to my heart rate, but I put it down to the fact that I'm rushed off my feet. He is handsome. God damn his eyes.

My next glimpse of him is ages later. I go to find a couple who've been hanging round in the bar patiently waiting for a table to come free. If I were them, I'd have departed long ago and would have gone to another pub. I'll reward their long suffering with a complimentary bread basket. Such is my power. I note that Shagger is behind the bar, sleeves rolled up, serving drinks. He winks at me in quite a sexy manner and I nod back, curtly. This isn't one of those films where the heroine, even though in peril, has the time to stop for a flirtation or a snog. I've got work to do. The time for fraternising is much later. I wonder if Mason will linger this evening and if we'll share a convivial drink or two together. Perhaps I'll risk something stronger than Coke and splash out on a taxi home. Reckless, that's me.

By the time we're quietening down towards ten o'clock and I finally have time to breathe, there's no sign of him. I wander over to the window as casually as I can and check for his car in the car park, but it's no longer there.

'Looking for His Highness?' Charlie asks as she's tidying up the menus and clearing the Specials board.

'Stop it,' I chide, though I feel as guilty as hell. 'Has he gone?'

'Yeah. About half an hour ago.'

Bugger. How did I miss that?

'He had a date to shag a supermodel or something,' she says over her shoulder.

'He said that?'

'No, but it oozed out of every pore.'

Charlie does make me laugh. Apart from anything else, Mason Soames is *way* out of my league. He's too young, too handsome, too sophisticated, too rich. And I'd do well to remember that when my tummy flutters every time I see him.

Chapter Twelve

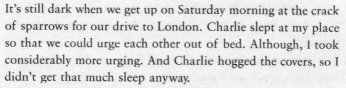

It's still dark when we get up on Saturday morning at the crack of sparrows for our drive to London. Charlie slept at my place so that we could urge each other out of bed. Although, I took considerably more urging. And Charlie hogged the covers, so I didn't get that much sleep anyway.

With Gary Barlow on the menu, Charlie was up and raring to go. We are now elbow-to-elbow at the sink in my cramped bathroom. She's already working her way through Take That hits in a startlingly chirpy manner, also proving that you can sing and clean your teeth at the same time. She's currently belting out 'How Deep is Your Love'.

My love for her at this moment in time is definitely not that deep.

'I never usually get up at this time unless I'm going to catch a flight,' I mutter under my breath.

'You'll be glad that you did when we're at the front with Gary winking at us and his lush bum is wiggling an inch from my nose.'

Is that to be considered a good thing?

As one, we turn round to look at my new cut-out Gary

Barlow, who has taken up residence in the corner of my bedroom. Charlie makes a squeeee noise. 'You like your present?'

'Love it.'

'You're not just saying that?'

'He's fabulous. I'll tell him all my secrets.' If I'm truthful, I find it a bit creepy to be sharing my home with cardboard Gary, but I don't tell Charlie that. It's the thought that counts, isn't it? I've always liked Kylie, but never thought to buy an effigy of her for my lounge room. It seems that I have, in fact, been a veritable lightweight on the fan scene. Buying an overpriced ticket or two for each tour just doesn't cut it.

'£29.99 off eBay. Bargain. He'll give you hours of fun. No home should be without one,' Charlie tells me sagely as she looks wistfully at The Barlow. 'I get great comfort from him. No licking him though,' she warns. 'The ink comes off on your tongue.'

'Can't say that was my plan and I'm not even going to ask how you know that.' I nudge her out of the way so that I can see the mirror. What stares back isn't looking good, though I simply can't apply make-up at this time of day as my face might fall off. I'll have to do that in the queue. I settle for brushing my teeth and a rub of the facecloth round my chops. 'Couldn't someone have stood in line for us?'

Charlie gasps. 'One of the unwritten rules. No one cuts the line. Pushing in is *totally* bad form. You queue, you do it for yourself.'

Fair enough, I suppose. Though, at this point, I'm wondering why I'm not just going to be sitting on my sofa watching it on telly with a mahoosive glass of red and a bag of Thai Sweet Chilli Sensations. Instead, I'm going to be standing in the dark and – I glance out of the window – rain for most of the day to see a band I like but am not mad keen on. I think better than to voice this.

'I've got T-shirts for us too.' She toddles off, so I hog the mirror. When she comes back, she's holding them up. They're white and have *Let it Shine!* in silver emblazoned across the front along with lots of spangles.

'Fabulous.' She throws mine to me and I pull it over my head. 'Do you have the world's largest collection of Take That fangirl T-shirts?'

'Probably.' Charlie tugs hers on too. 'I should start a museum. God, that'd be great.' She smooths *Let it Shine!* over her ample bosom and pouts at her reflection. 'Lovin' the tee, but it hides my tattoo.'

Charlie has recently had yet another inking. This one is the Take That logo just above her breast and the words *Relight My Fire!* in fancy script. She has half a dozen or more about her person – there are lyrics to 'Rule The World' across her lower back; a friendship bracelet with five beads, one for each of the guys, and a charm featuring Gary's face hanging from it around her ankle; and his signature graces the inside of her arm along with two kisses. I can't remember what else but I think they show a certain amount of dedication to the cause.

'Maybe you'll get to show him in a private meeting,' I say, wickedly.

My friend sighs. 'Wouldn't that be a thing?'

I'm sure that happy little thought will sustain her all day.

'Come on, Ruby, we'd better get going. We don't want to miss out. I had a quick look at the Facebook page and there are people queuing already. Maybe we should have gone straight from work last night.'

I'm not sure I could cope with spending a night on a pavement for anyone.

'I've queued for three days before now just to make sure I get a good spot. It's madness,' Charlie adds.

We're agreed on that.

So I grab a packet of HobNobs to take with us in lieu of breakfast and we jump into Charlie's car, which appears to be more reliable than mine. Minutes later we're heading off towards London.

Chapter Thirteen

It's a little past six o'clock in the morning when we reach the Maida Vale studios. I'm still half asleep and the HobNobs have long gone. It's just about light and, despite being nearly summer, it's bloody freezing. I wish I'd put on a fleece or thermal knickers. At least it's stopped raining. For now.

We walk along the length of the queue which already snakes along the pavement and Charlie says hello to nearly everyone. Clearly these are the hardcore fans. Some have chairs and flasks. At the front there are even pop up tents and sleeping bags in evidence, so obviously the queuing started in earnest last night and those fans have endured the cold and rain to be at the front.

We take our place at the end of the line. Charlie gets plastic bags out of her pocket and we put them down on the damp pavement so that we can sit on them. I wish I'd brought more HobNobs. I admit that I'm amazed to see that there are many, many ladies here before us. Many ladies and one solitary man.

'Hi, Paul,' Charlie says as he comes alongside us. 'All right?'

'Yeah. Good to see you. I saw on Facebook that you were coming. Mind if I join you?'

'Be my guest,' Charlie says. He unfolds a small camping chair and sets it up beside us. 'You take this, Charlie. I'll have the plastic bag.'

'If you're sure,' she says, but is very quick to swap with him. Paul settles on the plastic bag next to me.

'Hiya.'

'This is Ruby.' Charlie flicks a thumb at me. 'A Take That virgin.'

'Nice to meet you,' he says.

'You too.' He's a nice-looking guy. Shortish but kind of slender with fair hair, kind eyes and, even at this ungodly time of the day, a warm smile.

'You're not a fan?'

'I do like their stuff, but I probably wouldn't be up at dawn to see them if it wasn't for Charlie.' I confess with a grimace.

He laughs at that. 'This is how it begins.'

'I'm prepared to be converted. Have you always been a fan?'

'Yeah,' he admits, shyly. 'I realise that I'm a thorn among many roses, but the good ladies of the GB Army tolerate me.'

'We love you,' Charlie says. 'You balance out the oestrogen level a bit.'

He laughs. 'I'm not sure about that.'

'What time does the show start?' I ask.

'Seven o'clock.'

I think I must gasp out loud as they both laugh.

'We're in for the long haul,' Paul says.

'You have to be dedicated,' Charlie adds. 'Once we've got our entry tickets we can leave and come back later. So we're not stuck here all the time. They open the doors about four o'clock so that we can watch the sound checks and the end of the rehearsals. We usually try to nip to the Chinese restaurant down the road and have a set meal. Does that sound OK?'

'You've obviously done this before.'

'Many times,' Paul concedes.

'So how come you're such a big fan?' I ask him.

'I was an aspiring performer,' he says. 'I went to stage school as a kid and wanted to be in a boy band. Take That were my heroes. Even now I could show you all of their routines.'

'That would be a sight worth seeing,' Charlie quips.

'I just wasn't good enough,' he admits, with a hint of sadness. 'I was there with the future David Tennants and Olivia Colemans. I'm afraid that I was one of the also-rans.'

'Harsh,' Charlie says.

'But true. I had a few bit parts as an actor and a few in the chorus of musical theatre which didn't really live up to expectations or open the door to stardom. I could have spent the next twenty years chasing a dream and having walk-on roles in *Holby City*, but I decided to do something lucrative instead. I'm an accountant by day, but I'm in a band even now. I play bass in a pub a couple of nights a week which keeps me sane. The rest of the time, I follow Take That.'

'We're both going to try to get to their gig in Paris this summer if I can blag some extra shifts,' Charlie says. 'You should come.'

Then a bunch of ladies walk along the queue, chatting as they go. When they see Paul, they stop to hug him. While he's distracted, I whisper to Charlie, 'He's very nice.'

'Yeah.' She glances in his general direction and says rather non-commitally, 'He is.'

'Is that it?'

Charlie checks he can't hear and then whispers to me, 'He wears Tom Ford's Neroli Portofino just like Gary does.'

'Does he? Is that a good thing?'

'Are you mad?' she says in disbelief and shakes her head at me. 'It smells like paradise and a basket full of fluffy kittens.'

I spend the next hour trying not to sniff him. We wait some

more and then, at two o'clock – when we've been waiting for a mere eight of our human hours – we get our valuable golden tickets that allow us to go into the studios at four o'clock where we can enjoy another three-hour wait for the show to start.

'We can go and get some food now,' Charlie says, folding Paul's camping chair.

'Fantastic.' I'm up and off my plastic bag quicker than a flash. 'I'm starving.'

This show had better be good for all this effort. I tell you, at the very least, I want twenty-four-carat gold dust raining down on me from above and a chance to sit on Gary Barlow's knee.

Chapter Fourteen

We're seated at a window table at the Golden Phoenix next to the obligatory waving cat. Over a set meal for three, Nice Paul tells us more about his life. He's single, no lurking children – not that he knows of, anyway. Always good. He seems solvent and sane. He's ticking a lot of boxes. He has an easy, self-deprecating way about him – the polar opposite to Mason Soames.

I wonder what Mason's doing this weekend. I bet he's not queuing in the cold to see a band. Mason is the kind of guy who knows someone, who knows someone else who'd get him into the VIP Gold Circle – and not standing tickets either.

Then, fortified with rather excellent Chinese food, we head back to the studio. The second we're allowed in, I follow Charlie and Nice Paul in a rush down to the barrier in front of the stage to bag a prime space. The atmosphere is crackling with anticipation and I'm really excited to be here, so Charlie and Nice Paul must be about to wee themselves with ecstasy.

As the small theatre fills up, sound checks for the acts start, so there's plenty to keep us occupied while we wait and I hardly notice the pain in my back and my feet. Charlie hands out bottles of water to us.

'Go easy how you drink it,' she says with a wink.

I take a sip and realise that my 'water' is neat vodka that has survived the bag search. Well that's certainly going to go some way towards easing the pain.

'You're driving,' I remind Charlie.

She shakes her bottle at me. 'Mine *is* water.'

The show starts and it's fabulous. The fans are in a frenzy before anything happens so when Gary, Mark and Howard are joined on stage for the opening number by Robbie Williams the place goes wild. I look over at Charlie and she's in complete rapture, her face shining with joy. I feel my own face may be a little flushed with pleasure too. Nice Paul, I have to say, is watching Charlie as much as he is the band. They're right in front of us and I can now see why we've been here since the crack of dawn. The boys play their new songs and some of their most loved favourites and, by the end of the evening, I'm a Take That convert.

The rest of the evening is dedicated to a range of boy bands competing to take centre stage in a new musical about Take That. They go through two or three numbers each, all accompanied by slick dance routines. I have no idea which of the wannabe boy bands wins and I don't really care as they all seemed great to me. To this crowd, they're very definitely the secondary attraction. Then Take That do a final number and a mass of peri-menopausal women go into meltdown. I include myself and Charlie in that. We might be in our thirties, but it won't be long before our oestrogen leaves the building. We throw ourselves into singing and screaming and dancing with abandon.

Then it's over. The lights come up, the stage crew start to take away the equipment and break down the set. It's been a long and happy day. The vodka has kicked in and seems to double in potency as the fresh air hits us. We stagger back to the Tube – me, Charlie and Nice Paul – arms slung round each other singing 'Could It Be Magic' at the top of our voices. I've had far too much to drink and I've only just remembered that I've got to be up early tomorrow morning to go on this flipping dive outing. How much am I regretting that I signed up for that now? I'd be much happier staying in my PJs all day watching Take That DVDs with Charlie.

Still, this is what it is to be single and having fun. I'm out there giving it large. I'm not only embracing it, but I'm bloody well enjoying it.

Chapter Fifteen

The alarm goes off and I want to die. Not just die a little bit, but seriously, properly die. I try to lift my head off the pillow. Actually, I think I might have died already. I open one eye and tilt the iPhone towards me so I can check what time it is. I'm sure it's more blurry than it used to be. Another early start in succession. I'm *so* not built for this.

I haul myself out of bed and force myself to perform my ablutions so that people don't think I'm a total skank. The water in the shower hurts. I am meeting lots of new diving buddies today and I wish I was doing it with less vodka in my tanks. It was all happyhappypartyparty last night, but good grief am I paying for it this morning. I think once you reach your thirties your ability to process strong alcohol severely diminishes – yet every time you have strong alcohol you somehow forget that.

I pull on jeans and a T-shirt, then drag a comb through my hair. I can't do make-up. My face is too hurty. The sheer weight of mascara would just make my eyes close again. Besides, the natural look is fashionable. I think. Maybe that was last year.

While I'm still trying to make myself swallow Weetabix in an attempt to put a layer in my stomach and quell my faint vodka-based nausea, a car pulls up outside and a quick glance out of the window tells me that my ride is here. Maybe I shouldn't call Joe that, it could be misconstrued. Though I do like punctuality in a man.

Giving him a quick wave from my balcony window – which sounds considerably more grand than it is – I grab my bag and a bottle of water, then run downstairs. To be honest, the running is more akin to a painful tiptoe. But in my head, it's running. Every movement of my skull makes it throb. I hope I've got some paracetamol lurking in the bottom of my bag.

I slide into the car next to Joe and am not so hungover that I fail to notice, once again, that he's a very handsome man. I also clock that there's a whole heap of scuba-diving gear on the back seat.

'Hi,' I say.

'Rough night?' he asks.

So I clearly look as bad as I feel. It's a good job that I'm not trying to impress this man. 'Vodka was taken.'

'Ah. I remember late nights and getting hammered,' he says fondly. 'Just about.'

'I was in London with a couple of friends watching Take That at the Maida Vale studios yesterday.'

'Big fan?'

'Yeah.' I nod and instantly regret it. 'Well, I am now.' It was great fun – apart from the queuing part – and I can see why Charlie and her friends are so dedicated. Up close and personal they've got great energy and charisma. Would that someone might say that about me.

'I'll drive slowly,' Joe says. 'Not too many fast bends. It's mainly motorway. We've got plenty of time to get up there.'

'I don't even know where we're going,' I admit. Not only did I not read the small print, I didn't take much notice of the big print either.

'Quarry Hill Cove,' he tells me. 'A nice dive centre in the Midlands. It's a flooded gravel pit and there's a sunken boat in the water and the cockpit of a plane.'

I raise an eyebrow at that. 'Why?'

'It makes the dive more interesting,' he explains. 'There are things to look at and explore. Otherwise, it's just an exercise in getting wet.'

If you're like me, you'd have imagined that, once qualified, I'd be diving in aquamarine seas with dolphins and pretty angelfish and shit. Metaphorical shit, not *actual* shit, obvs. Destinations like the Maldives, the Seychelles and the Caribbean were my dreamed-of go-to places. A gravel pit in this country wasn't necessarily *that* high on my list.

Joe laughs, clearly able to read my mind. 'It's a great place,' he insists. 'Wait and see.'

'I'll take your word for it.'

'If nothing else, it'll give you a good chance to meet some of the other members of the club. They're nice people. We always have a laugh.'

'I'm regretting the vodka frenzy now,' I admit. 'I wish I was at my sparkling best.' I start to rummage in my handbag. 'Painkillers,' I mutter. 'I'm sure I've got some buried in here.'

'There's a packet in the glove box,' he says. 'I'm a dad. I can always supply aspirin, tissues and plasters. Though now the kids are getting older, it's usually only money that they need. Unfortunately, that's in shorter supply.'

'Where are they today?'

'I've dropped them off at Gina's yesterday. She's got them for the whole weekend. She remembered this time, which is never a given.' He gives an unhappy snort. 'Sometimes they come on the dive days with me. Very reluctantly, it must be said. They get bored quickly and I can't concentrate properly while I've got one eye on them. Daisy's at the age where she just wants to be at the shops with her mates and trying to drag Tom away from his computer is a life's work.'

'They sound like most children.' As if I know.

'They're good kids,' he says, thoughtfully. 'Though it is nice to have a day to myself for a change.'

I find the painkillers in the glove box, knock back a couple and wonder how long they'll take to kick in. Not long, I hope.

We turn on to the M1, but swinging left and heading north today rather than right and into London.

'Close your eyes if you want to,' Joe says. 'Have a nap. We can listen to some music.' He grins at me. 'I haven't got any Take That.'

'I've got pretty eclectic taste.'

'Ed Sheeran?' he suggests. 'My kids hate it. They call it Old Fart music. I have to listen to One Direction when Daisy's in the car and some hideous, headache-inducing rapper grime stuff when Tom has control of the iPod.'

'Ed Sheeran's fine.' He flicks on the music and 'Shape of You' fills the car. He turns it down to a civilised level.

I text Charlie to thank her for a great day. In return she sends two kisses and a selfie of us both with Nice Paul in which two of us look all pink and drinky. Then I let my head rest back and that's all I can tell you.

Chapter Sixteen

I jerk awake as we come to a halt in the car park.

'We're here, sleepyhead,' Joe says.

I try to blink myself to full consciousness.

'Feel better?'

I'm struggling to marshall my thoughts into cohesive speech, but eventually croak out, 'I think I will do when I've had a cuppa. Or two.' Suddenly, my stomach springs into life and rumbles noisily. 'And maybe a bacon sarnie.'

'Now you're talking my language,' Joe says. 'I'll just check in with the kids to see if they're behaving.' He punches a couple of text messages into his phone while I go about the business of waking up – stretching, yawning, all of that. When Joe's done, he shows his phone screensaver to me. 'My babies.'

They both have dark, glossy hair matched with olive skin and possibly favour their mother, though they look like Joe around their eyes. 'They're good-looking kids.' And they are. I'm not just making pleasant noises.

'They take after their mum. Gina's Italian. They've got my brains though,' he quips.

'Poor devils,' I tease.

He rolls his eyes. 'That's about right.'

'Are they both OK?'

'They've not killed each other yet,' he tells me. 'Always a good sign.'

'Do they get on well?'

'Not that you'd notice,' he admits. 'Tom's fifteen and finds everything annoying, especially his little sister. She, in turn, does her very best to wind him up.'

'Happy families, eh?'

He shoves his phone in his pocket. 'There's not been much of that recently.'

'Time's a marvellous thing,' I offer. 'They'll get over it.'

'Yeah.' He doesn't sound convinced. 'Anyway, that's enough of me. We've got some diving to do.'

Now that I've finally got my eyes to do focusing, I note that Quarry Hill Cove is, indeed, a lot prettier than I'd imagined. The former quarry is secluded, surrounded by trees, and tranquil. It's still not the Caribbean though. It's just after nine now and the sun is already doing its best to warm the day. The rays dance on the water, which is trying very hard to sparkle. Though it's not exactly turquoise – more of a murky brown. But it's a nice spot and the perfect place to spend a lazy Sunday. And it's not raining or cold. Bonus.

'Let's go and see the others,' Joe says and gets out of the car.

There are a number of vehicles parked close by and, already, their occupants are unloading diving gear. I follow Joe and we walk over towards them.

'Hi, guys.' He claps a few of them on the back. 'This is Ruby. She's come along today to see what goes on at a dive outing. She had her first session in the pool last week and did really well.'

I get that little glow of pride again. 'Hi,' I say, shyly.

'Hi, Ruby.' A few of them wave and say hello, then someone arrives with a tray of takeaway drinks and says, 'Tea?'

When I nod, he hands one to me and I take a grateful gulp of the tea; it tastes every bit as good as champagne. Joe and I stand and chat to the members of the group while we drink and there's much joshing and laughter. They discuss the condition and temperature of the water which goes over my head. It sounds cold, is all I know. Very cold.

'We should get the gear out of the car, Ruby. Want to give me a hand?'

So I go to the car with Joe and heave out all manner of stuff. Wetsuit, tanks, fins, demand valve, a dive knife, so many hoses that I've no idea what he'll do with them all and a face mask. This looks like a flipping expensive sport. Even if I do qualify as an open water diver, how would I afford all this kit? I suppose you can rent some of it, but still. Maybe I'll have to take up running instead. All I'll need then is a pair of trainers and some nipple cream.

While I fuss about, not really knowing what I'm doing, picking up stuff and putting it down again, Joe heads off to the changing rooms with his wetsuit. While I'm still fussing, he comes back. He's clad in tight neoprene from the waist down and is bare-chested. I tell you, I have no idea where to look first. He has a very fine physique and I feel myself getting all flushed. I think my hormones are still a bit awry after that oestrogen overload at the Take That gig.

Joe sits on the lip of the car boot while he eases himself into the rest of his suit and I assist him, as best I can, with putting on his belt and tanks. 'Pass me that please, Ruby.' I hand him the massive torch he nods at. 'You can't see a hand in front of you without this.'

'So what's the joy of diving in water like this?'

'You'll see when you try it,' he assures me.

This is not sounding thrilling. 'Any fish?'

'Some,' he says. 'Pike – a few big ones. Perch, roach, fresh-water crayfish. No sharks.'

I guess he's teasing about the last bit.

We go to the water's edge and I help the divers to launch the boat they call the RIB – which must mean something, but I'm too tired to ask what. The divers climb in and I squeeze in beside them, then we head out into the middle of the water. It feels good to be scudding across the lake, breeze in my hair. I could definitely get used to this, even if I never make it to the bottom of the quarry.

When we stop, there's more faffing as Joe pulls on his fins and his face mask. 'See you shortly,' he says. 'Enjoy the sunshine.'

One by one, the divers drop over the edge of the boat and disappear beneath the waters of the lake until I'm left with just one of the guys. 'Now all we have to do is wait,' he says.

So I sit back in the boat and close my eyes, enjoying the peace and quiet. Loving this diving lark, so far.

It's probably half an hour or more before Joe and his diving buddies come back and we help them to climb on board. We head back to shore where they have their tanks refilled and dive again, this time from a platform.

I find a suitably sunny spot where I'm not in the way and lie back on the grass, dozing. This is the most relaxed I've felt in a long time. In my half-dreaming state, I pick over the wreckage of my marriage as I do when I've got nothing else crowding my mind. To my surprise, I start to feel small strands of contentment weaving their way in. I've been hurting for so long that I began to worry that it would never stop.

Sometimes, I find myself dwelling on what Simon might be doing now. Are he and the Crystal Queen still loved-up? Good luck to them if they are. I truly believe that I could have done nothing more to save our relationship. I was a good wife. I kept the house clean and tried to make it a home. We ate nice meals. Not so much in the week as we were both busy, but I cooked something special every Saturday night and Friday night we'd get a takeaway and open a bottle. I knew exactly how he liked his steak cooked. Not the high-life, I grant you, but isn't this what makes couples tick? I watched one of the *Sex and the City* films again recently – which I love – and Carrie Bradshaw was ticked off and in fear of her marriage because Big didn't want to go out to dinner every night. That's not real life, is it? Well, perhaps it is in Manhattan, but it's certainly not in Costa del Keynes. Marriage is rubbing along very nicely together, isn't it? Snuggling up on the sofa, sharing a bar of Cadbury's, having sex twice a week if there's nothing better on the telly and being each other's best friend. Or am I missing the point?

What did Joe's wife want from her marriage, I wonder? What has she found with her new man that's made her want to walk out on her husband – who looks pretty good on paper – and her lovely kids? Had they just got into a rut together or was it something more? Perhaps marriage is always more of a struggle than floating on a cloud of romance. I wonder what she found that she didn't have with Joe? He looks pretty perfect to me. Then I chide myself. I must not think that way.

I'm footloose and fancy-free and he very much isn't.

Chapter Seventeen

When Joe eventually comes back, he looks happy and that makes me smile.

'That was great,' he says as he shrugs off his tanks. 'Nothing like coming nose-to-nose with a monster pike to sharpen the senses.'

'I have watched *Jaws*, *Jaws 2*, *Jaws 3-D* and *Jaws: The Revenge*,' I tell him. 'I am suitably impressed.'

'I'm impressed that you could sit through all of that nonsense.'

'*Jaws* was a classic,' I protest. Though, in fairness, it was all a bit downhill from there.

'I'm a man who's sat through more Disney films than you can shake a stick at,' he says. 'So I'm not really in a position to throw stones.'

'Did you see anything else down there?'

'The tug was fun to go through even though I've done it a dozen times before.'

And this is the thing with diving – do I really want to be crawling through what is essentially wreckage? And mixing it up with pike? I'm pretty sure they have sharp, bitey teeth and evil eyes. My vision of diving was more akin towards *Finding*

Nemo or *The Little Mermaid*. I decide against mentioning that.

Joe goes off to get changed so I help some of the guys with their gear again and generally hang around until he appears, freshly showered and changed. He smells of citrus aftershave and not of murky pond water.

'Ready for something to eat?'

I've hardly worked up an appetite, but I never knowingly turn down food. We head across to the pub with the rest of the group and enjoy a convivial meal with much banter and fun. I watch Joe, surreptitiously, as I eat my fish and chips. I like the way he acts in a group. He looks after everyone and he's clearly popular as a result of it.

His phone pings and he checks a text. He sighs and a world of frustration is expressed in it. Then he turns to me. 'I need to get back for the kids,' he says.

'Is everything OK?'

'Gina wants to drop them off early. There's a surprise.' He's keeping a lid on his temper, but I suspect he's seething. 'I can get someone else to take you back, if you're not ready to leave.'

'No,' I say. 'That's fine.' A night in front of the telly won't do me any harm even though I'm supposed to be searching for the new party-party life.

So we load up and drive home. This time Brandon Flowers keeps us company and I notice that Joe is a bit quieter on the drive. An hour or so later, we pull up outside my granny annexe.

'Do you want a quick cuppa?' I ask.

Joe checks his watch. 'I'd better get back. Gina will be dropping them off shortly and I don't like to leave them alone for long otherwise they start to kill each other.'

'Thanks for a great day. I've really enjoyed it.' Even though I didn't actually have to trouble myself with the business end of diving.

'See you at your lesson this week?'

'Looking forward to it already.'

I go to open the car door and he puts a hand on my arm. 'You're a great girl, Ruby. We've had a good laugh today and you're easy company.'

I'm glad he added the word 'company' to the end of that sentence.

'I have to put my kids first though,' he says. 'Above everything.'

'I know. It's what dads do.'

'I'd like us to be friends.'

'We are, aren't we?' What on earth is he on about? Then the penny drops and, once again, it sounds as if he's trying to warn me off. WTF? Well, there's really no need. 'I like you, Joe. But I'm only recently divorced myself and I'm not looking for commitment. I'm not *looking* at all,' I stress. 'If I were, I'd want someone with more freedom.' And *fewer children*, but I don't think I need to spell that out. We both know exactly what I mean.

'I just didn't want you thinking there could be more.'

'You should be so lucky,' I quip and we both force a laugh. But, in truth, that stings. We hardly know each other. I don't feel that there's any need to put a stake in the ground so soon. He's the one who asked me to go to the pub, the one who invited me to the dive day. I've done nothing to indicate that I'm interested in him.

'I should go.' I jump out of the car before this conversation can become any more embarrassing.

'See you, Ruby,' he shouts after me, but I don't reply.

I climb the staircase to my granny annexe, fiddling with the keys, as Joe sits there for a second too long before he turns round and drives off. I don't even watch him go which I hope shows him how very unconcerned I am.

Then, with the rest of the evening to myself and the world

at my feet, I dump my stuff, pour myself a big glass of wine and fall into the sofa. I watch *Ant and Dec's Saturday Night Takeaway* and while the perky duo do their best to be hilariously entertaining, I lie and wonder whether I'll actually go to my dive lesson this week. I'm never going to be able to afford the Caribbean and I certainly don't want to go and play among the pike in a gravel pit every weekend.

I don't think that diving is really me after all. Probably best if I try another kind of hobby. Wonder if I'd be any good at cake baking?

Chapter Eighteen

The downside of divorce is that you have to do your own DIY. All of it. I have had very little experience of power tools in my life, but I'm having to get to grips with them now. Thank you for that too, Simon the Knob. Today is putting up shelves. I gave up last time I attempted it and drank gin instead. I wish my dad was one of those dads who comes round to decorate for his daughter, but he's not. My dad, though I love him dearly, hasn't a practical bone in his body. If my mum wants any little jobs done round the house she has to 'get a man in'. I want to try to avoid going down that route. Women can do anything these days and that includes putting up shelves.

This morning I've been onto YouTube and watched many, many videos of people putting up shelves – only getting slightly distracted by videos of Take That and cute cats doing foolish things. Anyway, on the shelf-putting-up videos, they make it look easy. I can do this. I am woman. Hear me roar.

First, I'll have some more toast.

I'm feeling quite flat this morning and I don't know why. I had a lovely weekend, spent time with nice friends, ogled Gary Barlow and Co., and hung out with a lot of guys in neoprene.

What's not to love? So why do I feel like a deflated balloon inside? I'm on my third coffee and still I'm not getting that lift I need. I add two chocolate digestives to the mix and wait. Still nothing. Then extra-extra toast does nothing either. This is serious.

Maybe Joe warning me off has left a weird taste in my mouth. It was a real sideswipe. We hadn't even got into full-on flirting. I don't want to get involved with someone like him, anyway. Why does he even think that? He might be handsome, he might be nice, but he's not exactly without complications, is he? Two of them in particular. Perhaps it would be different if I had my own children and was looking to form a blended family, but I'm not so why should I be in a hurry to take on someone else's offspring? And there are other handsome, nice men out there. I'm sure there are. Also, I really do want to embrace this whole single thing. I've been a serial monogamist since the age of fifteen and I want time finding out who I am when I'm not in a couple. Plus, I'm not getting any younger and this might be my last time to play the field. Don't they say that women over forty become invisible to the opposite sex? That means I've got, at best, a few years to have some unfettered fun. Actually, that's quite depressing.

I should look for something else to do besides diving. Something with less testosterone. I pull my iPad towards me – and two more chocolate digestives for good measure – and Google 'hobbies for women in their thirties'. This is the list. In alphabetical order. I kid you not.

Acting. I'd get hives if I even thought about going on stage.

Biking. Mountain or road. Me and Lycra are not a good mix. At least in dive gear I'm under water where no one can see me.

Birdwatching. Seriously? Apparently, 85 million Americans enjoy this particular hobby. I didn't even realise there were that many Americans.

Blogging. I have no life, ergo nothing to blog about.

Bowling. Described as a 'fun group activity'. I'd rather eat my own face.

Calligraphy. Camping.

Canning. I have no idea what that even is. Oh. 'The preserving of leftover fruit and veg.' Not on your nelly. Surely no one can get their kicks from that?

Cards. And not even poker. Bridge is what they suggest. I didn't think you could play bridge until you were over seventy.

Chess. *Chess*! 'Wonderful for staving off Alzheimer's to which women are particularly vulnerable.' Oh, joy.

I skip through dancing, embroidery, floral arranging, gardening and geneology.

I dip back in at quilting. And straight out again. Did I accidentally Google 'hobbies for women in their nineties'?

They suggest spending time with family and children. Is that even a hobby? That's just life, no? A hobby is what you do when you need to take yourself out of your life. Or find friends. Or give yourself a thrill with something that isn't out of an Ann Summers shop.

W is wine tasting. Now you're talking! This is the most interesting one so far. Though solo wine tasting every night seems not to be recommended. It stresses, rather heavily, 'occasional and social drinking'. I don't know about you, but I'm always *much* more sociable when I'm drinking.

Y equals yoga. Strictly for vegetarians and people who wear Crocs without shame.

Nothing for Z. No zoology, zorbing or ziplining. Not even Zumba, which I have already tried and at which I failed.

What is a lady in her thirties to do? Even the so-called expert hobby bloggers have written us off.

Now I'm really fed up. I can't even face putting up my shelves. For the four hundredth time. Still, I'd better do it soon or my landlord might change his mind and rent this place out to a DIY whizz. I finish the last of the choccy biccies and set to. As I've seen on YouTube, I mark with a pencil where I want the holes for the screws. So far, so good. People do this day in, day out all around the world. How hard can it be? I get out my fancy new drill and switch it on. God it terrifies me. Still, if I don't do this no one will. I lean in and drill two holes in the wall. Not bad, if I say so myself. I blow the dust out of them and am surprised to see that I have a lovely view of my bedroom through them. Looks like I've drilled into the wall and straight out the other side. Bollocky bum. Didn't see that on YouTube. There must be a special and different way of tackling paper-thin walls. I put the drill away. I'm clearly not an independent and capable woman with power tools. I'm a stereotypical DIY disaster zone. Damn. I should do what my mum does and 'get a man in'.

I call Charlie. She'll cheer me up. We organise to have a coffee before we both head into work. I'll fix the holes in the wall later. Or tomorrow. Or somehow turn them into a feature.

Chapter Nineteen

Charlie makes me laugh and she's feeling all loved-up as she's still basking in the Gary Barlow afterglow. By the time I start my shift, I'm feeling better again too. More or less. We're busy, as always, and the evening flies by. We finally start quietening down at about ten o'clock and that's when Mason rocks up.

Nudging me in the ribs, Charlie says, 'Shagger's here.'

This, I already know. We have fancy cars galore that turn up here, but my ear seems to have very quickly become attuned to Mason's motor. Knowing Charlie, she probably calls it the shagmobile or something.

'Is he?' I try to sound disinterested. My heart says otherwise. It's doing the heart equivalent of running round waving its pants above its head.

Mason swings through the door and, when he sees me, holds up a hand in greeting. He looks great, as he always does. He's wearing a light blue shirt, open at the neck, and dark jeans, but they're designer stuff, well cut. 'Nicely turned out' as my nana always says. My stomach, stupid thing that it is, flips a bit. I know that I shouldn't be pleased to see him, that he's an out-and-out smoothie, but clearly the message is not getting

77

through to my vital organs. To teach them a lesson, I walk off in the opposite direction to clear a few tables. When they do manage to make me follow Mason – *minutes* later – I take a tray of empties through to the bar. Mason is talking to Jay, the manager, and I squeeze past them both to find a home for the tray.

When I turn to go back out into the restaurant, Mason steps in front of me. 'Hello, Ruby. How are things with you?'

'Cool,' I say. 'We've been mad busy all night. I'll be glad to sit down for five minutes.'

He lowers his voice. 'Stay for a drink,' he says. 'When everyone else has gone home.'

I'm assuming by that he means Charlie too. I'm about to make an excuse not to when I think 'sod it'. Why shouldn't I have a drink with him? Just the one won't hurt. Surely? Probably best if I don't tell Charlie though. She'll have a fit with her foot in the air. Or she'll want to stay too. Then I wonder why I don't want her to – which is hardly fair of me as she includes me in everything she does. I should go home. That's what I should do.

When I finish, I head to the staffroom. Charlie already has her coat on. 'I've got to swing into the Tesco Extra before they close,' she says. 'No loo roll. No coffee. No bread. One of those things I can't manage without.'

'Coffee?'

'Ha, ha. Very funny. Catch you tomoz?'

'Yeah. We on the same shift again?'

'Lates for me.'

'Me too. We could go somewhere for brekky in the morning.'

'Sounds like a plan,' Charlie says. 'Text me.'

'OK.' I fuss about, not getting my coat.

'Love you. Laters!' she trills and bounces out.

What do I do now? I didn't notice where Mason was on my

way in here and I don't want to look as if I'm hanging around waiting for him. That would be too desperate. I think I'll get my coat and make for the door as if I'm going to leave. If he asks me again then I might stay. Only might.

Leaving work never used to be so complicated at the council finance department, I tell you. But then my boss had dandruff and halitosis, so no contest really.

I get my stuff out of my locker and head out. In the bar, Mason is sitting at one of the tables, arm thrown casually over the back of his chair. He always looks so sharp, so hot – no wonder more impressionable females fall so easily for his rather obvious charm. 'Join me for a glass of wine?'

'Don't mind if I do.' So much for me playing hard to get. But then he did say the magic word. Wine.

With far too little persuasion, I take the chair opposite him and he pours me a glass. I hold it up and we clink glasses. 'Cheers.'

'Another busy night,' Mason says. 'The pub's doing really well. Number one in the chain.'

'It's on account of the charming staff,' I quip.

'I wouldn't disagree with that,' he bats back. 'You give great TripAdvisor.'

That makes me laugh and Mason smiles too. He has good teeth. Expensive ones. Like the ones you see in reality shows about trendy young things. Gleaming. It makes me realise that I'm probably overdue at the dentist.

'I like the pub when it's empty.' Mason has dimmed the lights and it's obviously just the two of us.

'It is nice,' I agree. 'Peaceful.'

'This place was built as a farmhouse originally. It's been here for about four hundred years. The farmer used to give out beer to the labourers from the back door.'

'I like the thought of that.' We both take in the blackened, rugged beams in the bar area, the sturdy hearth that once would have been the centre of a home and exchange impressed glances. 'It feels as if we're a little part of history.'

'Yes,' he agrees. 'The custodians of the past and for the future. We should do something to celebrate.'

My heart does a little pitter-patter. Remember that CCTV, Ruby Brown!

'Let's go to a club.'

'It's Monday night.'

'Oh, I think they open then. But only for depraved souls.' He swigs his wine and fixes his eyes on mine. 'I know a little place. Very exclusive. I'd like to show it to you. Fancy it?'

I look at my watch, uncertain.

'What have you got to get back for?' His eyes twinkle in the low light. 'You're not going to turn into a pumpkin are you, Brown?'

'It feels very wicked on a school night.' I suck in an anxious breath. 'What will the boss say?'

'Oh, I think he'd be all in favour.'

Then I remember I'm in my uniform of black trousers and white shirt. 'I'm not exactly dressed for clubbing.'

'You look gorgeous,' he says, lightly. 'We can snuggle up in a cosy corner.'

Charlie's right. He's an outrageous flirt.

'I'm driving too.'

'Let's leave our cars here. I'll call us a cab. They'll be all right here overnight. There's CCTV.'

Yes, I know all about that.

'Have I convinced you?' he asks.

I knock back my wine feeling more than a little reckless. 'Let's do it.'

Quick as a flash, Mason phones for a cab and I head off to the loos where I fluff my hair – which makes absolutely no difference at all to improve my general scruffiness – and make a token effort with a lippy. By the time I'm back in the bar, the cab has arrived. Mason turns off the lights and gently ushers me outside while he sets the alarm and locks up. I stand in the car park, shivering in the cool night air, feeling both a little bit sick and ridiculously excited. But, most of all, I'm wondering exactly what I've just agreed to.

Chapter Twenty

A short while later and we're in one of the posh hotels in the city centre, heading to the top floor in the lift. I'm very aware that we're close together in a confined space. We both stand and listen to James Blunt crooning.

'I didn't even know there was a club up here,' I say to Mason.

'Ah.' He taps the side of his nose. 'It's only just opened and it's very exclusive. Members only. You have to be in the know.'

'Or know someone who knows.'

He grins at me. 'Or that.' A tasteful stainless steel plaque on the wall announces that the hidden club is called the Vibe Lounge. His hand rests on my hip as he opens the door for me and steers me inside.

It's a beautiful place: small, intimate, and well out of my usual league. No wonder I don't know about it. I bet Charlie doesn't either and I'd normally credit her with knowing every-where. It's so sophisticated in here and, even in my uniform, I wouldn't be mistaken for staff. The waiters in here are hipsters wearing red waistcoats, the waitresses are in slinky red velvet dresses and vertiginously high heels. I hope that Mason doesn't think about introducing this dress code at the Butcher's Arms. My feet would die within ten minutes.

We're greeted by a guy who looks like a model. 'Hi, Mr Soames,' he says. 'Good to see you.'

'Thanks, Callum. Busy tonight?'

He nods. 'Word is spreading.' Then he shows us to a blood red chesterfield sofa by the big, stone fireplace where a fire roars in the grate. The room is seductively lit, the main illumination provided by small chandeliers that hang over the side tables. All along the fireplace is a row of elegant church candles and above them is a huge modern painting depicting a coat of arms. There are more candles clustered, artfully, on a silver plate in the centre of the dark wood coffee table. Next to them is a vase of scarlet roses. On the far side of the room there's a bar, also lit so low that I've no idea how they can see what they're doing. In the corner there's a DJ playing smooth tunes and a dance floor the size of a pocket handkerchief.

'Well, this is all very lovely,' I whisper.

'You like it?'

'It's fab. You say it hasn't been open long?'

Mason shakes his head. 'A couple of weeks. This is one of our ventures too.' I can't help but notice the pride in his voice. 'Well, it's my baby, really,' he adds. 'We're aiming it at couples who want something a bit out of the ordinary and are prepared to pay for it. We want it to be classy, a cut above.'

'You've certainly done that.' I bet membership here costs a fortune.

'We haven't even had a proper launch party yet,' he says. 'I wanted to give the staff chance to find their feet. You'll have to come along when we do.'

As if I'm going to say no. I'd go to the opening of an envelope and perhaps my one desperately underused party dress will get an airing.

The waitress comes over. 'Hello, Mason. Nice to see you.' She gives him a winning smile and they exchange an intimate glance. Hmm. Wonder if this one is another of his many conquests. 'What can I get for you?'

'Hi Cindy, I'd like a Jack Daniel's on the rocks, please.' He turns to me. 'For you, Ruby?'

'I'd like a Hendrick's gin with Fever-Tree tonic and a slice of cucumber. Thanks.'

Cindy dips and puts out two cocktail napkins and a small bowl of wasabi peas. I realise that I haven't had anything to eat all evening and fall on them.

'We should get some food,' Mason suggests.

'I haven't eaten all evening. I could kill for some chips.'

'I'm sure we could organise that.'

When Cindy comes back with our drinks, he orders two club sandwiches and fries. I'm getting to like this man more and more. And they say the way to a man's heart is through his stomach. There's a short cut straight to mine.

I settle back into the sofa. 'This is beyond cool,' I marvel. 'Thanks *so* much for bringing me here.'

'I value your opinion. You're very straight-talking, Ruby. I like that.' Mason glances round the room and I can see the pride on his face too. He's clearly pleased with his little self and why not? It's fab. Most of the tables are full, with couples or small groups of friends, but there's no lairiness like there is in so many clubs now – one of the main reasons I don't go to them. Plus I'm about twenty years older than the average clientele. Here, the atmosphere is great. 'If it goes well, then I'll roll it out in a few other cities.'

'Bye-bye Butcher's Arms?'

'Jay is doing a great job. I'm really surplus to requirements there. I know a lot of the staff feel that way.' He gives me a wry glance and I say nothing. Mason is obviously more shrewd than he appears. 'I've had a very privileged life, Ruby, and I've spent a lot of time jetting about, shirking my responsibilities. Now I'm ready to step up to the plate and I've managed to let my father give me free rein with a few of my own projects. I want to take on a new role in the company and make my mark. This is my first chance.'

'Looks like you've done it with good style.'

'I've put my heart and soul into it. It needs to succeed. My old man might have once had a soft spot for the black sheep of the family, but even he's run out of patience. He won't cut me any slack if this place flops. It's his dosh behind it.'

'I can't see that it will.'

Mason smiles. 'Thanks for your confidence in me. I have a lot to prove. Both of my brothers are successful businessmen and my sister is a barrister. I'm the no-good waster of the family.'

'I wouldn't say that.'

'My dad does and what he says is law. He's a very difficult man.'

I think of my own family, who are as soft as putty and have ceaselessly supported me through all my trials and tribulations.

'I have a lot to prove,' he continues. 'My family look down on me and I've played along with it just to wind them up. One of the reasons I spend so much time away is to avoid their scrutiny and their censure. It doesn't work though.' He shrugs his shoulders. 'Now I've got to grow up and make something of myself. I can't sponge off my parents for ever.' Then he grins at me. 'They've said as much themselves.'

I laugh at that and we clink our glasses together. 'Here's to growing up.'

'How boring,' Mason says, but we down our drinks anyway.

I'm surprised that he's being so candid with me, but I like this softer, more thoughtful side of Mason.

The waitress brings our food and Mason orders more drinks. We busy ourselves with eating and, when we've finished, we settle back in the sofas.

'I've talked enough about me. What about you, Ruby Brown? What do you want from life?'

'I'm still trying to work that out too,' I confess. 'I'm recently divorced and am finding being single more difficult than I thought I would.' Perhaps the gin – both doubles, I'd guess – is loosening my tongue. Mason is also surprisingly easy to talk to. Perhaps it's the convivial surroundings. If I was part of a couple with plenty of cash, I'd definitely sign on the dotted line for membership here. 'I just know that I don't want to get into another relationship. I want time on my own to have some fun and try new things.'

'Such as?'

'I'm open to anything,' I tell him. 'The more life experiences the better.' Annoyingly, I get an unbidden flashback to Joe in his diving gear. Well, the particular bit where quite a lot of him wasn't in his diving gear. I don't really want that when I'm here having a perfectly nice time with Mason. 'I've taken up scuba-diving.'

'Cool,' Mason says. 'I did my dive training out in the Maldives.'

Of course he did. Not the bottom of Wolverton swimming pool for the likes of Mason Soames.

'I've let my licence lapse now,' he admits. 'I've been more into skiing these last few years. My family have a chalet in Switzerland which I go out to.'

Hey, and my family like Toblerone, so we have something in common.

'I'm not sure diving's really for me,' I admit. 'The Maldives are beyond my meagre income.' Then I realise that it's Mason who provides my meagre income. 'I didn't mean it like that,' I add hastily. 'I like working at the Butcher's Arms, but I don't think it's my forever job. Though it does mean that I'm going to have to consider a cheaper hobby unless I want to dive at a gravel pit in the Midlands.'

Birdwatching. Embroidery. Bridge.

He clinks his glass against mine. 'Here's to life experiences.'

'To life experiences,' I echo.

We polish off our drinks and then I find myself stifling a yawn. 'I should go. I have work tomorrow.'

'Me too. I thought we might have a dance before we leave. We haven't checked out the dance floor yet and I can throw some great shapes.'

He's a funny one is Mason. One minute, he's all swagger, the next he seems to be eager to please, almost seeking approval. Perhaps having a daddy who's as rich as Croesus but is a complete bastard means that you're always trying to live up to unrealistic expectations. I don't know. It's late and I'm a bit pissed.

Chapter Twenty-One

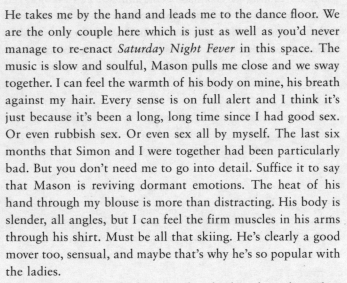

He takes me by the hand and leads me to the dance floor. We are the only couple here which is just as well as you'd never manage to re-enact *Saturday Night Fever* in this space. The music is slow and soulful, Mason pulls me close and we sway together. I can feel the warmth of his body on mine, his breath against my hair. Every sense is on full alert and I think it's just because it's been a long, long time since I had good sex. Or even rubbish sex. Or even sex all by myself. The last six months that Simon and I were together had been particularly bad. But you don't need me to go into detail. Suffice it to say that Mason is reviving dormant emotions. The heat of his hand through my blouse is more than distracting. His body is slender, all angles, but I can feel the firm muscles in his arms through his shirt. Must be all that skiing. He's clearly a good mover too, sensual, and maybe that's why he's so popular with the ladies.

I don't go home. We have another drink and another. Then we dance again. I feel light-headed and loose. Loose as in relaxed not in, you know, the other kind of loose. OK, I feel a bit loose in that way too. Mason is one hell of a sexy man and, despite vowing not to, I can see myself falling under his spell. Definitely no more gin for me.

When the song ends, I take the cue to move away from him. If I don't go now, I never will. But he keeps me pressed against him and my resistance is low.

'It's late,' I say, reluctantly. 'I really should be going.'

'You could stay,' he murmurs softly, his lips so, so close to my ear. 'I have an apartment on the next floor.'

I shake my head. 'Bad idea. You should never sleep with the boss.'

'I was only asking you in for coffee, you hussy,' he teases. 'What kind of boy do you think I am?'

A bad boy, Mason Soames. 'I'll call a cab.'

He stands away from me and gives me a reproachful look before saying, 'Let me.' So, as we walk to the door, he punches a number into his phone and orders a car for me. 'We have an account with them. The bill will be sorted.'

'Thanks. That's very kind.'

'My pleasure.'

When we reach the lift, he says, 'Do you mind if we say goodnight here? I'd take you down to the lobby, but I'd like to go back in and have a word with the staff before they finish for the night.'

Cindy, probably. And then I chide myself for being so stupid. What if he does manage to persuade Cindy to warm his bed instead of me? It's no skin off my nose. I've had a nice evening with Mason. Better than I'd expected and I feel that he enjoyed it too. He's good company and the world's most accomplished charmer.

He presses the button for the lift. 'Sure you won't change your mind?'

'No. It's been a lovely evening though. Thank you for bringing me here.'

'Let's do it again,' he says.

As we stand and wait, he kisses me softly on the lips and, I'm not joking, I think my head might explode. My lips tingle where his mouth has been and I feel like I'm on fire. We both intensify the kiss and my head swims. He holds me tightly and, at this moment, I could stay. I could throw caution to the wind and spend the night with him. Insert all of the things here that I said before about not getting enough/any sex. I have condoms in my handbag which are calling to me.

I know that I'd have a great time with Mason. I just know it. He is definitely a man who knows how to please a woman. Of that, I have *no* doubt.

Then the lift arrives and the doors bing open. Quickly, I scuttle into it before I lose my senses. It would be utter madness to let this go any further. I know what he's like. I've been warned. But, my word, he's got my motor running.

Mason touches his fingers to his own lips. 'Wow,' he says.

'Goodnight.' I don't think I've ever been more flustered. My cheeks are burning and, as the doors slowly close, we both look at each other – with what? Lust? Longing? There's definitely some chemistry going on here. 'I'll see you at work.'

'You should never kiss your boss, Ruby Brown,' he teases. 'And, my goodness, you just did.'

Chapter Twenty-Two

When the taxi dropped me home, I fell into bed. But sleep eluded me. I kept going over and over what had just happened. One kiss and I've turned to jelly. A particularly rampant jelly. Honestly, my nipples tingled all the way home. I probably should have had a cold shower. I might have got off to sleep quicker.

The sky is lightening over the lake when I finally close my eyes and nod off. What feels like about ten minutes later, my phone rings and it's Charlie.

'Are we still doing cooky brekky, chummy?'

I groan. 'I'd forgotten all about it.' I look over at my clock. It's gone ten. I let my head drop back on the pillow. I feel as if I've been drinking when I really haven't had that much at all.

Scrap that. When I recall the number of cocktails we downed, it was loads.

'You sound like shite.'

'Late night,' I confess. She'll probably find out anyway. That woman misses very little.

'Doing what?'

I have to bite the bullet and tell her, don't I? We are friends and, as such, should not have secrets. Sitting up, I wrap my

91

duvet around me. 'I went out with Mason last night after work.'
I brace myself for the backlash.

'Shagger?' I hear the incredulity in her voice. 'You went out
with Shagger?'

'For a drink. Or two. That's all.' I might be fessing up, but
I'm still not telling about our steamy goodnight kiss.

'He's not in bed with you now, is he?'

'Of course not.' I try to sound as indignant as I can whilst
realising that I really don't occupy the moral high ground here.

'Are you mad?'

'Possibly. But it was fun. He asked me to go to a club that
he's just opened in the city. What else was I going to do on a
Monday night?'

'He's opened a club?' Now Charlie's interest is piqued.

'Yeah. It's a lovely place,' I say. 'Very classy. The Vibe Lounge.
Have you heard of it?'

'No,' she admits.

'Well, it's fabulous. And he was the perfect gentleman.'

Charlie makes a harrumphing noise.

'He was. I had some gin, some chips and he paid for my taxi
home.' I get an unexpected warm glow when I think of it.

'Sounds like the perfect date,' Charlie agrees, grudgingly.

'It wasn't a date. He wanted my opinion on the club. He's
surprisingly insecure.'

'Beneath all that twattery.'

'He does hide it well,' I concede. 'But he's a really nice guy
when you sit and chat to him.'

'Now I definitely need to see you for brekky,' Charlie deter-
mines. 'I want a minute-by-minute account. Get up, get
showered, your presence is required at Café Rouge in half an
hour. This definitely needs to be discussed over a sausage.'

'OK,' I say, tiredly. 'See you soon.'

I fall back onto my pillow again and yawn. Charlie likes to

know chapter and verse. She won't be happy until she knows every single detail about my outing – not a date – with Mason. It won't just be the sausage that's grilled.

We are in Café Rouge. At a window table. Overlooking the water fountain in the pavement that squirts on and off and regularly catches unsuspecting people passing by. That's why we like coming here.

The waitress puts two full English breakfasts in front of us and we both fiddle with our tea, toast, eggs.

As Charlie slices into her bacon, she says, 'I'm waiting for you to start.'

'I'm confused,' I tell her.

'You're a muppet.'

'I didn't mean to go out with him. It just kind of happened.' I toy with my brekky even though I thought I was hungry when I ordered it. 'It felt very natural.' And a little bit reckless.

'Did you spend the night with him?'

'No way.'

'I bet he asked you to though.'

She's not wrong. Charlie never really seems to be. 'It was in the heat of the moment. We'd both had a lot to drink.'

'Ah, sparkly coloured drinks. The root of all evil.'

My headache agrees with her. If Charlie'd been there then she might feel differently. He treated me nicely, we had fun and he's a bright, ambitious guy. 'I kind of like him.'

'No.' Charlie holds up a hand. 'You can like anyone else in the world except Shagger Soames.'

'Can't I just have a little bit of fun with him?'

'No.'

'I promise I'd tell you everything.'

'Urgh. I wouldn't want to know.'

'You *so* would.'

She cracks. 'You're right, I would.'

'Since Simon left, I've lost all of my confidence. Mason makes me feel young and sexy again. Desirable even. Is that so wrong?'

'He's playing you, Ruby. You're my dearest friend, I don't want to bring you down, but he does it to everyone.'

I know he has a reputation. I know that. But he seems so sincere too. Can you really fake a reaction like we both had after The Kiss? It seemed genuine enough to me.

'I just don't want you to get hurt,' she adds. 'My bad-boy antennae is on red alert with him.'

There's no doubt that he's on the naughty side, but maybe that's what I need right now. Joe is lovely, no doubt, but he's weighed down with cares and commitments. I don't want to take those on.

'Sometimes you have to take risks though, don't you?' I ask her. 'I don't want one mistake to define the rest of my life. Sometimes you have to trust your instinct. Isn't that what love is about? Otherwise, we'd both end up in love with cardboard cut-out Gary Barlow for ever.'

'There are worse things,' she says.

'Mason ticks a lot of boxes. The main one being that he doesn't have any baggage. No children, no tricky ex-wife. That has to count for something. My instinct says that Mason Soames is an OK bloke.'

'If you're going to insist on falling in love again, I don't want you to fall for a bloke who's OK. He has to be totally fabulous.'

Maybe that's the impossible dream though. Like Charlie holding out for Gary Barlow. While I'm pondering this, she leans over and nicks my sausage. When I open my mouth to protest, she holds up a hand. 'You're looking far too smug with yourself,' she says. 'This is your punishment. Take it on the chin.'

So I let Charlie eat my sausage and wonder what will happen next time I see Mason Soames.

Chapter Twenty-Three

What happens is that Mason doesn't come into the pub for the next few days – which I think may be a good thing. I can't help having a surreptitious glance at the car park whenever a throaty car roars in though, which unsettles me slightly. Charlie's words have struck home. She's right. I should keep Mason at arm's length. I know that I shouldn't be thinking about him as much as I am. And I know that I should never have kissed him. I like this job. I *need* this job. If it all goes wrong and he starts being funny with me, I could be out of work. Remember that, Ruby Brown.

Also, I'm thinking of not going to my scuba-diving lesson tonight. I know that I'll have wasted the money I spent on the course, but . . . well . . . err . . . gahdohmehgrrrpfft. My head feels all scrambled. I'm thinking about Mason, I'm thinking about Joe. It's a good job I'm not at work as no one would be getting their right orders today.

I should go to my diving lesson, shouldn't I? There must be a saying about not giving up in the face of adversity. If there is, I can't think of it. I want to change my life, but my plan was to simplify it and have some fun. Instead, I seem to be making it more complicated by the minute. I'd ask Charlie, but I'm not sure I'd like her advice. Oh, God. Life should get easier once you leave the playground, but it doesn't. Then you think you'll have it sorted in your teens and you don't. So you hurtle into your twenties when you're sure you'll crack the meaning of life. Yet here I am in my late thirties and I'm still all at sea. I haven't even got Relationships sorted.

It's my day off and I need to grab some shopping as there is nothing but wine and wilted lettuce in my fridge. I need some fresh air too. Usually, I try to do a lap or two of shuffling around the lake during the week, but there's a stiff breeze blowing today and I'm not feeling like being biffed about by the wind. Yet a bit of a walk will help to clear my head and burn off some of those calories from that late-nite chip and gin fest earlier in the week. So, instead of heading into the shopping centre, I go up to our nearest little market town on the outskirts of Milton Keynes. Stony Stratford has an old-fashioned high street with quirky little independent shops.

There's a great cycle shop/café combo there which I love. They do the best cappuccino in town and always have cool tunes playing. When I was first divorced, I hated to go into cafés by myself. I felt as if everyone was looking at me and wondering why I had no husband, no mates. Now it's become second nature. I like the time that I spend alone, deep in contemplation – or, more likely, looking at Twitter on my phone to see what Ryan Gosling is up to. The other thing I like about this café is that it's not full of the pram set. You'll not find a toddler crawling beneath your table with the remains of a chocolate croissant spread round its mouth. Instead, it's always populated by fit Lycra-clad cyclists talking about pedals and headsets and handlebars and stuff I don't understand – nor particularly want to. Perhaps I should chat up one of those.

Yet, when I swing in today, it's full of glamorous lady

pensioners who look like they're having a book group meeting. Maybe they like to look at the firm thighs of cyclists while they talk about Anita Shreve novels. Perhaps I should join a book club even though I haven't read a novel since I was about fifteen. That's the kind of thing single women do. I don't recall seeing it on that internet list of hobbies though.

I have a nice relaxing coffee and listen to the mellow sounds. I think about texting Mason, then I realise that I don't actually have his number. Then I double-realise that it would be a bad idea to text him. If there's going to be any texting then it should come from him. Besides, he strikes me as the kind of guy who'd like to do all the running.

Clearly, the whole chillout thing works as, when I reach the last bit of froth at the bottom of my cup, I've talked myself into going to my dive lesson. I shall be cool but friendly with Joe. I won't flirt or go all giddy when he holds my hand underwater. I won't go to the pub afterwards to socialise. I shall be an island. I'll complete the course, learn to dive – of a fashion – and then tick the box marked 'done' and move on. That's exactly what I'll do.

After the coffee stop, I go round to my parents' house. Dad is at work keeping the wheels of the banking industry turning at Santander, but it's Mum's day off from her job-share as secretary at a local school. I stick my head round the door and shout, 'Hiya!!'

'Hello, love,' Mum shouts back. 'Just dead-heading the plants in the conservatory.'

Giving them a death sentence, more like. My mum tells everyone she's got green fingers but between you and me, she can kill an orchid stone-dead in a week. It's a gift. One which I have inherited.

She comes into the kitchen, wiping soil and random bits of petal from her hands. 'It's like the Sahara in that conservatory,' she complains. 'I'm having to water every day. I'm trying to persuade your father to get a proper roof put on it, but he likes the sunshine. He can fall asleep in a nano-second in there.'

I kiss her cheek while she's still muttering on.

'Do you want lunch?' she says. 'I've only got cheese or ham. Or there's some chicken from last night. Or I could get a pizza out of the freezer. Or whip you up a Caesar salad. I haven't been to Sainsbury's so there's no cake.'

My mother feels as if she's failed in life if you haven't eaten after you've been in the house for more than thirty seconds.

'A sarnie would be fine.'

'Cheese? Ham? Chicken? Or I can open a tin of tuna. Or boil some eggs. Your father's got some pork pies hidden from me at the back of the fridge. You're welcome to them, but on your own head be it.'

'Cheese. Don't go to any trouble.'

'It's no trouble.' She kisses my cheek. 'How can making lunch for my favourite daughter be any trouble?'

'I'm your only daughter.'

'And I don't see enough of you.'

'I'm busy at the pub. I've been doing some extra shifts.'

'Don't let them take advantage of you,' she warns. 'You're too easy.'

I think she's means easy-going. I'm sure of it. Though if she'd seen me letting my boss take advantage of me the other night, then she'd have a point.

'No young man on the horizon?'

'I'm not fifteen, Mum.' I've been in the house for about three minutes before we get on to my chequered love life, so this is even a record for Mum. See what I mean about them sometimes being *too* close?

'I want to see you settled,' she says as she washes her hands and delves into the fridge.

'What you mean is that you want me to knock out a couple of grandbabies.' And as soon as possible.

'You're not getting any younger.'

'Thanks for pointing that out.'

'By the time I was your age you and your brother were both teenagers.'

Probably about the same age as Daisy and Tom are now.

As she butters bread in a ferocious manner and slaps some ham on it, even though I'm pretty sure we'd settled on cheese, I say, 'It's different now, Mum. Everything takes longer. We don't settle down until much later. I'll probably be a pensioner before I can buy my own home.'

'You leave everything too late. We didn't have holidays in Mexico or go out drinking cocktails. We saved up and got married.'

'I tried marriage,' I remind her. 'Didn't quite work out.' It still pains me to discuss it with my parents. I know they had high hopes for me and Simon. If I was taken in by him, then they were too. They adored him. My dad used to walk down to the local pub to play darts with him – the ultimate accolade. I think it hurt them nearly as much as it hurt me when they found out he'd been cheating on me. So I never tell them how I'm really feeling. You don't, do you? You get to a time of life when it's your turn to protect your parents, not vice versa.

'You give up too easily. Do you think my life has been all ha-ha-hee-hee with your father?'

'I don't think Dad ever shagged the woman at the local One Stop Shop though, did he?'

'Your father's no angel,' she says, darkly.

For the record, my father is an angel. My mother's idea of a heinous crime is for him to put the empty cereal packet back in the cupboard rather than in the bin. Which, in fairness, he does sometimes do. Dad has barely put a foot wrong for the

99

forty-odd years they've been together. He is a paragon of virtue. If someone had a notion to show my dad their bejewelled vajayjay, he'd run a flipping mile.

'Simon went off with another women. Even if he'd begged to come back – which he didn't – I could never have forgiven him for that.'

'It's not like my days.' My mother shakes her head, clearly perplexed by the ways of the modern world. 'I just want you to be happy. '

'I am.' But you can see why I don't say anything about Mason or Joe or anyone of the male variety who crosses my path. I daren't even tell her about cardboard cut-out Gary Barlow or she'd be looking at hats.

Still I'm glad that I have a supportive family, who are here for me. Like I said, they went through as much agony as I did when I divorced. My pain was their pain. It was truly awful to watch them suffer too. I couldn't put them through that again. I feel for Mason who has a tyrant as a father and a judgemental family and for Joe whose parents live too far away from his young family to be able to help. I'm lucky. I know that.

I just wish my mother would chill out when it comes to me finding myself another future intended. I'd like to confide in her about Mason or chat to her about Joe and his kids or my attempts at scuba-diving, but I daren't. It's way too early. Even I realise that one heady kiss with Mason does not a boyfriend make.

Chapter Twenty-Four

Later that evening, I'm at the swimming pool again. I'm not keen and I think that's probably written all over my face.

'Hey,' Joe says. 'Good to see you. I did wonder if you'd come back for another go.'

'I like to see everything through to the bitter end,' I lie through my teeth. Honestly, I thought about turning round and going home when I got to the car park.

'You're enjoying it that much?' Joe laughs.

'I'm not sure that I'm a natural in the water.'

'You're doing fine,' he says. Then he looks over his shoulder at the group of guys by the poolside. 'I've paired you with Bob for tonight. He's very experienced.'

I confess that I get a heart-sink moment. Of course, I thought that I'd be with Joe again. Why wouldn't I be? Looks like he's decided to play it cooler than me.

Bob comes over. I'm not being fatist, ageist or sexist or anything, but he's a fat, old bloke. Actually, I probably am being fatist, ageist *and* sexist He's bald too. Maybe that's hairist. He has a nice smile and a friendly face though and I hang onto that thought.

'Ready, love,' he says and we go through the same procedure of getting into the pool. I still experience the same amount of terror. Though I care less about putting my bum in front of Bob's face. We sink to the bottom and sit beneath the surface. When Bob squeezes my hand to check if I'm OK, I don't feel quite the same thrill as when Joe did it. And that's a good thing. That's a very good thing.

I take more notice of the silt on the bottom of the pool and wonder when it was last cleaned. Properly cleaned. A spent Elastoplast floats by. Gross. I wonder how many children have done a wee in here this week? How many teenagers have hopped in with verrucas? I might scrub myself with bleach when I get home.

Bob encourages me to try a little swimming and I follow him to the deep end, listening to my own breathing in my ears, the hiss of the bubbles which I think should be soothing, but is vaguely horrifying. When I get out of the pool with all the elegance of a seal on land, Bob is full of praise and, I have to say, he's been a great instructor, very patient with his somewhat reluctant pupil. He just doesn't look like he's going to make Mr March of the Diving Hotties annual calendar any time soon.

Joe is chatting to some of the other guys at the end of the pool. I think he catches my eye, but turns away. Well, two can play at that game. I am the Queen of the Cold Shoulder. I dump my gear and head to the showers where I give myself a triple wash with Zingy Lime shower gel.

While I let the water cascade over me, I think about Joe. He's great and there's no doubt that my heart is quite impressed by him, but if I'm going to set my cap at anyone then it should obviously be Mason Soames. Joe is still too embroiled in his old life for him to be able to take on a girlfriend too. He said as much himself. And that's fine. It was totally unnecessary of him to spell it out. And rather clumsy of him, I thought. Still, he's playing it cool with me and that's fine. I might have had a few stomach-flipping moments with Joe, but that kiss with Mason was sensational and, if it was up to him, it wouldn't have ended there. No reluctance on Mason's part. Oh no.

When I'm finished, I grab my stuff and head out to reception. I don't have the same sense of exhilaration or achievement this week – even though I've probably done quite a bit more. My determined step stutters a little when I see Joe hanging around by the door. He's looking very tousled and I hadn't realised that tousled is a good look on a man. And I want to make it really clear to you right here, right now, that my mouth only goes dry because of all the damn chlorine in the water. Right? Let's park that one straight away. I had a conversation with myself in the shower about it not five minutes ago.

'How did it go tonight?' he asks.

'Great,' I say. 'I really enjoyed it.' Diving is *so* not for me.

'Are you coming to the pub?' He sounds hopeful when he adds, 'A few of us are going down there.'

'Not tonight. I've got *loads* to do.' Make a cup of tea, have a sandwich, watch telly. Mister, my life is all busy, busy, busy. 'Thanks for asking though.'

'See you next week, then?'

'Wild horses wouldn't keep me away.' Sub-text: hell would have to freeze over before I'll ever get in that swimming pool again. This is me *so* done with diving. And diving instructors.

'Great.' His smile brightens his face. 'Maybe we could pair together again.'

'I'm quite happy with Bob,' I say, so sweetly that I nearly make myself sick. 'He's lovely.'

As I breeze out of the leisure centre and walk to the car, I'm sure that I can feel Joe's eyes on my back and I make my step just a little more jaunty.

Chapter Twenty-Five

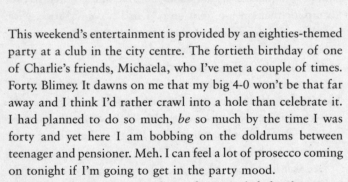

This weekend's entertainment is provided by an eighties-themed party at a club in the city centre. The fortieth birthday of one of Charlie's friends, Michaela, who I've met a couple of times. Forty. Blimey. It dawns on me that my big 4-0 won't be that far away and I think I'd rather crawl into a hole than celebrate it. I had planned to do so much, *be* so much by the time I was forty and yet here I am bobbing on the doldrums between teenager and pensioner. Meh. I can feel a lot of prosecco coming on tonight if I'm going to get in the party mood.

We're only going to get there after our shift finishes as we daren't ask Jay for a Saturday night off together, so Charlie's taken our outfits into the staffroom at the close of play in order to get changed. My feet are killing and it would take very little encouragement for me to give this a miss and go home. My bed is calling me and I don't really know anyone else at this party, other than Charlie and the birthday girl.

My friend pulls two day-glo costumes out of a crumpled plastic bag. 'Ebay,' she says by way of explanation. She holds one of them up in front of her. 'Cheap.'

I would never have guessed. Our outfits comprise of a yellow net top with a perilously low neck. I'm quite well blessed in the chest department, and I think this is going to have trouble containing my girls. Maybe I shouldn't have been rash enough to give Charlie free rein when it came to outfit choice.

'You've got your black bra?' she asks.

I nod. 'In my bag.' The tops are also very see-through.

The skirt is shocking pink and of the ra-ra variety and, as such, accentuates every single inch of hip. Of which, I have many. I hold it up to me and baulk at the lack of fabric. I tell you, they barely skim our bottoms. As if that isn't bad enough, the outfit is accessorised with hot pink leg warmers and a rainbow-coloured wig that's more Cyndi Lauper than Madonna. It's topped with a big, pink satin bow.

'You don't really want me to be seen in public in this, do you?'

'We'll look fab,' she insists.

'We might get arrested.'

'Only if we're lucky,' she quips. 'Come on, get changed. We haven't got all night. Everyone else has been at the party for hours. We've got a lot of catching up to do. We'll have to self-medicate with Vitamin P.'

At least we're agreed that prosecco is the way forward.

Reluctantly, I part with the sensible white shirt and black trousers ensemble required for the serious business of waitressing and wiggle into the ra-ra skirt and canary-yellow tart's blouse. Frankly, it could have done with being a size bigger. Maybe two. As predicted, the skirt barely covers my modesty. Actually, I don't think it does. My modesty seems very much on show. I try to pull it down at the sides.

'If you've got it, flaunt it,' Charlie instructs.

'I don't think I have got it. I'm pretty sure it went a long time ago.' I put my wig on. Charlie bursts out laughing and not in a good way. 'I'm having second thoughts about this.'

'We look *fabulous*, darling,' she assures me. Then she stands in front of the mirror to put her wig on and catches sight of herself. 'Bloody hell. They are short. Did we really go out in these?'

'I was about four when I last wore a ra-ra skirt and I don't think showing my knickers then was as much of an issue.'

'Oh, God.' Charlie tries in vain to make her skirt longer. 'If I bend over you'll be able to see what I had for breakfast.'

A car pulls into the car park.

'That must be our cab.' Charlie stops fussing with her skirt and jams the rainbow wig on her head.

But it's not a cab. I recognise the throaty sound of that car instantly. Dammit, Mason has just rocked up. I can hardly fess up to Charlie that I know the exact engine note of our boss's car by heart, so we grab our bags, turn off the staffroom lights and head out.

Mason is coming through the door of the restaurant as we hit the bar. He's looking really lovely in a tight-fitting black sweater that may well be cashmere, and grey jeans. He hasn't shaved and even that suits him. I wish I was looking more scrubbed and polished.

Not surprisingly, Mason recoils in horror as he sees us. 'Whoah.'

I hold up a hand. 'Say nothing.'

'What have you two ladies come as? Pepsi and Shirley?'

If he wasn't our boss Charlie would tell him to sod off. I can see it written all over her face. He's trying very hard to suppress his grin and is failing miserably. 'Going somewhere nice?'

'Well, I don't think we'd get into your club looking like this.'

'Definitely not,' he agrees.

'Eighties party,' Charlie informs him. 'We thought you were the cab.'

'I'd run you there, but I've only got room for one.' He gives me a meaningful look which I hope Charlie misses.

'We're off to Wilton Hall,' she says sharply. 'It'll only take five minutes.' Another set of headlights appears outside the window. 'Our chariot's here now.'

'Have a great time, ladies. I'll lock up.' He turns his attention to me and gives a wink when he adds, 'Catch you later.'

'Hold your skirt down,' Charlie instructs as we scuttle out. 'I don't want that lecherous bugger getting an eyeful of my bum.'

It's fair to say that I feel exactly the same.

Chapter Twenty-Six

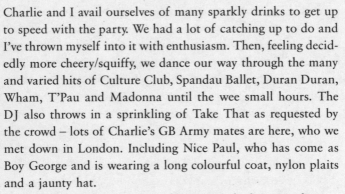

Charlie and I avail ourselves of many sparkly drinks to get up to speed with the party. We had a lot of catching up to do and I've thrown myself into it with enthusiasm. Then, feeling decidedly more cheery/squiffy, we dance our way through the many and varied hits of Culture Club, Spandau Ballet, Duran Duran, Wham, T'Pau and Madonna until the wee small hours. The DJ also throws in a sprinkling of Take That as requested by the crowd – lots of Charlie's GB Army mates are here, who we met down in London. Including Nice Paul, who has come as Boy George and is wearing a long colourful coat, nylon plaits and a jaunty hat.

I've no idea what time it is, but it must be late. My feet are throbbing and I've had enough to drink to forget the sheer awfulness of my outfit. It helps that I'm surrounded by people who are dressed in similarly bad-taste clothes.

I'm giving it my all to 'The Only Way is Up' – if my memory serves me right, the only hit for Yazz and the Plastic Population – when my phone pings. It's lucky that I even hear it over the music.

I'm outside, it says. Mason xx.

That pulls me up short. I'm assuming that means he'd like me to go outside too. I know he said *catch you later*, but I didn't really think that he meant it. Does he think it's OK to sweep in like this and expect me to drop everything for him? Of course he does. And there's my dilemma. I really want to. I'm sort of done here and I need a sit down. Looking over at my friend, I can see that she's still in full party mode. I suppose it couldn't hurt to go out for a little while and see what Mason's up to?

I shout over to Charlie, 'Back in a minute,' but I'm not sure that she hears me as she seems to be quite engrossed with Nice Paul. Hmm.

So with only a modicum of apprehension, I head out of the main door. Sure enough, Mason's flashmobile is parked right out front in a spot that is very clearly labelled NO PARKING in big letters. He swings open the passenger door and, even though I try my best to get into the car like models do, I end up falling inside. The night has turned cold and I'm wearing nothing more substantial than netting. I attempt to pull said netting down to cover my legs, but it's going nowhere.

'I was feeling lonely, Brown,' Mason says with a pout.

'Come in. Join the party!' I sound a bit more slurry and a bit more shouty than I'd like.

'I feel a little under-dressed.' He gestures at his black sweater and jeans. He may have a point. One bloke in there has come as the Incredible Hulk. 'Let's go to the club.'

'I can't really go anywhere else dressed like this, can I?' My head is sweating under my rainbow wig and I'm torn between keeping it on and having wiggy hair. 'Plus I'm knackered now.' I check my phone and it's gone two o'clock. The party will be winding up pretty soon anyway. Having sat down, I don't think I'm going to be able to get up again.

'So what shall we do?' He runs a finger gently down my

cheek and I hear myself gulp. Mason smiles, turning on the full wattage.

I'm suddenly feeling the excess of prosecco and my long shift at work. I'm clearly not as young as I like to think I am. 'You could drive me home,' I say. 'That's really all I'm fit for.'

'Really? The night is young, Brown.'

'Yeah, but I'm not.' I unleash a yawn that I'm not able to stifle.

'I get the point. So you just want to go home?'

'Yes, please.'

He sighs at me. 'OK. My pleasure.'

'No funny business though.'

He laughs. 'None at all.'

I settle back in the plush leather seat and give Mason my postcode for him to tap into the Satnav. Then I text Charlie to let her know that I'm going home and she sends me back two kisses. She's in safe hands with Nice Paul who I'm sure will see her into a cab.

I close my eyes and lay my head back as Mason speeds along the deserted roads of Milton Keynes. His car is comfortable and warm, and I think I may have dozed off as, sooner than I imagined, we reach my estate and he pulls into my road. The moonlight shimmers on the lake. It looks positively romantic.

'Nice area,' he says.

'That's my place.' I point out the granny annexe.

'You could invite me in for coffee.'

'Nooooooo,' I say. 'That would be a *really* bad idea.' I think of Gary Barlow standing in the corner of my bedroom and know without a shadow of a doubt that Mason would think that was weird.

'We've got some chemistry going on here, Brown. I know that you feel it too.'

'You're my boss,' I remind him. 'Bad idea. Very bad idea.'

'You don't fancy a walk by the lake in the moonlight?'

'There are usually drunks down there.'

'Ah. We could sit here and look at it,' he says. 'I can do romance if that's what you're looking for.'

'I'm not looking for anything.'

He turns on the music and flicks through his playlist until something suitably smooth serenades me.

'Huh.' I try to sound unimpressed. 'Music to make babies by.'

'If I'm lucky.' Then he leans in and kisses me and my head spins. I think his lips must be supercharged, as the touch of them makes me tingle all over. Despite my earlier resolve, I feel myself responding. I can't even begin to tell you what a good kisser he is. So we kiss and soon it intensifies. Mason's hands become more bold. They slide up inside my ra-ra skirt, they travel down over the canary yellow top, maybe a bit inside it. And like it. I like it a lot. I haven't had decent sex for soooooo long. Or even *indecent* sex.

We move closer together and the kissing goes to another level, but then gearstick gets in the way and breaks the moment.

'This isn't going to be easy,' Mason laughs. 'Sports cars aren't made for lurrrrrve.'

To be honest with you, that stops me short and makes me realise what we're doing. I push Mason away and, slightly breathlessly, say, 'This is wrong on many levels.'

'Why?' He looks perplexed. 'I thought we were just getting started.'

'For one, I'm wearing a ra-ra skirt and a rainbow wig. Two – I haven't had sex in a car since I was about seventeen,' I tell him. 'It wasn't great then. And it was only because I had nowhere else to go.'

'But you have to admit that it felt great,' Mason says. 'In a slightly sleazy and ridiculous way.'

Pulling down my ra-ra skirt to cover my . . . ahem . . . modesty, I say, 'We should call it a night.'

'We could move into your place. That would be a lot more comfortable.'

'I don't think so, Mason.' My head is clearing slightly. I don't want to wake up in the morning full of regrets and needing to hand in my notice. 'I should be going. Thanks for the lift home.'

'Don't go, Brown.' He puts a hand on my arm. 'Let's talk about stuff.'

'Like what?'

'I don't know.' He looks at me, a teasing smile on those kissable lips. I should get out of the car. I should get out of the car *now*. Then he says, 'I do know! Let's go away somewhere. Come to Paris with me.'

I laugh. 'Paris?'

'I'm going shortly. A work trip. Once the club is running smoothly, my next project is to open a chain of French-style cafés. I'm going over there for research.'

'Nice work if you can get it.'

He acknowledges my jibe. 'Come then.'

'I don't have "Paris" money,' I point out. 'I barely make my rent each month. I don't have anything left over for holidays.'

'It's my treat. If it makes you feel better, I can put it down on business expenses. We can check out some great restaurants and cafés. You can give me your valued opinion. It would be so much better with you by my side.' That little bit of flattery brings a flush of colour to my cheeks and Mason clearly sees me wavering as he presses on. 'Then, when our work is done, we could take a romantic stroll along the Seine, go and see the Mona Lisa, climb the Eiffel Tower. Tourist stuff.'

'I don't do heights.'

That doesn't deter him. 'We can sit at pavement cafés and watch the world go by. Then we can make love all night with

112

the French doors open onto a little wrought iron balcony and the lights of Paris beneath us.'

It is actually sounding rather appealing.

'Have you been to Paris?'

'Never.'

'Ah, then you don't know what you're missing, Brown.'

'I can't come to Paris with you, Mason. That would be stupid.'

'OK.' He shrugs. 'But I could come in and discuss it further.'

I push him away. 'Nice try.' Then I kiss his cheek, a friendly peck. 'I'm going now. My bed is calling.'

'Your bed's calling me too.' He gives me pathetic eyes.

'I know bed language,' I tell him, firmly. 'And my bed is very definitely saying "Stay out".'

He grins good-naturedly and starts the engine of his car. 'I know when I'm beaten.'

I open the door and get out. 'Goodnight, Mason. Thanks for the lift home. I do appreciate it.'

'Think about Paris,' he says, then he roars off into the night and I check round to see if any of my neighbour's curtains are twitching.

'Paris,' I say with a scoff as I open my door.

In the bedroom, cut-out Gary Barlow is waiting for me. I throw myself onto the bed and sigh. 'What do you think about me going to Paris with Mason, Gazza Bazza?'

But, as always, Gary keeps his opinion to himself.

Chapter Twenty-Seven

Charlie and I are on the late shift together the next day. She looks as rough as I feel. We are sitting on what we've christened 'our' bench half an hour before we have to start work. Me with a coffee, Charlie with an e-cig and a hangover. The industrial bins hide us from the customers who are enjoying the sunshine in our beer garden, so we're not likely to be asked, inadvertently, for menus or something. We skulk here while we have our obligatory pre-shift natter.

'Where did you disappear to last night?' my friend asks, narrowing her eyes as she puffs out a cloud of vapour.

I could lie and, I have to say, that it's very tempting. I know that Charlie will be very disapproving and she has every right to be. But she has laser vision and can see right through me, so I'd better come clean. 'Mason rocked up outside – unexpectedly.' I want to make that very clear. 'He gave me a lift home.'

She frowns at me and nicks a sip of my coffee. 'I'm not liking the sound of this.'

'He's OK.' I insist.

'There's no way you got out of that car without snogging him.'

'We did have a bit of a snog,' I confess. 'In my defence, I had rather a lot to drink and was wearing a ra-ra skirt. I was feeling quite reckless.'

'He's an arch manipulator, Ruby. I've warned you. Shagger Soames likes getting his own way.'

'I'm a big girl and I'm treading very carefully. Trust me.' I pick at the rotting wood and marvel at the fact that we don't get splinters in our bottoms. 'Besides, who did you go home with?'

'I shared a cab with Amanda.'

I don't actually know who Amanda is, but I was fully expecting a different answer. 'Not Nice Paul?'

'Nooooo.' She shakes her head. 'Why would I go home with Nice Paul? He's just a mate.'

'You looked as if you were getting quite cosy.'

'Looks can be deceiving, my friend,' she says. 'Besides, you can't kiss a bloke dressed as Boy George. That would be totes weird. He was wearing more make-up than me.'

'You did think about kissing him then?'

'No. What is this, primary school?'

'I like him.'

'You go out with him then. Stop playing with fire with Shagger Soames.'

'I think you've got him all wrong.'

'Don't think so, love. What did he have to say for himself that gave you that impression?'

'Not a lot. I just get on OK with him. That's all.' I busy myself reorganising gravel with my toe. I don't mention Paris. Charlie would do her pieces. He was probably just joking, anyway. As if I'd really go to Paris with him. Ha! Then the phone rings and I rush to answer it, glad of the distraction.

We're run off our feet. Sometimes, I have no idea where all these people come from. I go out to dinner once every blue moon, but there are couples who eat in here practically every night of the week.

When Mason turns up – and, shame on me, I hoped he would – I'm busy on the phone. Every time I hang up, it rings again. We've got another steak night special that's proving ridiculously popular as it's half our usual price.

He gives me a slow, sexy wink as he crosses the restaurant and disappears into the bar. I hope no one else saw it. When I finally get off the phone, he comes over to me. My heart starts to patter, ridiculously – particularly for a woman of my age. It's a long time since I was a teenager and I must keep reminding myself as I thought I'd left this kind of stuff behind when I was a hormonally charged fifteen-year-old.

'Busy, Brown? That's what I like to see.' He leans on my desk.

'Steak special. It's gone mad,' I tell him. 'Clearly a lot of carnivores around here.'

'I enjoyed the other night, Brown.' He grins at me as he openly eyes me up and down. 'Preferred that outfit too.'

'Stop that right now.' I wag my finger at him. 'You should treat your employees with respect.'

'I'm not only treating you with respect, I'm trying very hard to spoil you.' He lowers his voice and checks that no one else is within listening distance. 'Come to Paris with me,' he cajoles. 'I meant it. We'd have fun. And it would be work too, of course. I'm booking it in the next few days. Premier class Eurostar, bijou little hotel with a perfect view of the Eiffel Tower.'

I go to speak, but he holds up a hand. 'I know that you don't like heights, but you won't get dizzy just looking at it. Tell me that it isn't sounding tempting.'

Sighing at him, I lower my voice and say, 'Of course it is.'

'Then what's the problem?'

Charlie is glaring at me from across the bar and, traitor

that I am, I turn my back on her. 'You're my *boss*. I'm your *employee*.'

'This hasn't escaped my notice.'

'A *junior* employee. It puts me in a compromising position.'

'Oh, I do hope so.' Then he looks at me sincerely. 'Do you have any idea how difficult it is to get good, reliable staff who the customers love?'

I confess that I don't.

'I don't want to lose you,' Mason assures me. 'This will *not* affect our working relationship.'

He sounds so very sure of it that he almost has me convinced.

The worrying thing is that I'm already imaging myself sitting at those pavement cafés, glass of red wine in one hand, a baguette in the other. I can see my hand in his, him moving above me at night. That's quite a strong imagine, if you must know. And we would have a good laugh together. I already know enough about Mason to realise that. It's just that . . . I chew my lip with indecision.

'I'll pay for everything,' he adds. 'Happily. It won't cost you a penny.'

My mother always used to say there's no such thing as a free lunch. What about a trip to Paris? What would the cost of that really be?

'I'm not looking for a relationship,' he leans close to me and speaks softly. 'We'd have a great weekend. Lots of fun. We're both adults. Where's the harm in it?'

'I'm not the sort of person who jets off to Europe for the weekend.'

'Then maybe you should become that woman.' Those blue eyes twinkle for all they're worth.

I think of the miserable time I've had recently. Don't I deserve a bit of fun? Paris with Mason sounds sophisticated and elegant. No one's ever taken me to Paris before. My ex took me for a surprise weekend to Alton Towers once, but that's hardly the same is it? If Simon can take up with a younger model, then why the hell shouldn't I? We could have a glamorous weekend of no-strings sex and gourmet food in the international city of love. This is *exactly* the sort of thing I should be doing as a newly divorced, single person. The whole of the world is out there for me to explore. I might as well start with France. Infinitely better than a gravel pit in Leicestershire, no?

'Yes,' I rush out. 'I'll come.'

Mason grins and it is the contented grin of a winner. Damn him, he knew I'd cave in. He's played me very well. I realise that.

'I could switch your shifts around and we could go this weekend.'

One of the benefits of fraternising with the boss, I guess. 'So soon?'

'I don't want you changing your mind.'

'OK, then.' Now my grin matches his. I feel as if I'm doing something really naughty. I know he's twisted me round his little finger, but at least he's made an effort to woo me in style. It's flattering. Head-turning, in fact.

'I'll book tomorrow and let you know the details.'

With that he swings out of the restaurant and leaves me there feeling both elated and terrified. I think I might have just joined the jet set.

I look round and see my friend's eyes locked on me. Oh, bum. I've no idea how I'm going to break it to Charlie.

Chapter Twenty-Eight

I'm still contemplating this matter later that evening while I'm sitting on the bottom of Wolverton swimming pool with Bob. I snuck out of work, avoiding a conversation with Charlie whereby I'd have to confess that I'd agreed to go on a dirty weekend with Mason to Paris. Do people still even call them dirty weekends? I don't know. I feel so out of the ways of dating and its associated minefields. Whichever way, Charlie will go bonkers when I tell her.

I know what I said about not doing any more diving lessons, but I felt as if I was being inexorably drawn here by a force outside myself. Ahem. Plus I sort of wanted to see Joe again. I was a bit childish after our last lesson and am feeling guilty. He's a nice guy and it wouldn't hurt to be friends with him. He could probably do with a friend right now. Plus, if I am going to finish this course, then I don't want there to be any friction between us. He's at the other side of the pool when I arrive helping a big, military-looking guy put his tanks on, so I give a friendly wave in greeting – that's all it takes, nothing more – and then I get on with the job in hand. Sort of.

Even though my mind is more on Paris than demand valves and whatever, I do quite well with my diving practice. Well, I manage to survive without drowning, which you have to agree is a good thing. Bob is less distracting as an instructor and I find that I do actually listen to what he's saying rather than just watching his mouth. All round, it makes for a better diving experience. And my heart rate stays normal. Bonus.

'Coming to the pub?' Bob asks when he's helped to haul me out of the shallow end. I'll never get used to how heavy all this gear is.

'Yes. That would be great.' I'm feeling quite uplifted after my session and a nice glass of wine would just put the finishing touch to a good day. 'I'll see you down there.'

So we tidy away the gear and I have a long, hot shower which relaxes me even more. I'm in quite a blissed-out state by the time I hit reception and see Joe standing there.

'Hey,' he says. 'I told Bob that I'd wait for you. We can walk to the pub together.'

'OK.' I can hardly cut and run now, can I? So we head out into the night and fall into step together.

'How did the lesson go?' he asks as we turn into the street.

'Good. I'm feeling more comfortable with being underwater.' That might be over-egging it, but I'm maintaining a positive frame of mind.

'The theory of it all will start to kick in soon. That's not so thrilling, but essential for safety.' We walk along for a moment in silence and then he adds, 'I thought I'd take over from Bob again next week. If you're OK with that.' He rushes on, 'We buddied up quite well and that's very important when diving.'

Hmm. That has the whiff of bullshit about it. I think I buddy up with Bob quite well, probably better as he's not so distracting in the loveliness department. What he probably means is that he'd rather do the damsel-in-distress thing rather than deal with someone who's beefier than he is.

'Whatever you think is for the best,' I say sweetly. Though, despite all my resolutions, I can't deny lessons with Joe hold more attraction than with dear Bob.

Joe holds open the door and we step into the noise of the pub. 'What can I get you?'

'A small glass of red, please.'

As we stand at the bar and wait for our drinks, Joe clears his throat before he says, 'I feel things ended badly after the dive day.' He hesitates before adding, 'I said some stupid things in the car. I wasn't thinking straight.'

'It really doesn't matter,' I say magnanimously. 'All water under the bridge.'

'How about I take you out to dinner by way of an apology? I have a rare free weekend. The kids are with Gina from Friday to Sunday. We could go somewhere nice. Your choice.'

What is it with men? They're like buses. Nothing at all on the horizon and then two come along at once.

'It sounds lovely and in normal circumstances, I'd be happy to.' I'm maintaining a friendly air, but I also want him to know that, despite his U-turn, he's too late for anything more. 'However, I'm being whisked off to Paris this weekend.'

'Oh.' He looks taken aback. As well he might. I'm quite taken aback myself. 'Paris, eh?'

'I haven't been before,' I confess. 'Though I've heard it's beautiful.'

'Well, I can't possibly compete with that.'

'It's just with a friend,' I add breezily. 'We're not in a relationship or anything.' How very modern do I sound?

'I hope you have a great time,' Joe says, but he sounds unenthusiastic. 'Shall we go and join the others?'

As we move across the pub to where the rest of the dive club are chatting, I feel that was churlish of me and, more than that, I'm weirdly disappointed that I turned down dinner with Joe even though it was absolutely my choice. At least I think it was.

Chapter Twenty-Nine

There's a beautiful and ancient wood near where I live. Even better, there's a little café tucked on the edge of it and I meet Charlie there for bacon butties the next morning. The sun is out in force bringing some meagre warmth to the spring day, so we brave it and sit outside on the terrace. They serve tea in mismatched china with decorative silver spoons that have place names on each one.

'Blackpool,' Charlie says and shows me the end of her spoon.

'Brighton.' I hold up mine.

'I've been to neither place,' Charlie says.

'I've hardly been anywhere on this planet,' I complain. Though I will be starting with Paris, very shortly. I keep my eyes averted so that Charlie doesn't see guilt written large.

We tuck into our butties and, when she's finished her mouthful, Charlie says, 'How was diving?'

'Good.' I wipe some ketchup from my mouth. 'I think I'm getting the hang of it now.'

'And hot stuff instructor?'

'Also good. I went to the pub afterwards and he asked me out to dinner.'

'Cool. You said yes?'

'I said no.'

'Twit. Why?'

I shrug. 'It's complicated.'

'The kids? The ex-wife?'

I nod. 'Something like that.' Then my phone pings, I dig it out of my handbag. It's a text from Mason. All booked, ma chérie! Will send you the details later. M xx. As I slip my phone away again, I know that I look guilty. I just know it.

Charlie raises an eyebrow in query. 'Hot stuff?'

'No. Nothing exciting,' I lie. 'More tea?'

I concentrate on my food and we talk about nothing in particular. Charlie doesn't mention Mason and I think I might have got away with it. When we are full of tea and bacon, I say, 'Shall we go for a walk in the woods?'

'Exercise?' Charlie looks horrified. 'In the fresh air?'

'It's a lovely day.'

She does an exaggerated shudder. 'But we're going to be on our feet from lunchtime until silly o'clock at work serving the great and good of Buckinghamshire. Isn't that exercise enough?'

'Come on,' I urge. 'It will do us good.'

'Red wine is good for you,' Charlie protests.

'Not in the quantities you drink.' I stand and button up my coat. 'You'll love it when we get going.'

So Charlie hauls herself out of her chair and I link my arm through hers and steer her towards the woods.

'Shouldn't we borrow a dog or something?' she says. 'We'll look stupid going for a walk without one.'

I love this place. It's a little pocket of solitude in the busy city. There's a pond as you leave the café filled with a mass of tadpoles at this time of the year. By the side of it there's a brass sculpture of a band made up of frog characters that always makes me smile.

The sun filters through the fresh green leaves, recently uncurled. The ground beneath us is soft and spongy with bark. As we turn along the path, we're greeted by a carpet of bluebells spread out ahead of us, threading through the trees as far as the eye can see.

'Nice,' Charlie says with an appreciative purse of the lips.

I nudge against her. 'Glad I dragged you in here now?'

'Yes, it's been totally brilliant.' Said in the manner of someone who didn't think it was brilliant at all. She rubs her hands together. 'Now can we go back to the café and have celebratory cake?'

I laugh. 'Of course. You must be quite dizzy with all this fresh air.' So we take a few snaps of the bluebells with our phones and turn to take a different route back to the café so that I can stretch out the walk for a little bit longer.

'I know you're hiding something from me,' Charlie says conversationally. 'I just haven't worked out what yet.'

'I don't know what you mean.'

'You do,' Charlie insists. 'I'm like Hercule flipping Poirot. I *will* find out, so you might as well fess up and save me the trouble. I know it's to do with Shagger. I've deduced that much.'

I sigh and don't turn to look at her as I spill the beans. 'I'm going to Paris with him,' I spit out. 'This weekend.'

'You muppet,' she mutters darkly. 'You right bloody muppet.'

'He's nice,' I say, defensively. 'We have a laugh when we're together. Besides, how many men have ever offered to take you to Paris? I was flattered.'

'I don't want to rain on your parade, but you'd better put your umbrella up, chummie.' Charlie fixes me with knowing eyes. 'There's no easy way to break this, but this is Shagger's standard play. He's already taken about half a dozen of the waitresses to Paris. Research for a new restaurant chain, romantic Paris, it would be so much better with you at my side.'

124

Yikes. That stings.

'Yada, yada, yada.' Charlie frowns at me. 'I take it you didn't know that?'

'No,' I admit. 'I didn't.'

'That's how he got his nickname.'

'Now I feel foolish.'

'Don't say I didn't warn you.'

She says it in a teasing voice, but I know deep down that she really means it. This would be on my own head. We walk along a bit more. 'Do you think I should cancel?'

'I've no idea, Ruby. That's up to you. I'm simply trying to tell you what he's like. You're too nice for him. I don't want to see him treat you the way he does most women.'

I let out a wavering breath. 'I'm not sure that I can back out now. He's bought the tickets. That was him texting me earlier. It might make things awkward at work.'

'Another very good reason for not shagging the boss.'

'Point taken.' We walk a few more steps. 'Did he ever ask you to go to Paris?'

'Of course he did. He asks everyone.'

'And you said no?'

'Yeah. I'm not that desperate.'

My friend gets a dark glare for that. 'Thanks, Charlie.'

She sounds exasperated rather than penitent when she says, 'You know what I mean. I'm only trying to explain to you what you're getting in to. Go to Paris, shag him senseless if you want to, but please tell me that you'll keep him at arm's length. He's a player. A charming one, I give you that – but a player, none-theless. This can only end badly and it won't be Shagger Soames who comes out worst.'

My heart feels as if it's dropped to my Converse.

Charlie puts her arm round me. 'He's supposed to be very good in the sack, if that's any consolation.'

'I think it makes me even more terrified.'

'I'm sorry if I've scared you, Ruby, but I am doing my best to protect you.'

'From myself?'

Charlie laughs. 'That too. What you need is a man like Gary Barlow. He'd never let you down.'

She's probably right. How could I have been so stupid to fall for Mason's chat-up lines? Am I really that desperate? Will I be the butt of all the jokes at work? Serves me right if I am. It looks as if I'm going to be just another notch on my boss's bedpost as Charlie warned me. I should have listened to her. So much for me being this sexually liberated *femme fatale*. Now I feel like a complete twonk.

I turn to her and pout. 'I need that cake now.'

'My treat,' Charlie says, trying to cheer me up. 'I'm sorry that I'm not deliriously happy for you, but I don't want us to fall out over it.'

'We won't. But you can buy the cake and I want a big bit,' I inform her. 'A *huge* bit. The chocolate one with the sprinkly things on top.'

'You're on.' Charlie looks relieved that I am taking solace in calories.

Frankly, I need something sweet to take away the sour taste that's suddenly in my mouth.

Chapter Thirty

I'm in Paris, the city of love and lovers, and I can hardly believe it. And I suppose I am with my lover. Of sorts.

I didn't ring Mason and cancel our trip. Obviously, you can tell that. Also, I will spare you the details of all the soul-searching and agonising that went on over the last couple of days. The amount of times I tapped his number into my phone to tell him that I'd changed my mind, only to then bottle the call. Packing alone had me in a turmoil of anxiety. I've got one small wheelie case, but I could have gone the whole Kim Kardashian and taken my entire wardrobe. Google said that Paris is best seen on foot, so I've packed comfortable walking shoes as well as heels. We're only here overnight, so I don't know how much sightseeing we'll be able to cram in. I spent hours dyeing my hair and defuzzing myself in all the little important places.

For your own sake, I'll skip the slightly awkward journey on the Eurostar where Mason was charm personified and I was more shy than my painfully shy teenage self. It felt like my first ever date and I'd rather that was consigned to the dustbin of memories. Three glasses of champagne helped to get over that bit, eventually.

We can't avoid the fact that I came over all shy because, essentially, I'm going to be spending the *entire* weekend with a man that I don't actually know very well. More fool me for agreeing to it. However, I'm here now, with the delights of Paris spread out before me and I should make sure that I enjoy as much as I can. I've been all over Google checking out what there is to do.

We take a cab from Gare du Nord to our hotel and I'm so excited to see the city whizzing by the windows. Even the cab smells French and I'm sure any minute now there'll be the sound of a street accordion playing and an onion seller complete with stripy jumper and beret will cycle by. Squee.

Mason is amused by my enthusiasm, but I don't care. I want to lap up every minute. This might be a standard thing for someone as well travelled as Mason but for me it's a Big Adventure!

The hotel is lovely. Small and elegant rather than overwhelmingly grand – perfect for a romantic weekend – and is in a street lined with attractive little cafés and pavement tables. Just as it should be. It would be nice to unpack and come down here for some lunch. I'm starving after our early start and, after all, our main mission is to try out menus for Mason's idea of setting up a chain of French-style cafés. I'm hoping that wasn't simply a ruse as Charlie suggested.

I feel self-conscious as Mason checks in for us and it's clear from the receptionist's reaction that he's a regular visitor. She's young, pretty and her smile for him is very warm, slightly secretive.

'*Bonjour*, Monsieur Soames. So lovely to have you visit us again.' Her accent is sing-song, sexy.

'Hello, Valerie.' Mason beams back at her.

Valerie, eh? First name terms.

'You have my usual room for me?'

'But of course.' She flicks her long, glossy black hair as she hands him the keycard. 'I hope you have a nice time during your stay.'

'I'm sure we will,' Mason answers and again, it sounds loaded.

Huh. I reckon he's had a little fling there or something.

'You know her well?' I ask as he carries our bags across the lobby.

'I've used this hotel for years,' Mason tells me. 'Valerie's been here for a while.'

We cram into the small wrought iron lift and we go up to the room. Mason's hand caresses my back. Inside, it's beautiful, the furnishing – all cream and black – chic and understated. Mason tosses our small cases on the bed and then opens the doors onto the balcony. The Eiffel tower is straight ahead of us. This is as French as it gets.

'Wow.' I'm impressed. 'That's some view.'

'Paris is one of my favourite cities.'

'I can't wait to see it,' I say. 'Shall we freshen up a bit and go straight out?'

'I thought we'd celebrate our arrival first,' Mason says and then I notice the bottle of champagne chilling on ice standing on the coffee table.

Oh, well. It would be rude not to even though I feel I've had enough booze for now and could kill for a cup of tea. With a side order of croque-monsieur and some frites, preferably. My tummy rumbles at the thought. However, I accept the glass that Mason offers me and we move out onto the small balcony. I drink in the atmosphere of Paris below me as I knock back the bubbles. Anything else would seem churlish. Mason's arm curls round my waist and he eases me closer to him, until I'm leaning along the length of his body.

'You like it?'

'I love it.' I pull a sheet of paper out of my pocket that I've scribbled on. 'I've made a note of some of the things I'd like to do. If we're able. You've probably seen them a million times, but it's all new to me. I'll do whatever you fancy really.' He is, after all, paying for everything and, to be honest, that makes me feel a bit weird. Indebted.

Then I realise that I'm gabbling and that Mason is regarding me with an indulgent smile on his face. He takes the piece of paper from my hands and tosses it onto the table beside us.

'We have plenty of time,' he says. 'Let's relax first. Get to know each other.' He turns and kisses me deeply and I know that the entire reason for bringing me here is to seduce me, but the speed with which he moves takes my breath away. We've barely walked in the door.

He takes the glass from my hand and holds me tightly. His arms are strong and it feels good to be held like this. Every fibre of my being responds, my head swims and I'm flooded with feelings that have been missing for so long. Yet why am I feeling so coy? I knew the score. I knew exactly what I was coming here for. Mason doesn't really want my opinion on the cafés or the food or the good wine. He wants to get down and dirty. As quickly as possible, it seems. Part of me wishes that I'd been able to prove Charlie wrong. I guess that was optimistic of me.

So I decide to go with the flow. I might as well enjoy myself too as Mason is obviously revved up. Hurriedly, we undress each other and, in the shadow of the Eiffel Tower and with the breeze from the French windows on our skin, we make love on the huge bed. I want to rush to orgasm, but Mason slows it all down, teasing my body mercilessly. Charlie was right, he is good. He's attentive and knows all the right places, all the moves. His body above me is taut, slender rather than muscled but he's definitely all man and, when he's ready, he makes me come with the ease of someone who's done this many times before – quite possibly in this room. Afterwards, he pours us more champagne and I lean against his chest as we drink it and admire the view – the one out of the window and the one lying next to me. It was good. Very good by any measure and, at this moment, I feel surprisingly content.

'I'll take a quick shower,' I say. 'Then should we grab something to eat?'

'Sounds like a plan,' Mason agrees and he kisses my hair.

I'm elated and still feeling more than sexy when I let the hot water wash over me. It will set me up nicely for a bit of culture. Probably a good thing to get it out of the way now so that I didn't have time to stress about it throughout the day.

When I go back into the bedroom, Mason is still sprawled out in the bed. 'I've ordered us some room service food,' he says. 'Come back to bed.'

'Oh.' I can't help but feel disappointed. All of Paris is out there waiting for me and I want to get up and at it. Rather than be in here and at it. Mason, it appears, has other ideas. Not entirely sure how to address this.

While I'm still prevaricating, the room service arrives. Mason slips on a dressing gown and takes the tray from the waiter to set it down on the table by the window. Then he brings me a dressing gown too and we sit at the table together. The noise of the bustling street below drifts up to us.

'Ta-da,' Mason says as he lifts the silver dome that covers my plate. 'I hope *madame* approves.'

It is, exactly as I would have ordered, a croque-monsieur and frites. This feels nice. Quite romantic. That lifts my spirits and I tuck in. Mason watches me as I eat.

'What?' I wipe melted cheese from my lips.

'I like you, Ruby,' he says as he regards me. 'I like you a lot.'

That makes me blush. 'Thanks for bringing me.' I want to make reference to the fact that I know other women have trodden this well-worn route before me, but I don't want to spoil the mood. Besides, we are both single and have no commitments so why should it be a problem? Mason has never pretended that it would be anything more.

After lunch, I get dressed. I slip off my dressing gown and put on my bra and pants. I bought new stuff. Lacy bits. Only from Primark but I couldn't let Mason see me in my best gym knickers, could I? You can't come to Paris for a romantic weekend and not wear lace, right?

'What do you fancy doing this afternoon?' I throw over my shoulder as I try to find my jeans. What's left of the afternoon, I should add.

'This.' He comes to wrap his arms around me, cupping my breasts. I'm not quite sure what happens next, but no sooner am I in my undies than I'm out of them again. Mason presses me against the wall and comes inside me, murmuring sweet nothings into my neck. I surrender to the sensations and think that the Louvre, the Seine, the lovely Eiffel Tower will all still be there tomorrow.

Chapter Thirty-One

We make it out of the hotel for dinner. You'll be pleased to know that. *I'm* pleased to know that. We eventually get out of bed and into clothes without another false start. Honestly, I've already had more sex in a day than I had in a year of married life. Mason is insatiable. I wonder if this is what it was like when my ex-husband went off with her of the jewelled vajayjay? Could he simply not keep his hands off her and, thereby, our marriage was doomed? But I won't think of Simon today, not while I'm living it up in Paris.

I should be present in the here and now. I confess that I'm liking the glint in Mason's eye, the sheer lust of his need. It's quite a heady feeling to be the object of so much desire. Was it like that with the women who came here before me? I should stop thinking about that, really, shouldn't I? It feels good to be wanted, even if it's for a fleeting moment.

'I've booked a table just down the road,' Mason says into my reverie. 'It's one of my favourite places. Good, traditional French cooking. You won't be disappointed.'

So we head out of the hotel and the pretty girl is still on reception.

'Have a nice dinner,' she shouts out to us in her sexy accent. '*À plus tard.*'

She and Mason exchange a glance, I'm sure. I'm no mug. What was that about? There's definitely history there, if you ask me.

The street is busy with people heading out for the evening and it's so very French that I could cry out with glee. The road is cobbled, pretty awnings cover pavement tables, couples share a bottle of red wine or sip at tiny cups of espresso – the sort of scene you see in every clichéd drawing of Paris. I love it. Mason takes my hand as we walk together down to the restaurant which, I have to admit, feels good too. Isn't it weird that, in this day and age, you can have had enthusiastic sex with someone – a number of times – yet never have held hands with them?

'You're quiet,' Mason says.

'Just thinking.'

'We can walk over to the Eiffel Tower after dinner,' he says. 'If you want to.'

'I'd like that.' As much as I've enjoyed our bedroom gymnastics, it would be great to see some of *actual* France while I'm here.

We're shown to a table in the window complete with candle in a bottle and a red and white gingham cloth. I feel as if I'm in heaven. Mason orders for us and we share a delicious bottle of red wine with pan-fried mussels from the bay of Locquémeau for me – which Mason assures me is a good thing – and steak tartare for him. Frankly, he looks like the type of man who would enjoy raw meat. Perhaps that's where he gets all his . . . ahem . . . *energy* from. Would a vegetarian bloke be able to go at it like that? It's not a study that I've ever undertaken. Is that a bit vegetarianist?

We both have duck leg confit for main course with black

cherry sauce, dauphinoise potatoes, pot-roasted carrots and French beans. The chocolate mousse for dessert is smooth and rich – quite like Mason. We get on well and laugh a lot. His leg rests against mine beneath the table. The wines goes down too easily. As we have coffee – milky and frothy for me, dark and strong for Mason – we watch as rain sweeps in, runs down the windows, turns the pavements slick with water.

Mason waves away my offer to pay for dinner and, when I see the bill, I'm relieved that Mason is settling it. Traditional French cooking, but at thoroughly contemporary prices. While Mason is paying, Charlie texts me. Have you shagged him yet? xx

Many, many times, I ping back.

Tart! comes straight back and several emoticons of a pie which I guess is the closest she could find to a tart. No doubt Charlie is going to want the whole chapter and verse the minute I get back.

How are you getting on with Gary? I ask. She was going to see the opening night of Gary Barlow's new musical tonight with the fan club.

Fab. Going to wait at the stage door afterwards to see if I can get a cheeky cuddle. xx

For all Mason's faults, I still think I'd rather be here with a flesh and blood man than waiting for a glimpse of an unattainable celebrity. Never tell Charlie I said that.

When it's time to leave, the rain is hammering down and we don't have an umbrella. We hover at the door of the restaurant looking at the gutters running with water and the rain bouncing back from the pavement.

'It's too wet for sightseeing,' Mason says. 'We still have all day tomorrow. Let's go back to the hotel for a nightcap.'

So he takes off his jacket and, very chivalrously, holds it above my head as we run back to the hotel in the pouring rain, laughing. In the small bar, we drink French brandy and play footsie on the bar stools.

Then, in the bedroom, fuelled with brandy and chocolate mousse, we rev it up again and are soon in the throes of passion. We're naked and Mason is doing pleasurable things to my nether regions when there's a knock at the door.

'Room service?' I quip with a laugh.

'Kind of.' Mason sits up. 'Just say if you're not into this, but I thought it would be fun. You said you wanted a bit of adventure.'

I give him a puzzled look.

'I've asked Valerie if she'd like to join us.'

'What?'

He holds up a hand. 'If you don't want to, that's cool. It's nothing heavy, just a little playtime.'

'A threesome?'

'Some people would call it that.'

There'd be three of us. What else would I call it? 'You've done this before?'

'Yeah. Occasionally. Valerie is fun. She knows the score.' He grins at me. 'Go on. Be a little bit naughty. Try it. You might find you like it. No one need ever know. What happens in Paris, stays in Paris.'

This is supposed to be the city of love, not the city of three in a bed, but I've drunk so much that it's clouding my judgement and I'm not exactly sure how to say no without appearing gauche. Never in a million years did I expect him to spring this one on me. Even Charlie didn't warn me about this! Oh, my Lord. What am I to do now?

'Have you done this before?' Mason asks.

'Never!'

'I want you to feel entirely comfortable, Ruby,' Mason stresses. 'But don't you feel a little bit tempted?'

And, I hate this, but he's right. I am tempted. Part of me wants to say yes. I've never done this before, never had the opportunity and I wonder should it be on my bucket list. I read *Cosmopolitan* – when I find it in the hairdressers. Isn't it the sort of thing that modern women do? Clearly it's what Valerie does.

'Be adventurous. No one need ever know but us. It can be our secret. You said you wanted to try some new experiences.'

I was thinking nice cheese or expensive wine. Not sharing my boyfriend with another lady. There's another tentative knock at the door.

Mason looks at me earnestly. 'I can send her away or she can come in. It's entirely your call, Ruby.'

When I can't really think of anything else to say, I bite down my apprehension and gulp as 'OK' pops out of my mouth.

Still naked, Mason opens the door and a second later Valerie is inside and stripping off her blouse. While I'm still wondering why the hell I've agreed to this, he helps her to undress and I sit there feeling more than a bit like a lemon. When Valerie's naked too, she climbs onto the bed and takes my hand, guiding it to her waist. I feel frozen with terror, even though she's soft and smiling. I have no idea what to do, but I'm pretty sure that bolting for the door isn't an option. I could stop this, I know I could, yet something inside me is letting this happen. Is it because Simon, during our break-up, told me that I was as boring as hell in bed? I'm not. I'm sure I'm not. But that kind of thing sticks with you. He certainly wouldn't say that if he could see me now.

While all this is knocking round my brain, Mason kisses me, then kisses her. Next Valerie's mouth is on mine. Strains of Katy Perry's song, 'I Kissed a Girl' go through my head. But I'm not sure I do like it. It just feels *weird*. Her lips are silky, her olive skin too. I can't help but notice that she has a fantastic body, taut and toned, and I can't say I've ever noticed that in a woman before. Rather than making me feel sexy, I think she's making me feel very old and cellulitic.

'Relax, Ruby,' she purrs, her voice husky. 'We'll just have some fun. You will enjoy this.'

Then she goes further and her hands are on my skin, her fingers exploring, her lips sweet and firm. Mason joins in. Soon we're a tangle of limbs – me, Valerie and Mason – and I'm not sure which bits are mine, whose hands are pleasuring me. Yet, God help me, I'm turned on even if I'm not certain that I want to be. However, it's too late to back out now. I'm in for a penny *and* for a pound – or a Euro in this case – so I close my eyes and let the new and strange sensations flow over me.

Chapter Thirty-Two

I wake up just as it's coming light. Valerie and Mason have all the covers and I'm cold, hanging onto about an inch of bed. I look at them both, comfortable in sleep, legs entwined and feel mortified. As I think of the things that we did last night a flush comes to my neck and a feeling of nausea hits my stomach. Breathe, Ruby, breathe.

Running a hand through my hair, I wonder how I managed to get myself in this situation. I am *so* out of my comfort zone. I thought it might make me feel as if I had one up on my ex, but instead I'm just kind of feeling tawdry and a bit unclean. Perhaps Simon was right all along. I'm just not the adventurous type. If he could see me now he wouldn't think I was a racy, daring woman. He'd think I was an idiot. And he'd be right.

If I could, I'd go straight to the station now and run away from this. Also, I have the motherfucker of all hangovers. My head throbs. I think it was the brandies that finished me off. I'm never touching the stuff again. I always thought that I got a bit reckless on gin, but brandy has taken me to a whole new level.

As quietly as I possibly can, I get out of bed and tiptoe to the bathroom, collecting last night's clothes from the floor as I do. I don't even want to pee in case I wake them, but needs must. Afterwards, I splash cold water onto my face which hurts – everything hurts. Deciding a shower will be too noisy, I wash my important little places, dress quickly and, pulling on my jacket still damp from last night's rain, creep out of the room into the grey Paris dawn.

I thank God for Google Maps as I head out into the un-familiar streets and make my way towards the Eiffel Tower. There are very few people on the streets, a handful of delivery vans unloading, someone sleeping in a doorway. A couple of streets away, there's a lone café open so I get myself a coffee – a latte, hot and milky – then sit at one of the metal tables on the street while I drink it. In reality, it's too cold to be sitting outside, but doing just this was on my Wish List for Paris, so I'm damn well going to. The trees are out in blossom and Paris in the springtime looks just as lovely as it's supposed to.

When my bones are starting to seize up with the cold and I've finished my coffee, I push on. Soon, I've negotiated the building traffic and am standing beneath the edifice of the Eiffel Tower, which is magnificently impressive. The delicate ironwork legs that stretch skywards do a good job of dwarfing every other building. Even at this hour, there are plenty of people here. There's a photographer doing a photo-shoot with a hand-some couple posing with a red balloon. Bit clichéd, I suppose, but it reminds me to take out my phone and snap a few selfies. Despite not being the biggest fan of heights I'd love to go to the top. It has to be done, no? But it doesn't open for another three hours and you'd probably be better to buy tickets in advance. Maybe I can come back another time. I'm sure Mason would know what was the best thing to do but, of course, he's otherwise engaged. I check my watch again. I'm sort of putting off going back to the hotel. What if Valerie's still there and they expect me to get down to it again? Shudder. Don't think I could do that in the cold light of day. That's definitely an activity best undertaken after too much champagne, red wine and brandy. That thought makes me feel slightly queasy.

I meander round the adjoining park and stroll down to take a look at the murky brown ribbon of the Seine. The sun is slowing rising higher now, warming my face. Then my phone pings and it's Mason. Where are you? I'm worried.

Just walking, I text in return.

Come back. Let's get breakfast.

While I'm hesitating over my reply, another one comes in.

Valerie's gone now.

The coast is, therefore, clear. On my way, I tap.

I'll see you here. Their croissants are the best in Paris. An address pings in too and, once again, I let Google Maps steer me to the right street.

Mason is already waiting inside the busy café when I get there. As I make my way towards him, he stands and fusses with his napkin. His face is the very picture of concern.

'Are you all right?'

'Fine,' I say, taking the seat on the other side of the table. 'I couldn't sleep, so I thought I'd do a little bit of sightseeing. The Eiffel Tower is very beautiful at dawn.' I sound forced and too cheerful.

He orders me coffee, which I'm grateful for. I bury my nose in the menu so I don't have to look at him. I'm not feeling in the slightest bit hungry even though it feels as if rather a lot has happened since my chocolate mousse at dinner.

'About last night.' He lowers his voice as he speaks, though I don't think anyone else here is paying us any attention. 'You're OK about it?'

'Fine,' I bluster. 'God, yes. Fine.' I don't really want to talk about it at all. The less said about it the better in my book.

141

'I was concerned when I woke up and you were gone.'

I probably should be glad that he even noticed. 'Hangover,' I say with a tinkling laugh. Which is, of course, absolutely the truth. 'Needed some fresh air.'

'I thought you might find it fun,' he adds. 'A bit of naughtiness away from anyone who knows us.'

It just highlights that Mason really doesn't know who I am and, to be honest, it makes me consider if *I* know myself. I thought I could be modern, liberated, enjoy a bit of X-rated sex with a new man, but I don't think this is for me. I'd rather be in Paris with someone who loves me, wants to be with me – and only me. This trip could have been so very different.

'It's not really your thing, is it?' Mason says.

'No,' I admit. 'I kind of like it the usual way.'

He laughs at that. 'I'm sorry, Ruby. It won't happen again. Will you forgive me?'

'There's nothing to forgive,' I tell him. And I sort of mean it. 'I went along with it.'

'It's not something I do often. Just when I'm in Paris. Valerie's a nice girl,' he offers when I don't reply. 'There'll be no awkwardness.'

I wonder why, if he thinks she's a nice girl, he brings other women for their playtime? Why doesn't he just come here to see her? Why drag someone else in the equation? But I don't ask any of these questions. What Mason does is his own business. As long as he doesn't involve me again.

'She's not working today,' he adds. 'Not at the hotel.'

Then the penny drops. Perhaps it's a business arrangement between them? Does he pay her for services rendered or does she do it for free, for the fun? I can't bring myself to ask him that either.

Instead, I try to quell the lurching feeling in my stomach by ordering Eggs Benedict and some freshly squeezed orange juice.

I figure that some extra vitamin C will get me back on track again. While I wait, I pick at the basket of butter croissants that Mason has previously requested.

'We can do whatever you like today,' Mason says.

He's trying so hard to be nice, but both he knows and I know that a line has been crossed. All I have to do is get through today then I can run back home and be boring Ruby Brown instead of trying to be someone I'm not.

'There's a flea market in Montmartre, if that's your kind of thing,' he continues. 'Or we can take a trip in a bateau up the Seine. It's up to you.' His hand covers mine when he says, 'I'm at your service, Ruby. I want you to have a good time.'

One that involves just the two of us, I gather from that. His concern is touching and I feel my disappointment recede. When Mason is like this, he's good company and the silly mistakes of last night start to fade away.

Taking a deep breath, I reason that there's no cause for this to continue to be difficult. We're both grown-ups. What happened, happened. I was a willing – if slightly inebriated – participant. I could have said no and didn't. I blame my own insecurities for agreeing to do it. I can't change what's happened, but I can simply brush it under the carpet, think of it as a life experience that I hadn't necessarily anticipated and set about enjoying what's left of the day. That perks me up considerably and, with a renewed lift to my spirits, I say, 'A boat would be nice.'

Chapter Thirty-Three

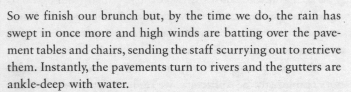

So we finish our brunch but, by the time we do, the rain has swept in once more and high winds are batting over the pavement tables and chairs, sending the staff scurrying out to retrieve them. Instantly, the pavements turn to rivers and the gutters are ankle-deep with water.

'We might as well stay put and have another coffee,' Mason says. 'Paris in the rain is appalling.'

I'll have to take his word for it. Though I'm up for Paris in any weather. I'm more than a little disappointed as I was hoping to get out and about today.

'We could go to the Louvre?'

'The world and his wife will be there,' Mason dismisses my suggestion. 'It will be hell.'

'Any other museums?'

'Yes, but not really my bag.'

'I suppose the boat's out of the question?'

He shrugs to indicate his lack of enthusiasm for the joys of the Seine *dans la pluie*. I think that's right – it's a long time since the French language and I were associated. 'You won't see Paris at its best.'

I won't see Paris *at all* at this rate, but I say nothing. I could go off on my own to explore, but that seems unfair. Mason has funded everything so far and I feel in his debt. It hardly seems right to leave him by himself and head out. So I'll do what he wants to do. Plus, it's still pouring down heavens hard and I have no umbrella. Or rain jacket. Or suitable footwear. In my attempt to pack light, I did not pack for all climatic occasions. I thought Paris would be hot and sunny. I thought I'd be strolling round all day under a cloudless sky. I was wrong on both counts.

'We could get a bottle of wine,' I suggest when all other options seem to be off limits. My hangover has just about abated enough to cope with more alcoholic input. 'Stay put for a while. Maybe the rain will pass.'

'A decent red sounds very appealing,' he agrees.

So while Mason orders us a decent red, I abandon any plans or hopes I had to see Paris in any kind of weather and settle in, trying to content myself with absorbing the atmosphere in this very traditional café. Perhaps I should just be happy to enjoy this time with Mason and get to know him better – or at least in a way that doesn't involve his gentleman's playthings. We had a nice dinner last night and I could try to recapture some of that mood.

Mason pours us the wine and, as it disappears too rapidly, the rain gets worse and worse. You could say it's raining *chats* and *chiens*. I know. I'll get my coat.

I study Mason as he talks to the waiter. His French sounds pretty good to me and he has the confidence that I so badly lack. There's a lot that I *do* like about him. He has loads of potential as partner material and has some great points. Despite the little erm . . . *interlude* . . . with Valerie, he's pretty hot in bed. So much to offer and yet, even though he's not that much younger than me in actual years it somehow seems like a vast age difference. He might be running a successful business, yet he still seems quite immature in so many ways.

If there's one thing that this weekend has taught me – apart from the fact that I don't particularly like kissing other ladies – it's that I want to be in a settled and secure relationship. I want to be part of a couple again. Not straight away, but I need to look for someone solid and dependable. Mason is too fickle, smooth and fly-by-night. All the things that Charlie warned me about. I'd probably like a family one day and, while time is running out for me, Mason seems to be a million miles away from that kind of commitment. He said he just wanted fun and he's certainly proved that.

As people soaked through to the skin rush in and a few brave souls dash out into the deluge, Mason and I stay hunkered down. We mainly talk about Mason's business plans for the future. He tells me a bit more about his family who sound like a totally fucked-up bunch despite their privileged lifestyle.

'My dad was never around when I was growing up. He was always at work, building his empire.' Mason gives a cynical snort. 'My mother spent her time at charity lunches and Doing Good. We were all packed off to boarding school. The minute I hit the age of eight, I was shipped out. We weren't even at the same school. As a result, we don't have what you'd call a close relationship.'

Fancy sending your kids off to school at eight. Why would you bother having them, if you're just going to farm them out to someone else to look after? Perhaps this is why he struggles with close relationships. I'm not trying to analyse him. It's just a thought.

'Didn't you miss them?'

'Yeah. I suppose. But I didn't know any different. Boarding school messes with your head. It did with mine anyway.'

I think of my nice little school that was just down the end of our road. The friends who all lived a short walk away and how there'd always be half a dozen of them at my house for tea at least one night of the week. It couldn't have been more different. I know that money doesn't buy you everything and Mason's living proof of that. Despite all his wealth, it makes me feel a bit sorry for him.

'You get on with them now?'

'Not that you'd notice,' he says, then brushes away further interrogation by adding, 'More wine?'

I nod and he fills my glass again. The wine brings a warm flush to my cheeks and I try to content myself by thinking that this is probably a very French way to spend a Sunday morning. If I'm being straight with you, I *really* like this side of Mason when he's been sincere and not showing off.

As he sits back in his chair, he catches me looking at him. 'You're not disappointed that we've been rained off? It wasn't a total washout? You've still had a good time?'

'Yes,' I say. 'I have.' Parts of it have been lovely. Some bits less so. 'Thank you for bringing me. Though I don't think we did a lot of research for your café chain.' I raise an eyebrow.

'Ah,' he says, acknowledging that I've seen though his bull. 'There's always another time. We could do this again and pray for better weather.'

'Yes,' I say. Yet, in my heart, I know that this will be my one and only weekend away with Mason. A small part of me feels sad about that. Would I feel differently about him if it had just been me and Mason and sunshine? 'Should we brave the rain and head back to the hotel then?'

'Good idea.'

I do feel a little upset that I've barely grazed the surface of Paris – one look at the Eiffel Tower doesn't really count for much – and, yet, too soon it will be time to leave. There's no doubt that I'd like to come back here one day. Preferably with someone I love.

We finish up the last dregs of our bottle of wine. Then,

conversation and alcohol exhausted, Mason asks the restaurant to phone a cab for us. They get no joy and tell us that the Metro is shut due to flooding. We decide to head out anyway and hesitate in the door before we plunge out into the street. It's lashing it down. Sheltering under the striped canopy, we look vainly up and down the street for a glimpse of a cab. No such luck. The road is like a river and there's nothing moving along here at all.

'This is showing no sign of letting up,' Mason says. 'Shall we make a run for it?'

'I think we have no option.'

So he peels off his jacket and, in his usual gentlemanly manner, holds it above my head as we dash out into the rain together. We run along the pavements which are awash with water, as fast as we can. Thunder rumbles across the sky and lightning illuminates the torrent of water running down the road. A lone car trundles past, water up to the sills. Mason's jacket proves to be an ineffectual umbrella and within minutes we're saturated, our hair and clothes plastered to our skin.

Chapter Thirty-Four

Not a moment too soon, we reach the hotel and stumble inside dripping wet, breathless and laughing. Valerie, as Mason had said, is thankfully nowhere in sight as we head to the lift. As we go up to the room, I start to shiver and Mason pulls me to him, rubbing my back to warm me up. I nestle against him, gratefully. Then his lips find mine and, before I know it, we're locked in a passionate embrace.

I've no idea how we get to the room, but as soon as the door is closed, we're stripping off each other's sodden clothes and Mason's chill, damp skin is against mine. He lowers me tenderly to the bed, and we make love again. Except there's no love involved at all, is there? I can't begin to pretend that after what happened last night. Yet, to my surprise, this time it's slower, sadder, more intense and neither of us says a word until Mason whispers my name against my neck as he comes inside me. It's the best sex since we arrived and, even better, there's no knock on the door from a third party. I feel as if I get another tiny glimpse of the real Mason Soames. Yet I feel oddly disengaged from it too, as if I'm observing rather than taking part and I'm left feeling weirdly hollow. Sorry, but that's the only way I can explain it. If I thought that fabulous sex was the way to fill a hole in my life, then I have to say that I'm sadly disappointed.

When we're finished we lie together, entwined, in the huge bed and Mason is quiet, thoughtful. Even though I'm tempted, I don't ask what's on his mind. Instead, I leave his side to take a hot shower before we have to catch our train. I wonder whether he might follow me into the bathroom, but he doesn't – even though some traitorous part of me wants to feel his hands on me again.

We pack and head to the station for our early evening train. Maybe part of the deal with Mason's receptionist friend is that we have a late checkout from the room or perhaps he paid extra for us to say longer – I don't know. The Eurostar whizzes us back to London and, while Mason busies himself with his phone, I doze on and off. The lack of sleep last night is now catching up with me.

When we finally hit Milton Keynes, it's getting late and Mason drives me home. We say little on the journey, but he turns to me as he parks up outside my place.

'I'm sorry it didn't go quite the way I'd planned,' he says softly. 'I've really enjoyed your company, Ruby. I hope you feel the same.'

'It was great,' I agree, but even I don't hear that conveyed in my voice.

'I'd like to see you again.'

'I'll see you at work, I guess. I'm on the early shift tomorrow.' Mason rarely comes in until late evening and I'll be long gone by then.

'Don't be obtuse, Brown,' he tuts. 'You know what I mean. I'll call you.'

Yet I imagine that he won't. Though I hope we can, somehow, maintain a civil, professional relationship now that he knows what colour my pants are and the sex noises I make. Ugh. I sigh at my own stupidity.

'Right then,' I say brightly. 'Best be off.' Now we're awkward with each other. I lean over and kiss him chastely on the cheek – this, the man whose mouth knows all my intimate places.

He gets my scruffy little weekend case out of the boot for me and I let myself into my flat as he drives off. The granny annexe feels empty, unloved – much like me. In the bedroom, cardboard cut-out Gary Barlow is standing guard. I throw my bag down onto my bed.

'Have I got some stories to tell you, Gazza,' I sigh at him. 'And I bet that you and the boys must have seen some things in your day.' I'll swear that he rolls his eyes at me. That's nothing compared to what Charlie will do. 'Your number one fangirl is going to be *sooo* cross with me.'

Chapter Thirty-Five

Charlie is already there when I get to work the next morning. I get the strongest of strong coffees, load it up with sugar and we take up our usual place at the back of the pub near the bins on the rickety bench that still hasn't made it to the tidy tip. It's not all that warm out here and I'm glad I've still got my coat on. The sky is grey and low, brooding. It matches my mood perfectly. I'm knackered and feeling very flat.

'Right,' Charlie says, charging up to vape. 'Tell Auntie Charlie all there is to tell.'

'You first. I'm knackered this morning and need a bit to regroup.'

'Is this entirely due to excess shaggage?'

'Yep. Pretty much.'

Charlie sucks on her e-cig. 'When he went there with Leanne – she worked here about six months ago – she said she never managed to get out of the hotel room.'

My heart plummets. Sounds all too familiar. To deflect attention from my extreme foolishness, I ask, 'So how was Gary?'

'Gorgeous.' She gives herself a cuddle and goes all dreamy. 'Oh, he's lovely. The musical was fantastic and all the boys were there. Well, except Robbie, obvs. And Jason.'

'Did your Nice Paul go too?'

'Yeah,' she says still wistful. 'He loved it too. We went to a burger place afterwards and then I got the Train of Shame back to the Keynes at some ungodly hour.' Then she glares at me. 'But he's not *my* Paul.'

Of course not. 'What did you do yesterday?'

'Worked.' She grimaces. 'I was knackered. I think every table got their order cocked up. It's a good job Mason wasn't in. I'd have been sacked. I bet you two lovebirds didn't even give me a thought while you were swanning around Paris.'

'We're hardly lovebirds. And I didn't really do a *lot* of swanning either,' I confess.

'But you did see some of it,' she says. 'The Louvre, La Tour Eiffel, all that *Fronch* stuff?'

Making an evasive-sounding noise, I say, 'It was great. Loved it.'

However, Charlie is not so easily deflected. 'That's not what your face is saying.'

Remind me never to take up poker.

She narrows her eyes at me. 'Tell Auntie Charlie all there is to tell,' she repeats more forcefully, 'and I won't have to hurt you.'

I sigh all my disappointment out. 'To be honest, Charls, we might as well have been at the Premier Inn down the road for fifty quid a night,' I tell her, frankly. 'The first day we didn't get out of the hotel at all – like the other girl you mentioned.' And probably many others whose names he's forgotten. 'That man is insatiable.'

'Cool,' she says, impressed.

Well, sort of. I press on. There's time enough for explanations of the tawdry truth. 'The second day, it totally poured down all the time. I did go out for an hour or so in the morning. By myself. But the rain was biblical. Everywhere flooded. We had brunch together in a café, but couldn't go really go anywhere to do sightseeing. We'd have drowned. They closed most of the metro stations in the area and we couldn't get a taxi for love nor money.'

'Sounds like the perfect excuse for staying in bed all day.'

'We did. Well, the whole afternoon,' I concede. 'I had hoped to see a bit more of Paris. From what little I did glimpse, it looked great.'

'So how did you get on with Shagger, though? Is he all he's cracked up to be in the sack? Or is it quantity over quality?'

'We got on fine,' I admit. 'Some bits of him are great.'

Charlie snarfs. 'Which particular bits are we talking about?'

'He's very sexy. No doubt about that.' Then I think that I might as well come clean. I don't know whether Mason will keep our adventures to himself or whether they will quickly become the talk of the pub. I wouldn't like Charlie to hear this from anyone else. She would kill me then. 'He's a little bit too . . . *adventurous* . . . for my tastes.'

'Aye, aye!' At that she perks up. 'Exactly how . . . *adventurous* . . . are we talking? Silk scarves, blindfolds, *toys*?'

I wince as I admit, 'We had a threesome.'

Charlie guffaws. 'Seriously?' She doubles up with laughter on the bench. 'You dirty mare. I can't let you out of my sight for five minutes and you're up to no good. What kind of threesome?'

'How many kinds are there?'

'Two guys?'

'No, no, no.'

'Another woman?'

I nod, unable to voice my shame.

'God, that is a bit kinky. Did you enjoy it?'

'Not really. It was well weird.'

She belly laughs again. 'Who'd have thought?'

154

'Not me,' I say firmly. 'It never crossed my mind that he'd be into that. In my defence, I'd had a lot to drink.' And, if I'm honest with myself, I really didn't know how to say no without causing a scene. It seemed easier to go along with it. Does that make me pathetic? I think perhaps it does. But you don't really have time to rehearse an exit strategy for these kinds of situations, do you? 'For the record, I'm never touching brandy again.'

'Was that her name?'

'Haha, very funny. She was called Valerie, if you must know, and was the receptionist at the hotel.'

'Blimey. Does she give all the guests a "happy ending"?'

'I've no idea and I don't want to know.' I feel myself go pink again at the thought.

Charlie giggles again at my discomfiture. 'No wonder you had no energy for sightseeing.'

'That's partly why I sloped off by myself in the morning. They were still sleeping and I needed to get out of the place. I couldn't face either of them.' I push away the image of Valerie and Mason still in bed while wondering whether they slept together when I left. Not that it matters. Far from it. 'I was mortified, Charlie.'

'I'm not bloody surprised.'

'It did mean that I saw the Eiffel Tower.'

'You could hardly bloody miss it,' Charlie notes. 'I could probably see it from here if I looked hard enough.'

'It's fair to say that my romantic weekend with our boss wasn't quite the resounding success I'd hoped for.' I clutch at my coffee for comfort. 'You did warn me.'

'Oh, Ruby,' she says. 'What am I going to do with you?'

'I can see why you stick to Gary Barlow now.'

'Gary would *never* have a threesome. He's far too wholesome.' She looks all faraway for a moment before adding, 'So, are you seeing Shagger again?'

'No. That was more than enough.' Though, in my weaker moments, I still have an image of the eight-year-old boy being packed off to boarding school tugging at my heartstrings.

'You've not developed a taste for the steamier side of sex?'

'No,' I say vehemently. 'I've learned my lesson. I'm only going out with nice men from now on.'

'You can't have Gary Barlow,' she says. 'Not even on your laminated list. That baby's mine. We're not going to share that one, you and your sleazy threesomes.'

I hang my head in shame. 'Don't remind me.' I think the problem is that I'm sure Mason would have been happy in Paris with anyone. It wasn't *me* he wanted to take. Despite what he said, he wasn't really hankering after my sparkling company. Mason just wanted some fun. By *fun*, I mean lots of sex. Anyone would have done. That doesn't make me feel so great.

'Take That are playing Paris in the summer. You and I should go there together. We'd have great fun. And we'd see stuff.' Charlie kicks her legs against the bench. 'The fan club are organising a trip. We could do some sightseeing. Take in all the tourist bits that you missed.'

'Sounds like a plan.' I would have a good time with Charlie. I know that. Then my mobile pings and it's a text from Mason. Hope you enjoyed the weekend. I'll call you. Let's have dinner soon. I turn my phone and show it to Charlie.

'Dinner, eh?'

'He's just being polite,' I say. 'There's no way he'll call and, even if he does, there's no way I'm having dinner with him.'

And I mean it. Honestly, I do.

Chapter Thirty-Six

Mason actually calls me a dozen times, maybe more. I let them all go to voicemail. There's nothing I want to say to him and there's certainly nothing I want to do with him of an intimate nature. I've had my head down for the last two days, just doing my job, earning a meagre crust. I've swerved out of work dead on time too so that I'd avoid him, but Charlie tells me that he hasn't been into the pub at the end of the day as he sometimes does. I can only hope that it's not going to be difficult between us when he does, eventually, rock up. We're grown-ups. We can handle this.

On Wednesday morning, when my phone rings again, I'm about to leave it unanswered then I glance at the number and it isn't Mason. It's Joe and my heart pitter-patters a bit even though I don't want it to.

'Hi,' I say when I pick up.

'Hi Ruby. It's Joe Edwards. Sorry to bother you, but I'm calling to say that I can't make our lesson tonight.'

'Oh. I thought Bob was teaching me now.'

'He's not able to make it either. We're short-handed so we've had to cancel the session. It doesn't happen often and normal service should be resumed next week. I'm sorry.'

'I hope nothing's wrong.'

'Work-related issues for me. We're doing our first film show for the public at the centre – I managed to raise some funds. My colleague was due to be on duty, but she's sprained her ankle and is laid up for a few days. I've stepped into the breach.'

'That's very noble,' I say. 'I hope you enjoy the film.'

'I'm not sure it's my bag,' Joe laughs. 'We decided to let the residents choose what we show. This one's going to be *Love, Actually*.'

'Oh, that's a great movie. One of my favourites.'

There's a pause which goes on a bit too long, before Joe says, 'Would you like to come along? As my guest. I'd be glad of your support.'

Before my brain has time to process the invitation, my mouth already says, 'Yes. That would be lovely.'

'Are you happy to come along by yourself? I've got to get there early to set things up and I'm sure you don't want to hang around, otherwise I'd pick you up. The film starts at eight o'clock, but we're serving drinks in the bar beforehand.'

'I'm working until seven, so I'll come along straight after that.'

'Perfect. I'll see you later.'

Then I hang up and wonder if I've actually just organised myself a date. I can't have. Can I?

Chapter Thirty-Seven

The Sunshine Woods community is to the south of Costa del Keynes which makes it handy for me to drive to when I leave work as it's barely ten minutes from the Butcher's Arms. I get changed quickly in the staffroom – clean white shirt, beige cigarette-cut trousers, black heels. I fluff my hair, spray myself with a waft of Viktor & Rolf Flowerbomb and put some lippy on too. Looks as if I'm saying I made an effort, but not too much. I hope so, anyway.

Now I swing into the complex and park up. It's bigger than I'd imagined with a couple of dozen small houses arranged around a pretty courtyard. Each one has a French door that opens onto a small lawn and there are well-tended flowerbeds in full bloom with the last of the spring flowers. There's a café here too, closed now, and I can see a small hall ahead of me. A sign in slightly wonky writing says, FILM, THIS WAY!, so I pick my way through the manicured garden. In the foyer there are a few people already gathering and as I step inside, I see Joe all spruced up in a white polo shirt and black jeans standing with one of the residents. He smiles when he sees me and it's filled with a warmth so genuine that, for a moment, it takes me aback.

'Hi Ruby,' he says. 'I'm glad you could make it. I wasn't sure you would.'

'I said I'd come.'

'Billy,' he says to the man with him. 'This is my friend, Ruby. Say hello and ask her would she like a programme.'

The man is probably in his forties and has Down's Syndrome. 'Hello, Ruby. Would you like a programme?'

'I would. Thank you.'

He hands one to me with a smile. 'I like you. Have you got a husband?'

That kind of question still manages to take the wind out of my sails. I expect everyone thinks I'd be happily settled down by now. 'No,' I smile. 'Sadly not.'

'I don't know why. She's nice, isn't she, Joe?'

'Yes, she's lovely,' Joe agrees. 'Let me get you a drink. Remember to say hello to everyone who comes in, Billy. Don't ask all the ladies if they've got a husband.'

'OK.' He grins at us both.

Joe steers me towards the bar. 'Sorry about that. Billy's great, but sometimes he's a bit over-familiar. He wants to marry everyone he meets.'

'Ah. And I thought it was just me.'

Joe laughs and slips behind the small bar in the corner to join a young barman standing stiffly with a tea towel over his arm. 'What can we get for you, madam?' Joe asks. 'Wine? Red? White?'

'I'd better not while I'm driving. A Coke will do.'

'Happy to do that, Eamon?' The barman nods enthusiastically. 'Don't forget to ask if your customer would like ice and a slice of lemon.'

'Ice? Lemon?'

'Yes, please.'

When it's done, Eamon lifts the glass as if he has a nest of delicate bird's eggs in his hands and places it in front of me with a satisfied beam.

'Excellent,' Joe says. 'That's great, mate. Well done.'

Eamon proudly smooths down the front of his shirt.

'I'll come back when you have your next customer.' We walk towards the window which looks out onto the garden. 'All our residents need assistance to be independent. This sort of thing helps with their confidence and interpersonal skills, but we've never attempted anything on this scale before. Everyone's a bit over-excited. Except me,' he adds. 'I'm a bag of nerves.'

'It looks like a lovely place.'

'Yeah,' Joe says. 'On the whole, it is. We have our ups and downs like anywhere, but they're a great bunch of people who live on the campus and we have a good team. It's a privilege to work here. Which is just as well as the pay is shocking.'

'Like any vocation.'

'The only difficulty is that I can't always swerve out of here on the dot of five or whenever my shift ends.' He tries to keep his eye on all of his charges as he talks. 'Juggling childcare is an art form. One I've not quite mastered. Still, the kids are getting older. It won't be long before they can start to look after themselves a bit more.'

'Where are they tonight?'

'With Gina.' He glances over his shoulder. 'I've reserved seats for us on the front row, right by the aisle – just in case I need to pop out quickly. It's a small audience tonight – only about thirty people. Mainly friends and family of the residents. We wanted to run this as a trial to see if it works out OK before we unleash it onto the general public.'

'Everyone seems to be doing well.' There's a girl in her twenties selling sweets. Someone at the door taking tickets.

'Two of the residents who are in a relationship have chosen

161

the film tonight. We wanted to make sure as many of them as possible were involved.'

'Sounds like a great idea.'

'I can't take any of the credit for it,' he admits. 'It was my colleague who came up with this one.' Then he sighs. 'All I'm doing is talking about myself. I haven't asked you how your weekend in Paris was with your partner.'

'He's not really my partner. It's more of a casual thing. I'm not even sure we're friends as such.' Joe raises an eyebrow and I realise that sounds wrong. 'Paris was OK.'

'You're not bowling me over with your enthusiasm. Shall I cross it off my bucket list?'

'It's a long story, but it wasn't quite what I expected.' He looks as if he wants to ask me more, but I'm not really keen to reveal much more about my trip. To explain what Mason and I are to each other seems way too complicated. 'It rained a lot.'

'Oh.'

Then a couple head towards Eamon at the bar and I'm quite relieved when Joe says, 'Mind if I leave you for five minutes to help out? Go through when you're ready or you can chat to some of the residents.'

'I'll get us some sweets.' The foyer is filling up now, so I go to the counter and buy a box of Maltesers and chat to the young girl about the film.

Over by the bar, Joe claps his hands. 'Ladies and gentlemen, our film will be starting shortly, if you'd like to take your seats.'

Making my way to the door, I then linger until Joe is free to join me. I can tell that he's torn between spending time with me and making sure that everything goes smoothly for the evening. I quite like that. It's sort of cute. I can see that he's a genuinely kind and caring person.

Eventually, he comes towards me and takes my arm. 'Let's go and see what Hugh Grant has to offer.'

'This isn't your kind of film?'

'I don't mind a rom-com. Years of being married has brain-washed me, but I'm feeling too cynical to buy into a happy ending at the moment. Plus I still prefer something with a car chase and Vin Diesel doing bad things,' he says with a smile. 'At least the kids have stopped watching wall-to-wall Disney and Pixar. There was a time when I knew more about *The Little Mermaid* than a man should.'

I laugh at that. Joe looks like a man who'd be comfortable watching Disney and Pixar films. Unbidden, I get a flashback to my . . . er . . . torrid time . . . in the hotel with Mason and think that, as men, they couldn't be more different.

'If you're good,' he says. 'I'll buy you an ice cream in the interval.'

'I have snacks to keep us going until then.' I hold up the Maltesers.

'My kind of woman,' he says and, for a moment, part of me hopes that I am.

Chapter Thirty-Eight

Two of the residents sit at the front of the auditorium in front of the screen. They're middle-aged and are holding hands tightly.

'I'm Emily,' the woman says, beaming shyly. 'And this is my boyfriend, Graham.'

'This is our favourite film,' Graham says. 'It's the film we saw on our first date.'

'Second date,' Emily corrects. 'On our first date we went bowling.'

'That wasn't really a date as there were other people there,' Graham insists. 'We watch it every week.'

'Twice a week,' she corrects.

'My girlfriend likes Alan Rickman.'

'I don't,' Emily chips in. 'He cheats on his wife.'

'Only in the film,' Graham counters.

'He buys a necklace, but it's not *actually* for her,' Emily tells us.

'It's a good job you've seen it,' Joe whispers to me.

'I thought you liked him.' Graham is clearly piqued. 'You said you did.'

'I didn't.' She's very affronted now. 'I only like him in Robin Hood.'

'You said this was your favourite film.'

'I like *Notting Hill* better.'

'Guys, guys,' Joe says. 'Not a good time for a domestic. Introduce the film.'

'This is *Love, Actually* by Richard Curtis,' Graham says. 'We hope that you enjoy it.'

As we applaud, they stand up and take their seats in the front row. Emily takes the opportunity to dig her beau sharply in the ribs. The lights go down and the film starts.

I know it's cheesier than a ripe Camembert but I love this film. Even the opening sequence makes me feel all warm and fuzzy. It's not high art, I get that, but it pushes all my buttons. Unrequited love, heartbreak, misunderstandings, longing, loss – frankly, all of my life is written large here. I'll cry at the end, I know I will. I always do. I check that I've got a tissue in my back pocket.

It feels weird sitting here with Joe in the dark. Weirdly nice. His arm is resting lightly against mine and I don't know if it's deliberate or whether the seats are just too close together. The warmth of his big solid body is comforting. Maybe it would be nice to go on a proper date with him, I think – as Graham views it. Just us and no one else. A date where we aren't doing something like scuba-diving or he's working. Perhaps it might happen, in time. If he sorts himself out with his ex and his kids. I wonder how long that will take? I could be on one of those wheelie walking frames by then. I offer him the box of Maltesers and he dips in.

We get to the bit where Martin Freeman and that nice girl off *Gavin and Stacey* are in the buff acting out a porn scene and a voice shouts out from the back. 'Are they having SEX?'

'Pipe down, Billy,' Joe says with a smile.

Huge stage whisper. 'They *are* having sex.'

Joe turns to me. 'I think I need to vet the film more carefully next time.' We both smother a laugh.

So it goes throughout the film, every time someone kisses, shows skin or does venture towards having sex, Billy shouts out, 'They're doing it AGAIN!'

Which kind of detracts from the film and adds to it at the same time. I think Billy definitely needs a girlfriend. We have ice cream at the interval and when the film ends, despite having seen it a dozen or more times, I still cry at the end.

In the foyer afterwards, I wait while Joe says goodbye to some of the families and I help Eamon to tidy up behind the bar and then give the girl with the sweets a hand in packing them away.

'Sorry about that,' Joe says when he's finished.

'No worries. You're working. I understand that.' Then I take my courage in both hands. 'Do you fancy going for a drink or a coffee somewhere?'

'Now?' Joe looks as surprised as I feel.

'It's not late.'

He hesitates for a moment before saying, 'I can't. I'm sorry. I need to see that the residents are safely home. One or two of them like to wander off when no one's looking. Plus I'm on the clock with Gina. The kids are in school tomorrow.'

'Oh, I thought they were staying overnight with her.'

He gives a hollow laugh. 'I should be so lucky.'

'It doesn't matter. It was silly of me to ask.' Wasn't it just.

'Another time though,' he adds quickly. 'It would be great.'

'Yeah. Of course.' I try not to sound disappointed but it's never going to happen. He has commitments. Loads of them. I get that. 'Thanks for a nice evening.'

'I bet you go home and watch it in peace now without Billy's commentary.'

'That made it much more fun,' I say earnestly. 'You have some very nice people living here.'

'I'd better go.' Joe glances over his shoulder, distracted. 'I'll see you at scuba-diving?'

'Yeah. Sure.'

'Thanks for coming, Ruby.'

'My pleasure.' I have to say this is possibly *the* most chaste date I've ever had. It's not exactly a date though, is it? Never was.

As I turn to leave, he catches my wrist and kisses me lightly on the cheek. 'I mean it about coffee,' he says. 'Let's do it soon.'

'OK.' Then he dashes off to help someone carrying chairs.

I stand and watch him for a moment longer. And as I walk to the car, I have to stop myself from touching my cheek where he kissed it.

Chapter Thirty-Nine

I drive home with a stupid smile on my face. Despite the refusal at the coffee fence, that was a good evening, all considered. Good film, Maltesers, cold ice-cream, hot man. The promise of a coffee-based date? Maybe. I'm still grinning when I pull up outside my granny annexe. That's until I see Mason's fancy car parked there.

I turn off my engine and sit in my car for a moment, wondering what to do. I'm going to have to get out, aren't I? I can hardly sit here all bloody night. He knows it's me in my slightly mouldy Mazda. With a sigh, I open the door. I've no idea what to say to him.

By the time I'm out of the car, Mason is standing leaning against my bonnet. It's fair to say that he's looking pretty hot. He's wearing a crisp, white shirt, designer jeans and shoes that are most definitely handmade rather than from Next. He folds his arms and gives me a direct stare. 'You're avoiding me, Brown. Why's that?'

'I'm not.'

'I've called you dozens of time and they've all gone to voice-mail. I've left you invitations for dinner and yet nothing. Have you stopped eating?'

'I'm busy. I did mean to return your calls.' That sounds as lame as you think.

'Like hell you did.' He's clearly not buying my excuses, yet he's smiling when he says it. 'I'm not used to being given the run around.'

'That's not my intention.'

'Then come out with me now.'

'Now?'

'I'm going up to the club. Get your gladrags on and let's hit the town. The night is young.'

'It's nearly eleven o'clock.' That didn't seem to bother me when I was asking Joe for coffee, did it? 'I've got work tomorrow and I have a boss who's pure evil.'

'I've heard he's a pussycat. And extraordinarily handsome.'

'I can't come to the club, Mason. It's late and I'm tired.'

'Charlie said you'd gone to watch a film.'

Thanks, Charlie. Remind me to kick her in the shins tomorrow. 'Yeah, I did.'

'A date?'

'Not exactly,' I say. 'Not that it's any of your business.'

'What did you see?'

'*Love, Actually*.'

'What kind of date is that?' He turns up his nose.

'A nice one. I enjoyed myself.'

'So why home so early?'

'I told you, it's none of your business. It wasn't a date, anyway.'

'I can do nice, cheesy dates, if that's what floats your boat. Come on,' he wheedles. 'Don't make me beg. Play out with me. I'll drive you home afterwards. You can have as many sparkly cocktails as you like.'

'I'm not that easily bought.' Though he already knows, to my eternal shame, that a weekend in Paris is my price. 'I don't think this is a good idea, Mason. We should continue our relationship on a purely professional footing.'

'Bollocks,' is his view on that. 'We're good together and you know it. Come on, Brown. Let your hair down. See what I did there? I'm a poet and I didn't even know it.'

I can help but smile which only encourages him.

'Go and get changed. Or come as you are. You look great either way.'

I sigh. I have no idea why but Mason is wearing me down. His club is nice, sophisticated and I think that one drink – or maybe two – wouldn't hurt. I know what he's like now. There's no way that I'm going to get suckered in again. Besides, what am I going to do? Sit indoors by myself thinking about Joe and a date that might never happen? What if he was just trying to be polite? What if he has a change of heart and decides to warn me off again? Oh, man. This is doing my head in. I'm young – sort of – single, and I can either have an early night or live dangerously. I shouldn't sit here waiting for a man that's too busy to see me. Right? I'm looking to you to enable this.

'An hour,' I say. 'That's all. I want to be in bed by midnight.'

'I can arrange that too,' he deadpans.

'By myself,' I stress. Not with you. Not with Valerie or similar. 'Will I do like this?'

'You look fabulous.'

'Now I know that you're lying.'

'Get in the car,' he says. 'There's a Porn Star Martini with your name on it.'

I shake my head at him. 'Charmer.' Yet I get in his car, nevertheless.

The Vibe Lounge is busy for a weekday, but we're shown to a reserved sofa in the corner. For the record, I have three sparkly cocktails – two more than I had pledged would pass my lips.

What can I say? I have a weakness for the coloured drink. And for Mason Soames too, it seems.

We have a great laugh. He's fun and naughty and it's hard not to get caught up in his enthusiasm. He chides me again for not returning his calls. He makes me feel on top of the world and, when he takes me in his arms on the dance floor, we move well together in time to the smoochy music. Damn him. When he's like this, I like him. A lot.

When I look at my watch it's one in the morning. I groan. 'It's waaaaay past my bedtime. I'm never going to get up in the morning.'

'Come on, Cinders, I'll take you home.'

'I can get a cab.'

'Won't hear of it.' So I take the last sip of my drink, grab my bag and we head to his car.

My eyes close as we drive through the deserted streets of Costa del Keynes and Mason turns up the stereo. Adele fills the car with hit tunes and I think I might sing along in a slightly drunken way.

When Mason pulls up outside the granny annexe again, I feel that I'd be happy to sleep in these comfy leather seats all night.

He turns to me and strokes my hair. 'Here you are, Brown. Safely delivered before you turn into a pumpkin.'

'It was the pumpkin that turned into Cinderella's carriage,' I inform him.

'Whatever.'

'Clearly, you're no Prince Charming,' I laugh.

He's suddenly serious. 'I could be. If that's what it takes.' Then he leans over and kisses me.

I think it's the sparkly drinks, but my resistance is very low. When his hands move over my body, it takes all my effort to say, 'I should go.'

'Let me stay the night,' he murmurs against my neck.

'No, no, no.' I shake my head and my brain hurts. 'Seriously bad idea.' I grasp for the door handle to make my escape before reason deserts me.

'We're good together. You know it.'

'We're not. You're my boss. I'm your minion. You're upstairs. I'm downstairs.'

He shakes his head at me. 'I have no idea what that even means.'

Obvs Mason doesn't stay in at night watching crap telly.

'Let me stay.' His lips move over my neck. 'I know all the funny little noises you make now and I want to hear them again.'

I push him away and wag my finger at him. 'You don't know *all* my funny noises.'

'I don't?' He looks shocked. 'There are more?'

'That's something you'll never know,' I tell him.

Mason sighs ruefully. 'You're making a big mistake, Brown.'

'I'm so not. See you at work, Mr Soames.' I lurch out of his car, totter up the path and then clamber up the stairs to my granny annexe eyrie. Blimey. I don't remember the stairs being this steep. Do you think the landlord has had them changed while I was out?

As I fumble with my key in the lock, I hear Mason's car roar off into the night. I go through to the bedroom and fall onto the bed face first.

'I had a very narrow escape,' I mumble to cardboard cut-out Gary Barlow, turning my head to look at my guru. 'He's *such* a good kisser. But if I'd let Mason stay the night Charlie would have killed me, resurrected me and then killed me again.'

And, with that thought in my head, I greet oblivion.

Chapter Forty

I haven't heard from either Joe or Mason. Seriously, it's either feast or famine here. Two men in one night – not in the biblical sense of the word, obvs. Given my slight aberration in Paris, I feel the need to reiterate that. Then not a word. Since our late-nite impromptu clubbing get together Mason has stopped the ten phone calls a day and he's only been into the pub when I've not been on shift. I wonder if that's deliberate or whether he's tied up with the Vibe Lounge. Joe didn't turn up to scuba-diving again this week, so I had Bob. Again, not biblically. Bob said he thought Joe had to go to parents' night at school for one of the kids or something. He might have rung me himself and explained that though. No? And the promised coffee date? Not a sausage.

Still, I don't care. Men are more trouble than they're worth. I don't understand them at all and yet women are supposed to be the tricky ones. Pah.

I haven't seen Charlie all week as our shifts haven't coincided – which is a rare thing as we normally persuade our manager, Jay, to put us on the rota together. Though he doesn't take much persuasion as he calls us the Dream Team and not in a sarcastic way.

However, we're both off work today and are going on an outing together. There's a Gary Barlow festival on at a local hotel – GaryFest. Even the rubbish name can't put us off. Charlie has got us Platinum tickets which include a glass of prosecco, tickets to all the talks about all things Barlow and a performance by a well-known tribute act. Though I have to say I've never heard of him.

We're getting ready at Charlie's place. I have my *Let it Shine!* T-shirt on again. Charlie's instructions. She takes a photo of us pouting at her phone. I comb my hair, put my lippy on and think that I should, at least, listen to the new album before we go to GaryFest.

'I've just tweeted the photo to Gary to let him know where we're going and he tweeted me back!'

'What did he say?'

'*Cool.*' She shows me the tweet.

'Is it really him? He has over four million followers. Surely he has a team of minions to do it for him?'

'Gary wouldn't do that. He follows me, you know. That's as big a deal as it gets.'

'Why? What do you tweet about?'

'You shagging our boss.'

I asked for that. 'I'd like to point out that I haven't had so much as a phone call from Mason since our night at the club.'

Charlie screws up her eyes and stares at me. 'What night at the club?'

Ah.

'I sort of went out with him to the Vibe Lounge again last week. We had a nice time. I thought everything was OK between us again.'

'What are you like? You could give Mrs Gullible lessons in being gullible.'

'I know. That's it though. I'm finished with him.'

'I don't mean to be mean, but it sort of sounds like he's finished with you.'

'Thanks, Charlie.'

She puts her arm round me. 'Don't be down, we're going to be immersed in all things Gazza Bazza and you won't be able to stay miserable for long. A little dose of Gary cures all ills.'

So we head off to the hotel and I'm surprised to see that it's already packed when we get there even though it's not yet eleven in the morning on a Sunday and, by rights, as I'm not at work I should still be in bed. Take That music fills the air.

There are a few hundred women of all shapes and sizes, many of them wearing similar T-shirts to our own. Amid the women, I spot a solitary bloke. Nice Paul is standing chatting in a little roped off area reserved for those fans bearing the covered Platinum ticket. 'Hey,' I say. 'Your mate is over there.'

'Oh,' Charlie says and, if I'm not very much mistaken, she brightens considerably.

We queue to exchange our tickets for two wristbands and, as we finally head towards Nice Paul, he sees us and swiftly brings over two glasses of prosecco. Might as well start as we mean to go on.

'Good to see you, girls.' We clink glasses together. 'Here's to a great day,' Paul says.

So we drink prosecco, go to talks about Gary and his life, buy Gary memorabilia – not me, but Charlie and Paul. I watch them, heads together, cooing over old photos of Gary, autographed posters or coasters with Gary's photos on them as if they were priceless antiques. All of the Barlow stuff you could ever require is here to buy. While they're busy I grab them both a mug that says 'Keep Calm and listen to Gary Barlow' and quickly pay for them, before secreting them in my handbag. They will soooo love them.

At lunchtime we avail ourselves of the barbecue buffet and

sit outside on the grass while the fluffy clouds drift above us in a sky that's, quite fittingly, sky blue. We listen to a set by one of the foremost tribute acts and, I'm no expert, but he certainly gives it a good go. Mr Barlow's fans seem more than appreciative.

We are all proseccoed out by mid-afternoon and in desperate need of the more traditional British refreshment – a good cup of tea. So Nice Paul goes off in search for one for us.

I lie back on the grass, enjoying the feeling of the sun on my face and realise that I spend far too much of my life indoors. 'He's nice,' I say.

'Yeah,' Charlie agrees. 'He's not Gary but he's pretty good.'

'I don't mean the tribute act. I mean Paul.'

'Oh. Yeah. He's great too.' Though she still sounds quite non-committal about him. Surely his quiet charm must be having some effect on her?

'I'm having a lovely time,' I start, 'and I get that Gary is a totally fabulous human being.' All these ladies can't be wrong. 'But why spend your life following someone unattainable when there's a great bloke right next to you?'

'Paul?'

'Who else? He seems so nice and you patently share the same interests.' Actually make that 'interest' in the singular. 'He clearly likes you. It could be the start of something special.'

'I've been married, you know.' Charlie picks at her fingernails.

I look at her aghast. 'Seriously? I thought you were resolutely single? All the time I've known you and yet you've never said a word about that?'

Charlie looks at me with tears in her eyes. 'There's a very good reason for that, Ruby.'

Chapter Forty-One

My brain tries to make sense of this unexpected revelation. I've known Charlie for months now. She's my best mate in the world and I'd no idea she was hiding this from me. As she said, there must be a very good reason. I thought we told each other everything. She knows all about my dismal marriage, especially Simon and the Crystal Vajayjay. She's had chapter and verse on that. She probably feels as if she's seen it herself. I know I do.

Charlie looks down at her feet as she continues. 'I try very hard to pretend that he doesn't exist, that he was never in my life at all. I don't even like to say his name. '

'Oh, Charlie, why? Was he that bad?'

She nods, clearly upset to be recalling their time together. 'A shocker.'

I can tell from her expression that it's clearly painful for her, so I put my arm round her. 'My poor girl. No wonder I've never heard you talk about him. But we're friends. You know you can tell me anything.'

Charlie gives me a sideways glance. It looks as if she wants to tell me.

'You know about my tacky threesome,' I remind her with a nudge. 'It can't be any worse than that.'

She tries a laugh. 'Nothing's worse than that!'

'There you go then.'

She sighs at me. 'He was a nightmare, Ruby. A *proper* nightmare. Abusive in every way that you could think – emotionally, physically.' I feel sick that she hasn't been able to confide in me until now. 'I didn't mean to keep it a secret. I just never tell anyone.'

'He sounds like a total shit.' At least with all our troubles, Simon never threatened me. I don't know how I would have coped with that. 'He's gone now though.'

'Yeah. At least I hope so. Knob.' She tries to make light of it, but I can tell that it still hurts her. 'Even though the bruises had long gone and I had new locks on my door, it still felt as if he was in my life. He'd ground me down for so long that I struggled to manage without him.'

'Oh, Charlie.'

'Seems a stupid thing to say, right?' I look at the tears welling in her eyes and want to brush them away. 'It's OK. Everything's fine now. His job took him to another part of the country – thank God – and slowly my life returned to normal. More or less.' Charlie studies the floor. 'There are still times when some small thing reminds me of him and I'm right back there. I feel sick just thinking about him. Unless it's happened to you, you don't know how it feels. How it saps your confidence, drains every ounce of joy out of life. It took me so long to recover, I couldn't return to that.'

'I don't blame you.'

'So that's why I stick to Gary. He's never going to hurt me or let me down. He's never going to break my ribs or knock out my teeth or pull out chunks of my hair. Gary sings me to sleep every night and I don't have to do a single thing in return.

I don't have to worry about what mood he's going to come home in because he's never going to do that.'

'You've got so much to offer though. It makes for a lonely life keeping everyone at arm's length. Don't you want to settle down, to have children?'

'The only saving grace of our relationship was that we never had kids, otherwise I'd never have been entirely rid of him. I've got a friend in a similar situation and she has a son. Every week she has to take him to a supervised visit to play happy families with the man who tried to choke the life out of her. At least I don't have to do that.'

'I'm sorry, Charlie. I had no idea.'

She shrugs. 'Like I said, I don't talk about it if I can help it. That's the other thing, they make it feel like it's all your fault. If only you were funnier, prettier, better in some way then this wouldn't be happening. It took me years to come to terms with the fact that he was an out-and-out shit and there was nothing more complicated than that about it.'

'So Nice Paul's on a hiding to nothing? He's not the same man, you know. Wouldn't you even give him a chance?'

'I can't risk it again,' she says, sadly. 'Perhaps I'm just not over it yet. Maybe I never will be. It leaves scars, stuff like that. Some you can see, some you can't. The false front teeth are a permanent reminder of the damage that rushing into a relationship can cause.' She taps a finger to them. 'Paul's a great mate. I like him a lot, but . . .'

She doesn't need to say any more. I won't talk about it any longer or even tease her. If it's not to be, that's Charlie's choice. I just want her to be happy and if even it means that she's most contented by herself, then so be it. I'll always be there for her, as she is for me. I put my hand on her arm. 'Thanks for telling me.'

'Thanks for being a mate,' she says in return.

Then, before I can say anything else, Nice Paul comes back, still smiling affably, balancing three teas on a tray, and my heart goes out to him.

'The queues!' he exclaims as he sits down beside us and hands out the tea.

I don't think Nice Paul has it in his heart to hurt anyone, but then what do I know about men? I currently have too many of them or none at all.

'I have a gift for you both,' I say and I delve in my bag to find the 'Keep Calm and listen to Gary Barlow' mugs I bought. 'This has been a lovely day. Thanks for including me.'

I hand them over and they both go into throes of ecstasy.

'This is *so* cool,' Charlie says and kisses me. 'You're not to borrow it when you come to my house.'

'Wouldn't dream of it.

'The perfect mantra to live your life by,' Paul says with a grin as he admires his present.

They both kiss me again and I think it's such a shame that they'll never get together as they're so well matched.

I think of Mason Soames and Joe Edwards. Both nice guys. Both with complications. I should be like Charlie and be content on my own. I don't need a man. Of that, I'm sure. The tribute act starts up again and we kick back to enjoy the set. Gary Barlow's going to be the only one for me too.

As Alan Banks from Barnsley croons 'It Only Takes a Minute' I think, sadly, that it's going to take Charlie a hell of a lot longer than a minute to fall in love.

Chapter Forty-Two

Despite my affirmation that Gary Barlow is going to be the only man for me from now on, I still find myself rushing to my scuba-diving lesson, heart a-flutter, stomach in knots – something that last happened when I was about fifteen – only to be disappointed that I've got Bob again. Three weeks in a row. Joe, on the other hand, is nowhere to be seen.

To be honest with you, there's nothing wrong with Bob. He's a good, solid instructor with the patience of a saint. It's fair to say that I am not one of scuba-diving's naturals. I can't remember what to do with what thing and I wonder if I'm ever going to be good enough to let loose in open water. Yet I'm probably learning more about scuba-diving with Bob than I would with Joe as I don't have the unbridled urge to stare at him wistfully or long to see his naked bottom. I keep telling myself that I'm much better off with an instructor who has a pot-belly and a comb-over. I go to the pub with them all afterwards but, frankly, it's just not the same.

I miss Joe. That's the truth of the matter. I think about him a lot. When I'm in bed – even though cardboard cut-out Gary Barlow is available – when I'm in the bath, when I'm serving in the pub. Which means that a lot of diners are inadvertently getting someone else's chips by mistake. My bad.

Before work, Charlie and I sit on what we lovingly call 'our bench' and discuss the situation. It's pushing on towards summer with a vengeance and Jay has put out a load of new hanging baskets all round which look a bit pathetic now, but I'm sure will soon be heavy with the type of flowers you put in hanging baskets. Gardening isn't among my skill set either, in case you were wondering. He bought one too many, so had a spare which he's put round by the bins to cheer up our 'office', as he calls it.

'You're as miserable as sin,' Charlie remarks as she vapes. 'Look at you. Just because I'm sworn off men, it doesn't mean that you still can't dabble.'

'I dabbled with Mason Soames and look where that got me.'

'Ben behind the bar says he's been doing the Grand Prix season. I don't even know if that's a thing. Apparently, he's jetting off here, there and everywhere to watch the racing.' She looks at me bewildered. 'Why do that when you can watch it on telly?'

'Atmosphere,' I say knowingly when, in reality, I know nothing at all.

Charlie rolls her eyes.

'Besides, it's not Mason that I miss.' Though I do wonder how Ben behind the bar knows his every move when I, who have recently shared his bed, don't. 'I like him and we have a great laugh together, but he's not relationship material. Joe on the other hand . . .' I take the opportunity to go all dreamy.

'Is a family man with a whole heap of commitments,' Charlie chips in.

Trust reality to intrude.

'You've not met these mythical kids yet?'

'We haven't even really had a proper date. It's far too soon to be thinking of all that.'

'You might hate them. They could be little shits. The kind of kids who run around restaurants and cough with their mouths open.'

'They're teenagers. Wouldn't they be past that?'

'Teenagers?' Charlie shudders as if I've said 'axe murderers'. 'They might have even worse habits.'

'I like kids,' I tell her, even though I'm not really sure that I do. 'At my age, I'm not going to find that many men without them.'

'Except the Shagger Soameses of the world.'

'Indeed.'

'So you like Joe. Make the first move. He might just need a little persuasion if he's been out of the dating game since the time when the dinosaurs roamed the earth. It's pants out there. If you wait for him to come to you, it might never happen.'

'That thought is *too* depressing.' I pull a leaf off the hanging basket and set about tearing it into pieces. 'He said he'd phone me for coffee, but weeks have gone by and he hasn't.'

'Maybe he's got cold feet? Maybe he needs a little persuasion? It shows you that he was up for it, if he said that.'

Charlie could be right. 'Perhaps.'

'Then grasp the whatsit by the horns. We're modern women,' she states, 'we should take the initiative. Bake him some cakes. They say that the way to a man's heart is through his stomach.'

'Yeah, perhaps I should have knocked up a Victoria sponge for Mason rather than have a threesome with him.'

'Thank goodness it wasn't a threesome *and* Victoria sponge. That would have been *too* weird.' Charlie laughs and it lifts my mood.

'I'm no domestic goddess,' I confess. 'I can't bake to save my life. I don't think I've actually switched on the oven since I moved into the granny annexe. I'm a microwave kinda gal.'

'For heaven's sake, woman, use your imagination,' Charlie

says. 'Buy some cake from Sainsbury's. Take them to that place where he works as a pressie for the residents. Show him your sharing, caring side rather than your pants.'

I hate to admit it, but that sounds like a damn fine idea and I wonder why I didn't think of it myself.

Chapter Forty-Three

So the next day, before I'm due on shift, I find myself buying nice cakes in Sainsbury's. Not the ones in boxes down the aisles, but proper ones from the bakery – cupcakes with little fiddles and twiddles on them – squares of fudge, drizzles of sweet sauce, chocolate flakes and mini marshmallows.

As I turn up at the Sunshine Woods community campus, I can see that Joe is helping a group of the younger residents to tidy up the raised flowerbeds in the garden. Armed with my supermarket-bought cakes, I feel nervous as I walk towards him. Yet when he glances up and sees me, he smiles widely – and looks more than a little surprised.

'Hi,' I say. 'I come bearing gifts.'

'Anyone with cake is welcome,' Joe says and leans on his fork. 'I'm just showing the guys some gardening skills. We're currently struggling to differentiate between a weed and a flower.'

'You too!' one of the young men says, affronted.

'Yeah,' Joe agrees pleasantly. 'Me most of all.' He strips off his gardening gloves. 'Gardening is not my forte. Guys, can you spare me for five minutes to take a pretty lady for coffee?'

Much enthusiastic nodding from all three of them.

'Come to the café. We can have some coffee to go with the cakes.'

Damn. I hadn't thought it through that there was a café already here. I have, in fact, brought coals to Newcastle.

'How about you pick a bunch of flowers for our guest, Richie,' Joe suggests to one of the young men. 'Just a few flowers. Not all of them. Some of these.' Joe points to some orange flowers which, if I knew my flowers, I'd be able to name.

'OK,' he says and picks up a pair of secateurs.

'Careful with those,' Joe reminds him. 'They're sharp.'

'OK, Joe.'

'Shall I wait while you cut them?'

'No.' A toothy grin. 'I'm OK.'

'Well, just shout if you need my help. I'll only be over there.'

So we head towards the café, me clutching my cakes and trailing in Joe's wake.

'Let's sit here,' he says, pointing to a shaded table on the patio. 'I can keep my eye on them from here. What can I get you?'

'Skinny cappuccino?'

'The perfect accompaniment to cake,' he teases and I give him a wry smile. He has a point.

He walks to the counter and I can't help but take in an eyeful. He is one fine-looking man. Where Mason is slender and angular, Joe is muscular, well built. He wears jeans and a tight T-shirt very well. Even with muddy handprints on the bottom, I'd be tempted follow that to the ends of the earth. Though I do wonder exactly what I'm doing here. When I don't see him it's hard to remember that he's too complicated for me right now and that I actually don't need this in my life. He hasn't called me and I should have just let it go. I watch him queue at the counter. I can hardly leg it now.

While he's being served Charlie texts me. How's it going? xx. No idea what I'm doing here! I text back.

Is he still HOT? There's a row of many emoticons – sunshine, sunglasses, beach, barbeque, flames.

I send her one back – a smiley face with hearts for eyes.

That's why you're there! xx

Joe comes back with the coffee and turns to face the guys who are still concentrating on their gardening. I open the cakes and Joe takes a chocolate thing covered in marshmallows. I go for the one that I think was salted caramel. It's lush whatever it is. Nice one, Sainsbury's.

'I've missed you at diving.' No point beating about the bush. An appropriate moment for a gardening pun, no?

'I'm sorry,' he says. 'Busy. I've been covering extra shifts at work and the kids always seem to have something on. I'm on permanent taxi duty. Is Bob looking after you well?'

'Brilliantly. I've learned the knack of making my ears go pop on demand.'

He grins at me. 'Good for you. It's one of the most important skills.'

He's patronising me, of course, but I don't care.

Then he takes a glug of his coffee and looks thoughtful. 'I'm thinking that I might have to give up taking the lessons. I vowed that I'd keep my diving time as "me time". That's the modern thing, right? My daughter seems to need it every time there's homework looming.'

So, essentially what he's saying is that I'm stuck with Bob for the foreseeable future.

'I'm hoping that I can keep up going out with the club on weekend dives, but that depends on Gina.'

'Still not around much?'

'No.' He looks at me over the top of his sunglasses, his voice tight. 'She and her new boyfriend haven't yet exhausted the romantic capital cities of Europe. Though they have done quite a few of them now.'

'Oh.' It makes me think of my weekend with Mason. I wonder how much Joe's ex is actually seeing of the sights at all. Probably best not to mention that.

'The kids are way down on the list of her priorities, which is why I'm trying to be Superdad. I don't want them to suffer.'

'I understand that. I just wanted to make sure that I hadn't done anything wrong.'

'Seriously, it's not you, it's me.' Then we both laugh. 'That sounded pathetic.'

'Pretty much.'

Joe takes a deep breath. 'You're a lovely woman, Ruby. At any other time . . .' He looks off into the distance. 'What I'm trying to say – very badly – is that I can't get into a relationship now. I'm not in the right place. All this with Gina has left me raw. It's always there under the surface. I'm not ready to get involved with anyone else. It *really* isn't you.'

'I get that.' It's a shame, but he can't be fairer than that. 'We can be friends. If you ever find yourself with a free night and at a loose end, call me. We can go for a drink or a curry. No strings.' And I know that it would be a very different 'no strings' to Mason's idea of 'no strings'.

'Thanks, Ruby. That's very kind. I just don't want you waiting for something that I can't offer.'

Now all I want to do is leave as I feel a bit stupid.

Perhaps sensing the change of mood, Joe says, 'Let's go and get you those flowers.'

I follow him back towards the young lads who are snipping away. One of them hands me a big bunch of the orange flowers, some greenery which is very pretty and the whole thing is set off with a sprinkling of dandelions.

'Well done, Richie.'

He blushes as he hands them over to me.

'Thank you. They're lovely.'

'Thanks for the cakes.' He pulls on his gardening gloves and picks up his fork. He hesitates before he gives me a peck on the cheek. 'I'll see you around, Ruby. Good luck with the diving.'

'Yes, sure. I'll let you know if I ever make it to open water.'

Then I walk back to my car muttering 'Damn-damn-damn,' under my breath. And I know in my heart that both my interest in diving and my chances with Joe have just died.

Chapter Forty-Four

So, it was all over with Joe before it had even begun. Dust yourself off, Ruby Brown, paint on a smile, move right along, nothing to see here. I don't go back to my diving lessons and I don't miss them. I only miss my instructor and you can gather here that I'm not talking about Bob.

Two weeks have gone by and my life is a wilderness filled only with disappointment and shifts at the Butcher's Arms. Eat, sleep, work. That's all I do. Dramatic, I know, but I do feel down and that's not really like me. Even cardboard cut-out Gary is failing to cheer me up. I know that he's all Charlie needs to be happy, but I am finding him wanting in the boyfriend and companion stakes.

'What do you think, Gary?' I ask him.

No answer. Then I realise that I'm talking out loud to a cardboard cut-out and wonder what has become of my life.

So I decide to take a bit of action. I have a few hours before work, so I'm going to get out in the world and give it all I've got. Exercise is the way forward! I can expend all my excess energy – not that I have any of it – and while away a pleasant few hours to boot.

I swipe my boldest red lipstick on as I pout at the mirror. Then I remember that I've just decided to go running and think about swiping it off again. I don't want to be one of those women running round the lake in full war paint. Actually, I don't want to be one of those women running full stop. I don't like the feeling of everything jiggling around. Yoga sounds more appealing, as you get to sit down a lot. But all my money has been blown on stupid scuba-diving lessons which means I can't afford classes and running is free. So running it is. Where I live I can literally run out of my door and be right on the path around the lake. That has to be some kind of incentive. Plus exercise releases endorphins and I am desperately in need of a few of those.

So here I am in my ratty old jogging bottoms – I'm sure they weren't this tight when I last wore them – and a vest top that's seen better days. But I'm only going to get all hot and sweaty so who cares what I look like. I scrape my hair into a scrunchie and am all good to go. When I come back I'll have to wash my hair and put on my slap ready for work. It would be nice if all the walking I do while waiting tables kept on top of my calorie consumption, but it doesn't. So needs must. I can't slide into middle age without at least trying to make a valiant effort. Basically, I'm running out of time to get this relationship shit together. No pressure at all.

There's been no contact from either Joe or Mason. Not even a measly phone call. I am back wandering round the eternal desert of dating. I'm even considering Tinder – that's how desperate I am. I'm not sure anyone on Tinder would swipe left because I don't have toned thighs. Many of the men on there seem to set their criteria quite low.

'What do you think of Tinder, Gary?' I ask The Barlow. 'Shall I give it a go?'

As usual, he keeps his counsel.

In the absence of any useful relationship advice from my cardboard friend, I grab a bottle of water from the fridge and head out to the lake. It's a glorious summer Saturday morning. The sun is already high in the sky and it's a day for barbecuing or something like that. Everything looks better with a bit of sunshine on it. That's probably why I've got this ridiculous urge to run. The circular path around the lake is already busy with folk enjoying the weather. Dotted around the edge of the sparkling water are fishermen with their tents and paraphernalia already set up for the day, families out for a stroll and the ubiquitous Lycra-clad cyclists.

I pop in my headphones, flick the iPod to 'Running Music' – though I think the Trade Descriptions Act might have occasion to rebuke me for calling what I actually do 'running' – and set off at a sedate lumber around the lake. Within seconds I'm gasping for breath. I can't remember last when I did this, but I'm sure it wasn't quite so painful or pitiful. I stagger past the kids on *Star Wars* scooters and pink bikes with stabilisers and sparkly streamers from the handlebars. I dodge the dog walkers and the daydreaming dawdlers, all the time puffing like an old train. No one should need to humiliate themselves thus. Why can't you get fit by lying on the sofa with a good glass of Pinot and a box set of *Breaking Bad*? It seems to me that, as a species, we have some very basic design flaws.

By the time I reach the opposite side of the lake to my granny annexe – the point of no return – my face is the shade of a ripe tomato, there's a fire in my lungs and I think I might actually expire on the spot. I stand doubled over, trying to catch what very well might be the last breath in my body. I've got a stitch under my ribs, calves that are threatening to cramp and thighs that are wobbling like jellies. Oh, the indignity of it all.

As I'm bending over, attractively dripping sweat on the floor, I feel a nip on the back of my leg and shoot upright. As I whirl round there's a black-necked Canada goose an inch behind me. It hisses at me and I step back, only to find that it's brought all its mates with it too for backup. They are the thugs of the goose world as, in a flash, they have me completely surrounded, honking and hissing in a threatening manner. They're clearly hungry and in search of bread. They must think I've got some secreted down my joggers or perhaps I eat so much bread that I carry the air of it about my person. Whichever way, they obviously think I'm holding out on the carb front.

'Shoo,' I say and the ringleader nips me again. 'Ouch.' I try stamping my foot while looking as menacing as I can, but it rears up and flexes its wings. Bugger. I'm the one who backs down. The goose gives me the evil eye. His glinty-eyed expression says 'Unless there's bread, lady, you're not getting out of here alive.'

I try edging away from them, but they're immoveable and bold. A few more have a test nip at me. Perhaps these aren't bread-eating geese, but have morphed into cannibals and are looking to eat me instead of a bit of stale Warburtons' Toastie. Shit. I'm a townie and live in the middle of a city, but Costa del Keynes is a hotbed of wildlife. They're everywhere – ducks, woodpeckers, kingfishers, foxes, you name it, and, of course, these wretched geese.

'Nice geese,' I say and have another go at breaching their defences, but they have me corralled.

I think they are pretty useless as geese go. I don't think you can eat them and they poo everywhere. What exactly is their purpose in the food chain? While I'm contemplating this, another one bites me and it's a proper bite this time, not a nip.

'Fucker!' I jump up and down a bit, but that only attracts more geese. Soon, I'm in a sea of them, marooned in the middle. I lift up my arms and wave them, but that only makes them stand taller and some of them come right up to my chest. I'm thinking about shouting for help, but don't know if anyone would hear me above all this threatening hissing and honking. I might have to jump in the lake and swim for it, but then I remember that geese are fully capable of being water borne too. Yikes. What on earth am I going to do?

Then I hear a voice say, 'Come on, boys. Leave the nice lady alone,' and I spin round. Joe is approaching in a purposeful manner, he claps his hands in a very manly way and strides towards me.

The geese scatter instantly. Bastards. Why didn't they do that for me? In an instant, they're looking innocent again, foraging on the bank of the lake, gliding about serenely on the water. Yeah, butter wouldn't melt in your mouths, evil geese. I know differently.

'Thanks for that,' I say with genuine relief. 'I thought I was a goner.'

'Always available to rescue a damsel in distress,' he says with a twinkle in his eye. 'I couldn't leave you there being goosed.'

Quite.

'I'm not good with animals. I try to avoid them at all costs unless they're on my plate. It's a good job you came along when you did.'

'We're just out for a walk.' He looks over his shoulder and there are two children hanging back. Both of them looking as if they'd rather be anywhere else. 'I wanted to drag them away from their computer screens for an hour.' The boy has head-phones in and both have every atom of their being concentrated on their phones. 'I thought it would be fun.' He raises his eyebrows. 'I'm beginning to realise that I'm in the minority.'

Wow, so these are actually Joe's children. Until now they've been a kind of abstract concept. There in the background, but not exactly three-dimensional. I did, indeed, begin to wonder if they might be imaginary kids, but here they are, flesh and blood. Joe's flesh and blood even. They're certainly good-looking kids. They're dark-haired like Joe and have his eyes. They look even more like him in real life than they did in the photo he showed me on the dive day. I'm sure Joe has also told me all about them, but I can't quite remember the details. I should have paid more attention, but perhaps I never really believed that I'd ever meet them.

The girl, Daisy I think, looks about twelve. Her curly hair falls to her shoulders and she's heartbreakingly pretty. She's tall for her age, but as thin as a pin. Her pink sweatshirt, leggings and sparkly pink trainers announce to the world that she's the girliest of girly girls – and no harm in that. As you know I'm partial to a bit of girly stuff myself. Maybe we'd get along just fine.

The boy, Tom, is about fifteen and is tall, rangy, uncomfortable in the way he holds his body – as only teenage boys do when they're not quite sure whether they're a man or still a boy. His hair is gelled within an inch of its life in an attempt to tame his curls, I'd guess. He looks pretty cool in his Superdry T-shirt and skinny jeans and I bet he's the school heartthrob.

It's the first time I've seen Joe with his children and it seems weird. Until now I've only really seen him as a single entity hottie, now here he is as a family man and a father. Although we've discussed it enough, it suddenly feels like a step change. A bit like when you see your dentist out of uniform at the pub and, for a minute, you don't quite recognise the person you think you know.

Joe shouts over his shoulder, 'Daisy, Tom, come and say hello to Ruby.'

They barely look up and both mutter 'Hi,' in my general direction.

'Hi, kids.' I sound overly chirpy, like a CBeebies presenter.

Neither of them looks impressed and I wish I'd bumped into

all of them while dressed in proper clothing, in full make-up and not being mugged by greedy geese. I know that Joe's told me that he's not ready for a relationship as he has commitments and wants to put his kids first after what they've been through. I understand that. But it's different seeing them here in front of me. He does have other priorities. I get that now. Keeping two traumatised teenagers happy must be a full-time job.

'I've been showing Ruby how to scuba-dive,' Joe explains to them.

Clearly, this doesn't rock their world. Eventually, Tom tears himself away from his screen and glances up through his fringe. 'Cool.'

'How's it going?' Joe asks.

'I haven't really been going,' I confess. 'Busy and all that. I should phone Bob and explain.'

'That's a shame. You were doing well.'

I shrug. 'You know how it is.' Somehow I have lost the incentive.

Then we're a bit awkward with each other and Joe has half of his attention on the kids.

'I'd better carry on before they come back,' I say, one eye on the geese who are waddling determinedly in my direction again. Though I don't really want Joe to see how much of me jiggles when I jog. 'Thanks again. I'll see you around.'

'Yeah.' He looks thoughtful when he says it. 'Bye, Ruby.'

I wave and set off again, trying to look like a proper runner and not like a slug. I hope to God and all that is good that he's not watching me.

'Damn,' I mutter to myself again. 'Damn.' I like him and, in different circumstances, I think he might like me too.

Chapter Forty-Five

Then Joe calls after me: 'The kids are going to Gina next weekend. I'm free on Saturday night, if you're around.'

That stops me in my tracks. I'm working and have no idea how I'll get out of my shift as no one, NO ONE, wants to swap a Saturday shift. 'Yes, I'm free too.' I shout back.

'Great. Pizza or something?'

'Perfect.'

He grins at me. 'I'll pick you up at seven.'

I refrain from saying, 'It's a date,' because, quite obviously, IT IS a flipping date! Yay! Go me! I have a date with the rather delectable and previously reluctant Joe Edwards. Clearly, he can't resist my skanky running look.

Now his kids are paying attention too. They've both looked up from their phones and are gaping, slightly open-mouthed. Take that, teens! The oldies still have it.

Waving, I set off again. IhaveadateIhaveadateIhaveadate! I also have wings on my feet all the way back to the granny annexe and, until I collapse gasping on the steps up to my flat with oxygen debt, I barely notice that I'm in complete agony.

Chapter Forty-Six

'Swap shifts with me,' I beg Charlie on our bench.

'No.'

'Pretty please.'

She sucks on her e-cigarette. 'No, no, no. Thrice no.'

It's too cold to be sitting out on the bench today, but I don't want any of the other staff overhearing this conversation, particularly not our manager. Charlie and I huddle together and she pulls her jacket around her. Our summer is coming and going as British summers are prone to do. Yesterday, shorts and scorchio. Today, cold enough for coats. The sky is as flat and dreary as Farrow and Ball paint.

'I can't miss this date with Joe.' I try to sound as pathetic as I can. 'He could be the love of my life, the one I've been looking for.'

'He'll wait,' Charlie says.

'He might not.' I do my imploring face. 'He hardly ever gets any free time to himself. He's always got his kids and his ex-wife yanks his chain.'

'That should tell you something.'

But I don't listen to that bit. 'I'll swap you one shift for two shifts. Double bubble.'

'No. And don't even think about phoning in sick and dumping your work on the rest of us.'

'I would *never* do that.' I was thinking of it.

'I'll grass you up to Shagger Soames.'

'It's just one little Saturday. I'll never do it again. I promise.'

She sighs. 'Have you ever heard of playing hard to get?' Charlie fixes me with a stern gaze. 'First you go running off to Paris with Shagger and we both know how that ended up.' She makes lascivious movements with her fingers, giving me a flashback to the night of my threesome with Mason as my dear friend had intended.

I hold up a hand. 'Don't.'

Unperturbed, she continues, 'Now you're chasing after this bloke who's saddled with a couple of surly kids.'

'I'm not chasing him,' I point out. 'He's the one who changed his mind.' I hug my knees to my chest and try to pretend I'm not on the verge of shivering. 'The thing is, there are so few good guys out there that I want the chance to grab one while I can.' I don't mention that I think Charlie is letting one of the good guys slip through her fingers. And I don't mean Gary Barlow. She could have a lovely relationship with Nice Paul but, for very good reasons, she's closed herself off to any possibility of that happening.

'I can't keep up with you,' Charlie says. 'One minute it's all on with Shagger. The next it's Joe. I don't know how you cope.'

'I confuse myself,' I admit. 'Though, in fairness, I haven't even had a proper date with Joe yet and I haven't seen Mason for weeks. I'm not in a mutually exclusive relationship with either of them.'

'Mutually exclusive, eh? Big words. Sounds as if you've swallowed a copy of *Cosmo*. I should also point out that you're not exactly in any sort of relationship with either of them.'

'Good point, well made,' I tell her.

The trouble is, I want to be cautious and not get involved with the wrong sort again. I know, like Charlie, you're thinking of my dalliance with Mason – but that was me having fun. Although it didn't quite turn out as I expected and I learned my lesson. This time, I'm staying away from the baddies. I've realised that I can't do sex without strings. I like to be in a relationship. I'm coming to understand more of who I am and, at fast approaching forty years old, that has to be a good thing, right?

'I want you to know that I'm doing this under extreme duress,' Charlie says. 'Also, because I have two Gary events on the calendar that I might need you to cover.'

'I'll do it,' I say without hesitation.

'OK. I'll swap shifts,' she says. 'I'll leave you to tell Jay.'

'I love you.'

Charlie waves a hand, dismissively. 'Cupboard love.'

'Let's hang out after we finish work tonight,' I suggest. 'We can watch a crap film and crack a bottle of something. My treat.'

'Sounds like a plan,' Charlie says. Then she fixes me with a stare. 'You're my best friend and I love you but don't come crying to me when it all goes horribly wrong, Ruby Brown.'

'I won't. Cross my heart and hope to die.' Besides, and I'm only telling you this, I have a very good feeling about this one.

Later, much later, I'm behind the bar pulling a pint when Mason rocks up at the pub. I've kind of been dreading seeing him and wondering why I haven't at the same time.

'Evening, Ms Brown,' he says. 'What are you doing behind the bar?'

'Ben didn't turn in for his shift. It's all hands to the pump. Literally.' Clearly our boss has finished his taxing stint at the Grand Prix season for the time being and is coming to see what his minions are up to. 'The place has been madness.'

'I'll take over,' he says.

'I'm fine,' I say a bit tartly. 'I can manage.'

Mason sighs at me. 'Brown, no need to fight me on everything. Let me help.'

So I capitulate and he finishes pulling the pint with expert skill. 'I should have called,' he says. 'I've been busy, but it was very remiss of me.'

I shrug as if I couldn't care less. Which I almost don't. 'I've been busy too.'

'Come to the club tonight after we've finished here. We can catch up over cocktails.' He puts a hand on my waist.

I slap his hand away. 'That's sexual harassment. Hands off the workers.'

'You didn't seem to protest too much in Paris,' he reminds me and he gives me a cheeky squeeze. Part of me – a *tiny* part – is pleased to see Mason back in the pub and it's not simply because we're so short-handed tonight.

'Ah. That was then. This is now.'

Mason laughs. 'God, I've missed you, Brown. You and your pithy repartee. Come to the club. Let's get drunk together.'

'Can't. I've promised Charlie I'll watch a film at her place.'

'Riveting. You can do that anytime. Bring Charlie too. *Dirty Dancing* can wait.'

'Not tonight. But thanks for the offer.'

'I want to know what you've been doing without me.'

'Nothing.' I decide to fess up. 'My social life is a wasteland through which no one wanders.'

He frowns at me. 'Then why are you looking so pleased with yourself?'

'I'm not.' Though I can't suppress the smile on my lips.

'You look like you're harbouring a smug little secret.'

'Sorry to disappoint you, but I'm not.' Though I flush as I say it. Mason needs to know nothing about my love life as I need to know nothing about his. Though I do wonder whether he had another little *ménage à trois* on his travels. I expect so.

'I'm having an official opening for the Vibe Lounge,' he tells me. 'Say you'll come to that.'

'I might. If you ask nicely.'

'I just did.' He narrows his eyes. 'There's something going on with you. I know it. I just don't know what.'

Then to deflect attention from myself, I say, 'Are you going to make yourself useful behind this bar or not?'

Mason grins at me. 'I do like a bossy woman, Brown. Never forget that.'

I roll my eyes at him and grab the waiting tray of drinks before the people on table four die of thirst.

Chapter Forty-Seven

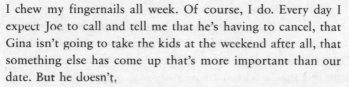

I chew my fingernails all week. Of course, I do. Every day I expect Joe to call and tell me that he's having to cancel, that Gina isn't going to take the kids at the weekend after all, that something else has come up that's more important than our date. But he doesn't.

Saturday arrives and The Big Date is still on. I've no idea what to wear. We're going for a pizza, so the only party dress I own is immediately ruled out but all else is to play for. I rifle through all my clothes. ALL of them. My entire wardrobe is found wanting, so I make an emergency dash to Primarni. I'm flicking ever more frantically through the rails when my phone rings. It's Charlie.

'Hi, babe.'

'I'm sick,' Charlie croaks. 'Really sick. Both ends.'

TMI.

'I can't cover your shift tonight, Ruby.'

'Nooooooo,' I cry down the phone.

'Is that sympathy for my severe illness?' she asks flatly, 'or disappointment at having to ditch your hot date?'

'Both,' I say while I actually think *What bloody awful timing*.

'I've called Jay,' Charlie says. 'I think I'm going to be out of it for a couple of days.'

I'm trying to feel solicitous, but inside I'm screaming. 'Can I get you anything? I'm at the retail park at the moment.' Trying to buy something hot for my now non-existent date. 'Shall I swing by on the way home?'

'No,' she moans. 'I'm just going to crawl back into my pit, pull the covers over my head and quietly die. I'm going to listen to Gary, so that if I do in fact die then he'll be the last thing I hear.'

'Drink lots of fluid,' I try, helpfully. Though I've no idea if that's really helpful. 'I'll call you in the morning. Not too early.'

'Sorry to let you down,' she says. 'Gotta go. Bathroom calls again.' She hangs up.

I stand in Primarni staring at my phone. Buggerbuggerbugger. What now? I look down and, true fact, I have the most perfect dress in my hand. It says fun, flirty but is chic too. Even better, it's less than a tenner. I have to have it. And, more than that, I *have* to go on this date.

In the car park, new dress in my bag, I sit in my car, a mass of seething indecision. What's more important: work or my love life? Then I make my mind up. What I'm about to do isn't pretty. Please don't judge me.

I call Jay. 'I can't come in tonight, Jay,' I say, putting on a croaky voice much the same as Charlie's. It's a voice that says I have vomited too many times and may not have much longer on this mortal plane. 'I'm really sorry.'

'We're desperate, Ruby,' Jay says sounding like a man broken. 'Charlie's phoned in sick too.'

'Has she?' I feign innocence. 'Must be a bug going round. Hope it's not something we picked up in the kitchen.' That will give him something bigger to think about. 'I've got to go, Jay.'

'OK. OK.'

I hang up. Blimey. What did I just do? I must really like this guy to lie to my boss so that I can see him. I've never done that before. I'm usually the most steadfast and reliable employee. I hate to hear Jay sound so harried, but they'll cope. It's not the first time it's happened, though it's not usually me and Charlie who are off sick. We are normally the stalwarts.

I drive home feeling more guilty than Mrs Guilty from Guiltytown. On my next shift I'll work triple hard to make up for it. I'll give all my tips to charity for a month. Well, maybe a week. Call it psychosomatic but I even begin to feel slightly nauseous.

Still, I put my duplicity to the back of my mind, have a long, luxurious bath, shave all the important little places, moisturise until I'm like an oil slick and wash my hair, lashing in the coconut conditioner so that I'll smell like an extra-tasty tropical cocktail.

I'm just about finishing my make-up when my doorbell rings and my heart jumps to my mouth. It's only six o'clock. I like a punctual man but surely he can't be this early. I check my watch to make sure that it hasn't stopped. While I'm basking in indecision, the bell rings again – with a slightly more impatient tone. As I haven't time to get dressed, I pull my dressing gown over my undies and head to the door.

Instantly, I recognise the outline of my visitor through the glass pane and it isn't Joe. It is, however, Mason Soames.

Damn.

'Open the door, Brown,' he says. 'I come bearing gifts for the sick.'

Oh, shit. Mason's the last person on earth that I'd expect to come visiting. I press myself against the wall, hoping that he hasn't spotted me too.

I stand and hyperventilate for a bit. What do I do? I can hardly pretend that I'm not here when I'm supposed to be in my sick bed.

'Brown!' he shouts again. 'Have you died? Let me in.'

Eventually, reluctantly, and simply because I have no other choice, I open the door a fraction and peep out. A wave of embarrassment engulfs me. Now I do actually feel hot all over and more than a bit clammy. 'Hi,' I croak.

He looks at me suspiciously. 'Jay has called in the cavalry tonight,' he says. 'Both you and Charlie have gone down with something, so I've cancelled my prior arrangements and I'm riding to the rescue. Thought I'd drop in some essentials on the way.' He holds up a basket covered with cellophane and tied with a ribbon. 'Flowers, fruit, carton of soup, Immodium.'

'Thank you.' I try to sound on the verge of death. At this point I really wish I'd gone to stage school. I'm not a natural liar and the words stick in my throat – which, in effect, adds to my act. 'Very kind. Sorry to let you down.'

'Are you going to keep me standing here, Brown? Or are you going to let me in?'

'Might be infectious,' I warn. 'I'm all hot.'

'Are you sure it's not the menopause?'

'Thanks, Mason.' A bit too crisp. 'It's *definitely* not the menopause.' Cheeky sod. 'I think I caught it from Charlie.'

He takes a step back, but there's an expression of concern on his face. 'I'm worried about you.'

'I'll be fine,' I assure him. 'I'll probably have bounced back by tomorrow. Probably a twenty-four-hour thing.'

His eyes narrow. 'I'll leave the basket here then and be on my way. Wish me luck.'

If I could, I'd allow myself a smile. Waiting tables is well below Mason's pay grade.

'Thanks, Mason,' I say, genuinely grateful even though he's on a fool's errand. 'It's kind of you to pop by.' Unexpectedly.

'If you don't mind me saying, you look more like someone getting ready for a night out rather than someone on their sick bed.'

'Looks can be deceiving,' I say, voice a hoarse whisper once more.

'Hmm,' he agrees. I know I'm not sick and he knows I'm not sick. 'Shall I call in on the way home? Make sure you're still alive.'

'No, no. No need. Early night,' I tell him. 'In bed by nine.'

'Lucky you,' Mason says. 'Think of me dealing with the hungry hordes in your stead.'

'Thanks, Mason. I owe you one.'

'You do,' he says. 'I'll be considering ways in which you can redeem yourself.'

'Better go.' I put my hand to my mouth and do a bit of a *bleurgh*.

'I'll see you, Ruby.'

I close the door and stand with my back to it, sweating. I hear the slam of Mason's car door and then watch him as he drives away. It was so kind of him to come. If I'd truly been ill, I would have been touched by his thoughtfulness. I hadn't expected that in the slightest and, when he shows his softer side, I can't help but like him. It's easy to convince myself he's an arrogant, self-centred twat. Then he does something like this. Nevertheless, I'm still hoping he doesn't feel the need to check up on me later or I'm in deep trouble.

Chapter Forty-Eight

Joe picks me up at seven. I'm quite nervous going out to his car in case Mason is hiding in the bushes waiting to catch me out. This date could very well get me the sack.

It might be worth it though as I've never seen Joe looking more handsome. He's obviously freshly showered and shaved. His dark curls are still slightly damp and his face is flushed with warmth. We look quite the dandy pair with him in a white shirt and faded jeans and me in my new Primarni frock in pastel shades.

'You look lovely,' he says and I'm glad that I bought it. A tenner well spent.

We go for pizza at a small restaurant out of town rather than a busy chain. I've not been here before and the atmosphere is great, but we can still hear each other speak rather than having to shout over the noise. It's also quite useful to be away from the centre of Costa del Keynes where someone from work might spot me. This is how subterfuge makes you think. It must be exhausting to have an affair.

Once I relax and stop feeling guilty that I'm not actually ill and am out on a date, Joe and I have a great evening and laugh a lot. He's easy company to be with and not too shabby to look at either.

He talks a lot about Daisy and Tom, showing me photographs on his phone. He's obviously a proud dad and why not? It makes me sad to think that this little family have broken up and I wonder what pressures they've been under to have brought them to this point. I'd ask, but I don't want to spend the whole of our evening talking about his ex or bringing him down with talk of his divorce. So we skip over the surface of it and move onto films, music and life in general. He doesn't drink as he's driving and I limit myself to a couple of glasses of wine, even though my nerves think they would like a lot more.

It's eleven o'clock when he looks at his watch and says, 'Wow, is that the time? The evening has flown by.'

I'm hoping this is a good sign as I really do like Joe. He's wholesome, considerate and obviously a caring person.

'I can't think last when I was out this late on my own,' he laughs. 'I thought it would get easier when the kids were more grown-up, but the demands seem even more. They're both high on hormones and most of my life is spent ferrying them about to parties and sleepovers. Their social life is ten times better than mine.'

'It seems to be the way of the world now.'

'I know I talk about them a lot,' he says. 'I'm sorry if I've bored you, but they're my life. Everything I do, I do for them.'

'I understand.'

'That makes it harder for me to come to terms with what Gina has done. She puts herself ahead of everyone else.' It's the first time he's mentioned her all evening and, as I suspected, his mood changes when he does. 'I thought she'd find an excuse to back out of this weekend, but so far, so good. The kids were really excited to be going there. She lives in a big, posh house now and kids' heads are easily turned.'

'It will come right, I'm sure. All you have to do is persevere. Soon they'll be off enjoying their own lives, maybe at university or travelling. The pain of this time will recede.'

'Wise words,' he says. 'When you're in the midst of it, sometimes it's hard to retain your perspective.' Then he laughs. 'Before I get too maudlin, I'll pay the bill.'

'Let me split it with you.'

'Wouldn't dream of it,' he says.

'My treat next time.'

He fixes me with a warm gaze. 'I like the sound of that.'

'Me too.'

'I have to take this slowly,' he says. 'I'd like us to see each other again, but I have to think of the kids. They've been through too much for me to cause any more disruption. I don't want someone coming into their lives only to crash out a few months later. I have to be sure.' It seems as if he's been thinking about this a lot. 'It's not an excuse. I really do want to see you, but can we agree to take it one step at a time?'

'That suits me fine.' That's clearly the sensible thing to do. And we are both very sensible grown-ups.

Then he drives me home and we park outside the granny annexe. We sit awkwardly in the car together, turning towards each other.

'Thanks for a great evening, Ruby.' Joe leans over and kisses me softly. 'I'm out of practice with all this.'

'It seemed all right to me,' I admit, head spinning.

'I'd better be off then.'

We both linger and then kiss some more. It feels so right to be in his arms.

My mouth goes dry when I say, 'You said the kids were away tonight?'

'Yeah.' Our eyes meet and, hesitantly, he says, 'I could stay for longer.'

I try to sound nonchalant. 'If you don't have to rush back for the kids.'

'This isn't really taking it slowly, is it?'

We both laugh at that. 'No, it's not,' I agree. 'But maybe we have to seize the moment.'

This time, without pausing, he blurts out, 'OK.'

So, with an indecent amount of haste, we get out of the car and climb up my stairs together.

Chapter Forty-Nine

We're kissing again before I even open the door. In the living room, I make no pretence of offering coffee and we fall on each other hungrily, his mouth on mine, his hands exploring my body. We fall onto the sofa together and continue our fevered exploration. I fumble with the buttons of his shirt and he struggles with the zip of my best Primarni. We are half-naked, rumpled and revved-up when his phone rings. He looks at it with indecision and I want to say 'don't answer it', but I know that it might be one of the kids and he can't ignore that.

'Sorry,' he says. 'Really sorry.' He holds up a finger as he grabs his phone. 'Don't move a muscle.'

But I do. I rearrange my clothing so that it's slightly more decorous.

'Hi,' Joe says into his phone and then mouths at me 'Daisy' as he moves away from me to pace the living room floor, head shaking as he does.

Hopefully, it's nothing too serious. Maybe she just wants to say goodnight to him. Though the pacing may suggest otherwise. Surely her mother could deal with it? I keep my fingers crossed and my mind wanders while he murmurs into his phone. This has been going well, very well. We could move to the bedroom, I think, when festivities resume. Though I'd have to turn Gary Barlow to the wall.

'Yeah. Yeah,' he continues his pacing while running his hands through his hair. 'I'll meet you there.' He hangs up and turns to me. 'Sorry. Sorry.' His face is bleak. 'That was Gina. Daisy's slipped on the stairs going up to bed and has landed awkwardly. Her hand has ballooned. Gina's worried it might be broken, so they're waiting at A&E now. I'll have to go down there and see if she's OK. Sorry.'

'Don't apologise,' I say. 'It's important.' Though inside I'm cursing the bad timing of this.

He starts to button his shirt, embarrassed now.

'You could come back,' I offer, trying not to sound desperate.

'I don't know how long this will take. A&E on Saturday night will be like bedlam. We could be in for a four-hour wait with the drunks.' He sighs. 'Plus she might want to come home with me rather than go back with Gina.'

'Can I do anything to help? I'll come with you, if you like. I don't mind. Really.'

'Thanks for the offer, but I'd just better shoot off. Sorry to run out on you like this.'

'Do what you have to do. It's not a problem. Your daughter's well-being is the most important thing. You need to be there or you'll only worry about her.'

There is something approaching despair in his expression. 'I've enjoyed it though, Ruby. Can we do it again?'

'I'd like that,' I say. In fact there's nothing I'd love more. I wish he didn't have to dash off and that we could spend the night in each other's arms. But it's not to be. Not yet.

'I hope that Daisy's all right. Text me when you know what's wrong.'

'I will.' He gives me a peck on the cheek, but I can tell that the moment has gone and that his thoughts are already elsewhere.

'I'll call you,' he says and he dashes out of the door, his footsteps heavy on the stairs, his tyres screeching as he accelerates away down the road.

'Damn,' I say to no one but myself.

I have a cup of tea and stay up watching rubbish telly. When it's two o'clock and I still haven't heard from Joe, I resort to the best comfort food of all, cheese on toast, even though I'm not remotely hungry after our lovely dinner. I check my phone a million times but there's no text to let me know how Daisy is. Maybe the signal at the hospital is useless or maybe he's had to turn his phone off.

Eventually, when there's no call or text, I give up waiting and go to bed, but I lie there fidgeting and twitchy. It would be too sad to get cardboard Gary Barlow in bed with me for a cuddle, wouldn't it? I just want to be held, feel strong arms around me. The sad thing is that while I'm lying here restless with longing, I could phone Mason. I know I could. He would come at the drop of a hat. He wouldn't care that he was just a booty call. My fingers are a hair's breath away from punching his number in. They toy with my phone. I know that you'll think badly of me. I think badly of myself and Charlie would kill me stone dead. It's a good job that I remember that I have pretend sickness as I really don't want to go down that road.

Chapter Fifty

'Glad to see you're better, Brown,' Mason says when I turn up for work the next day. 'Miraculous recovery.'

'Shut it, Mason,' I retort.

He rolls his eyes. 'You simply can't get the staff these days.'

'What are you doing here? Haven't you got a Grand Prix to go to or a tennis match or Badminton Horse Trials?'

He laughs. 'Yes. Want to come with me?'

'No. Unfortunately, I've got to stay here in the Butcher's Arms and serve chips to the proletariat.'

'Me too,' Mason says. 'Your friend, the one who is *actually* sick, is still off work. I'm her stand-in.'

I called Charlie this morning and she sounded terrible, so I'll drop in on her on the way home. I also called Joe, but it went straight to voicemail and I wonder what happened with Daisy last night and whether she's OK.

'So what were you up to last night?' he says.

'Nothing. It was just a tummy bug or something.' I try to look innocent or at least not the very picture of guilt. 'I went to bed early and slept it off.'

He still seems unconvinced. 'Well, I'm very glad to see you.'

'Same here,' I bat back.

Then he sidles up next to me and whispers, 'I miss you, Brown. It's boring without you. Come away with me again. It was fun. You can choose where. Rome is good for a weekend. Barcelona too. Or we could do Venice. I know some great boutique hotels.'

I wonder if there's a 'Valerie' in each of those places too.

'I can't, Mason. I'm not one of the jet set. You know that my shifts here don't allow me many weekends off.' I can't help but smile. 'Plus, I'm seeing someone.'

'Seriously?' He looks as if you could knock him down with a feather.

'Deadly.'

'I knew there was something going on. You're being un-faithful to me?'

'Hardly that.' However, I do think it's time to come clean.

'I'm wounded, Brown. Who is this man who's stolen your heart? Look at your contented little face. You're like the cat who's got the cream and it's nauseating. I need to know who my love rival is?'

My phone rings and my heart jumps when I look at the screen. 'His name's Joe. That's him now. Excuse me.'

Mason looks affronted. 'You can't take personal calls in work time, Brown!'

'Sod off,' I say and I make my way outside so that Mason can't hear. I sit on our bench in the sunshine.

'Hi,' Joe says. 'Is this a good time?'

'Perfect.' I sound too pleased to hear from him. 'I'm glad you called. How's Daisy?'

'We were at A&E half the night as I thought,' he said. 'So we all had a lie-in this morning. Good news though – at least her hand wasn't broken. Thank goodness. It's just badly sprained.'

'Poor Daisy.'

'She's moping around like a misery guts and her hand is black and blue, but she'll be as right as rain in a week or so with some well-aimed painkillers and rest.'

'That's good to know.' Then a beat. 'The kids came back with you?'

'Yeah. Daisy wanted to be at home with me.' He lowers his voice as they are obviously within earshot. 'I'm sorry to run out on you last night.'

'Just as it was getting interesting,' I tease.

He laughs at that. 'Yeah. Perfect timing.'

'I can't stay long,' I tell him, though I'd happily talk on the phone for hours. 'I'm about to start work.'

'When can I see you? I think we have unfinished business.'

Hurrah, more flirting! 'As soon as you're free.'

There's a heavy breath from the other end of the phone. 'That might prove to be the tricky thing. Finding a night when I'm free and you're free and the kids are out may not be that easy.'

'But we can do it if we want to,' I point out. 'Some things are worth waiting for.'

'I'll call you,' Joe says. 'I promise.'

'I'll look forward to it.' I hang up with a smile on my face and in my heart. I breeze through service, chatting to all the customers – even the regulars who I don't like that much. From the other side of the room, Mason watches me through narrowed eyes and they still stay narrowed even when I blow him a kiss.

Chapter Fifty-One

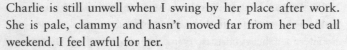

Charlie is still unwell when I swing by her place after work. She is pale, clammy and hasn't moved far from her bed all weekend. I feel awful for her.

Though if you have to be ill in bed, Charlie's bed is the place to be. She has a white, wrought iron bed head threaded through with pink feathered fairy lights and a wispy curtain that hangs down from the ceiling on either side also threaded with white lights. The duvet is pink and white patchwork and she has enough cushions to be able to sell some to Next. She's listening to Take That on her iPod.

I smooth the hair from her face and ask, 'Can I get you something? Could you manage a bit of toast? Or some tea?'

'Yes,' she says. 'That sounds good. I'm actually feeling a bit hungry. The first time since Friday.' She puts her laptop to one side. 'I'm on the GB Army forum. Keeping up with my boy.'

'Is that making you feel better?'

She nods. 'You're never alone when you're with Gary.' She has the very same cardboard cut-out as I do in the very same corner of her bedroom. We both give him a smile. 'Paul's on there too,' she adds more coyly.

Oh, yes? 'That's cool.'

'He's called me a couple of times as well. Just to make sure that I'm OK.'

I'm liking the sound of that. See, definitely Nice.

'So what did I miss at work?' she asks with a yawn.

Confession time. I prepare myself for a dressing down when I say, 'I phoned in sick on Saturday so that I could go out with Joe.'

Charlie tuts at me.

'I know, but I *so* wanted to go. Don't tell Mason, promise me.'

'As if I'm likely to.'

'He covered both of your shifts.'

She laughs at that. 'Seriously? It won't hurt him to get his hands dirty. About time that lazy sod did some work and appreciated what his minions do to keep his business afloat.'

I know we're supposed to be on the same side, but I hate it when Charlie disses Mason. He's not as bad as she makes out. Really, he's not.

'So what was the date like? Worth lying through your teeth for?'

'Great.' I'm in grave danger of going all dreamy even though I'm a woman approaching a certain age. 'He's fun and I really like him. It all ended a bit prematurely when his daughter was rushed to A&E with a suspected fracture.'

'Yikes.'

'She was OK. Just a sprain in the end, but he spent the rest of the night at the hospital instead of in my warm, cosy bed.'

'You'll always come behind the kids in the queue,' she says. 'You know that.'

'Yes. It's how it should be.'

She makes a harrumphing noise.

'I think he's worth it, Charlie. When you get to our age

219

whoever you hook up with comes with history of some sort. That's something we have to learn to accept. On both sides. Otherwise we will both end up with no one but cardboard cut-out Gary Barlow for company.' I get up from her bed. 'I'll go and make some toast.'

'There's bread in the freezer, if the loaf in the bread bin is manky. You're going to stay around for a bit?'

'Of course, I will. We can binge-watch some Take That DVDs if you fancy it. Budge yourself up and make room for me on the bed.'

'I don't think I'm infectious now.'

As I head for the door, I say, 'Remember, that's never a great opening line for a date.' Then I duck as Charlie throws one of her multitude of cushions at me.

Chapter Fifty-Two

I'm just going to skip the next few weeks because if I tell you about all the long, late-night and a little bit lovey-dovey FaceTime calls with Joe, you might just want to puke. We slowly, steadily get to know each other via the media of technology. But this is modern dating and we have to embrace it. In my mother's day you had a few dates with the boy next door or one from your class at school and then you married them. There was none of this hooking up with strangers who you happened to like the look of from their profile picture only to find out that they were, at best, socially inept or at worst, a latent serial killer. At least I have met Joe in person and, if we have to work round the constraints of his family, then I'm prepared to do that. It's infinitely preferable to throwing myself on the mercy of Match.com or eHarmony. No?

We have also managed a few real dates in that time. We snatched breakfast one morning after the school run and before we both had to start our shifts. That's quite civilised, I think you'll agree. We tried one more scuba-diving lesson with Joe as my instructor again, but our hands were straying to places that they shouldn't at the bottom of the swimming pool and my mind wasn't fully on my demand valve. Good job Bob didn't try that or I'd have blocked his snorkel. Not a euphemism.

Joe and I haven't had an opportunity to take our relationship onto a more . . . ahem . . . physical plane simply due to the fact that I can't go to Joe's house as he doesn't yet want me to be 'formally' introduced to the kids and he can't stay at my place as he has to be at home for the kids. Yet that's no bad thing is it? Is it better to wait and enjoy the slow build-up to consummation or to hop into bed with someone you've met at a night club – someone who you don't know a thing about and who couldn't care less whether you have a good time or not? That said, I wouldn't be adverse to it happening sooner rather than later. My nipples are permanently on red alert.

Anyway, that's why you find me today on another outing with the good folk of the Costa del Keynes dive club. We're out in force today as about a dozen members have come along. I'm still not safe enough to be let out in open water myself and, to be honest, I'm not in the slightest bit bothered. I'm not proving to be a natural diver. I'm not all that keen on getting wet or going into water where I don't know what else might be in there. A bit of a drawback for a diver, I think you'll agree. I maybe should have gone for photography instead or taken a course in Thai Massage.

So I'm sitting in the sunshine overlooking Quarry Hill Cove gravel pit in deepest, darkest Birminghamshire or somewhere, on one of those deckchairs you buy in service stations for a tenner, my thoughts as warm as the summer's day. Joe has completed one dive and is currently on the jetty shrugging off his air tanks and kicking off his fins. I'm very happy just to take in the view. Sigh.

I'm content for the first time in a long time. Sometimes we hurtle through life, don't we? I'm rushing off to work or racing round the supermarket, doing a dozen other things that I really don't want to be doing and it's easy not to stop and simply take a breath. That's what Joe has done for me, he's brought an enrichment to my life which is, in turn, creating a feeling of settling deep in my core. No, I've not been reading self-help books, but it's how I feel. Can't help it.

Then I realise that this is a lot like love feels. That sends a jolt through me. I look at Joe as he chats to the other members of the dive club and feel my heart swell. There was no thunderbolt moment when we met, but over the weeks that I've known him there's increasingly been a quiet knowing and a certainty that he is a good man.

He comes towards me, rubbing a towel over his hair. His wetsuit is unzipped and peeled down to his waist. I shield my eyes against the sun to better look at him.

'What are you grinning at like a Cheshire cat?'

'Nothing,' I say. 'Everything.'

'You're not bored?' He flops down on the grass beside me.

'Far from it. It's nice to be able to spend time together.'

'Yeah.' He runs a finger gently along my arm and makes me shiver with delight.

His phone rings and I pass it to him. On the screensaver, I can see it's Daisy calling.

'Hi, sweetheart,' he says. 'What are you up to?'

I zone out so that he can carry on his conversation with his daughter in private. I know that she's with her mum today and that the plan was for them to go shopping. I get a little pang of envy. Things are going so well with Joe and me, but I feel that he's still holding me at arm's length. I think it's time for me to meet his children properly. So far, we've still only exchanged a brief, disinterested hello.

Joe hangs up. 'Daisy has new shoes. All is well in her world.'

I laugh at that and then think that this is probably as good a time as any to bite the bullet. 'I'd like to be more involved with your life,' I say, tentatively. 'If I met your kids then we could spend more time together and do stuff with them too. They're part of you and I'd really love to get to know them. Maybe we could all have a day out together.'

Joe frowns. 'It's a great idea . . .'

His tone doesn't match the words.

'But?'

'They're at a difficult age,' he says. 'It's easier, I'm sure, with younger kids who are more malleable, but teenagers are strange and fragile creatures for all they pretend not to be. They're both toughing it out, but I know inside that they're still hurting. What happens if I bring you into our lives and they're happy to accept you, then in a few months, we break up?'

'Isn't that a risk worth taking?'

'I don't know, Ruby. I can understand where you're coming from but, for me, it's a big step. If you decide you don't want to be with a family man and put up with all that entails, you can just walk away without looking back. I'm the one who'll be left picking up the pieces again.'

'We could take it really slowly,' I say.

Joe laughs. 'Look what happened last time we said that.'

'True, but we both mean it this time. We could go out to dinner with them or to a film. Nothing heavy. See how we get on. I'm really happy with you but, at the same time, I feel as if I'm in one small compartment of your life. We're having to snatch small moments when we can. If we are going to take this forward, then I'd like to be more than that.'

'Joe!' One of the club members shouts him from the jetty. 'You're up again.'

He holds up his hands.

'Go,' I say. 'That's fine. Just tell me you'll think about it.'

'OK,' he agrees.

I squeeze his hand. 'Thank you.' He stands and brushes the grass from his wetsuit. 'Be careful out there.'

Then he bounds down to the jetty and I settle back in my deckchair. The sun's on my face, the breeze is in my hair, life is good and I can't help but smile.

Chapter Fifty-Three

I'm on the train with Charlie and we're heading up to London. The barriers were open at the local station so we didn't buy a ticket and are hoping that there's no ticket inspector on the train. I'm working on the theory that the prices are normally so flipping expensive that if I manage a freebie every now and then, it balances it out and brings train travel down to the realm of just over-priced rather than outright extortion. What we'll do at the other end, I'm not sure. However, I'm leaving Charlie in charge of our criminal activity.

'Tell me again,' I say. 'We're doing what?'

She looks up from painting her fingernails. The whole carriage smells of pear drops from the polish and people are tutting in that particularly passive/aggressive British way.

'We're going to hang round the hotel that the boys are probably staying in.'

'*Probably?*'

'Someone swears she saw Mark there this morning and so we're going to check it out.' She gives me a fixed stare. 'There'll be lots of Thatters there.' The collective name for Take That fans. Sometimes, not surprisingly, known as Mad Thatters. 'You'll have to pretend that you really like them.'

'I do.'

'But in the way that *I* really like them, not in the half-hearted oh-I-buy-all-their-CDs way that you like Kylie.'

'I go to Kylie's concerts. As many as finances will allow.'

'Ah, but if it was a choice of eating or buying a ticket for a Kylie concert what would you do?'

'Eat, obviously.'

Charlie gives me a smug look. 'I rest my case. You are a merely a fairweather fan. I stuck by Gary even through the wilderness years.'

'Yes, but I'm sure Gary wouldn't want you to go hungry for him.'

'I am *very* hungry for him,' she quips and then laughs lasciviously at her own joke, frightening the elderly man sitting next to us. Poor bloke.

'Don't they get annoyed by all their fans chasing them around?'

'We've been with them from the start,' Charlie says. 'Some of us. Effectively, we've bought their houses, their posh cars, their places in the sun. There are bricks in Gary's walls that I have personally paid for. I think they owe us a little of their time, don't you?'

Fair point.

'If we all suddenly dropped them and started following, say, *Spandau Ballet*, where would they be?'

'That's never going to happen, is it?'

Charlie grins at me. 'Not while there's breath in my body.' She holds out her nails for me to admire.

'Nice.'

'I was going to get them painted with butterflies for *Wonderland* and all that, but I ran out of time.'

'Work gets in the way of a lot of things,' I agree. 'We could try to get some stick-on butterflies in Accessorize at Euston.'

'Sounds like a plan,' Charlie says.

So we manage to sneak out of an unguarded side entrance to Euston station and get our journey for free.

'That's a good omen,' Charlie assures me.

Our odds are further increased when we do manage to find some butterfly transfers to go on her nails. Result. One dirty, crowded Tube journey later – that we have to pay for – and we rock up at the five-star hotel where Take That are reportedly ensconced.

It's very nice. I can't think that I've been anywhere quite so smart before. Even the posh hotel that Mason took me to was more understated than this. It's all wall-to-wall black marble and modern art. And I'm not even going to say where it is as everyone will then be heading down here and Charlie would kill me.

These days, I seem to spend a lot of time worrying about being murdered by Charlie.

Already, there are a dozen fans taking up the sofas in the bar area. Their Take That T-shirts are a bit of a giveaway. Charlie recognises them instantly as girls from the fan forum and they all have a group hug.

'This is Ruby,' she says. 'A newbie Thatter.'

'Hi. I am on the forum,' I add, in case they think I'm an imposter. Though I have been lurking on there rather than contributing.

We order cocktails – at prices that only A-list celebrities would be comfortable with – and sit down. We hang out for the rest of the afternoon, talking, drinking more heinously-priced cocktails and gradually, we get more and more mellow.

'Joe's agreed that I can meet his kids,' I tell Charlie. 'I'm pleased, but it's a bit scary too.'

'Kids are not just for Christmas, they're for life.'

'What do you think we should do? Where do you take a teenage boy and girl so that they're not bored out of their heads?'

'Nando's,' is Charlie's choice.

'Noooo. That's really dull. There must be some sort of activity they'd like.'

She shrugs. 'Shopping?'

'I thought about wakeboarding or that iFly skydiving thing in the city centre.'

'Sounds hideous.' Charlie wrinkles her nose.

'What about crazy golf or climbing?' Charlie looks horrified that I could even think such a thing. 'I want them to see me as a fun-loving, adventurous person.'

'Why?'

'Because their dad is becoming an important person in my life.'

'If I were you, I'd stay clear of the children altogether. Just shag their dad whenever you get a chance.'

'But that's sort of the point. Unless I integrate with the family as a whole I don't even get the opportunity to do that. I don't want to be nothing more than a booty call for him.'

'You don't seem to mind that when it's Shagger Soames.'

'I haven't seen him for weeks,' I remind her. 'He's not been in the Butcher's Arms much lately either.'

'Exhausted by his handful of shifts, he's probably off swanning round the Med on a yacht to recover while dating a supermodel or something.'

I sigh and don't really know why. Probably because Charlie might be right.

'I'd like to have a proper relationship with Joe and if that means taking on his children, then I'm prepared to do it.'

'Madness.'

I don't like to point out that we're spending our afternoon sitting in a hotel just waiting for the outside chance of catching sight of an unattainable man. I know that Charlie is terrified of commitment and for good reason, but it would actually be less hard work to have a *real* boyfriend. It would take a braver woman than me to tell her that though.

Then, as some of the ladies are thinking of moving on, a couple of seriously slick limousines pull up at the front of the hotel. And that's our cue. No one needs even to speak. As one, we're out of that reception like greyhounds out of a trap. The minute we hit the pavement, Take That appear from a side entrance.

'Garrrrrreeeeee!' Charlie screams in my ear. He turns and smiles. She clicks her phone camera. Got him!

Security guards hustle them towards the waiting limos. We're on them, crushing together in a pack. The boys hold out their hands and high-five the nearest women, sending them into fevered ecstasy. With practised ease, they're in their cars in a flash and, before the doors are barely shut, they speed off with us in hot pursuit, tottering along the pavement in our heels after them.

'Did you see that?' Charlie turns to me. 'Did you flipping see that?' She jumps up and down and I jump up and down with her. That was actually bloody awesome!

'I get this,' I tell her. 'I *totally* get it.'

Charlie and I high-five each other. 'I think you can officially call yourself a Thatter now.'

I allow myself a giddy little giggle. 'Cool.'

Then arm-in-arm we Thatters go back to the bar, high on adrenaline, flushed with the thrill of the chase, bubbling with excitement and chattering like a flock of colourful birds. We are true fans, the unshakeable. We came, we saw, we got our photos for social media. And even the fact that someone has cleared away about a hundred and eighty quid's worth of our cocktails cannot quell our spirits.

Chapter Fifty-Four

Joe's kids don't want to go wakeboarding. They don't want to go to iFly and pretend they're skydiving either. Arial Extreme Adventure is ruled out as being naff too. Cinema – nothing they both want to see. Big Rock Climbing – lame. Ice-skating at Planet Ice – get real. Bounce trampolining – so last year. Hollywood Bowling – the shoes smell. Indoor skiing at the Snozone – too cold. Mr Mulligan's Pirate Crazy Golf. Woburn Safari Park. Daytona karting. No, no, no.

We go to Nando's.

Chapter Fifty-Five

I smile brightly as the kids sit opposite me scowling. Both Joe and I are trying too hard to be jolly and it's excruciating.

We know it's excruciating. They know it's excruciating.

Daisy is the picture of pre-teen resentment, whereas Tom clearly thinks he's too cool to be wasting his time on me. It's a heady combination and I'm wilting in the face of it.

'What do you fancy to eat, kids?' Joe asks, rubbing his hands together in an over-enthusiastic manner. 'I'm starving.'

Daisy exudes *ennui*. 'I don't think I like chicken any more.'

'They have other things, Dais,' Joe says. 'What about a veggie burger?'

'I don't like vegetables any more,' she sighs.

He tries his other offspring to see if he has better luck. He doesn't. 'Tom? Have you decided?'

Tom hasn't even opened his menu yet. 'A burger.'

'What kind?'

He shrugs. 'Don't care.'

This is my one day off in two weeks when it has actually coincided with seeing Joe and this is my big chance to impress his children. So far, it's not going well. They seem to have decided that they hate me and I haven't even done anything yet.

The sun is beating down outside and we're in a noisy, busy, air-conditioned restaurant that's chilled to below zero and two of us are finding the food selection wanting.

Daisy slumps forward on the table, the exertion of choosing food apparently all too much for her. 'Mum always lets me have the choc-a-lot cake instead of dinner.'

'Well, I'm not your mum,' Joe points out. 'If you finish your main course, then you can have a pudding. Daisy, you're twelve. You know the score by now.'

She closes her menu with dramatic finality and pushes it away from her as if it's poisoned. 'I'm not hungry.'

'OK, but I'm not cooking later,' Joe says. 'I've got the ironing to do.' He turns to me and grimaces. 'It's my most hated chore of the week. Ten school shirts for these two and five of my own for a kick off.'

I'm realising that I know nothing about his life. How little I appreciated all that he has to deal with or what it is for any single parent to manage their children alone. Now that they're sitting here in front of me, reality punches me in the guts and I realise that they may be a mountain I'm unable to climb.

The waitress comes and, by some miracle, we all manage to order. Joe looks relieved. Under the table his hand finds mine and he gives it a reassuring squeeze which is very timely as every fibre of my being is telling me to get up and leave. However, I've resolved to give this tricky initial get-together my best shot. I have to remember that this is the first woman other than their mum that they've ever seen their dad with and it will take some coming to terms with. It's all new to them as it is to me. But I am in his life whether they like it or not and we're all going to have to find a way to deal with it.

I take a deep breath before I say, 'So what kind of music do you guys like?'

They look at me aghast and a profound silence descends on the table.

'Daisy?' Joe prompts.

Her look says *whatever* and she still doesn't reply.

'You love Taylor Swift and Harry Styles, don't you?' he presses on.

'They're OK,' she says with disdain. 'A bit childish.'

'Tom?' Joe gives his son a direct look. 'Ruby asked you a question.'

'Grim Sickers. MoStack. Lethal Bizzle. Stormzy,' he answers flatly. Tom's expression says *you're none the wiser, are you?*

I wonder if he's actually just made the names up. They're certainly not on Radio 2.

'It's all a terrible noise,' Joe says with an attempt at a light-hearted laugh. 'Give me Coldplay any day. Something with a tune.'

'I've recently become a big fan of Take That,' I tell them brightly. 'My friend is a huge fangirl and she started taking me along to gigs and stuff. Now I really like them.'

They both stare at me blankly.

I flounder around thinking of something else to say and fail.

Our food comes and the conversation, if humanly possible, is even more stilted. Joe makes a valiant effort at keeping it going and I try to chip in too, but it's like talking to two brick walls. All my efforts are bouncing right back off them.

As we eat, my food nearly chokes me. Every question is met by a rebuff or outright stonewalling and it's quite possibly the longest meal of my life. I knew this would be difficult, but I didn't realise they'd be quite so deliberately hurtful. Don't they want to see their dad happy again? Can't they see that I'm making an effort here?

After the main course has been cleared away, Tom picks up his phone.

'No phones at the table,' Joe says.

His son, with a look that could curdle milk, puts it down again with an exasperated huff. Let him use the phone, I think. Let's end this misery for all of us.

'Anyone for dessert?' Joe says, optimistically.

I turn to him and whisper, 'I think I should be going.'

It's the first time that I see the children smile.

'Are you sure?' His look of concern makes me want to cry.

'Yes, you all enjoy the rest of your day.' I go to stand up and he puts a hand on my arm.

'Hang on.' He faces his kids. 'You've both been really rude to Ruby today and I'd like you to apologise.'

The children gape at him, faces full of unbridled hostility.

'They're not normally like this,' he tells me. 'They're good kids. I don't know what's got into them.'

'It's fine,' I assure him when it patently isn't. 'I have things I should be doing.'

'I'll walk you out.' He wags an angry finger at his children. 'You and I are going to have words when I get back.'

It only makes them sulk more.

'Bye, Tom. Bye, Daisy.'

'Bye,' they mumble in unison and with equal amounts of grudging.

It's never really been put to the test, but I always thought that I quite liked children; maybe I don't. Babies are cool, but I'm not sure that I'm keen on teenagers at all.

'Sorry,' he says as we leave the restaurant. 'I'm really sorry. They've behaved appallingly. They're not normally like this.'

'It's OK.' I knew that they'd put me to the test and they certainly did. I never expected them to embrace me with open arms, but neither did I imagine such direct opposition and I have crumbled in the face of their rudeness. Teenagers, one. Ruby, nil.

'It isn't OK. They've been awful. That was painful.'

Probably one of the most painful experiences of my life and, believe me, I've had a few. 'You were right, Joe. I was wrong. It's too soon.'

'They'll have to get used to it,' he says, sounding determined. 'I need a life of my own too.'

I have an awful feeling that I've made things even worse by insisting on meeting them. They were supposed to think I was a fun, friendly person and yet they didn't give me a chance. Breaking into this family could be like trying to crack a walnut with a feather.

Joe catches my hand in his and we swing them between us as he accompanies me to my car. He kisses me softly and makes my head spin, but it's tinged with sadness. I so wanted this to go well. I wanted the kids to think I was the kind of cool person who would enhance their lives, but my best efforts fell woefully short. They despised me and made it glaringly obvious.

'I'll call you,' he says. 'Give me a couple of days and we'll sort out another night out. By ourselves.'

'You're a good man,' I say, heavy of heart.

'I'd better get back.' He looks over his shoulder towards Nando's and the ties that bind him.

I could cry when I kiss Joe goodbye. I sit in the car and watch him walk back to his children, hands in his pockets, shoulders hunched.

That's it. There's no way that this relationship will ever work. I'm simply not up to taking on his hostile kids. And I liked him. I really did.

Chapter Fifty-Six

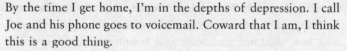

By the time I get home, I'm in the depths of depression. I call Joe and his phone goes to voicemail. Coward that I am, I think this is a good thing.

I leave him a message telling him that I don't think that this will work between us. I explain that I've really enjoyed knowing him, but that now he needs to concentrate on his family. I tell him that he was right that it's too soon to introduce another person into the mix. I wish him well and then hang up.

I sit and shake for a bit, wondering exactly what I've done. I think perhaps Joe will call me when he picks up the message, but he doesn't.

Chapter Fifty-Seven

At work that night Mason is all over me like a rash. The more I push him away, the keener he is. He asks me to go to his club with him when my shift ends. And I think sod it, why not? I've had a shit day and I deserve some fun.

We dance, drink too much and, afterwards, I go up to his flat with him drunk as a skunk. In bed, he blindfolds me, ties me up and pours champagne over my body which he laps up like a cat. The things he does with his tongue are totally obscene. And I love every fucking minute of it.

Just don't tell Charlie. Please don't tell Charlie.

Chapter Fifty-Eight

As if she's psychic, Charlie phones me in the morning. I'm still in bed next to Mason. The ties and blindfold are still on the pillow. I get a flashback to our night of passion and feel an unwanted rush of desire for him.

'Hiya,' she says, brightly. 'What are you up to this morning, Chummie?'

I look across at my companion who's stirring from his sleep. 'Err. Not much.'

Call me fickle, but I want to get up and out of here as fast as I can before Mason can do any more damage.

'Meet me for brekkie,' Charlie says. 'Then we can go straight to work.'

'OK. Give me an hour.'

'We'll meet at the café in the woods?' One of our favourite haunts.

'Sounds like a plan. See you later.' I hang up.

Mason opens one eye. 'Good morning, Brown.'

'Sorry my phone woke you. It was Charlie. I'm meeting her for breakfast.'

His hand snakes under the sheet and round my waist, pulling

239

me to him. His leg rests over mine, pinning me to the bed. I get a vision of him above me last night, my hands bound and held over my head. 'Don't go,' he says. 'Stay. I'll make you breakfast. I am the king of scrambled eggs.'

He's probably had lots of practice, I think. I wonder how many women have already been in this posh apartment with him. You don't keep a blindfold for yourself, do you now?

'I should go.' I wriggle away from him and out of the bed.

Mason sighs at me. 'Last night was fun, right?'

'Yes,' I say. 'It was great.' Just what I needed, apparently.

'So why are you running out on me this morning?'

'I'm not running out, I'm just leaving.'

'I can't read you, Ruby.' He shakes his head. 'You're always keeping me at arm's length.'

'I'm in your bed.'

'But you're not entirely here, are you? You're already somewhere else.' He stares at me, levelly. 'I think we could be good together.'

'I'm looking for more, Mason.'

'How do you know that I can't give you more until you try me?'

I've no idea what to say to that, so I deflect, 'Charlie's waiting for me. I have to go.'

Mason flops back on the bed. 'Tonight?'

'Working.'

You see, in the cold light of day, I can rationalise that I don't want to be with someone like Mason, but there's no doubt that I have a weakness for him.

'At least let me make you some tea.'

'I'm fine. Honestly.' After what we did last night, for some reason I'm embarrassed to be naked before him. I find my clothes, scattered about the floor alongside Mason's in our haste to undress. The thought of it brings a flush to my cheeks and my loins. And I really didn't even think I had loins.

While I pull on last night's underwear – inside out, give me some credit – I look round the room. It's so masculine, so Mason. The bed is chocolate brown leather and there's a leather chair in the corner. Above the bed is a huge painting of a vintage cycle in sepia tones, the bedside tables bear anglepoise lamps. There's not a thing out of place anywhere – he's the tidiest sex addict I know. Yet, stylish as it undoubtedly is, it looks more like a hotel room than a home. Unlived in and a little bit unloved. I know we made our way through the kitchen and living room in our rush to bed, but I've no idea what either of those look like. I imagine that they're both as achingly trendy.

When I'm dressed, I go to kiss him on the cheek. He tries to pull me back down onto the bed, but I ease myself out of his embrace.

'Catch you later,' I say. 'Thanks again.'

'That's it?'

I shrug. 'What more do you want?'

There's an exasperated note in his voice when he says, 'I'm not going to pursue you for ever, Brown.'

'OK.'

He pouts like a toddler. 'What am I going to do with myself for the rest of the day?'

'I'm sure you'll think of something. I'm going to meet Charlie.'

And I leave him in his swanky leather bed looking distinctly disgruntled.

Chapter Fifty-Nine

Charlie is already waiting for me at the café. She's bagged one of the tables on the terrace that overlooks the pond on the edge of the woods. It's another glorious day and maybe summer will be here to stay for more than a day or two this time. We've had too many false starts this year. Making the most of the weather, the dog walkers are out in force and we're lucky to get this spot. 'I've ordered us two full English brekkies.'

'Good. I'm starving.'

'You look like shit.' You can always count on Charlie to be candid. 'Did you have any sleep at all last night?'

'Not a lot.'

'Joe?'

'Complicated.'

'Ah.'

With convenient timing, our breakfasts arrive and we busy ourselves with buttering toast and administering the correct amount of ketchup.

'Al fresco cooky brekky! Does life get any better?' Charlie exclaims.

'Al fresco cooky brekky with The Barlow?'

'Ah, yes. Everything is better with a bit of added Barlow.'

So that Charlie didn't get the scent of my scandalous indiscretion, I did manage to go home after leaving Mason's place and have a quick run round the shower. I also washed my hair and put on my work stuff, so I'm not still wearing last night's clothes. I'm sure that she won't be able to tell that I spent the night with Mason.

'I had some great news this morning,' she says. 'I got free tickets to the Take That concert dress rehearsals in Manchester. Me and Paul are going up together. Yay! Go me!'

'Cool.'

'You don't mind that I asked Paul instead of you?'

'No. I'm glad. He'll appreciate it more than me.' Plus, I rather like the idea of her going with Nice Paul. He'll look after her. I know it. 'You must be thrilled.'

'I like to imagine that Gary personally hand-picked me.' Charlie goes all dreamy-looking.

'I'm sure he did.'

'How did the first family date go yesterday?' Charlie asks between mouthfuls.

'It was disastrous with a capital "D".'

'That bad?'

'Shocker.' I pause to contemplate while chewing my bacon. 'The children, far from being the little sweethearts that I'd conjured up in my head, were evil. They were determined to hate me on sight.'

'You're trying to steal their daddy away from them.'

'I'm not.'

'But it must feel like that.'

'Anyway, it's irrelevant now. They got their wish. Joe and I are over before we really started. I can't see it working. It would be like pushing water uphill to try to make a go of a relationship

243

with him. Without even giving me a chance, they were dead set against me.'

'They'll grow up. In a few years they'll be leaving home.'

'Daisy's only twelve. Even if she goes straight to uni, that's six years. Six years! There's no way I could cope with all those resentful faces for so long.'

'Go easy on them, Ruby. Their mum hasn't long left. It must be tough for them. They don't need another mum right now.'

'I know. I have no intention of trying to replace their mum. I just hoped that I could be their friend. Joe was right. It's too soon. He has to focus all his attention on them.'

'Maybe it's not over just yet. Give them a bit of time. They may come round to the idea.'

'I called him and ended it,' I tell her. 'That's definitely it.'

'What did he say?'

'Nothing. I didn't actually speak to him. I just left a message. I thought he might call me back but he hasn't.'

'You muppet,' Charlie sighs.

I might be a little bit hurt, but I'm not entirely surprised. After yesterday, he'll probably view it all as too much hard work. Quite frankly, I wouldn't blame him.

Chapter Sixty

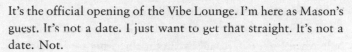

It's the official opening of the Vibe Lounge. I'm here as Mason's guest. It's not a date. I just want to get that straight. It's not a date. Not.

I pulled my new Primarni frock out of the wardrobe again which makes me think of my date with Joe a bit. That was a nice evening. I had high hopes after that. Fool that I am. Of course, I've heard nothing from him after our disastrous lunch with the kids and my subsequent message on his voicemail. Nothing at all. It's probably a good thing. I'm not potential stepmother material. We've probably both come to that conclusion.

Still, I won't let thoughts of my failure there spoil tonight. I feel good in this dress, but its impact is slightly weakened by the amount of designer labels on show. Are all these people from Costa del Keynes? They seem too sleek, too sophisticated. Where do they normally go in their Alice Temperley dresses with their Mulberry bags? I never see them in Lidl.

Having exchanged my invitation for a glass of champagne, I'm now hanging round at the door not knowing quite what to do with myself. We've already established that I don't know anyone else here, so I feel like Billy No Mates. I should have asked Mason if I could bring Charlie, but then she would have only taken the piss.

I catch a glimpse of Mason at the other side of the room. He's busy schmoozing, as I knew he would be. After all, it's the thing he seems to do best. Then I remember our recent night of passion and revise it to second best.

The music is mellow – no idea what, except it's not Take That. Hipster waiters drift by with platters laden with tiny, ultra-cool canapes. No cocktail sausages here, love. One of them stops in front of me and proffers his tray. 'Chicken and mango skewers with basil raita.'

'Oh. Thank you.' I take one and it tastes great. Though I feel really self-conscious eating it as everyone else seems to be waving the waiters away without partaking of their fayre. It's only when I've eaten it and I've not a clue what to do with the remaining wooden skewer that I realise why. Clearly they are veterans of these things and I am not.

I inch closer into the room and, surreptitiously, stick my skewer into the nearest vase. So, if food is off the menu, now what? Moving through the crowd, I go in pursuit of Mason – who seems to just keep moving ahead of me. There's tinkling laughter filling the space, lots of bling on show, more designer label outfits than I have ever seen in one room. This is the life I could have with Mason Soames. I could become a social butterfly and flit from event to event. I could be his life and business partner – an indispensable party hostess, right at his side. I think we could do that well together.

Eventually, as I'm about to give up and go to the bar in search of more booze, Mason turns and sees me. He breaks into a smile, excuses himself from the group he's talking to and comes over to me. He kisses my cheek in greeting, places a comforting hand on my arm and my confidence grows just from being with him.

'I didn't notice you slip in,' he says. 'Glad you could make it.'

'As if I wouldn't.' I glance around me again and I can make a full appraisal now that I'm not alone and anxious. 'The great and the good of Costa del Keynes are here.'

'It's going well,' he says and Mason sounds slightly tense too, though he has no need to. As parties go, this seems to be a resounding success. 'We just hope it translates into people signing up for membership.'

'They'd be mad not to,' I tell him and get a sudden rush of affection for him. Like the rest of us, Mason is only trying to do his best in the world.

'Thanks, Brown,' he says. 'Can I get you a drink?' He grabs one from a passing tray with a skill that's clearly been honed by years of extreme socialising and hands it over. I glug it, grateful that I got a taxi instead of driving. 'Let me introduce you to some people.'

We join a group of women, probably my own age. Clearly life has been kinder to them. They're all as thin as a pin, groomed, tanned and toned. I don't really know my labels – I was blagging earlier – but even I can spot a Chanel handbag and there's at least one on show. And it's *definitely* not a fake. The tan is, though.

'Hey, Mason,' one says. 'Come and spend some time with us.'

'I'm all yours,' he schmoozes and air kisses both of her cheeks. Then, as I try to hang back, he eases me forward. 'Ladies, this is my good friend, Ruby.' They all look at me with haughty disinterest. So much for the sisterhood. 'This is Charlotte, Honeysuckle, Emmaline and Serena.'

Now I feel that being called Ruby makes me sound like a charlady. 'Hello.'

They look me up and down a bit more. As they do, someone calls for Mason and he says to me, 'Back in a second.'

Before I can shoot off with him, he leaves me standing there with *Sex and the City*-lite. They all look at me blankly. To fill the awkward silence, more than anything, I ask, 'How do you know Mason?'

They all giggle, girlishly as if I've asked them what colour knickers they're wearing.

'We've been friends for years,' one of them answers. Except she says 'yars'. 'We ski together.'

I wonder if that's all they do together. Then there's another excruciating pause until one of them deigns to ask, 'What do you do, er, Ruby, was it?'

'I'm a waitress. At Mason's pub, The Butcher's Arms.'

They all look at me horrified. I don't know what they do and am not the slightest bit interested. It looks as if they spend all day in the gym, if you ask me. Which no one did.

We all stand and look at each other, conversation clearly exhausted. With friends like this, Mason really doesn't need enemies.

'Excuse me,' I say. 'I need a refill.' And, thankfully, when I hold up my glass as proof, it is actually empty. I slink away and then wonder what to do with myself. Might as well find another drink, I suppose.

So I head to the bar and, when I get there, am relieved to find that Ben from behind the bar at the Butcher's Arms is moonlighting here. There's a queue and Ben and one other barman are struggling to keep up with pouring drinks and mixing cocktails. I don't mind queueing though as it gives me something to do.

'A friendly face, finally,' I say when I stand in front of Ben.

'Ruby!' He looks as relieved to see me as I am him.

'I didn't know you worked here.'

'The odd shift. But I might move here permanently. What can I get you?'

'A glass of white. Large.'

'We're drowning here,' he says. 'Typically, Shagger hasn't considered the logistics of catering for this many people.'

'Want me to roll up my sleeves?'

Ben's stressed face brightens. 'Would you?'

'Why not?' So I ditch my idea of another drink, go behind the bar and set to in serving the thirsty partygoers.

They say time flies when you're having fun. It also flies when you're serving behind a busy bar, trust me. When the last of the customers have been served, Ben high-fives me. 'Thanks, Ruby. We couldn't have managed without you.'

'No problem. Let's clear up and go home.'

The glitterati are drifting away now, the club is emptying nicely. I wash glasses, tidy the bar, think how much my feet hurt and how foolish I was to wear vertiginous heels. I might get home before midnight, at this rate.

Suddenly, Mason swerves up, looking horrified. 'What are you doing, Brown?'

'Helping. You didn't have enough bar staff. Ben was over-whelmed.' I point in the general direction of the retreating crowd as I polish a glass. 'That lot seem determined to drink the place dry.'

'It went well, though?' He still seems worried.

'A resounding success,' I assure him. 'They'll be flocking to sign on the dotted line.'

'I really appreciate you stepping in, but you shouldn't be doing this.' He lowers his voice. 'You're here with me.'

Except I wasn't. I was standing round like a lemon on my own and keeping busy was definitely preferable.

I pick up another glass. This is probably my designated role in life. I'm not one of the party people, I'm more suited to being behind the bar at glamorous events. I don't know what makes me think of Joe, but I wonder where he is now. He'd be my equivalent. I'm sure he'd rather be rolling up his sleeves and getting stuck in rather than standing posing in a dinner jacket.

When Ben moves away, Mason says, 'Let me finish here. I won't be long and then we can go up to my apartment and I'll make it up to you.'

'Yeah, sure.' But that certainly isn't on the cards tonight.

'I promise I won't be long.'

'You go and do what you have to do,' I tell him and he hurries off to chat to some of the guests as they depart.

I polish my last glass, dry my hands, kiss Ben on the cheek and say, 'See you at work.'

'Cheers again, Ruby.'

Then, without Mason noticing, I head out of the door and go home.

Chapter Sixty-One

The next morning I get flowers delivered. Can't remember when that last happened. I think when I had my appendix out. Not surprisingly, they're from Mason. Red roses. Two dozen. They're gorgeous.

I text him to say thanks.

Then realise that I'll have to go round to Mum's to borrow a vase because I don't possess one and I can't really leave them standing in the sink.

Chapter Sixty-Two

A couple of days later, when I'm chucking the wilted roses in the bin, Joe calls me out of the blue and asks me to meet him for a coffee.

In truth, I'm reluctant to go as I'll only like him again. However, as my default setting is to say 'yes', I've agreed to meet him before my brain can work out how to turn him down.

So later that day after we've both finished our shifts, we meet in the city centre at the Queen's Court. Joe buys us iced coffees from the trendy stainless steel wagon that pops up in the summer months and we take up residence in the red-and-white-striped deckchairs set out to face the sun. It's a beautiful day and this courtyard is a little grassy oasis in the busy shopping centre. There are a few other people dotted around – a young couple smooching, two elderly ladies with their shoes kicked off on a break from shopping, a family with a boisterous boy who's charging around while they try to relax. Me and Joe.

We're shy with each other, a bit stilted, conversation awkward. It's fair to say that our last meeting wasn't a resounding success and my subsequent phone message is clearly hanging in the air between us.

Still, I sit back and close my eyes for a second enjoying the rays on my face and the brain-freeze from my ice-laden coffee. I decided that I was going to be cool, aloof, but seeing Joe again has made my heart soften. He's a good, solid guy and they don't come around that much these days.

'I'm sorry about our lunch with the kids,' he says. 'I was pretty sure you wouldn't want to hear from me again. Then I got your message.'

'Sorry about that, but I thought it was for the best.'

'They were unspeakable,' he says. 'I've never been so mortified.'

'It's difficult for them,' I say magnanimously, even though they were both little horrors. I understand why. Truly I do. I'd probably be the same in their circumstances. They want their dad all to themselves, not sharing him with some random woman. If they see him moving on, then it's a dead cert that their mum will never come home. Sad. I get that.

'I've missed you.' He looks over at me and, tentatively, takes my hand. 'I know that you said you'd had enough, but I'm not ready to give up yet. Do you want to keep pushing on and see if my monsters learn to love you? I know it's not an easy ask, so it's entirely your call.'

And I guess that this is a defining moment of our future relationship. Do I say yes and commit to Joe or stick to my guns and simply walk away? I don't think that there can be any half measures. You can't dabble with a guy who's got kids. Not that I'm the dabbling kind anyway. Except with Mason. It's probably fair to say that I've dabbled with him.

'You're hesitating,' he says, anxiously.

'What can I do to get in their good books, though? They made it pretty clear that I wasn't welcome. How could I possibly break in? What do they like? I'm not really au fait with the World of the Teenager.'

'That brings me to my idea.' He sits up, animated. 'Daisy turns thirteen next week and has just announced that she wants a party.' Joe rolls his eyes. 'Gina's away with work – supposedly – and I thought it might be fun if we organised a party together.'

I must look vaguely horrified.

'I know it's short notice, but I seriously need help,' he confesses. 'I haven't a clue what to do for a teenage girl and I don't want to let her down. I'd like it to be something cool. Gina and I are still at the stage of competitive parenting. Plus, as Gina's away for her birthday, I genuinely want to make it feel special.'

Chewing at my lip, I say, 'I'm not sure that party planning is my forte.'

Joe holds up his hands. 'No pressure. It was just an idea. I thought it might be a chance for you to get to know her better.'

It could be. He's right. If I put on the party of the century for Daisy, then she might learn to like me. The only downside is that I'm totally rubbish at this kind of stuff. This could be my big opportunity, though. Shouldn't I give it one last chance? Needless to say, I have some sort of mental aberration and, before I can fully examine the pitfalls, say, 'Of course. Great idea. I'd love to do it.'

His face brightens instantly. 'Thanks, Ruby. You don't know how much that means to me.'

'What sort of thing does she like?'

'Oh, I don't know,' Joe admits, raking his hair. 'Pink, girly stuff. Princesses. Usual thing.'

'Anything more?'

He shrugs. 'Can't think of anything. The normal stuff.'

Very helpful. Sounds like I have my brief, though. I might be useless, but Charlie is good at this kind of thing. I'll get her roped in too.

'OK,' I say. 'I'll give it a go.' Already my mind is whirling with ideas. 'How many guests?'

'Ten, max. I don't think I could cope with any more girls than that. Girls en masse are hell. Trust me, I've done this before.'

Unlike me.

'I'll give you carte blanche,' he adds. 'Buy whatever you need. I'll pay the bill.'

'No, no. This will be my treat to her.' Yes, of course I'm trying to buy her friendship. What of it?

'You're a wonderful woman. This time, it will be better,' he assures me.

Then he kisses me and any misgivings fly right out of my head. I should be with this man. I know it. Every ounce of my being tells me that. I've just got to win round his kids.

Chapter Sixty-Three

Charlie and I. Our bench. Before work.

'I'm thinking unicorns, fairies, princesses. All of that shit,' I tell Charlie.

'You don't think a Take That themed party would be spectacularly good?'

'Charlie, I hate to disappoint you, but girls of that age don't even know who Take That are.'

She shakes her head and says mournfully, 'That's because they are young and foolish and have yet to learn about the finer things in life.'

With the best will in the world, Take That are also middle-aged men, old enough to be their dads. And dads, as we know, are *never* cool.

'Joe says she's a really girly kid. Pink and all that.'

'Aren't they all?'

My knowledge of what goes on inside the heads of teenage girls is negligible. I wrack my brain, but can come up with nothing better. 'Unicorns and fairies it is, then?'

'Fab.' Charlie nods in agreement. 'Sounds like a plan.'

How did I manage to agree to this? I'm pooping myself

already at the thought of it. 'Do you think we can pull it off in a week?'

'Tough call,' she says, 'but, with some well-aimed shopping, we'll ace it. I'll hit the internet. We need a Pinterest mood board too.'

Mood board? Blimey. Sounds terrifying. 'We're not frightened of a few hormonal teenage girls, are we?'

'Certainly not,' Charlie declares.

'Actually, I think I am.'

'Faint heart never won round a divorcee's kids,' my friend says.

'You're right.' I still chew my nails. 'And you're absolutely sure that this is a good idea?'

'None better.'

We high-five each other. It's less than an hour later before blind panic *really* sets in.

Chapter Sixty-Four

At the weekend, it's Daisy's thirteenth birthday and we're all set to go. With Charlie's help, I've produced a full-on magical theme, embracing Joe's somewhat vague brief – unicorns, fairies, princesses. What's not to love? I'd like this party myself, thank you very much.

Charlie and I spent a whole morning on our day off scouting out the perfect location for a picnic party spot. Then I prayed all week that the good weather would hold. It did.

We found this clearing in a small wood on the outskirts of Costa del Keynes. It's by a car park that's better known for evening dogging activities and a good kebab van, but on a Saturday afternoon it's all fine and dandy. I just hope we're not overrun with dog walkers. Or the doggers don't turn up early.

I had to beg Jay to let me have the time off work and, in the end, I've taken it as unpaid leave. I'm not in his best books at the moment. I wanted Charlie to help me with it, but he wouldn't hear of us both being off together, so here I am by myself setting up Daisy's surprise birthday bash. Joe is bringing her along at the appointed time, so he couldn't be here either. Which is fine as I think it would have made me stress even more. I just hope that I've got enough time to do it single-handed.

Loaded down with essential party goodies, I make my way along the narrow paths through the trees until I come to the well-chosen and secluded clearing. Shimmering sunlight filters through the leaves, illuminating the trees and ferns below, making it look truly magical. There's a circle of cut tree trunks where the party guests will be able to sit.

It's perfect. The ideal place to have a magical birthday party. I give a spin round to try it out for size. She'll love it. I'm sure she will. What more could a teenage fairy princess want?

Time is marching on and I'm expecting ten twelve/thirteen-year-old girls in just over an hour, so I'd better get a move on. I gave eBay and my credit card a serious battering and have bought up ALL the magical party goodies that I could get my hands on. I make a couple more trips to the car and hope that there aren't fairy-minded thieves about to pinch all the stuff I'm piling up in the clearing as I have no one to guard it.

I've got a huge pink picnic blanket for the centre of the circle which I lay down and scatter with sparkly silver cushions. Then I hang white, yellow and lilac paper lanterns from the lower branches of the trees, fairy bunting and a banner which says I BELIEVE IN UNICORNS. There are pink tiaras for the girls studded with blingtastic multi-coloured rhinestones and plus they've got a set of delicate white-and-silver fairy wings each. And a pair for me too, of course. Today, I'm going to be chief fairy, come hell or high water.

I've made creamy pink mocktails with strawberry milkshake and white chocolate that I've brought along in a cool box and will serve in jam jars with rainbow straws. I've bought cupcakes iced with jazzy frosting and set them all out on a picnic table that I've borrowed from my folks. Rushing round, I manage to get it all together in time. I've made a new playlist of stuff for my iPod featuring things that I think teenage girls will like and I hook it up to a portable speaker.

Standing back, I admire my handiwork. I've got it all ready in the nickiest-nick of time. It looks flipping amazing, even though I say it myself. Considering I've pulled it all together in a week, I'm so chuffed. If Mason ever gives me the sack from the pub, I could very well try my hand at event planning. I tell you, I have previously undiscovered talents. I can only hope now that the birthday girl loves it too.

A text comes in from Charlie. Good luck, chick! Hope it goes well! xx Plus a gazillion emoticons of unicorns, fairies, princesses and kisses. Oh, my word, I wish with all my heart that she was here with me. Charlie would know what to do. She'd make sure the party goes with a swing. With some effort and a bit of advanced contortion, I manage to put some fairy wings on myself. Yay!

Then, before I know it, I hear footsteps and I turn to see Joe behind me. He's holding Daisy by the shoulders and she has both of her eyes covered.

'We made it,' Joe says. 'Though it was a close run thing. Outfit issues.'

I stare at Daisy, horrified, and my mouth drops open. All the girly pink stuff, the embroidered sweatshirts, the skinny leggings – gone! The sequined trainers have been dispensed with, only to be replaced by footwear that look remarkably like Doc Martens. She's wearing a white T-shirt, black biker-style jacket, black jeans and a faceful of make-up. Her curls, as unruly as her father's, are now poker straight. You know in *Grease* when transformed goody two shoes Sandy turns up to meet bad boy Danny in her spray-on trousers, red lippy and looking at least thirty years old? That.

Joe, seemingly oblivious to this, gives me the thumbs-up and I nod, numbly. 'Open your eyes, Daisy,' he says.

When she does, Daisy stands there gaping in horror and then manages to say in a voice hoarse with shock, 'Thank you, Daddy.'

'It's not down to me, Princess. Ruby has organised it all for you.' He mouths to me. 'Fantastic job.'

And you have no idea how grateful I am for that.

'Wow,' she says, but not in a good way.

'Well, I'm off. I'm going to leave you two to have fun,' he says. 'I'll be back later.'

'Don't go,' I say, panic-stricken. 'Stay.'

'I've got to pick Tom up from a music rehearsal. I promise I won't be long.' Then he winks at me. 'You girls have fun. Lovin' the fairy wings, by the way.'

I am thirty-eight and I am wearing fairy wings. I think it shows that I am youthful and fun. Daisy is clearly looking at me and seeing a pathetic old hag who should know better.

Joe kisses Daisy on the head and then walks away from us.

'I hope you like it,' I try tentatively.

She turns to me open-mouthed.

'I thought it would be fun. Your dad said that you love unicorns and fairies. Princesses too,' I add, lamely.

'That was when I was twelve,' she replies, loftily. 'I'm thirteen now. I've moved on.'

'I can see.' Then I sigh with resignation. This is all a terrible mistake. I should have just booked them in for manicures somewhere. They'd have been in their element. 'Your friends will be here soon. Let's just try to enjoy it,' I offer. 'Do you want a tiara or some fairy wings to wear? Maybe both? You can never have enough sparkle.'

Daisy just stands and stares at me, hands bunched into tight, cross little fists. The look she gives me is the blackest of black and I'm surprised that I don't simply drop down dead on the spot. 'Seriously, do you think I'm *five*?'

'I'm sorry that you don't like it, Daisy. I thought you would.

It's done now and I think we should try to make the best of it. I realise that I've read this all wrong.' I feel awful that I'm actually going to ruin Daisy's birthday party when all I did was try my very best.

She is as still as a stone, radiating fury. 'That's because you don't know me. You might think you do, but you don't know me at all. And that's because you're not my mother.'

I don't point out to her that I'm here due to the fact that her mum is in Italy or Spain or somewhere with her new boyfriend, pretending to be working while they're probably shagging each other senseless in between bouts of sightseeing. I speak as someone who knows about these things. The only thing I know is that her mother's not bloody well here. I am.

But you don't say that to a traumatised thirteen-year-old, do you? Instead, I say more calmly than I feel, 'I don't want to replace your mum, Daisy. I'm doing this because your dad asked me to and because I'd like to be your friend.'

That is clearly cutting no ice with her. She views me as her sworn enemy. The woman who is trying to steal her father's affections away from her.

'Your friends are due in a minute,' I add. 'For their sake, we'll both have to make the best of it.'

She doesn't say 'fuck you' but I can feel it emanating from her pores. I'm simply going to have to plough on and hope for the best.

On cue, ten hyperactive, giggling girls arrive and all I can do now is try to get through this without both of us dying of embarrassment.

Chapter Sixty-Five

The girls troop towards us in an excited line, escorted by a couple of the mums. I'm just feeling awful now. This is a disaster waiting to happen. These young girls all look too cool for skool. Sassy and self-assured. I'm sure I wasn't that confident or grown-up at twelve. I'm not sure that I am now.

The mums drop them off and compliment me on my party-planning skills. I mutter some modest thanks. Little do they know that the birthday girl hates it all. Every bit of it. Daisy sits on one of the logs, still stony-faced despite my exhortations to try to enjoy it. When the mums leave, eager to get off to their retail therapy or coffee dates, and vowing to return in a couple of hours, I think that I might as well brave this out. 'Well,' I say, clapping my hands. 'Let's get this party started.'

'OMG! Daisy, this is soooooo cool,' one of the girls says as she takes in my magical glade. The others trill with excitement and run round, enthralled. They dance round the trees, try out the cushions, flop on the picnic blanket.

Daisy sits looking very perplexed at their reaction.

'Fairy wings!' one shouts and grabs a pair, twirling round. Another girl fastens them onto the back of her T-shirt for her and then they both squeal with excitement. Suddenly, they all want them and there's a frenzy of wing fixing.

'Tiaras!' a shout goes up and is greeted by giggles of glee. The girls all try them on for size and dance around in a circle together. Only Daisy is still frozen to the spot, outside of the group. My heart is in my mouth, yet perhaps I'm not the one who read this wrong.

I sidle over to Daisy. 'It's your party,' I say softly to her, trying to sound encouraging, 'and it looks as if it's a hit with your friends. You should join in for their sake. What do you say?'

She looks up at me, clearly wondering why she's so out of step with her chums.

'Can I get you a strawberry mocktail?'

She nods, mutely. I hand her a jam jar of milkshake and she swallows it down. Then I give them to the rest of the girls and dish out the cupcakes too. More delighted squealing.

I turn the music up and the girls start dancing. Daisy stands, staring at her guests as if she doesn't know them.

I try her with my box of goodies, whispering, 'There's a set of wings and a tiara for you too. Special ones.'

She looks down at them and there are tears in her eyes. 'Really?'

'Want me to pin the wings on?'

'Yes, please.' She takes off her new biker jacket and lays it carefully on a log before turning her back to me. Gently, I pin on the fairy wings.

'Gorgeous,' I tell her. 'Plus there's the biggest, sparkliest tiara for the birthday girl.' I slip it onto her head and straighten it.

'I wish we had a mirror,' she says, touching her crown.

'Take a selfie.'

So she pulls out her phone and, instantly, her friends crowd round to pose and pout.

'You look sooooo cool,' one of them says.

Daisy adjusts her tiara and starts to laugh. Soon they're all so giddy you'd think there was neat vodka in their drinks. Actually, that might not have been a bad idea. Joking! No need to call Social Services.

I let out a breath. The first one in about fifteen minutes. Now the girls don't even need me here. They're more than happy entertaining themselves.

'This so *totally* wonderful, Daisy,' I hear one of the girls say and my heart could burst with happiness. Who knew that the approval of teenage girls could feel so good, so gratifying and be so hard won? I'm so pleased to see that they're happy dancing, singing, pouting, taking enough pictures to drown social media.

It's going to be OK, I think, and get a rush of relief. It's going to be OK.

Chapter Sixty-Six

The mums come back and collect their daughters and friends. They all seem to have had a lovely time. I just want to lie down in a dark room and recover. Maybe drink heavily too. They all get pink glittery goody bags with hand-knitted unicorns in them that I found on Etsy. Even the most sophisticated of the girls are beyond delighted and this has restored my faith in unicorns. They go home completely hyperactive and floating on air. We should all have a little more magic in our lives, whether you're thirteen or thirty-eight. I think next time I'm sitting watching telly by myself on a Saturday night, I'm going to put a tiara on and see if it makes me feel better.

Despite being exhausted – emotionally and physically – I'm mostly relieved that it all turned out all right in the end. I snatched victory from the jaws of defeat. Go me! And it was great to see Daisy having a good time. I hope it's a birthday that she'll remember for a long time.

A few minutes later, Joe comes back to collect Daisy. My magical glade is totally trashed and looks like the aftermath of Glastonbury. There's stuff everywhere. It's going to take me an age to clear up, but I've got a few hours before my shift at work.

'Did it go OK?' he enquires anxiously.

'You'd better ask Daisy,' I suggest.

She meets my eye when she says, gratefully, 'It was the best party ever, Daddy.'

'Good.' Joe looks relieved too. We exchange a loaded glance. Mission accomplished. He gives me a slow wink. I hope Daisy doesn't notice. Although this was set up with an ulterior motive, I'm really pleased to have been able to do it for her. 'Thanks, Ruby. I really appreciate it.' We both know how much was riding on this. 'I'll help you to tidy up.'

'No need,' I say. 'You take the birthday girl home. I'll speak to you later.'

'If you're sure.'

I nod. 'I can manage.' I want them both to leave thinking that I'm an utter saint. Besides, Daisy still seems to be floating on a happy cloud and I don't want to spoil that for her by making her fill bin bags with rubbish.

So Joe takes Daisy's hand and I watch as they walk away through the trees. Then, after a moment, she turns back and runs down the path towards me.

To my surprise, she grabs me and holds me in a tight hug. 'Thank you, Ruby,' Daisy says and kisses my cheek without prompting. Then she races to catch up with her dad once more.

I resist doing the air punch that's inside me in case she sees. But it's there, nevertheless.

Chapter Sixty-Seven

Mason turns up halfway through my shift. He catches my wrist as I pass the bar and gives me a puzzled look. 'Why are you looking so pleased with yourself, Brown? I've never seen a more smug smile. What's going on?'

'I'm happy,' I tell him.

'Excellent. Let's celebrate at my club afterwards.'

'No thanks.'

He pouts. 'Then we can go back to my place and have sensationally sordid sex.'

'No thanks.'

'Don't you even want to think about it?'

'No thanks.'

'You ran out on me the other week after the launch party with no explanation.'

'I know. Sorry about that.'

He puffs out an exasperated breath. 'Playing hard to get is pointless when you get to a certain age.'

'I'll remember that.'

Mason stomps off.

So I serve polenta and couscous and other posh grub to my customers and am ridiculously busy until closing time and, by then, Mason has gone.

Chapter Sixty-Eight

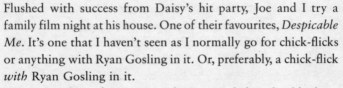

Flushed with success from Daisy's hit party, Joe and I try a family film night at his house. One of their favourites, *Despicable Me*. It's one that I haven't seen as I normally go for chick-flicks or anything with Ryan Gosling in it. Or, preferably, a chick-flick *with* Ryan Gosling in it.

We sit on the sofa in a cosy line, snuggled under blankets, hugging huge bowls of popcorn and unfeasibly large bottles of fizzy drink.

The house is a small, three-bed semi in Emerson Valley, one of the nicer areas of Milton Keynes. It's a modern estate, but built before the squeeze on land so the streets are tree-lined, the gardens more than handkerchief-sized and Joe's house backs onto some lovely parkland. Inside, it's very much a family home, a bit unkempt and much-loved. The hall is filled with discarded shoes and smells slightly of teenage boy's trainers. Joe says he's going to try to keep it on until they're at least eighteen, if he can afford it by himself, as this has been the kids' only home and moving them would be a trauma too far.

My relationship with Daisy has improved a lot. She's more relaxed with me and nestles nonchalantly against my side as we sit together. We have found some common ground in fairy wings and unicorns, it appears. Who'd have thought? The momentary appearance of Goth Daisy has been forgotten and she's back in head-to-toe pink. Earlier she let me paint her fingernails for her and I passed muster in that department too. At her suggestion, she put my mobile number into her phone so that she can text me. Progress indeed. I feel as if it's a series of tests that I have to complete to win her affections. Yet it seems to be working, in a small way.

Can't say the same about Tom, though. I've no idea how to reach out to him. You can't exactly throw a few unicorns at a fifteen-year-old boy and hope they'll stick. Although we're next to each other on the sofa, he sits as far away from me as humanly possible, making sure there is clear air, and sends regular death-stares in my direction. I do nothing but respond politely and kindly. He's a kid and he's hurting. I get that. But he's so sullen and hostile that it's bloody hard.

We like to think that children aren't affected by divorce, that they bounce back and cope with everything we adults throw at them. And they do. To a point. Yet who wouldn't be damaged by their mum walking out on them, no matter how many times that they're reassured that they're still loved? He sees me as a threat, obviously. Perhaps he thinks that I'm the one who is preventing Gina from coming home again, but that's far from the truth. They don't talk about their mum's new partner and I wonder if they're putting him through agonies too or are they more accepting of him.

It seems as if Gina is taking her responsibilities lightly in the face of finding new love. The kids are supposed to see her every other weekend and one night in the week, but Joe tells me that she often cancels at the last minute – leaving Daisy heartbroken and Tom angry.

I'm trying not to take sides or get too involved in their family dynamics. I take my hat off to anyone who can be a stepmum though and I do wonder if I'll ever manage to be fully part of their lives. However, I don't just want to see Joe away from his home as that's not real, is it? If I'm going to be part of his life, then we can't keep it all separate. Despite the comedy antics on the screen and the lovely, buttery bowl of popcorn to comfort me, my mood is quite low. If I'm perfectly honest with you, I like the feeling I get when I'm with them all. I've never done snuggling up with a family before – not since I was a kid myself, anyway – and I'm surprised how much I've enjoyed it. I want to do more of this. If only *both* of the kids would like me.

When the film finishes, Joe goes to make a cup of tea and Daisy troops after him to help. I'm left alone with Tom on the sofa. As he's finished his popcorn, I push my bowl between us. Miraculously, there's quite a bit left in there. 'Help yourself.'

He dips in, making absolutely sure that our hands aren't reaching in at the same time. Even that, it seems, would be a traitorous act against his mum.

I smile at him. 'That was a great film. I can see why you all like it.'

'It was mum's favourite,' he says pointedly.

'She has great taste.'

Then he looks at me squarely. 'You'll never replace her.'

'I'm not trying to, Tom. But I like your dad and he likes me. He's been through a difficult time too. Doesn't he deserve to have a little happiness?'

He doesn't answer me. Then Joe and Daisy come back and the moment is lost.

Chapter Sixty-Nine

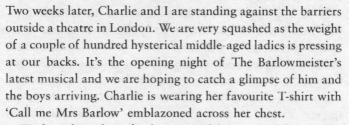

Two weeks later, Charlie and I are standing against the barriers outside a theatre in London. We are very squashed as the weight of a couple of hundred hysterical middle-aged ladies is pressing at our backs. It's the opening night of The Barlowmeister's latest musical and we are hoping to catch a glimpse of him and the boys arriving. Charlie is wearing her favourite T-shirt with 'Call me Mrs Barlow' emblazoned across her chest.

We have been here for hours. And hours. And hours. My feet are numb and I need a wee. I can't, however, go for a wee as the nearest loos are miles away and I'll lose the place I've been guarding with my life. I try to content myself with jiggling instead. It's not really working.

'Stop fidgeting,' Charlie says, 'or I'll have to kill you.'

'We've been here *for ever*,' I point out. 'How much longer?'

She checks her watch. 'The show starts in about half an hour, so he'll be arriving very soon.'

'Good. I can't last much longer.'

'Can I point out that some ladies have been camping out here on the pavement under the stars – or streetlamps – for three days to get the best spot on this barrier?'

'Three days! That's madness.' As much as I am coming to love Gary Barlow, I don't think I'll ever love him that much. Three hours, I think, is probably the limit of my adoration. I like the comfort of my own bed too much. Even now, I'm wishing I'd brought sandwiches.

Nice Paul is right here on the barrier next to her. He's been here for a long time too. We're going to have a meal together after we've seen Gary and Co. head inside. Then we're going to wait outside again afterwards until they come out at the end of the show. I think I might give the last bit a miss, if Charlie doesn't mind going home with the other fans rather than me. I don't think my dedication quite matches theirs yet.

'How's it going with Joe?'

'OK,' I tell her. 'One of his kids likes me now. Daisy's on side. She messages me regularly.' Silly little things from Snapchat mainly, but that's enough. 'I've still yet to win Tom over, but I'm prepared to keep trying.' I've done my best. Joe took me to watch him rehearsing for a music concert as he's a talented guitarist, but he studiously ignored me from the stage and when we met him afterwards. I wasn't allowed to go to the real concert as his mum would be there – though she did actually turn up for this one. Last Saturday morning, I also stood at the side of the road in the rain and cheered him along as he ran the Costa del Keynes half-marathon. He high-fived his dad and ran straight past me. I clearly have a lot of work to do yet.

'Shagger was asking about you.'

'I haven't seen him for ages,' I tell her. 'Last time we spoke, he wanted me to go to his club with him and I told him I wasn't interested. I'm not sure if he can cope with that. He's probably used to women falling at his Ted Baker-shod feet.'

'He seems pretty keen,' she says. 'He'd normally have moved on by now.'

'I suspect it's only because we haven't had any new waitresses for a while.'

'Ah,' she agrees. 'Probably.'

The stupid thing is that part of me likes the lack of complication offered by Mason – as long as you don't mind threesomes, obvs. Building a relationship with Joe is flipping difficult. It's hard to make yourself part of a tight-knit unit and I know that I'll always be second best. Joe's kids will always come first no matter what the demands. Maybe if Mason was older or looking to settle down then it might be a different matter. It's possible that we could have a future together. However, I'm at an age where I don't want to be someone's fuck buddy. Even the term makes me shudder. I need to be more than that.

'You've never been married, Paul?' I ask across Charlie – mainly because I want to stop thinking about my own tortured love life.

He shakes his head. 'I came close once, but I think I dodged a bullet there. It wouldn't have been right for either of us.'

'And now?'

'I'm waiting for someone special,' he says and we exchange a glance over Charlie's head and then smile at each other. I knew it! To coin one of my nana's phrases, he *is* sweet on her and Charlie is oblivious. Or pretends to be.

Then, before I can dwell on my friends' relationship potential, my suffering ends as a limo sweeps in and Gary, lovely wife on his arm, gets out. He waves to the crowd, poses for photographs and then works the barrier. Mrs Barlow is escorted inside while the man himself signs autographs, stops for selfies and chats to his fans. Charlie goes into meltdown as he gets closer towards us.

When he's right in front of us, Charlie lets out an ear-splitting shout. 'GARY!' Obligingly, he walks our way.

'All right?' he says to Charlie.

'Yes,' she breathes. 'I can't wait to see the show.'

'You know what, it should be a good one.'

He's so handsome close up and looks very debonair in his tuxedo. Even my heart goes all a-flutter and usually I'm quite content with cardboard cut-out Gary. For Charlie this is probably like achieving nirvana and I can understand why no ordinary man would live up to the standard he's set. She twists herself round for a selfie and he duly poses with her. Then he's off to the next set of fans to work his Barlow magic.

My friend tears her gaze away from his retreating back. 'That was good.' Understatement. Charlie sighs with happiness. She studies the resultant selfie and coos at it before she shows it to me and Nice Paul. It's a very good selfie. 'It's moments like that which make it all worthwhile,' she declares and hugs her phone to her chest.

And I get that now. It's such an adrenaline rush to touch the unattainable. Yet, despite the excitement, Nice Paul's expression is a little sad as he watches Charlie drool over her idol. I wonder if he's thinking will he ever have a chance with Charlie or whether she'll only ever have room for Gary Barlow in her life.

'We can go to dinner now,' Charlie announces. 'I can also die happy.'

'I'm going to skip off, if you don't mind,' I say to her. 'I'm tired and could do with an early night.'

'Wimp.' She kisses my cheek. 'Of course I don't mind. You'll miss Gary coming out though.'

'Take lots of pics,' I instruct. 'I'll live it vicariously through you. We'll catch up tomorrow.'

I kiss Nice Paul and he hugs me to him. I give him an extra squeeze. I want to tell him that it will all work out for him and Charlie, but I can't honestly see that happening. I hope I'm wrong.

Chapter Seventy

I buy a Cornish pasty at Euston station and a paper cup of luke-warm tea. Then I chug home on a train that stops at every damn station known to man. I think about calling Joe on the way home to tell him that our mission to see Mr Barlow was successful, but I remember that he's at work tonight and I don't want to bother him. They're still short-staffed and he's having to work extra shifts at the moment. I text him a little message instead to say that I'm on my way back but, as I expected, there's no reply.

I doze through some of the stations and I'm glad that I skipped out early on Charlie and Nice Paul as I'm completely knackered when I get to my granny annexe and it's not yet nine o'clock. I could do with a hot bath and a nice cup of tea. Actually, make that a large glass of red.

Not a moment too soon, I kick off my Converse. My feet are killing me and they need to be fully operational again before tomorrow's shift. A nice long soak should help to do the job. I start to run my bath, slopping in a good dollop of the posh bath foam that the ex bought me last Christmas. It doesn't have great associated memories, obvs, but it's a shame to let it go to waste.

In my bedroom, I kiss cardboard cut-out Gary. 'You're pretty hot in real life,' I tell him, but he doesn't seem impressed by my attention. So I strip off my grubby London clothes and slip into my dressing gown, pour myself a big glass of some cheap red that's already open and dig in the fridge until I find some chocolate. That's what's left of my night sorted.

I'm just about climb into the bath when my phone rings but, when I look at the display, I don't recognise the number. My first thought is to let it go to voicemail. So often these anonymous calls are trying to sell me something – and I neither require double glazing nor have the money for a new kitchen or funeral plan. But, call it instinct or something, this time I pick up.

Tom is on the other end of the line and he's sobbing. I can't even understand what he's saying, but my blood turns to ice and my stomach twists into a tight knot. For him to even consider ringing me, I know that this isn't good.

'What is it?' I say. 'What's wrong?'

'I didn't know what else to do,' he cries. 'I didn't know.'

'Are you hurt, Tom?'

'Yes. No.' More sobbing. 'A bit.'

'Are you at home?'

'No,' he says. 'I'm not.'

'Have you phoned your dad?' I realise that I sound as if I'm interrogating him, but I've no starting point to judge the gravity or otherwise of this.

'Yeah, but he's not answering his phone. Neither's Mum.' There's panic in his voice.

His tears are ripping my heart apart. It seems pointless trying to get any more information out of him over the phone as he's too distraught. I should just go and get him wherever he is. 'Where are you? Do you want me to come and get you?'

'Yes,' he manages. 'Yes, please.'

'Take a few deep breaths.' I hear him trying to calm himself down. 'Nice and easy.' When he's got his crying a bit more under control, I say, 'Now. Tell me where you are.'

'I'm not really sure.'

'OK. Describe to me what's around you.' Which he does. 'I think I know where you are. I'll be ten minutes. Hang on there. Try to stay calm. I won't be long.'

'Thank you, Ruby.' Tom's crying again, but his sobs aren't quite as heartbreaking. 'I didn't know what else to do.'

With one last look longingly at my lovely foam bath and my big glass of wine, I head out into the night to find him.

Chapter Seventy-One

It turns out that Tom's description of his location is pretty good. As I speed down the main grid road towards the city centre, I spot him sitting on the broad grass verge at the roadside. There's not much traffic about, so I pull up in the nearest layby, then jump out of the car to dash back to him. He's in one of the less salubrious areas and I wonder what he's doing up here.

'Tom!'

He stands up when he sees me and I feel relief flood through me even though I can see from here that he's got a black eye, a split lip and there's blood all over his T-shirt. I feel myself turn white. When I reach him, I hold him by his thin shoulders, looking him up and down, trying to assess the damage.

'What on earth's happened?'

'I've been mugged.' Tears run down his face. 'They took my bike, my money.' The floodgates open and he cries again.

Taking Tom in my arms, I rock him, making shushing noises. He feels so slight, insubstantial and it makes me realise that for all his attitude and posturing, he's still just a boy. 'It's all right,' I say. 'We'll sort it out.'

I don't want to panic him, but I really need to see where he's been hurt and how bad it is. When I've comforted him for a few minutes, I risk holding him away from me and ask, 'Where are you bleeding from? Can you show me?'

Tentatively, he lifts his T-shirt. His body is all white and angles. There are long scratch marks all over his skinny ribs and he looks like he's been attacked by a flipping tiger or something. The grazes are oozing blood, but, thankfully, they look much worse than they are, I think. His T-shirt must have ridden up during the attack or something as sharp nails have done this. I have another good look and they seem to be superficial and not deep. Though I'm hardly a medical expert.

'One of them threatened me with a screwdriver. They took my bike and my money. I've only got my phone because they dropped it.' The information comes out in gulping sobs and he shows me the phone. It's as battered and bruised as Tom is, the screen is completely shattered. 'They jumped me as I cycled through the underpass.' Our city is criss-crossed by a fabulous network of dedicated cycle paths which means that you can avoid the main roads, but they're not such great places at night – particularly for a kid on his own.

'How many?'

'Three of them.' He brushes fresh tears away with his arm. 'They pulled me off my bike and grabbed my stuff. They were punching and kicking me. I kicked them back, but I couldn't stop them.'

I think that he's probably been quite lucky if he was outnumbered like that. What if one of them had drawn a knife? I shudder at the thought. 'We should take you to the police station.'

'I want to go home,' he says.

I'm torn. If I was in his position I'd probably feel exactly the same. 'You might have vital evidence to help them to catch who did it.'

'I picked my phone up with a tissue I had in my pocket,' he says. 'In case there was a fingerprint on it.'

'Blimey. Good work.'

'I've also got a photo of them,' Tom says, helpfully. 'It's not the best. I took it as they rode off.'

'Seriously?' I'm not sure I could have managed such quick thinking in the same situation. 'You beauty!'

Tom shows me the phone again, but it's hard to see the image through the craze of broken glass. The lads who did this to him look as if they're in their late teens and you wonder what sort of people they are to do this.

I ruffle his hair gently and say, 'Good on you. Super sleuth.'

He laughs, but it's weak and watery. Then he cries again and sinks into my arms. 'It was horrible, Ruby. I didn't know what to do.'

'You've been really brave. To me it sounds as if you've handled it quite well,' I tell him as I stroke his hair from his eyes. 'But this is serious, Tom. We should definitely call the police.'

'Dad will kill me.'

'I think that's the least of your worries. Can I ring them?'

Tom nods, reluctantly. 'OK.'

So I punch in 999 and the call-handler tells me that they'll have a car with us straight away which makes me think that I've done the right thing.

'I shouldn't even have been up here,' Tom says, shamefaced – which comes as no surprise to me. 'I'm supposed to be looking after Daisy while Dad's at work.'

'Is that who you got my number from?' He nods. 'Is she at home on her own?'

'I thought she'd be OK.' He goes into petulant mode again. 'I've only been out for an hour. Two at the most. I wanted to meet my mates at the city. She didn't mind.'

But his dad will. I think Joe's going to be a bit more cross than I thought. 'Oh, Tom.'

'I was heading home,' he protests. 'And I've checked that she's OK. Twice.'

'Have you phoned your dad?'

'Dad didn't answer his phone. Mum's having a romantic weekend away with her bloke. Another one. It wasn't even worth trying her. She's never around now.' I can't help but hear the bitterness in his voice. 'I didn't know who else to call.'

'Well, I'm glad you phoned me.'

'Dad will go ballistic, won't he?' Tom turns frightened eyes to me. 'If this hadn't happened I'd have been home in loads of time. He would never have known.'

'For future reference, parents have a way of knowing. I'm sure he'll be more worried than angry.' Which makes me realise just how worried I am about Tom too. 'What time is he due home?'

'Not till eleven.' That's not too long. He hangs his head. 'This is the first time he trusted me to look after Daisy. I'm gonna be grounded for ever!'

'I'll try him again. Do you want to wait in the car?'

'I might bleed on your seat.'

'It doesn't matter. It's better than standing out here.' I help Tom to walk, but I think he's shocked rather than hurt and I don't want him to faint. He's definitely looking a bit green.

When he's settled in the passenger seat, I punch Joe's number into my phone as I sit on the kerb next to Tom. This time he answers straight away.

'Hi, Ruby. This is an unexpected pleasure.'

'Not exactly a pleasure,' I tell him. 'Now I don't want you to panic,' I sound as calm as I possibly can, 'but Tom's been involved in a bit of an incident.'

Of course, Joe panics immediately. 'What kind of incident? What's happened? Is he all right? Is he hurt?'

'He's OK.' I decide to give him scant details so that he doesn't jump straight in his car and drive here like a maniac and we end up with two incidents. 'He's had his bike stolen. Can you leave work?'

'My cover doesn't take over for another hour and I can't leave the place unattended. It's too risky. I'll ring and see if they can come in early. Tom's definitely all right?'

'Yes, just a bit shaken. We can explain it all when we see you. We're just waiting for the police.'

'Police?'

'There was a scuffle too.' That doesn't quite describe the ordeal that Tom's been through, but it will do for now. 'They're coming to take details. Don't worry. He's fine. Shaken, that's all.'

'Why didn't he ring me?'

'He did. If you check your phone you've probably got a missed call from him.'

'And Gina?'

'Away for the weekend.'

'Of course,' he mutters.

'Tom was sensible enough to get my number from Daisy and I came straight here.'

'Thanks, Ruby,' Joe says. 'I owe you.'

'Just get here as soon as you can.' I tell Joe where we are.

'He's where? What the hell is he doing up there at this time of night?' I can feel his fury coming down the phone.

'We can also talk about that when you get here.'

We both hang up. Tom looks at me gratefully.

'That wasn't too bad. He'll understand.'

'I've really fucked up, haven't I?' he say, woefully.

I consider offering some platitudes but, instead I say, 'Yeah.

It's not the end of the world though. You're relatively unharmed. Apart from the great shiner you'll have tomorrow.'

Tom risks touching his swollen eye and winces. 'Thanks for coming to get me, Ruby.'

'Not a problem. You did the right thing,' I tell him. 'And with your quick thinking, the police have a chance of catching who did it.'

'I'd like my bike back,' he says woefully. 'And a new phone.'

There'll come a time when Tom realises that, after an attack like that, escaping with only a stolen bike and a broken phone is actually a small price to pay. It makes me feel nauseous to think it, but what happened could have turned out so much worse.

Chapter Seventy-Two

Less than ten minutes later, a squad car pulls up. They go through the details with Tom and then we both get in the car and drive round the nearby streets in case we see the thugs on his bike, but we don't. After that, we're asked to accompany them to the station so they can take DNA swabs and check if there's anything useful that can be gleaned from the photos on Tom's phone.

Joe hasn't yet arrived, so I call and let him know that he should meet us there. We head down to the station in my car. In the passenger seat, Tom lets his head go back and he closes his eyes. He looks exhausted.

At the station, we sit together in the waiting room – Tom getting paler by the minute.

'Do you feel sick?'

'A bit,' he admits.

'What about that eye? Is it hurting?'

'Throbbing,' he says. I move his fringe aside to have a proper look. His eyebrow is cut and is thick with dried blood. 'We'll put some ice on it as soon as you're home and get you some painkillers.'

'Thanks, Ruby.'

Maybe we need to take him to A&E to get him checked over, but that will be Joe's call.

Then Joe arrives and he has a face like thunder until he sees the state that Tom is in, then he crumbles. Tom stands up on shaky legs and Joe takes his son into his arms and crushes him into a bear hug.

'I'm sorry, Dad,' Tom says, crying again.

'No harm done. But you and I need to have a talk when this is sorted.'

Tom nods.

'They want to take DNA swabs,' I tell Joe. 'They'll be with us shortly. Is Daisy still at home alone?'

Joe shakes his head. 'I phoned her and told her to go next door and wait for us. We'll pick her up when we get back. Neither of them are going to make school tomorrow.'

An officer arrives and takes Joe and Tom into the depths of the station. So I wait round, drinking tepid brown water that's supposed to be tea from a vending machine, until the police have finished with Tom.

Midnight has long gone when they both reappear and relief lifts my heart. I feel grimy from just sitting here.

'How did it go?'

'Tom gave really good descriptions of the lads,' Joe tells me. 'The pictures aren't great but it seems they might be known to the police already. That might help to catch them.'

'Are you feeling OK?' I ask Tom.

'Knackered.' He does look fit to drop. 'Every time I move my mouth, my lip splits open too.' There's fresh blood there when he touches it.

'Let's go home,' Joe says and takes my hand. 'This has been too much excitement for one night.'

'Should we go to A&E?'

'I don't think so. I'm not sure either of us could stand it now. I've had a good look at him. I think he'll live to fight another day.' He hugs his son to him and Tom winces, but bears it stoically.

'I'll be off,' I tell him. 'Glad there's not too much damage done.'

'Come back with us,' Joe says. 'We at least owe you tea and toast.'

'I wouldn't say no to that,' I admit.

I watch Tom and Joe as they walk across the car park, Joe's sturdy arm slung round his son's slight shoulders. I hope that Tom has learned his lesson from this awful experience. Then I jump into my own car and follow them back to the house.

Chapter Seventy-Three

I take Tom inside while Joe goes to collect Daisy from their neighbour's house.

'Do you want something to drink?'

He nods.

'Hot chocolate would be my go-to drink at moments like these,' I tell him.

He tries not to smile and split his lip open again, but there's a glimmer of one. 'Cool.' Tom eases himself into a chair at the kitchen table, clearly hurting all over. 'There's some in the top cupboard.' He points in the general direction and, with a bit of rummaging, I find it.

'A nice hot shower will make you feel better too. Get all that blood off you.'

Then he puts his head on his arms and bursts into tears. I abandon the chocolate and go to comfort him.

'Hush, hush. It's all done now.' I sit down next to him and stroke his hair. 'It'll all seem better in the morning.'

'Nothing's been right since Mum left,' he sobs. 'I keep wishing she'd come back.'

That brings a lump to my throat.

'How could she leave *us* for *him*? Mums don't do that. There's nothing wrong with Dad either. Some of my friend's dads are real knobs, but my dad's not. He's OK. What does she want?'

'Sometimes people just fall out of love,' I offer as I hold him tightly. Yet I realise that it sounds rubbish. 'Of course, you're going to miss her, but she's still your mum.'

They all act so hard and grown-up, yet inside they're still frightened children who want their mother and my heart goes out to him. It's been an awful trauma for him and no one can make him better like a mum can.

I hear the front door open and Tom quickly wipes his eyes on his filthy, bloodied T-shirt. A few seconds later, Joe comes in the kitchen with Daisy. She bursts into tears when she sees the extent of Tom's injuries. I move over so that she can wrap her arms round him.

'I told you not to go out, idiot,' she wails.

He doesn't argue back.

'I'll put some toast on,' Joe says. 'I don't know about you lot, but I'm starving.'

I have a hollow feeling in the pit of my stomach too. I'm not sure that it's hunger, but giving it some toast can't hurt.

So I pitch in and make hot chocolate for Tom and Daisy while Joe fiddles with bread. Joe and I have tea when I really think that at least a double Jacky D is in order. The night has left its mark on all of us.

Joe makes a monster pile of toast and we all sit at the table tucking into it – poor Tom wincing every time it touches his lip. If it wasn't for what had gone before, this would be quite a pleasant interlude. I look around the table and think that I'd very much like to be a part of this family. Joe is such a strong and stable presence that he makes me feel safe and I can't say that I've felt like that before. The kids seem more accepting of me and, while I wouldn't have wished this to happen in a million years, it has helped to form some sort of tentative bond between me and Tom. At least, I hope so. When he needed me, I was there for him. I'm optimistic that counts for something.

Then Joe notices that the kids are both yawning, heads drooping towards the table. 'Time for bed, you two,' he says.

'Can I have a shower first, Dad?' Tom asks. 'I feel horrible.'

'Yeah. Do you need any help?'

Tom shakes his head. 'I can manage.'

Pushing away from the table, I say, 'I should be going.'

'You can't drive now.' Joe grabs my hand. 'It's late and you must be as tired as the rest of us. Stay.'

'Are you sure?' He doesn't say as much, but he's probably intending that one of us takes the sofa. Right at this very moment, even that seems preferable to getting in my car. My eyes are barely open. I'd need matchsticks if I was going to try and drive.

'Stay,' Daisy urges. 'Dad says we don't have to go to school tomorrow.'

Joe picks up the last piece of toast. 'What time's your shift?'

'Not until late afternoon.'

'I'll make you a cooked breakfast to thank you for looking after my boy.'

I smile at him. 'That's definitely swayed me.'

'Good. That's settled.'

Daisy gives me a hug and I kiss her goodnight. Tom, all awkward again, kisses my cheek. 'Thanks, Ruby,' he mumbles.

'You're welcome.'

Joe flicks a thumb after them. 'I'll just go and see them both into bed. Won't be long.'

So I make myself useful and tidy up the kitchen. Despite being bone tired, I get a flutter of anticipation of what the night might bring while I'm stacking the dishwasher.

Finally, he comes back into the kitchen and he looks grey

with exhaustion. For the first time this evening, Joe and I are left alone.

'Are they OK?'

'Daisy's already asleep and Tom had another good cry. It's going to take a while for him to get over this. It's a shock to the system. Plus it makes him realise that he's not as tough and as streetwise as he thinks he is. Poor lad.' He sighs at me. 'I'm sorry, Ruby. I didn't really imagine our first night together to be quite like this.'

'Don't apologise. I can sleep on the sofa,' I tell him. 'We don't have to . . .'

He comes to take me in his arms. 'I think we do,' he murmurs against my neck. 'It would be the perfect distraction and there's a big, comfy, double bed waiting for us upstairs.'

'That does sound like bliss.'

So he takes me by the hand and I follow him up to his bedroom. I feel a bit strange being here and can see that the decoration has been chosen by Gina with the choice of duck-egg-blue wallpaper and matching bed linen. Yet I try not to think of her and Joe in here together.

'Thanks for all you did for Tom tonight,' he says. 'It means a lot.'

'Not a problem. I'm just sorry that something like that had to happen. It can be a horrible world now. He's learned a harsh lesson by being in the wrong place at the wrong time.'

'Yeah. I'll read him the riot act another day for leaving the house when I told him not to. But he's home and he's safe. That's all that matters.'

'Have you heard from Gina?'

Joe shakes his head. 'No. I left a message on her phone. I hope she rings Tom first thing in the morning. He's hurting. Maybe she's got a poor signal where they are. They've gone to Devon or Cornwall for the weekend or somewhere. I can't remember what she said. This country though, at least.' He rolls his eyes. 'I've never known anyone to need so many romantic mini-breaks. And all I'm offering you is a night of passion in downtown Milton Keynes.'

That breaks the ice and we both laugh. 'I think I can cope with that.'

Then Joe take me in his arms and kisses me. All thought of the last few hours, the ex-wife and the fact that I don't even have a toothbrush with me, fly out of my head and it's just us, here and now.

He takes me to bed and makes love to me slowly and tenderly. I feel so emotional and exhausted that, afterwards, tears roll down my face. Joe wipes them away and holds me tightly against his chest until my crying subsides. Then we settle to go to sleep with him spooned around me and the sound of his steady breath against my hair.

Before I finally surrender to sleep, I think briefly of Mason Soames and how very different this is. With Joe, I realise that I actually feel loved – or something that comes very close to it. Surely no one can make me feel like this without meaning it. He snuggles in closer and I lose myself in the weight of his embrace.

Chapter Seventy-Four

Oh, shit, fuck, bugger. An alarm is going off by my ear and when I open my eyes, for a moment, I have no idea where I am. Then I hear Joe muttering and he reaches over me to switch it off. Turning towards him, I wonder if I've got mascara tracks down my face as the last thing on my mind was taking my make-up off.

'Morning,' he says, sleepily.

'Morning.'

'Forgot to turn the alarm clock off.'

That, I'd gathered. 'Have I got panda eyes?'

'Yes. But I've always had a thing for pandas.' He reaches for me under the sheet and pulls me close. I mould into him and his hand caresses my breast then slides between my legs. 'The kids won't get up for ages,' he whispers against my lips as he kisses me. 'I don't see why we should be in a rush either.'

So we make love again and this time it's even more sweet, caring and sensuous. I'd be quite happy to have sex like this for the rest of my life. I have no idea what Gina's new man is like but, quite frankly, he's going to have to go some to beat this. The woman must be mad.

Eventually, we hear the kids stirring and we go into Joe's en suite and take a shower together. A shower that takes rather longer than it should.

I borrow a T-shirt from Joe, put my pants on inside out and rub round my teeth with toothpaste on my finger. Skanky, I know, but what can I do? I'll have to change when I get home.

'I promised you breakfast,' Joe says, 'and I'm a man of my word.'

I touch his arm before he leaves the room. 'Thanks for last night.'

'The pleasure was all mine,' he teases.

'It felt nice,' I say sincerely – which is the biggest compliment I can give him.

He wraps his arms round me. 'You're the first woman, other than Gina, that I've slept with in many a long year. Thanks for not making me feel like an idiot.'

I toy with the buttons on his shirt and it takes all my strength not to start opening them again. He stays my hand. 'Time for breakfast, madam.'

'Sounds wonderful.'

'Come on,' he says. 'I need to face up to the kids and I'd rather we were in the kitchen than coming out of the bedroom together. I don't mind them knowing that Daddy had a sleepover, but I'd rather it was on my terms.'

'You think they'll be OK about it?'

'We'll soon find out.'

So we go downstairs and I'm put on toast duty while Joe gets the necessary bits together for our fry-up. We're working quite well as a lean, mean breakfast-making team when the kids emerge. Tom's black eye is livid purple and his lip is swollen. He's moving like a zombie from *The Walking Dead*.

'How are you doing, champ?' Joe asks, gently ruffling his son's hair as he passes.

'I hurt,' Tom complains, smoothing it down again as best he can. 'I hurt all over.'

'I have the cure for that,' Joe says cheerily and cracks eggs into a pan. 'One full English coming up. It will put hairs on your chest and lead in your pencil.'

Tom grimaces. 'Gross.'

Daisy, clad in pink 'I'm a Princess Get Over It' pyjamas, raises one hand in greeting. 'Hey.' It looks as if several birds have nested in her hair overnight.

They both slide into seats at the table and busy themselves on their phones. That, so it seems, is the full glare of attention that my first night in their family home warrants. Perhaps it was better happening like this than us both making a big fuss about it. Whichever way, I'm certainly glad that it did. I have a little bubble of happiness around me. While Joe multi-tasks with the breakfast, he winks at me and I smile back. First hurdle jumped, I guess.

We eat breakfast together and then Joe checks over Tom's injuries again and decides that a family outing to A&E isn't necessary. His wounds seem to look worse than they are and he's given painkillers and a coating of antiseptic cream. So Tom collapses onto the sofa in front of the television while Daisy is cajoled into helping with the clearing up. I'm just stacking the dishwasher when the doorbell goes. Tom, washing the grill pan in the sink, wipes his hands on the towel and heads to the door.

The next moment, a woman who can only be Gina bursts into the room. She's beautifully groomed in tight white capri pants, a black shirt and gold heels even though it's eleven o'clock on a Monday morning. She has Aviator shades perched on top of her long, glossy black hair.

'Where is he?' she says, breathlessly. 'Where's my baby?' Then she pulls up short when she sees me. 'Who the hell are you?'

Joe is at her shoulder, his face dark with suppressed anger. 'This,' he says, 'is my friend, Ruby.'

'Oh.' Gina looks me up and down and is clearly not enamoured by what she sees. I, in turn, am wishing that I had on designer clothes or at least not her husband's band T-shirt and yesterday's pants. Some make-up wouldn't go amiss either. I probably bear the look of a thoroughly shagged woman. Which I am. Stick that in your pipe, Gina the Ex.

Joe adds, 'She came to Tom's rescue last night.'

'Did she now?' She scowls at me and I'm glad that looks are actually unable to kill or I'd be a goner. Gina turns her attention to Joe. 'And where were you when our boy was in trouble?'

'At work,' he says calmly. 'Where were you?'

She purses her lips at that and is rescued from making further comment by the appearance of the walking-wounded Tom.

'Hi, Mum,' he says and is instantly swept into Gina's embrace.

'My baby, my baby,' she coos, then bursts into tears and cries all over him.

'I'm OK.' He tries to wriggle loose. 'Just don't hold me that tight, it hurts.'

She holds him away from her and exclaims, 'I couldn't bear it if anything happened to you. I came as soon as I could.'

Nobody points out that they've been trying to get hold of her for the last twelve hours or more, but it hangs in the air. Try as I might, I can't imagine Joe being with this glamorous but brittle woman. He's so down-to-earth and caring yet, even standing here with her broken son, she seems to want all the attention.

Not to be left out, Daisy goes and twines herself round her mother. 'My darling,' Gina purrs. 'How I miss you both.'

Joe looks at me over her head and raises his eyebrows.

'I should go,' I say. 'I'm in work later.'

Joe nods tightly.

How things change in an instant. It was all going so well and, despite me being the one who Tom turned to in his hour of need, I now definitely feel superfluous to requirements.

'I'll walk you to the door,' Joe says, embarrassed.

I hold up a hand. 'No need.'

'I'll call you later.'

Gina takes a moment from fussing over her son to shoot me another black look. Bitch.

Picking my bag up, I head to the door and close it softly behind me. I sit in the car in Joe's drive, gripping the steering wheel and I could cry. It was all so lovely and then, as quick as a flash, I'm suddenly outside of this tight little unit and by myself.

And I realise with blinding clarity that this relationship is never going to be anything but difficult.

Chapter Seventy-Five

I work my shift, telling Charlie everything that happened last night and this morning in short snippets whenever we manage to cross at the bar.

'She sounds like a bagful of trouble,' is Charlie's assessment and I fear she may be right.

'We had such a great night,' I whisper over my two plates of harissa lamb with minted couscous for table four. 'Why did she have to come back and spoil it all?'

'That's the job of ex-wives,' she says, sagely.

Joe hasn't called me and that has my stomach in knots. I'm feeling mean-spirited and disgruntled. I really, really want to see Joe again. Preferably tonight, wrapped up in the warmth of his arms. Well, it looks like that's not going to happen, is it? Sigh.

When I've finished moaning about Gina, Charlie tells me all about her dinner with Nice Paul and how they went back to the theatre and managed to catch The Barlow coming out. Her night, it seems, was more uniformly successful than mine.

We finish work a bit early as there aren't many people eager to be in the Butcher's Arms on a Monday night, which I'm grateful for. My feet are killing me and the lack of sleep from last night is definitely catching up with me.

Charlie is in a rush to leave. 'I'll catch you tomorrow, chick,' she says and heads for the door. 'I've got an appointment with a forum.'

'Laters,' I say and, as she's leaving with more haste than usual, I wonder if Nice Paul is part of it.

While I'm getting my bag out of the staffroom, I hear a noise behind me which makes me jump. When I turn, Mason Soames is leaning on the door frame.

'You look like shite, Brown,' he says.

'Your chat-up lines might need a bit of work, Mason. They're slipping.'

'What have you been up to?' He pouts at me like a lost little boy. 'I never see you now.'

'I'm always here,' I point out.

'Drink wine with me. Tell me your troubles.'

'You *really* don't want to hear them,' I say.

'I can pour you a decent glass of red here or we could go back to my place where I have lots and lots of wine.'

'This is a pub,' I counter. 'You can't have more wine than here.'

'Semantics,' he bats back.

I'm not ready to go home alone, yet I know that I can't go back to Mason's place. I really want to be held tonight and I know that if I go with Mason it will involve so much more than that. Yet my stupid, tired and easily affected heart says, 'Ooo, he's handsome, let's get cosy with him,' while my brain says, 'Stay out of trouble, Ruby. Whatever he says, go home now.' I need to stay away from this man. It's ridiculous, but he's like catnip to me. I'm starting to care more about Joe and I don't want to hurt him in the way that we've both been hurt before. This is the time to cut all ties with Mason. Except for our professional ones.

'I can see you positively quivering with indecision.' He comes towards me but I hold up a hand.

'Don't, Mason. I'm over-tired, my defences are weak and I definitely should be by myself.'

'But I *love* it when your defences are weak,' he protests which makes me laugh.

'There's something else too.'

When I hesitate, he says, 'I'm all ears.'

I guess there's no point beating about the bush. 'Joe, the bloke I was seeing? Well, it's more serious now. Sort of,' I tell him, frankly, and am surprised to see his face fall.

'Since when?'

'For a little while now. On and off. It's complicated.'

'Ah, that old chestnut.'

I decide to be honest with him. 'I really like you, Mason. Sometimes I like you a lot. I simply don't have the energy for all your sexual hijinks. I'm too old for it. Swinging from the chandeliers is all very well for a short time. You're young and full of fun, which is lovely, and I thought it was what I needed to get over my broken heart. But it's not. I'm looking to settle down and I might have a good chance with this man.'

Mason doesn't look that impressed by my candid assessment of the situation. 'So, who is he?'

'That doesn't matter,' I say. 'You don't know him.'

'You love him?'

'I think so.' This is the first time that I've admitted it to myself. But I might do. I might just love Joe.

Mason blows out an unhappy breath. 'God, Brown. I thought you and I were going to get it on.'

I never know with Mason whether he's joking or not. I decide to play it as if he's not. 'I need someone to rely on,' I tell him, sincerely, even though I probably don't owe him this level of openness. 'There are some nights that I just want to be held.'

'I can do that,' Mason says earnestly and, for a moment, I believe that he really means it. There's a catch in his voice when he adds, 'I can be that person. Give me a chance.'

I shake my head as I pick up my bag. 'We've had fun together, Mason. That's all it was, though. I thought I could do that, but I can't. When it comes down to it, I'm not in love with you and you're not in love with me.'

'I could be,' he says.

'I don't think so.' I push open the door to the bar.

'Don't go now! I'm baring my soul to you. Don't walk out on me, Brown,' he says. 'Let's talk about it. Let me *hold* you, for fuck's sake!'

Smiling, I head for the door. 'Nice try, Mason. But it will never work for us.'

So I go home, drink *two* big glasses of wine and lie down in bed next to cardboard cut-out Gary Barlow and cry myself to sleep.

Chapter Seventy-Six

I don't hear from Joe. All week. Not a sausage.

Monday   nothing

Tuesday – nothing. Though I fully expected a call.

Wednesday – still nothing. I could call him, but I'm not going to. It's a point of principle. He should have called me. Preferably as soon as Gina left. Isn't that the done thing?

Thursday – more nothing. Despite chanting all day 'He will ring' – a mantra that I read in a clearly flipping useless self-help book.

Friday – even more nothing. You'd have thought, at least, he could have phoned me to let me know how Tom was getting on after all I did for him. Bastard.

Saturday – acres and acres of bloody nothing. He's not a bastard. I really like him. I might love him.

Sunday – nothing. I have a good cry. A properly good cry.

That's it. I'm done with men. No more Mason. No more Joe. Like Charlie, it's only Gary Barlow from now on.

Chapter Seventy-Seven

If Joe doesn't call by tomorrow, I'm going to ring him. Something might be horribly wrong.

Chapter Seventy-Eight

Joe calls me. My heart soars. I try not to run round the living room doing a happy dance when he does. Instead, I say, 'Hi,' too brightly as if he's some kind of long-lost friend rather than a boyfriend who hasn't phoned when he maybe should have.

'I'm sorry I've not been in touch,' he says and he sounds so weary that I want to rush to him and give him the biggest hug there is.

'Are you OK?'

Long pause. 'I've had a lot going on.'

When there's nothing more forthcoming, I try to stay upbeat and ask, 'How's Tom doing? Recovering from his ordeal?'

'Getting there,' Joe says.

'That's good to hear. Give him and Daisy my love.'

'Can we meet up for a coffee tomorrow?' It's clear that he doesn't want small talk today. 'If you're free.'

'I start work at twelve, but I could do ten-ish.'

'I'll be working, but do you want to come up to the café at Sunshine Meadows?'

'Yeah, that's fine.' It means it will be a bit of a snatched meeting, but that's better than nothing. 'Look forward to it.'

'See you tomorrow, Ruby.'

When he hangs up, I do run round the living room doing a happy dance.

Chapter Seventy-Nine

I fly up to Sunshine Meadows with wings on my feet. Well, I drive, in my clapped-out Mazda, but that doesn't sound nearly as wonderful. It's a glorious day. The sort of day that we should all stop what we're doing and head to the beach. The sort of day where we should eat fish and chips and ice-cream and drink Pinot Grigio by the pint. Perhaps Joe and I can take the kids somewhere by the coast one weekend before the summer is over. It would be nice to get away for a few days together if we can. Finances are tight for both of us, but a couple of nights in a basic B&B shouldn't break the bank. It's a long time since I've felt sand in my toes and I can just visualise long romantic walks on the shore, hand-in-hand with Joe.

I've made an effort with my appearance today. A flippy, floaty summer dress in pastel shades, dainty sandals, a straw sunhat. I'm doing Earth Mother plus Felicity Kendal meets Festival Grunge and I feel fabulous, light of heart, mood sunny and bright. I'll seriously frighten my colleagues if I turn up to work still feeling like this. Charlie won't recognise me.

There's no gardening going on today when I arrive, instead the residents are relaxing in the garden, chatting and reading.

There are a few blankets spread out on the grass and it's the perfect spot for a picnic lunch. It all looks so pretty here with an array of colourful flowers out in full force – I've no idea what as, by now, you know I'm totally not green-fingered, but they look great. If I had a garden this is the vibe I'd want.

Then I spot Joe over in a corner under the shade of a tree that's out in white blossom. He's lying stretched out on his side on the grass, sunglasses on his head, and looks hotter than hell. When I get closer, I can see that he's showing two of the young women who live here how to make daisy chains and I get a rush of affection for him. I stand to one side where he can't see me and watch for a moment as with his big, strong fingers he makes little holes in the stem of one daisy before threading through another. His pupils watch with rapt attention, tongues out in concentration as they follow his moves. He smiles paternally at them both, guiding their efforts and high-fiving them when they get it right. The women are happy, giggly and are clearly quite smitten with him. I know how they feel.

I step into the shade of the tree with them. 'Hi, there. Can I join you?'

'Take a seat,' Joe says and I sit on the grass cross-legged with them. 'This is Stella and Kate. Ladies, this is my friend Ruby.'

'I like your dress,' Kate says.

'Thank you.'

'We've made three chains,' Stella says. 'It's not easy.'

'Looks like you've made a great job, though.'

She beams with pride.

'I haven't done this for years.' I pick some daisies and start to thread them myself.

'Gently,' Joe instructs. 'You don't want to crush the stems.'

I grin at him. 'I have to say that I'm very impressed by your talent.'

308

'You can't have a daughter called Daisy and not be an expert in the art of making daisy chains. I am practically Jedi,' he boasts.

The more I see of this man, the more I like him. I can just imagine him sitting patiently with Daisy as a toddler showing her how to do this. Sweet.

We make a few more chains and I fix circles of the flowers on Stella and Kate's hair. I drape them round their necks and fasten them to their wrists. Now I'm getting into the swing of this, it's all coming back to me.

'We need to make more,' Kate says. 'For everyone.'

'I'm not sure we have that many daisies,' Joe says. 'But you keep going. I need to leave you lovely ladies. Ruby and I want to have a chat.'

'Aww.' Stella and Kate pull faces.

'I'll be back later,' he says. 'You could show some of the others what to do now that you're so good at it. I'm sure Maggie and Lou would like to learn.'

'Yeah,' Stella shouts enthusiastically. 'Let's show them, Kate.'

'Ask them nicely,' Joe says.

'OK.' And they bound off in search of willing pupils to show off their new skill.

'You have some nice people here,' I say when we've watched them go.

'Stella and Kate came in about five years ago at more or less the same time. They're inseparable. They do really well.' Then he looks at me wryly. 'With only the occasional meltdown.' He takes my arm and even the touch of his hand on my skin thrills me. 'Let's get a drink.'

We go over to the terrace of the café where we went last time and, as it's so hot, we eschew coffee and both have fruit smoothies. The hit of fresh berries is sharp on my tongue and, languidly, I wipe away the condensation that runs down the glass.

Away from the ladies and our daisy chains, there's a change in Joe's demeanour. He puts his sunglasses on and stares out into the garden, not looking at me. The sun goes behind a cloud for moment and it makes me shiver.

Then Joe turns towards me and I can tell by the expression on his face that something is terribly wrong.

Chapter Eighty

'There's no easy way to say this, Ruby.' His hands grip the edge of the table and I feel my heartbeat thud in my chest. He blows out an unhappy breath. 'After all that happened with Tom we've been in turmoil as a family.'

'I can understand that,' I say. 'It's perfectly normal. He must have been traumatised.'

Joe nods. 'Thank you again for helping out. It was fantastic of you and I'm grateful that you had my back. I should have sent you flowers or something afterwards, but . . . well . . .'

'That doesn't matter. I did it for you, for Tom. I'm just glad that I could be there. In a weird way, I felt that it helped the children to see that I am actually a nice person. Hopefully, they'll be happier that I'm in their lives now.'

'That's what I wanted to talk to you about.' Suddenly, he looks as if he has the weight of the world on his shoulders and my stomach flips over. 'Seeing Tom like that has made Gina re-think her priorities. She's been round every day since.' He's uncomfortable when he continues. 'Not just to see Tom, but to see me too.' Joe is wrestling every word out. 'She realises that she's been missing the children.'

I'm too stunned to point out that she's had a very funny way of showing it.

'We've been talking a lot,' he adds, flatly. 'Some of it round in circles.'

My head is spinning too. I'm not liking the way this conversation is going and I don't know why. But my anxiety is growing and I'm apprehensive about what Joe will say next. I wait for what feels like an aeon.

'The upshot of it all is that she'd like to give it another go.' He runs a hand over the shadow of stubble on his chin. 'Give *us* another go.'

I feel as if I've been punched in the stomach. Out of all of the scenarios, this is the one that I could have least imagined. It's only natural that Gina would be wanting to cling to her son after what had happened, but I thought she was too happy, too loved-up with her new man to return home. It seemed as if she'd flown the family nest for good. Try as I might, I can't get my head round it. Does she think she can walk back in, just like that?

When I fail to speak, Joe pleads, 'Say something.'

But I'm not sure that I have the power of speech. I open and close my mouth a few times but nothing comes out.

'I have to do this,' Joe presses on. 'For the kids' sake. They want their mum back. You must see that.'

When I finally find my voice, I say, 'So let me get this straight. She walks out on you, on her family, makes scant effort to see her children and then, when she decides that all in the garden of love isn't rosy and she might be missing out on something, she clicks her fingers and strolls right back in again as if nothing's happened?'

Joe sighs. 'That pretty much sums it up.'

'And you're happy about that?' Outwardly, I sound calm but inside my heart is shattering into a thousand pieces.

'No.' He uses those strong fingers, so recently making delicate daisy chains, to massage his forehead. 'Of course not. I've hardly had a wink of sleep this week going over everything time and time again.'

He certainly looks anguished. 'Do you still love her?'

'I don't know,' he says, honestly. 'We've been together for so long, we have history. Should we throw it away if there's a chance we can salvage what we had? We're still married. Even though she left me for someone else, we've never actually finalised divorce proceedings.'

Fool that I am, I thought that was simply a matter of logistics rather than emotion.

'I have to do this.' Joe looks as wretched as I feel. 'Don't you see? Gina and I have a lot of work to do and I don't think for a minute it will be easy, but I feel as if I have to try for the sake of the family. If we can salvage something from the wreckage, then we have to give it a go.'

Noble words and, frankly, it's nothing less than I would expect from Joe.

'Daisy's only thirteen. It's a difficult age for a girl – you'll know that more than me. I know she'd be better off if her mum was home again. Neither of the kids like shuttling between houses, but it affects Daisy most of all. She needs Gina to be around for her.'

The sun's beating down on my head again, my neck, my shoulders, making me feel queasy.

'This isn't really about what I want, Ruby. You know that.' His fingers find mine across the table. 'In different circumstances, I think we could really have made a go of this.'

I get a flashback to our bodies entwined on the only night we spent together, the warmth and affection between us, the passion and, foolishly, I hoped for a lifetime of that. And not just *that*. Not simply the physical stuff. I like Joe, I *love* Joe

– his strength, his honesty, his kindness. Even now while he's trying to let me down gently, I admire him all the more for it. Where will I find all that again? What will I do without him? How can I admit that I never really had him at all?

Slow tears squeeze out of my eyes, when I really don't want them to.

'Oh, Ruby. Don't cry.' He thumbs away the tears from my cheek. 'Please don't cry.'

'I can't help it.' I'm already grieving for what I nearly had. I know I could have loved him more than his wife. I could have loved him better. But she's had his children and those ties can never be broken.

'Will it help if I tell you that I do love you?'

'No,' I say with a wavering sigh. 'I really don't think that it does.'

'You'll find someone. A man who's worthy of you. You're a wonderful woman.' He strokes my hand softly, tenderly and it breaks my heart. I'd give anything to have one last night, one last day with him. For it not to end here, like this.

Yet there's nothing else that can be said. Gina is taking up her place again in the family unit and I'm out in the cold. There's no point asking if we can still be friends as I couldn't bear it.

Standing, I pick up my bag. 'I hope it works out for you.' I sound so brave, that I almost believe it myself.

Joe stands too and, I can't help myself, I go to him and he takes me in his arms. He holds me tight, rocking me against him and I let my tears flow. He kisses my hair, strokes my face and I feel that I'll never be able to let him go.

When we've stood there for too, too long locked in our final embrace, unwilling to let go, he eventually says, 'Goodbye, Ruby.'

'Goodbye, Joe. Give my love to the kids.'

Then before I lose my dignity completely, I walk away. I get in my car and somehow, through a blur of tears, manage to drive round the corner until I'm out of sight of Sunshine Meadows. Then I pull to the side of the road and I cry and cry and cry until I feel that my eyeballs might drop out of my head.

Chapter Eighty-One

'Shit,' Charlie says when I tell her.

'Yeah.' I haven't gone into work as I can't stop crying. Mason will be hacked off with me but I couldn't care less. I may not have known Joe all that long, but I feel devastated.

Charlie came straight over and now we're sitting on the sofa bingeing on Take That DVDs. 'Gary will cheer us up,' she says, confidently.

So we watch the lads strut their stuff and sing along with them. I bawl my eyes out at all the sad songs – 'Back for Good, 'Love Ain't Here Anymore' and 'Pray' are particularly difficult. Though Charlie is slightly disappointed that I don't know all the lyrics off by heart.

'He told me he loves me,' I sob in Charlie's arms.

'Fucker,' is her verdict.

But Joe's not a fucker, he's a nice man and I've lost him.

We eat a tub of Ben & Jerry's each – Cookie Dough for Charlie, Baked Alaska for me – glug our way through a bottle of wine apiece, then scoff two bags of Thai Sweet Chilli Sensations and a bar of 70% Lindt.

Then, when that has made me feel no better, we send out

for pizza. Extra large ones. Hawaiian with extra pineapple for Charlie. Meaty Treat for me. And garlic bread. And coleslaw. Even though I don't even like coleslaw. We polish off the lot.

If this is comfort eating, it's not working. Charlie just wants to be sick and I still feel like crap.

Chapter Eighty-Two

Weeks go by. I haul myself through my shifts, struggling to find a smile even for the regulars who I like. Yet my tired heart hasn't stopped hoping for the call that says Joe has made a big mistake and it's me he wants after all. Yeah. Was that a pig I saw flying across the sky? Plus the weather has taken a turn for the worse and it's not like summer at all. It's more like December – cold with freezing rain. Even that's coming out in sympathy with me. No one should be this miserable in blazing sun.

Charlie shoots off straight after her shift as she's going to a concert with some of the people from her Take That forum including Nice Paul. I don't want to go home to my empty flat, so I hang around in the bar talking to Jay about nothing in particular and having a double espresso in the hope that an excess of caffeine might lift my flagging spirits.

Then Jay has to go off and tend to his accounts and I'm just thinking about gathering my stuff together when Mason comes in. He brushes the rain from his immaculate hair and strides across the bar towards me.

'Hey,' he says. 'I hoped to catch you.'

I hold up my hands. 'Consider me caught.'

He drops into the armchair opposite to me. 'I need to talk to you about the Christmas menu and possible events.'

'Get lost, Mason. It's not even August.'

'You know what it's like, the office parties will be beating the door down soon. We have to get ahead of the crowd.'

Even though I know he's right, I bat back, 'I don't want to talk about naffing Christmas. Come back to me in December. I might be in the mood by then.'

'Grouchy today, Brown,' he notes. 'And looking like a wet weekend in Weston-super-Mare, if you don't mind me saying.'

'Thanks. I *do* mind you saying.'

'Charlie said you'd been dumped.'

I look at him aghast. 'What?' All I can do is shake my head in disbelief. Wait until I see Charlie.

'Well, she may have dressed it up with more girlie words, but that was the gist of it. Is it true?'

'Yes,' I concur, 'I have been dumped.' From a great height.

He actually smiles. 'The good news is, I'm still available.'

'Whoop-de-doo.'

'You're lucky, Brown. I could have been snapped up. Only this week I took out Sherene Taylor from *Girls About Town*. She was very keen.'

'Really?' *Girls About Town* is a hideous reality show that Charlie and I are addicted to. Sherene is actually quite hot, but doesn't appear to have been allocated her fair share of brain cells. 'You're saying that I'm on a par with a Z-list celeb?'

'Look, I get it.' He sighs at me in an exasperated manner. 'Your heart's broken and all that guff, but come out with me. I'll take your mind off it. We can have some fun.'

'I'm not interested, Mason. I need to be left alone to lick my wounds.'

'I'm being serious, Brown.' He certainly looks like he is.

Mason's expression is earnest in the extreme. 'We always have a good time together.'

'Do we?'

'I know you think I'm superficial.'

'There are puddles that are deeper.'

He ignores my jibe. 'We can even do proper boyfriend and girlfriend stuff if that's what you like. Picnics in the park, long walks in the woods, mind-numbing marathon sex sessions. Oh wait, you've already told me that you "want to be held".' He makes quotation marks in the air which really gets on my nerves. 'Make that marathon *cuddling* sessions.'

I curl up in my armchair, defensively. 'If you're going to take the piss, I won't talk to you at all.'

'I'm not taking the piss, I'm pointing out the reality of your situation. Don't waste your time on someone who's not interested in you when there are plenty of guys – rather like my good self – who are.'

'I'm done with men,' I tell him and I mean it. 'I'm going to be happily single from now on.' Well, 'happily' might be stretching it a bit, at the moment. But, in the fullness of time, I will be happyhappyhappy again. 'Let's just confine ourselves to a purely professional relationship from now on. If you were the last man on earth I wouldn't go out with you.'

'Jeez, Brown. I just don't get you.' Mason stands up, shaking his head. He grabs his car keys from the table between us and marches into the backroom.

'I'm not sure that I get myself,' I say to his retreating back, but I don't think he hears me. My heart sinks. That was unnecessarily mean, but I'm hurting and Mason thinks that it's amusing to toy with my affections.

Still, I take his departure as my cue to gather up my stuff and go home. I don't want to face him again today even though I think Mason may have got the message now.

Chapter Eighty-Three

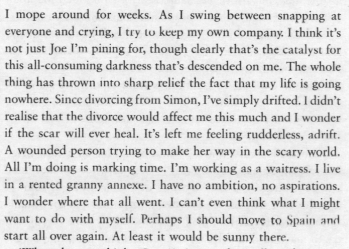

I mope around for weeks. As I swing between snapping at everyone and crying, I try to keep my own company. I think it's not just Joe I'm pining for, though clearly that's the catalyst for this all-consuming darkness that's descended on me. The whole thing has thrown into sharp relief the fact that my life is going nowhere. Since divorcing from Simon, I've simply drifted. I didn't realise that the divorce would affect me this much and I wonder if the scar will ever heal. It's left me feeling rudderless, adrift. A wounded person trying to make her way in the scary world. All I'm doing is marking time. I'm working as a waitress. I live in a rented granny annexe. I have no ambition, no aspirations. I wonder where that all went. I can't even think what I might want to do with myself. Perhaps I should move to Spain and start all over again. At least it would be sunny there.

'What do you think, Gary?' As usual, cardboard cut-out Gary Barlow has nothing to offer on the subject.

Plus, I spend my time talking to a cardboard cut-out of a boy band member. This is my life.

I need to get out of the house. I'm not working today, so I head into town to spend money that I don't have.

Drifting about, aimlessly, through the shopping centre, I pick up a few trinkets in Accessorize. Surely something sparkly might make me feel better. I'm just coming out of the shop, clutching my unnecessary purchase, when I catch sight of Tom and Daisy coming towards me through the throng of shoppers. Then, as I look up, following behind them I see Joe and Gina and all the breath leaves my body. They're hand-in-hand, both smiling widely. They are the very picture of a happy family.

He pulls her to him and kisses the top of her head. She beams up at him. A woman in love. This is heartbreaking. But only for me. They've clearly resolved their differences and are enjoying a second honeymoon. I'd like to be pleased for them, for the kids, but I just feel nauseous. Joe's forgotten me in an instant and I realise that I meant nothing to him after all.

And I'm trapped here. Any minute they'll be upon me and I have nowhere to go. What I'd like to do is turn and run, yet I'd draw even more attention to myself. I can't bolt back into the shop as I'd have to go right in front of them, but I don't want him to see me here. I *really* don't want him to see me. How could I bear to exchange bland pleasantries when inside I'm slowly dying?

With moments to spare, I scout round for an escape route but can see no way out. I'll just have to tough it out and hope that he's so loved-up that he won't notice me. Instead, I slowly crouch down behind the massive planter that's in the middle of the concourse with a palm tree sprouting of the top of it. I try to make myself very, very small. If I stay here, they might well pass by without spotting me.

Then, just as I think that I'm well hidden and that no one, in a million years, will ever notice me, a voice behind me says, 'What the hell are you doing, Brown?'

It's Mason. Of all the people, in all the world!

'Shush!' I say. 'Get down.'

He looks at me perplexed. As well he might be.

'Get down. Get down. I'm hiding.'

'Not very well, as it happens.' Nevertheless, he crouches next to me, his face close to mine and grins at me. 'I'm assuming there's a good reason for this.'

'What are you doing here?' I mutter at him. 'I didn't think you shopped where the proles shopped. I thought you went to Bond Street or something where the posh people get their retail therapy.'

'I normally do,' he concedes. 'Who knew I was missing out on so much?'

'Be quiet.' I watch as Joe draws level with me, unaware that I'm so close. My throat tightens and I grip the plant pot until my knuckles turn white.

'Is that him?' Mason fixes me with a stare. 'The one who broke your heart? Is that why you're hiding behind a big plant pot?'

'Yes,' I confess, miserably.

'Wow. He's not a bad looker,' Mason concedes. 'If I was that way inclined, I would.'

'Shut up.'

'Who's the woman? His new squeeze?'

'His wife,' I mumble.

'Wife?' Mason laughs. 'He's married? Oh, Brown. Schoolgirl error.'

'Yeah, well, he wasn't married when I started seeing him and then he was again. It's complicated.'

'He looks very happy.'

'Doesn't he?' I feel like crying. Yet I should be pleased that his family is reunited, that they've put the troubles they've had behind them. The kids will be happier, that's for sure. I hope Gina now appreciates how very lucky she is. Without even trying, I can still feel Joe's hands on my body, his mouth on mine, the comfort of his arms.

They continue walking past. Danger averted. I sit down heavily on the dirty floor.

'Bloody hell, Brown.' Mason frowns at me. 'You're in a bad way.'

'I know.' It's taking all my strength not to break down and weep. I feel as if I start crying then I might never stop.

'OK. What do women do when they're miserable?'

'Comfort eat. Get drunk. Talk to their mates.'

'Excellent,' he says. 'Let's do that.'

'It's a great idea, but I can't, Mason.'

'Why not? What else do you have planned?'

'Nothing,' I admit.

Mason hauls me to my feet. 'This isn't you, Brown. Let's get seriously pissed. Then you can dust yourself down and get on with your life.' He puts his hand gently on my cheek. 'I want to help,' he murmurs. 'Will you let me?'

I nod at him tearfully. So Mason puts his hand on my elbow and steers me out of the shopping centre. I don't know where we're going, I'm just grateful that it's away from Joe and his family.

Chapter Eighty-Four

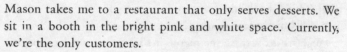

Mason takes me to a restaurant that only serves desserts. We sit in a booth in the bright pink and white space. Currently, we're the only customers.

I'm incapable of making a decision so Mason goes off to order for us both. While he's gone, I cry into the napkins and think how much Tom and Daisy would love it here. Then realise that I have to stop thinking like that or I'll go mad. Maybe I already am.

Our desserts arrive and Mason has ordered well. For me there's a classic banana split, filled with vanilla ice-cream, chopped nuts, chocolate sprinkles, and topped with toffee syrup, fudge cubes and a froth of whipped cream. Mason has an enormous knickerbocker glory which looks marginally more healthy than mine as, at least, it involves some fresh fruit. Strawberries are layered with chocolate and vanilla ice-cream, the obligatory overdose of fresh cream and strawberry syrup finished with a cherry and a wafer.

'Eat, Brown,' Mason instructs when I just sit there staring at it.

I push my tears back in and pick up my spoon. We don't

speak as we eat which is fine by me. I just sit here letting the coldness of the ice-cream give me brain-freeze.

When I finish my last mouthful, Mason says, 'Phase two. Come on.' He leaves a generous tip on the table, takes me by the hand and drags me down the street and into the nearest bar – one that's Cuban themed. It's normally bustling but, at this time in the day, there's just the tail-end of the lunchtime crowd.

We find bar stools. I feel so broken that I can hardly sit upright.

'What do you fancy?' Mason asks.

'Apart from unavailable men?'

He rolls his eyes and pushes the cocktail menu at me.

I stare at it, not really seeing anything. I can't even think what I'd like to drink.

'Shall I order for us again?'

'Yeah, sure.' I close the menu. 'As long as it involves lots of alcohol.'

Mason catches the attention of the barman. 'A Madhatter's Teapot, please.'

Salsa music blares out and the air smells of grilled chicken.

A huge teapot and two metal mugs arrive. Mason pours me a drink. 'Three different kinds of rum, passionfruit, lime. I can't remember what else is in there.'

Tentatively, I take a sip. 'Wow.' It nearly knocks my head off. 'This is lethal.'

Mason tries his. 'Tastes good though.'

'I'll be flat on my back in no time.'

'Excellent.' He grins cheekily at me and I can't help but smile back. You can't fault Mason for trying. 'Down the hatch!'

We clink mugs together.

As soon as we've knocked back the first mug, he tops us up from the teapot. The rum starts to numb my heart and loosen my tongue.

'Why are you interested in me?' I ask him.

'Because you're different, Brown,' he says, thoughtfully. 'You make me work hard for what little you dish out.'

I laugh out loud at that. 'I came to Paris with you the minute you clicked your fingers.'

He frowns at me. 'We got on OK there, didn't we?'

'Yeah.' I shrug.

His frown deepens. 'No matter what I do, I never feel that I get under your skin, Brown. Why do you keep me at arm's length? What has Family Man got that I haven't?'

'Let's not talk about him,' I say, worried to hear that I'm already a bit slurry. I clink my mug against Mason's. A bit too enthusiastically. Rum sloshes out on his jeans. He doesn't even look perturbed, he just grins at me indulgently. 'I drink to forget.'

'And you will forget.'

'Forget what?' I quip, then laugh like a drain at my own wittiness. We drink more and more rum.

When there is nothing left in our teapot, Mason asks, 'Feeling better?'

I shake my head. 'No. Not really.'

'We have to do it all over again then, Brown.'

So we go back to the dessert restaurant. This time I have Nutella pancakes smothered with chocolate sauce. Mason has toffee apple and pecan pie. When we've finished, we go back to the bar.

This time we share a Berry Big mojito which comes in something that looks like a flower vase. It's certainly the size of one and it's filled to overflowing with white rum, Chambord, muddled summer berries, mint and lime. If the teapot of rum wasn't there already, it would go straight to my head. I'm struggling to sit upright on my bar stool and keep sliding off. I cackle away. It's hilarious! Trust me.

'Whoah, there!' Mason catches me as I slide sideways once more. 'Steady on, Brown.'

'Sorry, sorry, sorry.' I start giggling and can't quite stop.

'Tell me that this is helping you to forget him?'

'Who?' I say. 'Forget who?' And that sets me off cackling again, even though I'm sure I've heard it somewhere before. But soon I'm not laughing and seem to be crying. I wonder where Joe is now and what he's doing. He's at home in the bosom of his family while I'm here getting slaughtered with Shagger Soames and can't even sit nicely on a bar stool.

'Time to go home,' Mason says and he helps me down off my stool as I don't seem to have legs that work any more.

He drags me outside and, when the fresh air hits me, I collapse into a heap. Mason heaves me onto his shoulder and flags down a cab, then bundles me in. This is a nice feeling of oblivion. I have no sensation anywhere. I feel as if I'm floatingfloating-floating.

I wake up as the cab stops outside my flat. I'm vaguely aware of Mason paying the driver but all I want is sleep, lovely sleep.

'Where's your key, Brown?' Mason roots in my handbag. It's in there somewhere, I'm sure. Eventually he says, 'Ha!' and then he starts to haul me up the stairs. 'Bloody hell, woman. You're like a sack of coal. Can't you move at all?'

I'd like to respond, but it all seems too much trouble.

'I think I may have overdone the drink element,' Mason is muttering to no one in particular. He opens the door and then manhandles me into the granny annexe. 'Straight to bed?'

I nod. 'I want sex with you,' I tell him.

'You don't,' he says. 'You want sex with anyone. That's not the same.'

Even in my drunken state, I think he's probably right.

So he picks me up and carries me through to the bedroom,

kicking the door open. He dumps me on the bed and I land with an 'oouff'.

He turns round and jumps when he sees my cardboard cut-out. 'Jeez, Brown. That thing nearly gave me a heart attack.'

That makes me giggle.

'I'm not even going to ask why you have a cardboard cut-out of a middle-aged man in your bedroom.'

'Issssss Gary Barlow,' I slur.

'That still doesn't explain it.'

I hold out my arms to Mason and he cuddles me. It feels nice to be in his arms, someone's arms and I really would very much like sex. 'Come to bed.' I try to look alluring.

'That's terrifying,' he says with a shake of his head. He prises me away from him and gets my duvet and tucks it around me. My eyes suddenly feel very heavy.

Mason sits beside me and strokes my hair tenderly. 'Comfy?'

'Thank you,' I manage

'Do you think you're going to puke up?'

I shake my head and that does make me feel sick.

'I'll be right in the living room if you need me. Just shout.'

'Don't go,' I say.

'I'll be here if you need me.' He kisses my forehead. 'Sleep tight, Ruby Brown.'

'Night, Mason,' I murmur back. And I think I'm asleep before he leaves the room.

Chapter Eighty-Five

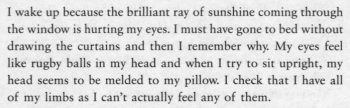

I wake up because the brilliant ray of sunshine coming through
the window is hurting my eyes. I must have gone to bed without
drawing the curtains and then I remember why. My eyes feel
like rugby balls in my head and when I try to sit upright, my
head seems to be melded to my pillow. I check that I have all
of my limbs as I can't actually feel any of them.

As quick as my head can manage, I turn to see if I am alone
in the bed and am relieved to find that I am. I'm sure Mason
came back with me. He must have left after he put me to bed.
Thank goodness. Sinking back onto my pillow, I let out a heartfelt sigh. That was quite some session. And it's all coming back
to me now. I have no idea how much rum that teapot held, or
the vase, but it was a fair bit. I'm rather proud of myself that
I didn't see my banana split or my Nutella pancakes again.
Hardcore.

I'm due at work later, so I need to get my act together.
Dragging myself out of bed, I lean on the walls of the shower
for a bit while the water does its best to revive me, pull on
some undies and, when I fail to find my dressing gown, wander
out into the lounge.

I recoil when I see Mason standing at my cooker as I've only got my undies on, but then he's dressed only in black underpants and my pink kimono. He doesn't even have that belted. 'Close your mouth, Brown,' he says. 'You're gaping at me.'

'I didn't realise you were still here. I should go and get dressed.'

'Put this on.' He takes off my dressing gown and tosses it to me. As it's a while since our last intimate encounter, I'd forgotten quite how fit his body is beneath his clothes. 'I'm here to make you breakfast. Hair of the dog and all that. It's what knights in shining armour do.'

'Pah,' I say.

'Sit down,' he instructs. 'How do you like your eggs? Scrambled or fried?'

'No eggs,' I manage.

'Bacon butty?'

Weirdly, that sounds like a very good idea. So I sit at my tiny kitchen table and try to resist the urge to lay my head down on it and go back to sleep.

When Mason has fussed a bit more, he puts a toasted bacon butty down in front of me. I don't point out that it's something of a miracle that I have the necessary ingredients. Bread usually being the trickiest of them all.

He sits opposite me and, in the cramped space, his toes rest on mine.

'Thanks,' I say. 'Much appreciated.'

'I feel we may have overdone it a bit,' he says looking suitably repentant. 'Apologies.'

'No, it was fun. Thanks. It was just what I needed.' I tentatively bite into the butty to test if I'm going to be able to keep it down. So far so good. 'Thanks for not . . . well . . . *taking advantage* of me. I was in a bit of a state.'

'You were most definitely hammered,' Mason agrees. 'And, strangely, I prefer my sexual partners conscious.'

I laugh at that.

'Whereas you, Ms Brown, seem to prefer your night-time companions made out of cardboard.' He raises an eyebrow.

'I like Take That. What can I say?'

'I always knew that your taste was dubious.'

'Blame Charlie,' I tell him. 'She's brainwashed me.'

'She's a big fan?'

'The biggest. They're playing in Paris soon. We thought about going. If we can get the cash together.'

Mason looks thoughtful, but says nothing.

'This is very good.' I wave what's left of my bacon butty at him.

'I have many skills. I wish you'd let me show you them.'

I snarf at him.

'Don't laugh. I'm serious. I could make very good boyfriend material.' He licks butter from his fingers and tries to look nonchalant as he adds, 'Why don't you give us a go? What have you got to lose?'

'I'm not in the right place for a relationship,' I tell him. 'My head is completely fucked. I'm even thinking about moving abroad. Starting somewhere completely new.'

'Don't do that,' he says. 'I'd miss you.'

'Yeah, well no one else would.' Though my mum might have something to say about it, actually. I finish my bacon butty and, thankfully, it seems to help my hangover. When I check the time on my phone, I can't believe how late it is. Most of the morning has gone. 'I'll have to get going soon. I have a date with the Butcher's Arms.'

'Never gets old, does it?' Then his fingers find mine and, for a second, we hold hands over the table.

'I had a nice time, Mason,' I admit. 'Thank you.'

'My pleasure. We must get utterly rat-arsed together again sometime. You're very funny when you're drunk, Brown.'

'Yeah. Hilarious.'

He lets go of my hand, even though he looks reluctant to. 'Mind if I take a shower?'

'Of course not.'

So I tidy up in the kitchen trying not to move too quickly – in case I dislodge the bacon layer on top of my banana split – and listen to the shower running through the thin walls. I think of Mason in there, naked, water streaming down his body and wonder, very briefly, whether I should join him. He's right. I could do a lot worse than him. When he's being nice, I like him. What's the point in pining for Joe? Seeing him with Gina yesterday should have put paid to that. I busy myself washing our plates.

Mason comes out of the bedroom ten minutes later, dressed in last night's clothes, hair washed. 'I've called a cab. Two minutes and I'll be out of your way. See you later at work.'

'Yeah. Thanks again, Mason. You're a mate.'

'I could be more,' he says lightly. He kisses me on the cheek, his hands warm on my arms and then his phone pings and it's a text from the taxi company to say they're outside. 'See you, Brown.'

'See you, Mason.'

He heads off down my stairs.

Standing on the landing, dressing gown pulled around me, I watch him go. As he gets to the cab, he turns and waves me goodbye.

I shout after him. 'I'll think about it.'

He looks puzzled. 'About what?'

'Us,' I tell him. 'I'll think about us.'

He grins at me and, smiling to myself, I quickly duck back inside before my landlord sees me and realises that I'm entertaining gentlemen overnight in my granny annexe.

Chapter Eighty-Six

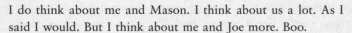

I do think about me and Mason. I think about us a lot. As I said I would. But I think about me and Joe more. Boo.

I'm thinking about him now. I miss him. I miss him for so many reasons.

If I'm honest with you, I don't miss diving. If I never see the bottom of a swimming pool again it will be too soon. But I do miss the outings with the dive club. They're a nice bunch of people – even though they get over-excited at the prospect of messing about in a murky gravel pit for fun. And I'll never see Joe again stripped down to the waist in his wetsuit which, frankly, is something that often troubles me in the wee small hours.

I'm sitting on the bench outside the Butcher's Arms watching a noisy bee trying to get some joy out of a garish pink flower that's growing by the bins. Maybe he's finding its nectar wanting as it just seems to be making him cross. At least he's not been fooled by one of the wasp catchers around the garden which are filled with sugar water to lure the wasps away from the diners' fish and chips or cheesecake. At this stage in the summer, they're already half-filled with a disgusting mulch of dead wasps and we haven't even reached the point where the wasps are bad-tempered and will sting anyone who looks at them twice. I don't know whose job it is to clean out the wasp catchers, but I'm glad it's not mine. It's half an hour before my shift and I'm having a cheeky roasted vegetable panini and a diet Coke to see me through the day. I know how to live.

I have been thinking about Mason too. A bit. We haven't seen each other since the night he stayed over at my place – on the sofa. That was fun and we do get on well, but . . . I don't even know what the 'but' is. But there is a but. If you know what I mean. We've been texting each other though – half a dozen times a day. Mason is busy with the club and another restaurant business that his father has started in London, so he hasn't been around. Which is fine. I don't want to rush into anything at the moment. I just want to nurture myself and hope the hurt will eventually go away.

Charlie's car pulls into the car park and I watch her as she walks towards me. There's a spring in her step, a sashay to her hips and I don't think it's just because Take That have got a new album out. Though it actually might be. She hasn't mentioned Nice Paul for days and I don't like to ask.

'Hey, chummie,' she says. 'What's occurring?'

'Not much,' I tell her – which is true.

She joins me on the bench, giving me a friendly dig in the ribs as she does. 'What are you doing out here on your tod?'

'Waiting for you. Thinking.'

'You do far too much of that,' she says. 'It's bad for you.'

'I know. I can't help it.' Somewhere in the dark recesses of my brain, I'm trying to form a plan for my future. *My* future and not a future that includes anyone else. But it's like trying to grab at gossamer strands that always seem to be out of my reach. I give up.

She roots in her handbag and pulls out all the vaping para-phernalia that lurks in there. 'You should try vaping. It's almost like meditating. Want a go?' She offers me her e-cig.

'No thanks. I think white wine works for me.' I break my panini in two. 'Do you want half of this?'

Charlie shakes her head. 'Fast day. I've just had a fresh air sandwich and a piece of virtual cake.' She leans back, pushing her sunglasses onto her head, closing her eyes and letting the sun warm her face while she puffs out clouds of vapour towards the sky. 'So what are you thinking about this time?'

I don't say Joe as I'm sure she's bored to death of me talking about him. 'Just wondering what to do with my life.'

She opens her eyes to look at me and pulls a face. 'Deep.'

'Mid-life crisis looming, probably. I'm at that funny age.' Charlie goes back to her sunbathing, even though she'll complain when her face is bright red later. 'Don't you feel as if you could have done more with your life?'

'Not really,' Charlie says. 'I like being a waitress. The world would fall apart without waitresses. This is a nice place to work. The pay's rubbish, obvs, but I get good tips. I don't want a Ferrari or holidays on a cruise ship, so it covers my needs. Mostly. I don't need to join a gym as I get enough exercise by being on my feet all day. And I go home after my shift and don't have to stress about work. When it's done, I'm done. There's a lot to be said for that.'

'I haven't really achieved anything. I haven't been anywhere.'

Charlie realises that she's not going to get any peace while I'm in this mood and sits upright, putting her sunglasses back in place. 'Where do you want to go?'

'I don't know.' I pick at my roasted vegetables, which have lost their appeal now. 'I've thought about packing it all in and going to Spain.'

'There's nothing in Spain.'

'There's not much here.' I think what I really want is to go anywhere that I'm not likely to bump into Joe and his family.

'I'm here,' she says. 'You can't leave me.'

'Perhaps I could take a course. Studying something.'

'What?'

I let out an unhappy breath. 'I don't know.'

Charlie laughs.

'It's OK for you,' I say more crisply than I intend. 'Gary Barlow is all that you need in your life, but I want more.'

'What you mean is that you want Joe.' She sighs at me. 'Well, lovely, you can't have him. That boat has already sailed.'

'I could say the same about Gary. You devote your life to him, yet he'll never be yours. How can that make you happy?'

'He's a fantasy,' she says. 'I know that. You know that. Part of the attraction is chasing that elusive dream. I don't have to put up with his moods or do his dirty washing. I don't have to listen to him moan or cook his dinner. I get Gary on *my* terms.'

'It isn't enough though, is it? Joe wasn't a fantasy. He's real-life flesh and blood. I want to be there for him when he's a grumpy old bugger or has man flu. That's what I want. And he was mine – if only for a fleeting moment.'

'Now we're both chasing what we can't have,' Charlie says and she sounds more sad than I've ever heard.

I hug her to me and kiss her cheek. 'Now I've made you miserable too.'

'You've made me think,' she says. 'That's different. But damn you all the same.'

'I guess we've just got to learn to be content with what we've got.'

'You will get over him,' Charlie says. 'In time.'

'I know.' But I wonder how long that will take.

337

Chapter Eighty-Seven

It's a few nights later when Mason turns up at the Butcher's Arms. He catches my arm as I'm rushing past with three sharing platters for table six.

'Can't stop,' I say. 'They've been waiting ages for these.'

'I'm sorry I haven't seen you, Brown,' he says. 'Work. Business. Life.'

'Me too. I'll catch you later.'

'Can you stay around when we close up?'

'Yeah,' I say. 'I'll put Ryan Gosling off.' And I'm away to deliver my platters before my diners complain and cut my tip.

Then I spend the rest of the evening rushing round and don't give Mason a second thought. I'm knackered and it's late when we finish.

He's helping to tidy up when I finally go through, stacking some glasses and setting out bottles on the bar. When he's done, he turns the lights down low and, as all the other staff have gone, we have the place to ourselves.

'You look knackered, Brown.'

'I am knackered. But thanks for pointing it out.'

'I have the very thing.' He flips a glass in the air and catches it with a flourish.

'Wow.' I find the nearest armchair and park myself in it.

'I've been on a bartending course,' Mason says.

'You didn't mention it.'

'I don't tell you *all* my secrets.' He does another fancy glass flip thing. I try not to look impressed, but I am. 'I'm thinking of sending all the bartenders at the club on a course, so I thought I'd try it out myself first. It was great fun. There are things that I can do with ice that would make your hair curl. I've mastered the technique of free-pouring . . .'

I look at him blankly.

'You don't use measures and I can handle four bottles at once.'

'Huh. I've been doing that with wine for years.'

Mason laughs at that. 'Let me mix you something.'

'I remember last time we had cocktails it ended very badly.' I think I might never touch rum again.

'I remember it ended with me having a bad back for days from sleeping on your rather small and inhospitable sofa.'

'Ah. Sorry about that.' And I am a bit as Mason was actually very nice that night.

'Live dangerously,' he urges. 'We haven't had a chance to see each other since then. I have stuff to tell you. Besides, it's work. I'm thinking of putting some of these on the menu.'

'My shift has officially ended. Does that mean I get overtime?'

'Whatever you like, Brown. Just say yes.'

'Taxi home too?'

'It goes without saying.'

I give in and grin at him. 'Yes.' I'm on the evening shift for most of this week, so if it all goes Pete Tong then I can have a lie-in tomorrow morning. 'You're a bad influence on me, Mason Soames.'

'Good.'

I have to smile. The man is shameless.

'What do you fancy? I have a repertoire of a dozen different cocktails.'

I hold up my hands. 'You choose.'

'A little Sex on the Beach for you then, madam.'

'Mason!' I look at him as you would a naughty schoolboy. 'Must you be so bloody obvious?'

'It's harmless enough,' he promises. 'And I'll make a small one so you can try something else. Vodka, peach schnapps . . .' He pours as he reels off the ingredients. 'Cranberry and a soupçon of orange juice.' He adds ice and a slice of orange before he brings it over to me.

'No colourful umbrella?'

'That's so last year,' he informs me.

I taste my drink. 'Hmm. Nice.'

'And it has three of your five a day,' he says.

'Nothing for you?'

'Oh, yes,' he says and peruses his bottles. 'A Singapore Sling, I think. Made to the original Raffles Hotel recipe. It's one of my favourites. I'll make one for you as a chaser too.' He concentrates as he pours a little of this, a bit of that. 'I'm seriously thinking of packing all this in and opening a beach bar in the Caribbean, Brown. I'd be quite happy doing this for the rest of my life. Coming with me?'

'Yeah. Why not?' It actually sounds quite appealing.

When he's finished juggling a dozen different bottles, he brings the drinks over and I take a sip.

'Blimey.' I give a theatrical cough. 'That's like rocket fuel. Just how much alcohol is there in that?'

'Maybe too much,' he says as he tries his. 'We'd have to charge a fortune for it. But it's good, right?'

'Very good.'

This is so strong that I can feel it melting my bones. But after a long, hard day on the front line of hospitality, it feels good to put my feet up and be waited on. Mason comes to sit next to me and he talks about what he's been up to, plans for the business, his bartending course and, to be honest, I don't really listen to him. I let it all wash over me and try to nod in more or less the right places but, if he notices, he doesn't seem to mind. It's actually nice to be sitting here with him getting slowly trollied. It's nice not to think about Joe for once. It's nice to have someone making a fuss of me.

When we finish our Singapore Slings, Mason rubs his hands together. 'Now what?'

And I don't know what possesses me, but I leave my chair, go over to sit on Mason's lap and kiss him deeply.

Chapter Eighty-Eight

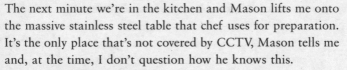

The next minute we're in the kitchen and Mason lifts me onto the massive stainless steel table that chef uses for preparation. It's the only place that's not covered by CCTV, Mason tells me and, at the time, I don't question how he knows this.

I can't tell you exactly how we got from the lounge to here, but we shed some clothes on the way, bump into furniture and the bar. My lips are bruised from some very enthusiastic kissing. Mason makes short work of unbuttoning my blouse and hitching my skirt up. As I'm struggling with his belt, his jeans, I think that chef would go mental if he could see us. I'm going to have to go over this with Dettol when we've finished.

We have rushed, drunken and sleazy sex on the table, my skirt rucked up round my waist, Mason's still wearing his socks. When we've finished, we lie on our backs and we both start to laugh.

'I'm glad you're my boss,' I say to Mason, giggling guiltily, 'because I would *so* sack my arse if I found one of my staff doing that.'

'You're such a tart, Brown,' he teases, fingers still trailing over my body. 'That was fun though. I must ply you with cocktails more often if this is the effect it has on you.'

'I think cranberry juice must be an aphrodisiac.' Though it may be the half a dozen or more shots of alcohol that we quickly downed. My head is certainly spinning.

Then there's a hammering at the front door of the pub, loud in the still of the night. My heart leaps to my mouth and I'm suddenly very sober.

'Shit,' Mason mutters. 'Who the hell can that be?'

I don't know, but whoever it is, I don't want them finding us here without most of our clothing. 'It can't be Jay, he'd have his key.'

He jumps down from the table and finds his jeans which were kicked off in the scrabble. 'Where are my fucking shoes?'

The knocking comes again. More insistent this time.

'Fuck's sake,' he grumbles as he pulls his jeans on. I see his pants on the floor, but he's not bothered with those. There's no sign of his shoes or mine. 'Keep your hair on!'

'Suppose it's burglars?' I suggest, heart pounding.

'Do burglars normally knock?' he asks as he hastily buttons his shirt.

'I don't know, but it's late.' I don't know what time it is as I've no idea where my phone went during our frenzy. 'Why else would someone come here at this time of night?' I don't like this. I don't like it at all.

'Shitshitshit.' Mason looks round and grabs a knife from chef's knife block.

'No, no! Not a knife,' I say. 'You might get hurt.'

'I'm planning on hurting *them*,' Mason points out.

'Take the rolling pin instead.'

'They might think I want to bake them a pie.' Nevertheless, he puts the knife back and grabs hold of the rolling pin in a menacing way. All the time the knocking is continuing. 'Stay here,' Mason instructs. 'If it sounds like it's going horribly wrong, phone the police.'

That will mean finding my phone. So I slide to the edge of the table and jump down as Mason heads for the door.

'Be careful,' I offer.

He rolls his eyes at me and mutters another curse under his breath.

Oh, God. Why did we ever think this was a good idea? I shimmy my bra back to where it should be, button up my shirt. My pants are entangled with Mason's so I leave them where they are. I've got hold-up stockings on which, currently, aren't holding up at all and are round my ankles. I yank them back into place, then pull my skirt down and smooth it. You'd never know what we'd been up to now.

I hear Mason unbolting the front door and think that I should be right behind him in case the burglars rush him. Plus I think my phone might still be on the table in the bar.

So, tentatively, I follow him and am glad to see that he's got the rolling pin poised for action. As he's opening the door I hear him say with surprise, 'Oh. It's you.'

Chapter Eighty-Nine

Joe is standing at the door, looking bleak. Mason stands aside so that Joe and I are facing each other.

He looks at me, then at Mason, then at me again. 'I'm sorry to disturb you,' he says and he sounds upset, cross and sad all at once.

When I find my voice, I ask, 'What are you doing here?'

'I wanted to see you.' He runs a hand through his hair. 'Sorry, Ruby, this was a really bad idea. I can see that you're . . . busy.'

My eyes follow his and I can see that he hasn't failed to notice that in my haste to dress, my blouse is buttoned up all wrong. One side is longer than the other, the lace of my bra very much on show. The fact that both Mason and I are both barefoot and looking dishevelled only adds to my air of being caught in the act. To help matters further, one of my hold-ups slowly slithers its way down my leg to my ankle. Both Mason and Joe follow its progress while I try to pretend it's not happening.

'I should go,' Joe says. 'It wasn't important.'

But I think that it must be if he's turned up here after closing time looking fraught.

'I'll make myself scarce,' Mason says, evenly. 'It seems as if you two have things to talk about and I have a pie to bake.' He holds up the rolling pin and then, with a glance at me, heads back to the kitchen.

'I'm sorry,' Joe says. 'Really sorry. I didn't mean to make things awkward for you.'

'It's fine,' I tell him when, quite obviously, all is far from fine. 'Shall we go and sit in your car?'

'We can do.'

So I follow him out into the night in my bare feet, trailing a stocking. I'd like to stop and take them off, but I think it would only attract attention to the fact that my stockings are not where they should be.

We get in Joe's car and sit side-by-side under the security light, both uncomfortable now. The fact that my blouse is misbuttoned is like an elephant in the room.

'I should have phoned,' Joe says again. 'Coming here like this was ridiculous.' He stares out of the window, not looking at me.

I touch his arm gently, but he moves it away from me. 'You still haven't said why you did.'

He rubs his face as if his eyes are tired. After what he's just seen, I should imagine that he'd want to bleach them.

'Gina's left. Again,' Joe says, eventually. 'We tried. For a few weeks I even thought we might make it.' His hands grip the steering wheel. 'Then I found that she was still texting her boyfriend behind my back. She hadn't given him up at all. Never intended to.'

'I'm sorry to hear that.' And I genuinely am. Joe's a decent man and deserves more than that.

'The thing is,' he says, 'I felt relieved when she went. I was putting my life, my feelings on hold for her and she threw it in my face.'

'Oh, Joe. Are the kids OK?'

'They're not great, but they're putting a brave face on it. I think they realise that we were trying to play Happy Families for their sake. They're upset that it didn't work out. That's the hard bit. They shouldn't have had to see her walk out a second time.'

He sucks in a breath and turns back towards me. 'I couldn't stop thinking about you, Ruby.'

I try a smile. 'I'm pleased to hear that.'

'Are you?' He gives me a hard stare. 'The kids were away tonight. Gina promised them that she'd see them more and believes strongly that a well-aimed pizza will fix anything. I was roaming round the house, not really knowing what to do with myself and I thought I'd come to tell you. I went to your apartment and, when it was clear you weren't there, I guessed that you might still be at work.'

'You were right about that.'

'I thought it would be a surprise.'

'You were right about that too.'

'I guess so.' He laughs without humour. 'I didn't mean to make things difficult for you. I never thought that you'd be seeing someone else.'

'We're just mates,' I tell him. 'Mason is my boss.'

'You seem to be quite friendly.' His tone is barbed and I can't say that I blame him.

'We do have a bit of history,' I confess. 'Tonight we had too many cocktails and got a bit carried away. It was stupid, but not against the law. I'm not in a relationship with Mason, if that's what you think.'

'If I'm honest with you, Ruby. I don't know what to think.'

'I'm single and have no commitments, Joe. As far as I knew you were back with Gina for good. I saw you in the shopping centre a while ago. You both looked very loved-up.'

'You did?'

I nod. 'It tore me in two. I've tried to move on.'

'Looks like you're making a good job of it.'

'Not really,' I admit. 'I've missed you too, but you've got to agree that this situation is complicated.'

'I wanted to ask you if we could give our relationship another go, but I've realised that it's too soon. I can't do complicated, Ruby. What I need is to be by myself for a while, to focus on me and the kids. They have to come before what I want.'

'I'm not with Mason,' I insist. 'He's a great bloke, but I have no future with him. He's young and irresponsible and we just have a good laugh together. Occasionally more. We've literally been friends with benefits.'

Joe risks a smile. 'That's way too modern for me.'

'And me. It's not what I want. It's not who I am. You're the one that I want to be with. Yet I didn't think there was any chance of that happening. If you'll let me, I would really like to try again.'

I can see the indecision on Joe's face, but also appreciate that he's only just had an abortive attempt at rekindling his relationship with his wife. He still must be feeling so raw. I can see that he wouldn't want to get involved with me again to protect his kids from further hurt. I could tear my hair out, gnash my teeth down to stumps, howl at the moon. This is totally pathetic timing. If only I hadn't got pissed with Mason. If only I hadn't been so keen for him to ravish me on chef's prep table. If only, if only. Why does life have to be so bloody difficult?

'Let's keep in touch and see each other as friends.' I'm starting to sound desperate even to my own ears. Perhaps I'd feel able to argue my case better if I didn't look as if I'd been thoroughly and soundly shagged. How mortifying. 'We don't have to rush into anything. Let's pretend that we've just met. I really believe that we could start all over again given time. I'd love to see the kids too.'

He shakes his head. 'I think maybe our moment has passed, Ruby,' Joe says, sadly. 'It was a mistake to come here. I'm sorry.'

'Please don't go. We haven't resolved this. I could come home with you so we could have a coffee and chat some more.'

'I'll have to pass on that,' Joe says, his voice filled with regret.

'I don't want to leave it like this.' But Joe stays immobile and offers no alternative. So, when there's nothing more left to say and I can't think of anything else to do, I kiss his cheek and say, 'Take care.'

'You too.'

Then I get out of his car and stand in the glare of the security light with my misbuttoned blouse and my droopy stockings and my heart aching. Joe drives away and I watch him, my heart feeling like a lead weight in my chest.

'You've messed this up big time, Ruby Brown,' I say to no one but myself.

Chapter Ninety

I go back into the Butcher's Arms, heartbroken.

Mason looks up. 'OK?'

'Yeah. No. Not really.'

'You love him?'

'What does that matter?'

'Has he gone?'

'Yeah.'

'You're not going with him?'

'No.'

He holds out my pants to me and, despite everything, that makes me smile. 'Want to come back to my place and finish what we started?'

'Yes,' I say.

Why not? That's what Single and Fabulous women do. They break hearts, they get their hearts broken, they sleep with unsuitable men nicknamed Shagger. They totally and utterly fuck up.

Chapter Ninety-One

So. Big jump forward. And here were are in Paris again. I've been seeing Mason properly for two months now. Ever since that fateful night in the Butcher's Arms. I know, I bet you never thought you'd hear me say that. Me neither. All I can say is that I tried nice and nice didn't work. I try not to think about Joe and, most of the time, I manage it. I'm only mentioning him now because I think you'd want to know.

To be fair to him, Mason's been trying really hard to be a proper boyfriend. He takes me out to nice dinners in fancy restaurants, he buys me flowers regularly and not just ones from supermarkets, but gorgeous arrangements from a posh florist. He remembers that roses are my favourites. He calls when he says he'll call – well, mostly. He's created a space for some of my clothes in his wardrobe. A small space, but it's there nevertheless. I keep a toothbrush in his bathroom. It's all a bit too good to be true. In fact, it's going so well that I've even had to persuade Charlie to refer to him as Mason now rather than Shagger.

She does so. Somewhat grudgingly.

He's even brought me on the promised return trip to the City of Love. And – double bubble – we're here to see Take That. Yay! Be still my beating heart. Mason, of course, managed to get VIP tickets through a friend of a friend of a friend. Seated. Gold circle. We're also having a pre-show Meet and Greet with Gary and the lads, plus unlimited champagne and I think I might just be in heaven.

Charlie and Nice Paul are here too. They're with the official fan club trip and are staying in a hotel a few streets away from where we are. We, as you will gather, are in a much posher hotel booked by Mason.

Our hotel is elegant, quaint and the room sumptuously furnished in jewel colours. We still have a view of the Eiffel Tower over the rooftops, but from a different direction this time. The hotel is on Rue du Faubourg Saint-Honoré, a quiet street off the Champs-Élysées and is home to a cluster of high-end boutiques and the beautiful Élysée Palace. I'm trying to persuade Mason to take a tour of it, if we've got time. Though I've already grasped the fact that he's not exactly a culture vulture and much prefers the cafés and restaurants to the palaces and museums.

I stand on our little balcony and look out over the city. This time the weather is kind to us – it's warm, sunny, the sky a muted blue, speckled with wisps of cloud. 'This is lovely.'

Mason looks up from his phone. 'Yeah.'

My only stipulation for this trip was that I absolutely refused to go back to the hotel where Valerie works. Actually, I had two stipulations – different hotel, only two of us in the bed at any time. Mason was happy enough to comply. We have, as is Mason's way, had a lot of sex – but maybe not quite as much as we did last time. These past few months have made me realise that it's never going to be the missionary position every night with Mason. He definitely likes his love on the edgy side – which is, on occasions, exhausting. Maybe TMI, but I wouldn't mind a bit of vanilla every now and again – especially when I've got to get up for work the next day. However, it's nice that he's keen and there's no doubt that he's a good lover.

A text comes in and it's Charlie telling me that they've just arrived. They came over on the ferry by coach, whereas we took the Eurostar. We organise to meet for a drink before the concert and I can't wait to see my friend. 'Charlie and Nice Paul are here,' I tell Mason.

He looks up from his phone again. 'Cool.'

Mason and I arrived yesterday and, unlike our other trip which was a bit of a washout, I've already managed to cajole him into doing some sightseeing. I've fallen in love with Paris. We went to the Louvre which was fantastic even though I'm not much of an art lover and we queued for France to get in. It's true that the Mona Lisa is much smaller than you think and it's shielded by bulletproof glass, but it's amazing and I'm glad that I know these things from personal experience.

After lunch at a little bistro, we went up the Eiffel Tower – which also took for ever and was crowded beyond belief. Despite my fear of heights, the view from over a thousand feet above the city was spectacular and well worth the effort. Mason wrapped his arms round me as we stood admiring the city and I felt the kind of contentment that I hadn't in a long time. Perhaps I can be happy with him.

'What are you smiling at?' He throws his phone on the bed and comes over to join me on the balcony, snaking his arms round my waist and pulling me close.

'I'm having a really great time,' I tell him. 'Thank you for bringing me back.'

'Only the best for you,' he says and nuzzles my neck. 'Shall we go and do some damage to a decent red, then take a bateau trip? We didn't manage it before.'

'That sounds like a very relaxing way to spend an afternoon and I want to conserve my energy for the concert tonight.'

So we head out and do just that. We hold hands and kiss as we go along the street, like a couple in love. I look over at Mason, well-groomed, as always, in his designer T-shirt and jeans and I feel a rush of affection for him. I feel as if I'm finally starting to see more and more of the real Mason Soames rather than the face that he puts on for the world and I very much like what I see.

Lunch is a croque-monsieur and a bottle of Chateau la Croix something or another, enjoyed outside at a pavement café. We chat, laugh, drink too much. Then we walk down to the River Seine, hop on board a Bateau-Mouche boat and find a place on the open-air viewing deck. We drift down the river, passing Notre Dame Cathedral and La Conciergerie, the distinctive glass pyramid of the Louvre and more views of the Eiffel Tower. Mason throws his arm round my shoulder and laughs at the amount of photographs I take on my phone.

'Selfie,' I say.

'Another?'

'When I'm old and grey, I want to look back at these and remember that I've been here.'

He strokes my face. 'It's nice to see Paris through your eyes, Brown. It's like seeing it through the eyes of a five-year-old.'

'I take it that's a compliment?'

'Yeah.' He laughs. 'Let's travel the world together and take selfies at all the best spots.'

I snuggle in next to him, my heart light. 'Let's do that.'

Chapter Ninety-Two

Too soon, it's time to go back to the hotel and get ready for the concert – but that's exciting too. I've never been to see a band abroad before, so I can chalk up another first. It feels like a very sophisticated thing to do. I can now drop, casually, into conversations, 'Oh, when I saw Gary in Paris . . .'

Life with Mason certainly isn't short on excitement.

I have a shower first. If Mason and I go in together, we'll never get out tonight and there'll be two empty seats in the VIP rows. I let the water wash away the dust of the day and then, wrapping myself in one of the hotel's fluffy towels, go back into the bedroom. 'Your turn,' I say to Mason.

He throws his phone down. 'Do you want to send for some tea before we go out?'

'No. I'm fine. We'll be hooking up with Charlie soon. I'll probably just hit the wine again.'

Mason slaps my bottom playfully as he passes. 'My kind of woman.'

So I towel myself down and smile as I listen to Mason whistling tunelessly in the shower. He sounds happy too and I really think that we can make a good go of this relationship.

Charlie gave me one of the tour T-shirts as a present and I'm thrilled to put it on tonight. If I'm going to shake the hand of The Barlow, I want to look not only as hot as I possibly can, but like a total fangirl. I get a flutter of nerves in my tummy.

Then Mason's phone pings on the bed and, without thinking, I pick it up and glance at the text that comes in.

I'll be waiting. V xx it says. My stomach drops.

I glance towards the bathroom, but Mason's whistling tells me that he's still in the shower and oblivious to the incoming text. I notice that my fingers are trembling as I scroll back through the previous messages. Clearly these are intimate texts. Ones that weren't intended for my eyes.

Mason to V. I'm in town, babe. Available?

Always for you. Where r u? Shall I come over? V xx

Mason to V. Valerie. It has to be.

He's tapped in our hotel name. Here with a friend. A friend? Is that how Mason sees me? Nothing more than that?

You or both tonight? V xx

Me. She's not interested in fun.

Good. I get to have you all to myself. When? V xx

I flick through them feeling both sick and guilty at the same time. All the time that I thought we were having a lovely romantic weekend and Mason has been texting another woman. And not just *any* other woman. It has to be Valerie. The one we shared a threesome with. And, for the record, I *am* interested in bloody fun, but the kind of 'fun' that only involves one other person.

Guiltily, I carry on scrolling. Though, if we analyse this, I'm not the one who should be feeling guilty. Supposed to be seeing Take That.

Afterwards? V xx

The sooner the better. I'll find some excuse not to go & come over to hotel. Same room as usual?

Then the first text I saw. I'll be waiting. V xx

I put down the phone. I should feel angry, raging, but I don't. Perhaps that's telling. I'm not even cross or surprised. There's a kind of inevitability about it all. I'm sad more than anything. Sad, weary and disappointed. Disappointed in Mason and in myself. I ignored all my instincts, all the warning signs and allowed myself to believe that this was for real when in my heart I knew it was too good to be true that Mason was a reformed character. Turns out I was right.

Chapter Ninety-Three

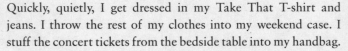

Quickly, quietly, I get dressed in my Take That T-shirt and jeans. I throw the rest of my clothes into my weekend case. I stuff the concert tickets from the bedside table into my handbag.

I look towards the bathroom door where, inside, Mason is still happily going through his ablutions. Perhaps he's making sure that his shave is extra close, putting on a splash more after shave, looking forward to tonight's entertainment. And I don't mean getting up close and personal with Gary Barlow. Mason has an entirely different form of entertainment on his mind. Well, good luck to him. I won't be part of it. I've had one cheating, shagging, bastard ex, I'll not have another one.

With only a brief glimpse round the beautiful room, I tiptoe out and close the door behind me.

Out on the street, I hail a cab and, when I'm settled in the back seat, I call Charlie and tell her that I'm on my way to their hotel. It's only then that I have a good cry.

Chapter Ninety-Four

The cab pulls up at Charlie's hotel where she and Nice Paul are sitting out at the pavement tables having a beer in the sunshine. I pay the driver and wheel my case over to them.

'I'm not liking the look of this,' Charlie says, eyeing my luggage.

I pull up a chair and sit down, then signal to the waiter that I'd like a beer too. In fact, I'd quite like a dozen or more. But, as I don't know how to say a dozen in French, I settle for one. For now.

When I take off my sunglasses, Charlie adds, 'You've got puffy eyes too.'

There's no point beating about the bush. 'Mason was texting another woman to arrange to see her tonight. I caught him out.'

'Seeing someone here?'

'Valerie.' I raise an eyebrow.

Charlie's eyeballs nearly ping out of her head. 'Valerie! Her of the . . . ?'

Please don't tell Nice Paul that I've had a threesome, I pray silently.

Charlie realises what she's about to say and waggles three fingers in a lascivious manner in the air instead. Unless Nice Paul is a complete dunderhead, I'm sure he'll gather her meaning too.

'Yes. That Valerie.' I still blush at the thought of it.

'Total bastard,' is Charlie's verdict.

'Yeah.' I can't really disagree. My beer comes and it goes down without touching the sides. Nice Paul orders us three more.

'Shall I leave you ladies to talk?' he asks. 'I can make myself scarce.'

I shake my head. 'No. Stay. You're an honorary girl.'

He laughs. 'I think that's a good thing.'

'Besides, I don't really want to waste any more breath on Mason Soames. We're here to have fun and fun we will bloody well have.'

'So, what's the plan?' Charlie asks.

'We'll go to the concert, have a lovely time and give this unpleasant little interlude no more thought.'

'I have to say you're taking this remarkably calmly.'

'Yes,' I agree. 'I am.'

'Perhaps it just says that Mason wasn't the right man for you, after all.'

'I think that pretty much sums it up.'

'You'll stay here tonight,' Charlie says. 'I've got a double bed in my room. You can bunk up with me.'

'Thanks.' Then, as my second beer arrives, my phone rings. Mason. I let it go to voicemail. Then a text comes in from him. Where ru? Why has all your stuff gone? I'm sure he'll work it out. Call me.

So we have many beers and enjoy the late afternoon sunshine. After Mason's third call, I turn the ringer off on my phone, but it continues to vibrate angrily on the table.

Later, I drop my case into Charlie's room and she says, 'The T-shirt looks cool.'

'Thanks.' I check myself out in the mirror. I look unhappy, so I make my smile wider, brighter. Mason Soames isn't going to spoil this evening for anyone.

We take the Metro out to the arena where Take That are playing. The crowds are already streaming in when we arrive and the atmosphere is electric.

'I'm so excited, I could wee.' Charlie dances with excitement. 'In fact, maybe I did.'

'Take these,' I say and pull our fancy VIP tickets out of my handbag. 'You'll appreciate them more than me.' If Mason had been a nicer person, he'd have got tickets for all four of us, anyway.

Charlie gapes at me. 'Seriously?'

'Give me one of your tickets. You might be able to sell the other one at the door.' Mason's certainly not going to be needing it. I did wonder whether he'd come down here and try to meet up with us, but there's no sign of him.

We swap tickets. Charlie stares at Nice Paul before she does a happy dance on the spot. 'We're going to meet Gary!'

'This is great,' Nice Paul says. 'But are you sure you don't want to go with Charlie?'

'No. You two enjoy yourselves. I'll be fine.'

He looks as if he can't believe his luck. 'Thanks, Ruby.'

'I'm glad that something good can come out of this.' I hug them both. 'I'll see you back here afterwards. Hit the free champagne and be sure to give Gary a kiss from me.'

Then we disappear our separate ways – Charlie and Nice Paul going for the VIP experience courtesy of Mason and me heading for the cheap seats by myself.

Chapter Ninety-Five

Charlie and Paul's seats are up in the gods. I climb a thousand steps and will probably need oxygen by the time I get up there. I think I'll have to grip the seat in front to stop myself feeling as if I'm falling forwards as this tier is dizzyingly high. The arena is vast and filling quickly. Someone beaming widely comes to sit next to me, so I guess that Charlie managed to sell their spare ticket which is great. I hope that Charlie and Nice Paul are enjoying meeting Gary, Mark and Howard. I feel a pang of envy, but it's only momentary. They deserve those tickets way more than I do and Mason Shagger Soames deserves to cough up for them.

Then the concert starts and I sing my heart out, jig my feet off, sway along, enjoy the fabulous show – even though the lads look like tiny ants on the stage. The light show is stunning and they've got the dance moves down to a tee. They faultlessly and fabulously go through all their old favourites and hits from their new album. Thank goodness I'm word-perfect due to Charlie. I only falter when they sing 'A Million Love Songs' and 'Why Can't I Wake Up With You' and then the words stick in my throat and I suddenly feel very alone, despite the joyous crowd, and I have a few tears. That bastard. I vowed that I'd never let another man do this to me. Meanwhile my phone continues to buzz in my pocket like an angry wasp. Well, Mason can ring all he likes, we're done.

The concert finishes with an encore of 'Never Forget' and 'Rule the World' and I finally feel like a true fan – a fully fledged Mad Thatter. Over the last few hours, I've fallen in love with Take That and perhaps I'll do as Charlie does and save myself just for Gary Barlow. There are worse things in life.

My ears are ringing when the concert ends from all the screaming around me and, despite my sadness, I feel quite light. This has done me the power of good. I might even get a Take That tattoo. A discreet one.

I stand outside the venue waiting for Charlie and Nice Paul, an earworm of 'Pray' going round in my head. I even feel moved to break out the dance moves. Eventually, I spot my friends in the crowd and wave frantically. When Charlie comes towards me I can see that an expression of pure ecstasy is written large on her face. Her hair is plastered to her head with sweat and she's pink in the cheeks. I also note that she and Nice Paul are holding hands.

'Was that not completely fabulous?' Charlie squeals. 'I think I've died and gone to heaven.'

'It was amazing,' I agree. 'They certainly know how to put on a show.'

'We were right at the front and both Gary and Mark grabbed my hand. Yay! Gary came down to sing to the fans and was jiggling his bum right in front of me! I'm *totally* in love.' She shows me video evidence of her close encounter on her phone.

'Wow.' Any closer and I think her nose would have been in his nethers. 'It's not only his bum that's jiggling. Has he got any undergrunts on?'

'Who cares? It was a magical moment. I thought about pulling him on top of me.' She gazes fondly at her screen. 'Your seat was OK?'

'It was great. Perfect.' In fairness, I can't say that I got an exceptional view of GB's testicles or botty, but I was happy enough. 'And your Meet and Greet?'

'I got to hug Gary and give him a kiss. He recognised me straight away.'

'That's fantastic.'

'He signed my arm.' She does a happy dance as she sticks out her arm for my perusal. 'I'm never going to wash again!'

'I can see another tattoo heading your way.'

'God, yes,' she breathes, ecstatically and gazes fondly at her own arm. 'It'll match my other one.'

Nice Paul smiles at her indulgently. 'I restrained myself to shaking his hand, but it was great. Thanks, Ruby.'

'My pleasure.'

'Have you heard from Shagger?' Charlie asks.

'Yes. Many times, but I haven't spoken to him.'

'Tell me that you won't.'

'No way.'

'You're a beautiful lady and will find someone nice one day. Someone just like Gary. But *neeeeeveeer forget*,' she sings the appropriate words, 'that I have first dibs on him.' Happily, Charlie links her arm through mine on one side and Nice Paul's on the other. They look at each other in a loved-up manner. 'Let's go back to the hotel and get absolutely hammered.'

Sounds like a jolly fine idea to me.

Chapter Ninety-Six

The hotel bar is filled with fans all wearing tour T-shirts, raucously enjoying a drink, swapping stories of the concert and showing each other the merchandise they've bought at ludicrously inflated prices. The hotel is worn, a bit grubby, the sort of place that caters for budget coach parties. This lot don't care at all. They're just happy to be here in the Take That stratosphere.

Charlie and I find a sofa on the edge of the melee. While she and Nice Paul chat away to the other fans, I sit and enjoy a large glass of restorative red wine and wonder what Mason's doing now. Valerie. That's probably what he's doing now. On my phone there are dozens of missed calls and a stream of increasingly apologetic texts.

The last text says, Forgive me, Brown. I'm a knob.

Finally, I text him back. At least we agree on one thing.

It wouldn't be too difficult for him to work out where I am and, if it really mattered to him, he'd be down here looking for me. But he's not.

When Nice Paul nips back to his room, I lean in to Charlie and say, 'You two are looking very cosy.' They haven't put each other down since they got back from the concert.

Charlie does a silent squee. 'I don't know what happened,' she says. 'I hugged Gary and kissed him, then I turned to Paul and did the same. He didn't seem to mind at all.'

I grin at her. 'Certainly looks that way.'

'I know you've been saying it all along, but he is a really nice bloke.' Then she looks a bit sheepish. 'I sort of said that I'd spend the night with him.'

'Tart!'

'I know. I hadn't really noticed him until now – not properly. You've got to seize the chance when you can, right?'

'I'm with you on that one.'

'There's just one snag.' She grimaces at me. 'He's got a single bed in his room and I've got a double.'

'What you're not so subtly trying to say is that you're blowing out your best mate for Nice Paul.'

'Yeah,' she agrees. 'Is that awful of me? You don't mind?'

I hug her. 'Of course I don't. Have a fab night.'

'I intend to.'

'Don't call out "Gary" at the wrong moment or there'll be trouble.' We both snarf at that. 'I know it isn't very romantic, but you have condoms?'

'I haven't. It's been a very long time since I needed those.'

'I've got some in my bag.' I fish around and, surreptitiously, hand them over.

'How very modern of you,' she says. 'But thanks.' Charlie looks anxiously at the packets in her hand. 'I hope I've got enough. He's *so* going to get it.'

We are still guffawing guiltily when Nice Paul comes back.

'Good to see you happy, ladies.'

'I've just been discussing our sleeping arrangements with Ruby,' she admits when she's got her giggles under control. I think that I might even see her blush. 'She's OK about taking your room.'

'Thanks, Ruby,' he says. 'As long as it's not putting you out.'

'No problem.' Given my previous history, they could have asked me for a threesome. 'I'm going to head up there now, if you don't mind.'

So Paul gives me his key and I pull him to one side. 'Be nice to her,' I whisper. 'I don't want to see her hurt.'

'It's the last thing on my mind,' he promises. 'I really like her. I have for a long time.'

'I think you two would make a great couple. Your mutual adoration of Take That has to be a great foundation for a relationship.'

'To be honest,' he murmurs back. 'Even though I do love them, the reason I travel all over the place to gigs is really to see Charlie.'

'Seriously?' I laugh at that.

'Don't tell her,' he says. 'Not yet, anyway.'

'My lips are sealed.' What a turn up for the book. I never realised that Nice Paul is more of a Charlie fanboy than a Take That devotee. I'm pleased though.

So I kiss them both goodnight then I leave the hardcore fans to their partying and head up to my room to lick my wounds.

In the cramped room with a view of a brick wall, I undress and take a quick shower. The tepid water drips out of an ancient tap. The bed's lumpy, the linen threadbare. I don't like to think of who's slept in here before. I lie on the bed, reluctant to get under the covers. Besides, the night is warm, clammy and there's no air-conditioning. Thoughts of Mason, Joe, my ex and even Gary Barlow swirl in my head, making sleep impossible. After a while, I abandon all hope of rest and get up again. I dress and head downstairs. It's late and there are just a few stragglers left in the bar. Of Charlie and Nice Paul there's no sign.

In the wee small hours of the night, I hit the streets of Paris.

The restaurants round here are closed up now, the cobbled streets all but deserted. It's nice, soothing. I walk without really knowing where I'm heading, just taking in the sights, the night. I put my earphones in and listen to Take That as I meander through the streets, passing the odd party of drunken revellers – many of them middle-aged women in Take That T-shirts.

I find myself on the Champs-Élysées once more and turn towards the Eiffel Tower. I'd like to see more of this beautiful city. It has so much to offer and a dozen weekend trips wouldn't even scratch the surface. I'd like to do it properly one day. Then I think that I have nothing to go back for. There's no one waiting for me at home. Mason has our train tickets and I've no intention of travelling back with him by my side, so I'd have to buy another one for myself anyway.

I look at the magnificent monument ahead of me, illuminated against the night sky. It looks like a beacon of hope. What if I didn't go home? Who would care? It would mean losing my job, but I can hardly work for Mason now, can I? I could do this. I could stay here for a few days, a few weeks, a few months even. However long it takes. I have nothing to go back for.

I get a thrill of excitement in my stomach as I contemplate the logistics of it. Is it even possible? Yet the more I think about it, the more I want to do it.

Chapter Ninety-Seven

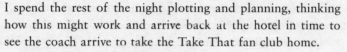

I spend the rest of the night plotting and planning, thinking how this might work and arrive back at the hotel in time to see the coach arrive to take the Take That fan club home.

Charlie's pacing the pavement. 'I've been out of my *tiny* mind,' she says when she sees me. 'I came along to your room to get you for brekkie, but there was no one there. You're not answering your phone either, you muppet.'

'Oh. I turned it off so that I couldn't hear Mason calling me.'

She tuts. 'Where have you been?'

'Just walking,' I say. 'And thinking.'

'Oh, God. Not that again.'

I laugh. 'I'm going to stay in Paris.'

'What?'

'I'm not coming home. Not yet. I'm going to stay here for a while and get to know the place.'

My friend looks horrified, as if I've told her that I'm not really mild-mannered Ruby Brown, but a mass murderer. 'For how long?'

'I don't know. As long as it takes. Until my money runs out.'

'You can't,' she wails at me. 'It's probably illegal or something.'

'I really want to and I'm not planning to be here for ever. Just until I get my head straight.'

'Come home,' she begs. 'We can get your head straight on cheap wine and chick-flicks. What will I do without you?'

'You'll be fine.'

'Plan this properly,' she says. 'Paris will still be here in a few months.'

'I want to stay,' I assure her. 'It's an adventure.'

'This is because of Mason, isn't it?'

'Partly,' I admit. 'But I have no ties, no commitments. I've never done anything wildly spontaneous in my life. There's a bit of spare money in my bank account. If I don't do this now, when else will I be able to?'

'Have you told that shagging shit?'

I shake my head. That's one call I can't make. If I never speak to Mason again it will be too soon.

'What shall I tell him?' Charlie asks.

'Tell him to fuck himself,' I suggest.

She shrugs. 'OK.'

I hug Charlie to me. 'I'll be fine. We'll FaceTime every day. You'll hardly notice I'm gone.'

'I'm going to have to leave the Butcher's Arms too, aren't I?'

'Don't rush into anything. You like that job.'

'I'll want to punch Shagger Soames every time I see him. I knew no good would come of this.'

'I should have listened to my bestie.' Then I check my watch. 'Your coach will be leaving soon.'

'I'd better go and help Paul. He's gone to get our luggage to bring it down to reception.'

'How did it go with him?'

She waggles her eyebrows mischievously. 'No condoms left.'

'None?' Charlie flushes. 'Wow. Good girl. Did you close your eyes and think of Gary Barlow?' I tease.

'No. I didn't.' She sounds surprised at her own admission. 'We had a great night. He's very caring.' A little sparkle comes to her eyes when she speaks about him. It's nice to see her happy and glowing. 'I like him, Ruby. *Really* like him. Do you think there's a chance it will work out for us?'

'I think you're lovely together. He doesn't even mind competing with Gary Barlow.'

'I know.' Then her eyes fill with tears. 'I'm frightened to let him close, Ruby.'

I take her by the arms. 'I fully understand why, my love, but give it a chance. He seems like one of the good guys.'

'He does.' She brushes away her tears. 'Come home soon. I'll miss you too much.'

I hug her again. 'I'll be back as soon as the money runs out.'

'Take That are playing the Albert Hall for Christmas. I've got gold circle tickets for us as a surprise pressie. You can't be away for that.'

'It sounds fantastic.' I kiss her cheek. 'I wouldn't miss it for the world.'

'You'd better not,' she warns.

Then Nice Paul arrives, struggling with all of their luggage. So we take some of the bags from him and Charlie say, 'She's not coming back with us.'

'Wow,' Paul says.

'Long story. Charlie will explain.' I walk with Charlie down to the coach and hug her again. She cries a bit more. 'Look after her,' I say to Nice Paul.

'Don't worry, I will.' Then I watch as he puts their cases in the hold and helps her onto the coach. That'll work out well. I know it will. I can feel it in my bones.

I stand on the pavement and wave madly at the coach until

it's out of sight. Then I look round at the streets of Paris, the little pavement cafés, the chi-chi shops and get a thrill of anticipation as I wonder where to start.

Chapter Ninety-Eight

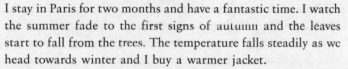

I stay in Paris for two months and have a fantastic time. I watch the summer fade to the first signs of autumn and the leaves start to fall from the trees. The temperature falls steadily as we head towards winter and I buy a warmer jacket.

Every day I pound the streets, finding my way round this beautiful city. I might be footsore but I'm light in my heart. I move to a room I find on Airbnb that's basic but clean. The house is perfectly located in the winding, cobbled streets of Montmartre, not far from the Sacré-Coeur. The landlady lets me use her kitchen and washing machine and it costs me less than twenty quid a night.

Montmartre is the place I love the most. It's quite possibly the most unashamedly romantic part of Paris that has a fab, arty vibe. I love climbing the quiet stairways, peering down narrow alleyways onto ivy-clad houses and sitting at pavement cafés watching the world go by. Every day it's thronging with tourists – like myself – and couples hand-in-hand. I won't deny it, I do get a few pangs of longing, but not for Mason. When Charlie told him I wasn't coming back, he called me every day for a week to beg me to reconsider. I never returned his calls. What do we have to say to each other?

No, the person I think the most about is Joe. He would love it here too and it would have been nice to come here with him for the romantic weekend that I never quite managed. I think about calling him and, once or twice, after too many glasses of *vin rouge*, I nearly do. But what would be the point? It didn't work out there and there's no good in thinking about what might have been.

I take in all the sights, eat in little cafés with surly staff and chic Parisian ladies. I learn a few passable phrases in halting French. I probably go to every single museum and art gallery in Paris. I take three trips to Versailles as I'm blown away by it. I buy a sketch book and pencils and have a go at drawing. I'm rubbish at it, but find it quite therapeutic. I sit wrapped up in the cool, autumn afternoons and try to capture my favourite landmarks. As a backup, I fill my phone with photos.

In the evenings, I relax in my room and read more than I've ever done in my life. I'd like to tell you that it's French literature, but it's not. I download cheap, chick-lit ebooks for my phone and find that I love them. I FaceTime Charlie every night before I go to sleep and tell her about my day.

I feel that I might be tempted to stay here for ever, but then, of course, my money does start to run out. I could look for a job in the gig economy but my heart's not really in it. I want to be a tourist here, not an employee. Then, even worse, my dear Charlie begins to nag me to come home. She reminds me that I have Take That tickets waiting for me and I can't miss that. I might even pine for my family a bit – although Mum has also FaceTimed me nearly every day too. Finally, when my landlord calls to tell me that he has a friend who's looking for a place to rent if I'm not going to return to my granny annexe any time soon, I book a ticket on the Eurostar, pack up my things, say goodbye to Paris and head back to Costa del Keynes.

Chapter Ninety-Nine

I need to fast forward a bit. Another year, another new me. We're in the grip of winter now. The mornings are freezing, the nights getting longer. My granny annexe is proving a bugger to heat. My car is even more reluctant to start. Nevertheless, I'm glad to be home.

When I came back from Paris, I dumped my stuff in the flat and cardboard cut-out Gary Barlow was still standing patiently in my bedroom. It was like I've never been away.

Except it sort of was, too. I'd changed. Something subtle inside me had shifted while I was giving the Paris pavements a good pounding. For the first time in a long while, it was just me in charge of my own destiny. Out there, I had no one to distract me or influence my thoughts. I think sitting at a pavement café for an hour or more every day watching the world go by with a glass of red and your own quiet thoughts is as good as any anti-depressant tablet you care to name. I thought about what I wanted from life and decided that, actually, I didn't really want all that much. You might have assumed, not unreasonably, that I'd have a blinding flash of brilliance and come up with some cunning business plan that would make me a millionaire before next year. No such thing. Instead, I realised that I have no interest in opening a café on a canal boat or a funky florist's shop or becoming an events planner. I'm glad that one successful fairy and unicorn party didn't turn my head on that score. It was such bloody hard work and too much stress.

No, I came to appreciate that I'm pretty much happy where I am in life. My dreams don't involve becoming an entrepreneur or emigrating and I'm kind of relieved. There's so much pressure on everyone to achieve now – to get a bigger house, car, designer handbag. What this has all taught me is that I'm an OK person and, when it comes down to it, I'm quite content where I am. It would be nice to have a partner to share all that, but not at any cost. I look at where I am and I think that I appreciate it more. I've got a great family, some wonderful friends and Gary Barlow. What more can you want in life?

So now I'm working in a café in Stony Stratford, a nice little market town on the very edge of the urban sprawl of Costa del Keynes. It's called Sweet Things and is very genteel here. I really enjoy it. The hours are much more civilised as we're only open from eight until five, so I have all my evenings free. Not that I do very much with them, but I could if I wanted to. The boss is really nice, an older lady called Florence who's never likely to try to put her hands down my pants – so that's all good as well.

Smoothing down my apron printed with pink cupcakes, I clear the tables. The café's all pink and gingham and flowery bunting with a bit of kitsch retro thrown in. The atmosphere is bright and sunny, as is my outlook on life. We serve fabulous homemade food to the good folk of Stony – fresh sandwiches, fantastic cakes. Being the antithesis of Mary Berry, I have nothing to do with baking the cakes we serve, obvs, but I do a lot of eating them and our good reputation is well deserved.

It's Saturday and, as usual, we've been busy all morning and I haven't really had time to turn round. Fortunately for me, I got the job the week I came back from Paris so my finances didn't suffer too much. There's not much – nothing – left for emergencies, but I'm slowing building my savings up again.

I haven't heard from Mason at all and I haven't ventured near the Butcher's Arms or his club. They're strictly out of bounds now. I heard through the grapevine that his father had sold off his chain of pubs and clubs for an absolute fortune and I did think about calling Mason to see how that had affected him. A second later, I thought better of it. Then I bumped into Ben the barman and he told me that he'd heard that Mason had bought a beach bar in Antigua. I wonder if that's Mason trying to fulfil his dreams too. I don't know. If it is, there was a time I would have been quite happy to go with him. Fool that I was.

Still, the other good news is that Charlie is working here too. She rushed from the Butcher's Arms as soon as another vacancy came up here and it's nice that we've still got each other for company. We miss our bench at the pub, but nothing much else about it. Here, as soon as our boss goes out, we change her choice of mellow music featuring Jack Johnson and Lana Del Rey to Take That. It's the only vaguely rebellious thing we do and our customers never seem to mind.

You'll be pleased to know that Charlie's still with Nice Paul and it's all going swimmingly there. Thank goodness. There's even tentative talk about them moving in together. I know! I do hope so as they seem very happy. I spent Christmas holed up with my parents, eating too much and watching rubbish telly, then let my hair down with Charlie and Paul at New Year. I was both melancholy and optimistic. Last year was quite the year. My *annus horribilis*. Well, parts of it. At midnight, as everyone was dancing and celebrating around us, I did think

377

about ringing Joe and wishing him all the best for the coming year, but I didn't. Probably just as well.

My social life isn't exactly a giddy whirl, but I'm cool with that too. I mainly hang out with Charlie and Paul. They're kind and treat me gently. We all go to Take That concerts and sundry events together and that's the only threesome you'll find me in these days.

'What's that dreamy look on your face for?' Charlie asks as she scrapes leftover sandwich into the bin.

'Nothing. Just thinking.'

'Flo's nipped out for an hour. Get that music changed over, chummie,' she instructs. 'Let's have a bit of the lads to get us in the mood.'

'For what?'

'Life,' Charlie says over her shoulder as she goes off to find more bread.

I change the music as instructed rather than face Charlie's wrath and go old skool with a playlist of their greatest hits. 'Patience' drifts out over the café – one of my favourites.

Singing along, I take a J-cloth to wipe down the tables during a momentary lull. As I'm leaning over table two trying to eradicate a particularly sticky patch of jam that a messy toddler has smeared into every crevice, the doorbell sounds and I wonder if we're in for another onslaught that will take us through to the lunch rush.

When I turn round, Joe and the kids are standing there.

Chapter One Hundred

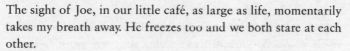

The sight of Joe, in our little café, as large as life, momentarily takes my breath away. He freezes too and we both stare at each other.

My heart clearly recognises him as well as it sets up an erratic and all-too-fast beat. They're all wrapped up against the cold, cheeks pinched to pink by the wind. Joe's in a dark jacket and gloves, his curls hidden by a beanie hat.

If he's even thinking about retreating, then he can't now. He's trapped.

'Ruby!' Daisy shouts and comes to hug me.

I squeeze her back. 'You are looking fab-u-lous,' I tell her.

'We miss you,' she says. 'I want another unicorn and fairy party.'

'That was fun, wasn't it?'

'The coolest! All the girls still talk about it.' She unwraps her long stripy scarf and slides into one of the seats. 'Mummy told us the cakes here were amazing, but we've never been before.'

At the mention of her mother my throat closes tightly. Perhaps she's left her boyfriend and is back in the family home once again, in Joe's bed. I try not to think of it.

Tom raises a hand in greeting. 'Hey.'

'Hi, Tom. How are you doing?'

He shrugs. 'OK.'

'Ever get your bike back?'

'Nah,' he says. 'The case goes to court soon though.'

It seems like a lifetime ago that all that happened, but I also remember it as if it was yesterday. That was the first night that Joe and I spent together. The only one, too, as it turned out. 'I hope it goes well.'

Then, clearly taxed by so much conversation, Tom goes back to studying his phone.

I can feel Joe's eyes on me and, when I regain my composure, I say as calmly as I can manage, 'Hi, Joe. This is an unexpected surprise. It's good to see you all.'

Joe looks as if he's struggling to find words too, but eventually comes up with, 'I had no idea you were working here.'

'I've been here a little while now,' I tell him. 'I left the pub ages ago.' I risk a wry smile. 'It's much less . . . *complicated* . . . here.'

'Ah,' he says and I hope that means he understands that I'm no longer with Mason either.

I'd like to tell him that I 'found' myself in Paris – but that sounds too ridiculous for words – that I'm a different person now, that I'm happy, that I've stopped bouncing around like a bloody rubber ball, that I might have found out what contentment is. I have to accept, though, that he might not be the slightest bit interested in my revelation.

Pulling off his beanie hat, he stands there looking dishevelled. He tries to ruffle his hair into some kind of tidiness and fails. I've never seen him look more handsome.

'Take a seat,' I say, brightly, as they strip off their coats. I whip them away and, as I hang them up, I'm sure I can feel Joe's eyes following me, but it could be my imagination. 'I'll bring some menus over.' Which I do in my most professional manner, despite the fact that my knees are shaking. I even manage to reel off the specials with a flourish. 'I'll come back in a moment to take your order.'

Then I bolt into the kitchen, close the door and lean heavily against it. 'Fuckfuckfuck.'

Charlie looks round. 'What?'

Usually such expletives are preceded by the smash of breaking crockery as one of Flo's favourite cups or plates accidentally hits the decks.

'It's him,' I hiss.

Charlie's eyes go round. 'Mason?'

'No, no, no!' I wouldn't have heart palpitations like this if it were Mason Soames. 'It's Joe. He's here with the kids. What shall I say? What shall I do?'

'Nothing,' Charlie says. 'Be cool. Be calm.'

Hyperventilating, I shove my pad at her. 'You go and take their order.'

'No.' She holds up a hand.

'I can't do it. I can't.'

'Grow some,' she growls.

'I'll love you for ever.' I'm not adverse to a bit of begging.

'Get out there, Ruby Brown. Don't be a wimp. He's just a bloke.'

'But he's a bloke that I really, really liked once – maybe loved – and I blew it.'

'Be lovely, then. Make him realise what he's missing.'

I mutter, 'Fuckfuckfuck' again and then turn and go out into the café, pad poised in hand. This is excruciatingly painful. I glide over to the table and pin on my most friendly smile. 'Now, what can I get for you?'

They reel off their order and I jot it down with shaky fingers. Then I hurry it back to the kitchen for Charlie to make up as I'm in total bits and can't concentrate.

Chapter One Hundred and One

I stand over Charlie while she prepares their order so that she gets it absolutely right. Which kind of annoys her.

She waves her knife at me. 'Sure you don't want to do this yourself?'

'No, no, no. I just need to know it's perfect.'

She tuts at me, but doesn't stab me, so she can't be too cross. I watch her butter the bread, make sure the fillings are exactly right. I don't want Joe and the kids to have found me in this café and then for the experience to come up wanting, do I? I don't. Trust me on that.

They're laughing together at the table when I deliver their sandwiches and jacket potatoes. I try not to make too much eye contact with Joe. I've found that it's never a good idea to slaver all over your customers. However, he is looking particularly handsome today. I think I might have mentioned that already. Yet he can't have got any more gorgeous in just a few months, can he?

Scuttling back to the counter, I try to make myself look busy while watching them all having a lovely time together. They're a nice family and it would have been great to have been a part of that, but it wasn't to be. I wonder if Gina is still with her new man. I'm guessing as she's not here with them that perhaps she isn't back at home again. Or maybe that's blind hope. Was Joe wearing a wedding ring? I didn't think to look.

Charlie comes and leans on the counter next to me. 'Stop staring.'

'I'm not staring.'

'Yeah? And I'm not fat and nearly forty.'

'Am I staring?' I straighten up.

'Yes, you've gone all googly-eyed and wistful.'

I make myself avert my eyes and lower my voice. 'I think he might well be The One That Got Away.'

'Really?'

I nod.

'Boo,' Charlie says. 'That sucks.'

'Big time.' I don't think that Charlie fully grasps the gravity of my situation. I feel that I might wander the earth for the rest of my days and never find another man like Joe.

She puts her arm round me and squeezes. 'Do you want some cake to salve your broken heart?'

'Nah. I'm good. We could drown my sorrows in wine later though.'

'Sounds like a plan. Paul's knocking together some Chinese food for dinner. We've got a film downloaded ready to roll. Can't remember what. Want to come over?'

'Please.' Nice Paul cooks too. Charlie's certainly hit the jackpot there.

Surreptitiously, we watch Joe for a bit longer. Then Charlie purses her lips and whispers, 'He does keep looking over here at you, though.'

'Does he?' That makes me brighten up, before I think, 'Maybe he simply wants more tea or something and is trying to catch my eye.' This is a café and I am a waitress, after all. I nudge her in the ribs. 'You go and check.'

'Don't make me do your dirty work. You should go.'

'I can't,' I say. 'My poor troubled heart couldn't stand it.'

'Drama queen,' she mutters. Nevertheless, Charlie goes over to them and chats as she clears the plates.

She breezes past me into the kitchen. 'No more drinks. But they're coming to get some cake. Can you cope with that?'

'No!' I hiss. Yet before I can dive into the kitchen to escape, the three of them troop up to the counter where our dazzling range of cakes are displayed.

Our star cakes today include a lemon meringue pie with a white topping that looks like a fluffy duvet, our usual carrot cake that's the talk of the town, a four-layered, rainbow-speckled sponge, layered with cream and blueberry jam and, my own personal favourite, lemon drizzle.

'The lemon drizzle is very good,' I tell them in a voice that comes out too high and makes me sound like a cartoon character.

'Sounds excellent,' Joe says and, it might be my imagination, but his smile seems particularly warm. Could be nothing more than wishful thinking.

The kids choose their cakes. The speckled sponge for Daisy and lemon drizzle for Tom. I make sure that they get extra big slices. Then I serve Joe.

'I'll have lemon drizzle too.'

'A fine choice, sir.' May as well try to keep it light.

While I busy myself fussing with the plates and napkins, Joe lowers his voice and, speaking in confidential tones, asks, 'How have you been?'

'OK,' I tell him. This is hardly the time and place to fill him in on the intervening months. Then, I can't help myself and blurt out, 'I went to Paris to see Take That in concert and didn't come back for two months.'

He looks taken aback, as well he might be. 'With that guy?'

'No.' I shake my head. 'Yes. Sort of.' I'm gabbling. I take a deep breath and try to organise my thoughts. 'We went out there together but ended up going our separate ways the next day.' I smile at Joe. 'It's a long story, best told over a bottle of wine.'

'Ah.'

'I did have a lovely time in Paris, though. I took in all the sights and fell in love with the place.'

'I've never been,' he admits.

'You should. It's wonderful.' I concentrate on not hacking the cake to pieces, then continue, 'I'm glad I stayed. Then I ran out of money and came home. I couldn't go back to the pub, so I ended up here.' I hand over the extra large slice of lemon drizzle. 'It's a really nice place to work. Plus Charlie came too, which was a big bonus. I'm really happy here.' I want to emphasise that. 'And you?'

'Good,' he says. 'All good. The kids have settled down again after Gina . . . well. You know the rest.'

I think I do, but I can never be sure. 'She's still with her new man?'

'No. That didn't work out either,' he says. 'Another long story.'

Which, at least, gives us both a laugh.

'It sounds as if we've both got long stories to tell each other,' I venture.

'Yeah. Seems that way.' He clings on to his cake, awkwardly. 'She's got a place on her own now in that big, new estate, Newton Leys. A little terraced house. Bit of a shoebox, really. She seems happy enough though and we're trying to keep it amicable for the kids. She sees them a lot more now, which is good for them and it means that I've actually got a bit of time on my hands.'

'You're still diving?'

'I haven't been for ages,' he admits. 'I'm hoping to get back to it. We've got a dive outing planned for next weekend and I want to make that. Do you think you'll ever give it another go?'

'Nah. I'm not a natural diver. I think I might try the glamorous world of flower arranging next. That's more my level.'

'I didn't have you down as a flower arranger.' There's a twinkle in his eye as he says it.

'You never know, I might have hidden talents in the horticultural department.' Then I realise I'm getting dangerously close to flirting with him and stop. 'It's been nice seeing you, Joe. Take care of yourself.'

'You too.' He takes his cake and goes back to his table.

I make myself busy so that I don't follow every crumb into his mouth and, when it's time to pay, I send Charlie over with the bill.

A few minutes later, he shouts, 'Bye, Ruby.'

When I turn, they're all booted and suited in their outdoor gear and are heading to the door. The kids wave to me and Joe holds up a hand. Do I see a bit of sadness in his eyes? I've no idea. I don't want them to go, but I can hardly lay down in front of them to stop them leaving. Instead, I make my mouth do smiling and wave back.

Next to me, Charlie says, 'Cute. Very cute.'

I sigh. 'Yeah.'

'You think that you might still love him?'

'Yeah.'

'That's a total bummer.'

'Yeah.'

'Do you want me to clear their table or do you want to do it?'

With a heartfelt sigh, I pick up my trusty J-cloth. 'I'll do it.'

'There'll be other blokes,' Charlie says with the chirpy optimism of a woman in love. 'You'll see.'

But there won't. Not like Joe. I know that.

Chapter One Hundred and Two

Joe has left the money on the table and a generous tip, which feels a bit weird. Perhaps they enjoyed their cake so much that they'll come in again and I can go all dreamy over him from afar once more. I hope so.

Picking up the receipt and the money, I then wipe down the table and head back to the counter, handing the cash over to Charlie to put in the till. She faffs about with the coins, then says, 'Oh, hello!'

I glance across to see her holding up the receipt. On it there's something scrawled in pen. 'For me?' I ask.

'Well, it's hardly going to be for me, is it?'

'Give it here then.'

Charlie, smiling, snatches it from my reach before, smugly, handing it over.

On the receipt Joe has written, 'Call me, please,' and his phone number. As if I've ever deleted it.

My heart thumps in my chest and I look at Charlie, stricken. 'What?' she asks.

I hand back the receipt and she reads the message. 'Wow. Nice work.'

'What shall I do?'

'Call him, you muppet!'

'When?'

'Now!'

'It's not too soon?'

'No time like the present.'

'I don't know what to say.'

'Perhaps you don't need to say anything at all. Do it, woman!'

'I don't know. What if it all goes horribly wrong again? What if his wife comes back a second time? What if his kids find out that they really hate me?'

'Then at least you'll know you tried.'

I chew at my fingernails, wracked with indecision. This is too important to mess up. Take That come on the iPod singing 'A Million Love Songs'.

'It's a flipping OMEN,' Charlie says.

The lyrics do seem particularly pertinent and a big ball of emotion lodges in my throat. How can I speak to Joe now?

'If you don't call him, then I bloody well will.' She goes to wrest my mobile from my hand.

'I will. I will. I'll call.' With trembling fingers, I find his number and punch the button. A second later, his phone rings.

Instantly, Joe answers. His breathing is ragged, uncertain.

'Ruby?' he says and there's a world of hope in the way he says my name.

I nod, which I realise is pathetic.

'Thanks.' He lets out a wavering breath. 'Thanks for giving me another chance.' I can hear the relief and the love in his voice.

'Me too.' My eyes fill with tears. We can make it work this time. I know that we can. 'Where do we go from here?' I ask.

'Look up,' he says.

When I do, I see him standing in the street outside the café

389

window and he's grinning right back at me. Next to him, the kids are running round, punching the air and cheering. And Gary Barlow sings about love, love, love.

CAROLE'S FAVOURITE LOVE SONGS

I probably could have actually chosen a million love songs, but
I was asked to restrict myself to my favourite twenty. What a task!
I'm sure I could have picked twenty belters by Take That alone.
I do like a good love song whether they're cheery and make you
grateful for what you've got, or sad ones about lost love that bring a
tear to your eye. I listen to music every day as I write and each book
synopsis I send to my editor ends with a quote from the wonderfully
soulful Luther Vandross: 'love, love, love.' So I hope you enjoy my
choices and add them to your list of favourite love songs too.

A Million Love Songs – **TAKE THAT**

How Deep is Your Love – **THE BEE GEES**

The Man Who Can't be Moved – **THE SCRIPT**

Never Too Much – **LUTHER VANDROSS**

Friday I'm in Love – **THE CURE**

Truly Madly Deeply – **SAVAGE GARDEN**

I Knew I Loved You – **SAVAGE GARDEN**

Something Like This – **THE CHAINSMOKERS** *and* **COLDPLAY**

Love and Affection – **JOAN ARMATRADING**

Heart – **PET SHOP BOYS**

It Must be Love – **MADNESS**

Marry Me – **TRAIN**

Loving You – **MINNIE RIPPERTON**

Always on my Mind – **ELVIS PRESLEY**

Tenerife Sea – **ED SHEERAN**

All You Need is Love – **THE BEATLES**

Got to be There – **MICHAEL JACKSON**

I Say a Little Prayer – **ARETHA FRANKLIN**

The Look of Love – **DUSTY SPRINGFIELD**

Jesus to a Child – **GEORGE MICHAEL**

If you enjoyed *Million Love Songs*, read on for an extract from Carole's bestselling novel,

Christmas Cakes and Mistletoe Nights

Chapter One

I watch a weeping willow dipping its branches into the canal, leaves ruffled by the breeze. Beneath it, a cow and her young calf are standing at the water's edge where the bank has been trampled flat by many hooves. Delicate, spiky-headed teasels, crisp and brown now after their summer flowering, harbour the last of the dragonflies. Behind, a lush meadow stretches away and, in the distance, the spire of an ancient church peeps above the tall trees that have already turned golden this year, parched after our long, hot summer. A couple of swans glide elegantly by. It looks as if it's been unchanged for hundreds of years. If I was an artist, I'd try to capture this scene in watercolour. But I'm not, so I take out my phone and snap a shot for posterity.

'Fay! Are you planning on doing anything with that windlass?'

Danny's shout brings me back to the present. 'Sorry!' He's waiting at the entrance to the lock for me to leap into action and open the gates. Which I now do. 'I'm on it!'

I've run ahead of him so that this would all be quicker and then wasted the time by standing here daydreaming for five minutes. I finish closing the top lock. Diggery, our little Jack

Russell cross, runs up and down barking his own instructions. He's wearing a skull-and-crossbones neckerchief today and looks very jaunty.

When I've finished my part, Danny steers *The Dreamcatcher* into the tight space, bumping the sides slightly as he does. *The Dreamcatcher* is a decent-sized narrowboat and takes some manoeuvring. Despite spending the last few months living on the canal together, we're still very much novices. There's no doubt that we're learning quickly, though. Every day seems to bring some new challenge or obstacle to overcome – I can now unblock a loo with a certain degree of competence, light a stubborn woodburner, and fill the water tanks without giving myself an impromptu shower. All of these things are life skills I didn't have a short time ago – or ever think that I'd need.

'No worries,' Danny says as he cruises past me on the boat and settles *The Dreamcatcher* into the lock. 'We're not in a hurry.' He jumps off the back of the boat onto the towpath and together we manhandle the heavy lock gates into place.

I tell you, I have arms like Popeye now after all this physical work. The canals are not for wimps. No gym membership needed for me!

'I was having a little daydream,' I admit as we work the lock, watching *The Dreamcatcher* rise on the turbulent water to the next level. 'This place is so lovely.'

Danny looks round and takes it all in. 'We can stay up here as long as you like. Hopefully, I can get some more work.'

And that's one of our main problems. The last of the gloriously hot summer has gone and we're well into the cooler days of autumn now. Christmas will soon be upon us and the seasonal work that's kept Danny busy on our travels is slowly starting to dry up as the days grow shorter and colder.

'There's enough to keep me busy on site for the next two or three weeks.' Danny's currently doing casual labouring on a building site, but as the weather worsens there'll be less available. 'But that's about it. They won't be taking on until after the new year. Maybe even spring, if we have a bad winter.'

His work has been bringing in some very welcome money, but only just enough to keep body and soul together.

'After that, I'm not so sure what will happen.' He turns his heart-warming smile on me. 'But something will come up. You don't need to worry about it.'

Yet, I do. I'm one of life's worriers. The fact that I'm here at all is nothing short of a miracle. I'd never done a reckless thing in all of my forty-two years – until, of course, I left behind everything that I know and hold dear to run away with Danny Wilde for an itinerant life on the waterways of England. Even though I'm telling you this, I can still hardly come to terms with it myself. I waved goodbye to my old life, my friends, my family, my lovely little café in the garden without a backward glance. Well, not much of one. I could well be having a mid-life crisis but if I am, it feels really rather nice. Well, most of the time. It's only when I look at my bank balance that I get the collywobbles.

'We've got our love to keep us warm,' Danny says.

'And a dwindling supply of firewood.'

'I'll get some later,' he promises. 'It's on my never-ending list of Things To Do.'

Life on the canal, as we're both finding, certainly isn't all about sitting back with a glass of wine and watching the world go by. It's hard graft, that's for sure. But, now that I've done it, I wouldn't change a thing.

We're in Wales on the Llangollen branch of the Shropshire Union Canal. It's the most beautiful part of the country and the temptation to linger here is very strong. It's taken us six weeks or more to work our way up here and the journey has been truly wonderful. I've never tried anything remotely like this before and I'm fully embracing the free spirit that's slowly emerging from somewhere deep inside me.

Together we open the other gates, me huffing and puffing like an old train, Danny doing it with consummate ease.

'Come on, Digs,' Danny calls. 'Back on board or we'll leave you behind.'

Taking no chances, Diggery bounds onto the boat and sits by the tiller.

Expertly handled by Danny, *The Dreamcatcher* floats happily out of the lock. It's a sturdy boat, getting on a little in age and slightly scuffed around the edges – much like my good self. A few bits are patched up and held together with string, glue, an extra coat of paint and crossed fingers which will need some attention when we eventually find some spare cash.

I close the lock behind the boat and climb on board too. I stand proudly beside Danny while he takes control of the tiller and steers us back along our route. Even now, there are times when I look at him and can't believe that we're a couple.

'What?' he says as I gaze at his face. 'You're looking all moony.'

I laugh. 'I *am* all moony!'

'Glad to hear it, Ms Merryweather.' He puts his arm round my waist and draws me close. He smells of woodsmoke from firing up the stove this morning to take the chill off the boat.

I didn't think my jaded, middle-aged heart was capable of containing this much love. But it does. Danny's young – much younger than me – handsome, and the nicest man that you could meet, to boot. And he's mine.

What can I tell you about him? He's thirty-two – a full ten years my junior, though I have to say I'm the least likely cougar on the planet. He's tall, skinny and muscular all at once. He never looks better than when he's wearing a tight T-shirt and black jeans. His hair's jet black, cropped at the sides but flop-ping every which way on top. I look at it now and think that it could probably do with a cut. Despite living frugally on the boat, Danny still likes to go to a barber rather than have me taking to it with the kitchen scissors. Today, because of the cool morning, he's wearing a black beanie hat and a faded grey denim jacket. He hasn't shaved yet and he subconsciously keeps smoothing the shadow of stubble on his skin. Originally, he's from Ireland – near Belfast – and even though he's lived in England for years now, he still speaks with a soft, sexy accent that makes my heart go all silly. He has dark, mischievous eyes and they make not just my heart but everything else go silly too. Actually, just take it as read that I'm as lovestruck as it's possible to be.

Danny Wilde came into my life at a time when I felt I had so little to look forward to. I'd completely lost who Fay Merryweather actually was or the woman she'd once hoped to be. I'd been in a relationship of sorts with the same man for years but, if I'm completely honest, I wasn't really in love. Anthony and I were together out of habit more than any great passion. He was more keen on his golf clubs than he ever was on me. My stepmother – a wicked one as it turns out – and her extensive range of illnesses had dominated my life. I was Miranda's prime carer and, for my sins, she made sure that it was a role I filled 24/7. I'd been forced to give up my job because of it and ran a café from our home by the canal, Fay's Cakes, that had developed out of necessity rather than any fabulously ambitious business plan. My ad hoc selling of cakes from our ancient canal boat, the *Maid of Merryweather*, became a success despite my daily struggle to hold it all together. Before long, I added light lunches and teas and my business grew into the garden when we put a few tables out under the apple trees. Then I took over the dining room and we had even more tables, so I hired Lija Vilks, my ill-tempered Latvian assistant, to help me keep my head above water. Lija turned out to be the most foul-mouthed and fastidious employee anyone could have and I have no idea how I would ever have managed without her. She's as feisty as I'm timid, and as lovely as she is difficult, but she's fiercely loyal to me and, well – just fierce, actually. Beyond all else, her cakes are flipping amazing. A slice of her lemon drizzle makes me overlook all her shortcomings in the customer-care department.

Yet, despite loving running the café, I still felt that I wasn't in control of my own destiny. Anthony and Miranda were controlling my life. When they said jump, all I did was ask, 'How high?' I got up, baked cakes, made beds, cleaned floors, pandered to Miranda's needs, baked more cakes, ironed shirts and sheets, pandered to Anthony's needs, fell into bed exhausted. Then got up and did the same thing the very next day. I was bumping along the bottom of my existence and that's never a good feeling. I'm in my forties and I should have been in the prime of my life – yet I was going nowhere fast. Little did I know how that was all about to change. Now I'm still going nowhere fast, but for very different reasons!

Our life on *The Dreamcatcher* is as far out of the rat race as you can get. Now we work to live, not the other way round. Danny had escaped the corporate life, buying the boat on a whim and taking to the canals for a great adventure. He came to the café looking for casual work – much in the same way that he's doing now. While Lija and I managed to stay on top of the daily upkeep of Fay's Cakes, the garden and repairs around the house were going to pot, so I found Danny some gardening and odd jobs that had been on my To Do list for ages, unaware that this seemingly small decision would turn my staid little life upside down.

Every morning, I thank my lucky stars that I did. If I'd decided that my fence could stay unpainted, my trees unpruned, then I could quite conceivably have drifted into marriage with Anthony and would have spent the rest of my life as a down-trodden golf widow with a husband who thought having sex once a month was being rampant. Instead, I fell madly in love, embarked on a whirlwind romance with my young and gorgeous gardener, left Anthony, gave up the café, and ran away to join Danny Wilde on his travels. Go, me!

I couldn't have acted any more out of character if I'd tried. Yet I'm so glad that I did. My new life is everything I'd hoped for and more. Danny and I have lived together in close quarters on the boat for a few months now and, so far, we've hardly had a cross word. Seriously, I have to pinch myself on a daily basis to check that it isn't all a beautiful dream.

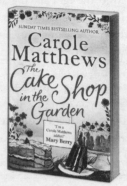

Fay Merryweather runs her cake shop from her beautiful garden. She whips up airy sponges and scrumptious scones, while her customers enjoy the lovely blossoms and gorgeous blooms. Looking after the cake shop, the garden and her cantankerous mother means Fay is always busy but she accepts her responsibilities because if she doesn't do all this, who will?

Then Danny Wilde walks into her life and makes Fay question every decision she's ever made . . .

'Perfect for lifting spirits' *HEAT*

Fay and Danny are madly in love and it's all Fay's ever dreamed of. But she left everything – including the delightful cake shop she used to run – to be with Danny on his cosy canal boat The Dreamcatcher. And as she soon finds out, making delicious cakes on the water isn't always smooth sailing!

Then Fay gets a call that sends her back to her friends and the Cake Shop in the Garden. It will be hard being away from Danny but their relationship is strong enough to survive . . . isn't it?

Christie Chapman is a single mum who spends her days commuting to her secretarial job and looking after her teenage son, Finn. It's not an easy life but Christie finds comfort in her love of crafting, and spends her spare time working on her beautiful creations. Soon, it's not long before opportunity comes knocking.

Christie can see a future full of hope and possibility for her and Finn – and if the handsome Max is to be believed, one full of love too. Christie knows that something has to give, but can she really give up her dreams and the chance of real love?

'I laughed and cried and marvelled'
CATHY BRAMLEY

Grace has been best friends with Ella and Flick forever. The late-night chats, shared heartaches and good times have created a bond that has stood the test of time.

When Ella invites them to stay for a week in her cottage in South Wales, Grace jumps at the chance to see her old friends. She also hopes that the change of scenery will help her reconnect with her distant husband.

Then Flick arrives; loveable, bubbly, incorrigible Flick, accompanied by the handsome and charming Noah.

This is going to be one week which will change all their lives forever . . .

To my dear friend, Hayley Butcher.

Shy person, black tooth, bag lady, mad flamingo fancier,
a fan of the filthy crochet, extreme worrier, super crafter,
sausage fondler, style guru and all-round nice person.
Happy Big Birthday. Again!

Acknowledgements

Thanks to my lovely Yvette Hughes for expert help and advice on all things relating to Gary Barlow and Take That. For being my designated carer on our outings. For always having your friends' backs. Your kindness knows no bounds.